Without Prejudice by Israel Zangwill

Israel Zangwill was born in London on 21st January 1864, to a family of Jewish immigrants from the Russian Empire.

Zangwill was initially educated in Plymouth and Bristol. At age 9 he was enrolled in the Jews' Free School in Spitalfields in east London. Zangwill excelled here. He began to teach part-time at the school and eventually full time. Whilst teaching he also studied with the University of London and by 1884 had earned his BA with triple honours in philosophy, history, and the sciences.

His writing earned him the sobriquet "the Dickens of the Ghetto" primarily based on his much lauded novel 'Children of the Ghetto: A Study of a Peculiar People' in 1892 and its glimpse of the poverty-stricken life in London's Jewish quarter.

As a writer he was keen to reflect on his political and social outlooks. His simulation of Yiddish sentence structure in English aroused great interest. His mystery work, 'The Big Bow Mystery' (1892) was the first locked room mystery novel.

Zangwill was also involved with narrowly focused Jewish issues as an assimilationist, an early Zionist, and later a territorialist. In the early 1890s he had joined the Lovers of Zion movement in England. In 1897 he joined Theodor Herzl (considered the father of modern political Zionism) in founding the World Zionist Organization.

Zangwill quit the established philosophy of Zionism when his plan for a homeland in Uganda was rejected and founded his own organisation; the Jewish Territorialist Organization. Its stated goal was to create a Jewish homeland in whatever territory in the world could be found for them.

Amongst the challenges in his life he found time to write poetry. He had translated a medieval Jewish poet in 1903 and his volume 'Blind Children' in 1908 shows his promise in this new endeavour.

'The Melting Pot' in 1909 made Zangwill's name as an admired playwright. When the play opened in Washington D.C., former President Theodore Roosevelt leaned over the edge of his box and shouted, "That's a great play, Mr. Zangwill, that's a great play."

Israel Zangwill died on 1st August 1926 in Midhurst, West Sussex.

Index of Contents

PART I

GOSSIPS AND FANTASIES

I

A VISION OF THE BURDEN OF MAN

And it came to pass that my soul was vexed with the problems of life, so that I could not sleep. So I opened a book by a lady novelist, and fell to reading therein. And of a sudden I looked up, and lo! a great host of women filled the chamber, which had become as the Albert Hall for magnitude—women of all complexions, countries, times, ages, and sexes. Some were bewitching and beautiful, some wan and flat-breasted, some elegant and stately, some ugly and squat, some plain and whitewashed, and some painted and decorated; women in silk gowns, and women in divided skirts, and women in widows' weeds, and women in knickerbockers, and women in ulsters, and women in furs, and women in crinolines, and women in tights, and women in rags; but every woman of them all in tears. The great chamber was full of a mighty babel; shouts and ululations, groans and moans, weeping and wailing and gnashing of false and genuine teeth, and tearing of hair both artificial and natural; and therewith the flutter of a myriad fans, and the rustle of a million powder-puffs. And the air reeked with a thousand indescribable scents—patchouli and attar of roses and cherry blossom, and the heavy odours of hair-oil and dyes and cosmetics and patent medicines innumerable.

Now when the women perceived me on my reading-chair in their midst, the shrill babel swelled to a savage thunder of menace, so that I deemed they were wroth with me for intruding upon them in mine own house; but as mine ear grew accustomed to the babel of tongues, I became aware of the true import of their ejaculations.

"O son of man!" they cried, in various voices: "thy cruel reign is over, thy long tyranny is done; thou hast glutted thyself with victims, thou hast got drunken on our hearts' blood, we have made sport for thee in our blindness. But the Light is come at last, the slow night has budded into the rose of dawn, the masculine monster is in his death-throes, the kingdom of justice is at hand, the Doll's House has been condemned by the sanitary inspector."

I strove to deprecate their wrath, but my voice was as the twitter of a sparrow in a hurricane. At length I ruffled my long hair to a leonine mane, and seated myself at the piano. And lo! straightway there fell a deep silence—you could have heard a hairpin drop.

"What would you have me do, O daughters of Eve?" I cried. "What is my sin? what my iniquity?" Then the clamour recommenced with tenfold violence, disappointment at the loss of a free performance augmenting their anger.

"Give me a husband," shrieked one.

"Give me a profession," shrieked another.

"Give me a divorce," shrieked a third.

"Give me free union," shrieked a fourth.

"Give me an income," shrieked a fifth.

"Give me my deceased sister's husband," shrieked a sixth.

"Give me my divorced husband's children," shrieked a seventh.

"Give me the right to paint from the nude in the Academy schools," shrieked an eighth.

"Give me an Oxford degree," shrieked a ninth.

"Give me a cigar," shrieked a tenth.

"Give me a vote," shrieked an eleventh.

"Give me a pair of trousers," shrieked a twelfth.

"Give me a seat in the House," shrieked a thirteenth.

"Daughters of the horse-leech," I made answer, taking advantage of a momentary lull, "I am not in a position to give away any of these things. You had better ask at the Stores." But the tempest out-thundered me.

"I want to ride bareback in the Row in tights and spangles at 1 p. m. on Sundays," shrieked a soberly clad suburban lady, who sported a wedding-ring. "I want to move the world with my pen or the point of my toe; I want to write, dance, sing, act, paint, sculpt, fence, row, ride, swim, hunt, shoot, fish, love all men from young rustic farmers to old town roués, lead the Commons, keep a salon, a restaurant, and a zoological garden, row a boat in boy's costume, with a tenor by moonlight alone, and deluge Europe and Asia with blood shed for my intoxicating beauty. I am primeval, savage, unlicensed, unchartered, unfathomable, unpetticoated, tumultuous, inexpressible, irrepressible, overpowering, crude, mordant, pugnacious, polyandrous, sensual, fiery, chaste, modest, married, and misunderstood."

"But, madam," I remarked—for in her excitement she approached within earshot of me—"I understand thee quite well, and I really am not responsible for thy emotions." Her literary style beguiled me into the responsive archaicism of the second person singular.

"Coward!" she snapped. "Coward and satyr! For centuries thou hast trampled upon my sisters, and desecrated womanhood."

"I beg thy pardon," I rejoined mildly.

"Thou dost not deserve it," she interrupted.

"Thou art substituting hysteria for history," I went on. "I was not born yesterday, but I have only scored a few years more than a quarter of one century, and seeing that my own mother was a woman, I must refuse to be held accountable for the position of the sex."

"Sophist!" she shrieked. "It is thy apathy and selfishness that perpetuate the evil."

Then I bethought me of my long vigils of work and thought, the slow, bitter years in which I "ate my bread with tears, and sat weeping on my bed," and I remembered that some of those tears were for the sorrows of that very sex which was now accusing me of organised injustice. But I replied gently: "I am no tyrant; I am a simple, peaceful citizen, and it is as much as I can do to earn my bread and the bread of some of thy sex. Life is hard enough for both sexes, without setting one against the other. We are both the outcome of the same great forces, and both of us have our special selfishnesses, advantages, and drawbacks. If there is any cruelty, it is Nature's handiwork, not man's. So far from trampling on womanhood, we have let a woman reign over us for more than half a century. We worship womanhood, we have celebrated woman in song, picture, and poem, and half civilisation has adored the Madonna. Let us have woman's point of view and the truth about her psychology, by all means. But beware lest she provoke us too far. The Ewigweibliche has become too literal a fact, and in our reaction against this everlasting woman question we shall develop in unexpected directions. Her cry for equal purity will but end in the formal institution of the polygamy of the Orient—"

As I spoke the figure before me appeared to be undergoing a transformation, and, ere I had finished, I perceived I was talking to an angry, seedy man in a red muffler.

"Thee keeps down the proletariat," he interrupted venomously. "Thee lives on the sweat of his brow, while thee fattens at ease. Thee plants thy foot on his neck."

"Do I?" I exclaimed, lifting up my foot involuntarily.

Mistaking the motion, he disappeared, and in his stead I saw a withered old pauper with the Victoria Cross on his breast. "I went to the mouth of hell for thee," he said, with large reproachful eyes; "and thou leavest me to rot in the workhouse."

"I am awfully sorry!" I said. "I never heard of thee. It is the nation—"

"The nation!" he cried scornfully. "Thou art the nation; the nation is only a collection of individuals. Thou art responsible. Thou art the man."

"Thou art the man," echoed a thousand voices: "Society is only an abstraction." And, looking round, I saw, to my horror, that the women had quite disappeared, and their places were filled by men of all complexions, countries, times, ages, and sexes.

"I died in the streets," shouted an old cripple in the background—"round the corner from thy house, in thy wealthy parish—I died of starvation in this nineteenth century of the Christian era, and a generation after Dickens's 'Christmas Carol.'"

"If I had only known!" I murmured, while my eyes grew moist. "Why didst thou not come to me?"

"I was too proud to beg," he answered. "The really poor never beg."

"Then how am I responsible?" I retorted.

"How art thou responsible?" cried the voices indignantly; and one dominating the rest added: "I want work and can't get it. Dost thou call thyself civilised?"

"Civilised?" echoed a weedy young man scornfully. "I am a genius, yet I have had nothing to eat all day. Thy congeners killed Keats and Chatterton, and when I am dead thou wilt be sorry for what thou hast not done."

"But hast thou published anything?" I asked.

"How could I publish?" he replied, indignantly.

"Then how could I be aware of thee?" I inquired.

"But my great-grandfather did publish," said another. "Thou goest into ecstacies over him, and his books have sold by tens of thousands; but me thou leavest pensionless, to earn my living as a cooper. Bah!"

"And thou didst put my father in prison," said another, "for publishing the works of a Continental novelist; but when the novelist himself comes here, thou puttest him in the place of honour."

I was fast growing overwhelmed with shame.

"Where is thy patriotism! Thou art letting some of the most unique British birds become extinct!" "Yes, and thou lettest Christmas cards be made in Germany, and thou deridest Whistler, and refusest to read Dod Grile, and thou lettest books be published with the sheets pinned instead of sewn. And the way thou neglectest Coleridge's grave—"

"Coleridge's grave?" interrupted a sad-eyed enthusiast. "Why, thou hast put no stone at all to mark where James Thomson lies!"

"Thou Hun, thou Vandal!" shrieked a fresh contingent of voices in defiance of the late Professor Freeman. "Thou hast allowed the Emanuel Hospital to be knocked down, thou hast whitewashed the oaken ceiling of King Charles's room at Dartmouth, and threatened to destroy the view from Richmond Hill. Thou hast smashed cathedral windows, or scratched thy name on them, hast pulled down Roman walls, and allowed commons to be inclosed. Thou coverest the Lake District with advertisements of pills, and the blue heaven itself with sky-signs; and in thy passion for cheap and nasty pictorial journalism thou art allowing the art of wood-engraving to die out, even as thou acceptest photogravures instead of etchings."

I cowered before their wrath, while renewed cries of "Thou art responsible! Thou! Thou!" resounded from all sides.

"A pretty Christian thou art!" exclaimed another voice in unthinking vituperation. "Thou decimatest savage tribes with rum and Maxim guns, thou makest money by corrupting the East with opium. Thou allowest the Armenians to be done to death, and thou wilt not put a stop to child-marriages in India."

"But for thee I should have been alive to-day," broke in a venerable spirit hovering near the ceiling. "If thou hadst refused to sell poison except in specially shaped bottles—"

"What canst thou expect of a man who allows anybody to carry firearms?" interrupted another voice.

"Or who fills his newspaper with divorce cases?"

"Is it any wonder the rising generation is cynical, and the young maiden of fifteen has ceased to be bashful?"

"Shame on thee!" hissed the chorus, and advanced upon me so threateningly that I seized my hat and rushed from the room. But a burly being with a Blue Book blocked my way.

"Where didst thou get that hat?" he cried. "Doubtless from some sweating establishment. And those clothes; didst thou investigate where they were made? didst thou inquire how much thy tailor paid his hands? didst thou engage an accountant to examine his books?"

"I—I am so busy," I stammered feebly.

"Shuffler! How knowest thou thou art not spreading to the world the germs of scarlet fever and typhoid picked up in the sweaters' dens?"

"What cares he?" cried a tall, thin man, with a slight stoop and gold spectacles. "Does he not poison the air every day with the smoke of his coal fires?"

"Pison the air!" repeated a battered, blear-eyed reprobate. "He pisoned my soul. He ruined me with promiskus charity. Whenever I was stoney-broke 'e give me doles in aid, 'e did. 'E wos werry bad to me, 'e wos. 'E destroyed my self-respeck, druv me to drink, broke up my home, and druv my darters on the streets."

"This is what comes of undisciplined compassion," observed the gold-spectacled gentleman, glowering at me. "The integrity and virtue of a whole family sacrificed to the gratification of thy altruistic emotions!"

"Stand out of the way!" I cried to the burly man; "I wish to leave my own house."

"And carry thy rudeness abroad?" he retorted indignantly. "Perchance thou wouldst like to go to the Continent, and swagger through Europe clad in thy loud-patterned checks and thine insular self-sufficiency."

I tried to move him out of the way by brute force, and we wrestled, and he threw me. I heard myself strike the floor with a thud.

Rubbing my eyes, instead of my back, I discovered that I was safe in my reading-chair, and that it was the lady novelist's novel that had made the noise. I picked it up, but I still seemed to see the reproachful eyes of a thousand tormentors, and hear their objurgations. Yet I had none of the emotions of Scrooge, no prickings of conscience, no ferment of good resolutions. Instead, I felt a wave of bitterness and indignation flooding my soul.

"I will not be responsible for the universe!" I cried to the ceiling. "I am sick of the woman question, and the problem of man makes my gorge rise. Is there one question in the world that can really be settled? No, not one, except by superficial thinkers. Just as the comprehensive explanation of 'the flower in the crannied wall' is the explanation of the whole universe, so every question is but a thin layer of ice over infinite depths. You may touch it lightly, you may skate over it; but press it at all, and you sink into bottomless abysses. The simplest interrogation is a doorway to chaos, to endless perspectives of winding paths perpetually turning upon themselves in a blind maze. Suppose one is besought to sign a petition against capital punishment. A really conscientious and logical person, pursuing truth after the manner recommended by Descartes, and professed by Huxley, could not settle this question for himself without going into the endless question of Free-will versus Necessity, and studying the various systems of philosophy and ethics. Murder may be due to insane impulse: Insanity must therefore be studied. Moreover, ought not hanging to be abolished in cases of murder and reserved for more noxious crimes, such as those of fraudulent directors? This opens up new perspectives and new lines of study. The whole theory of Punishment would also have to be gone into: should it be restrictive, or revengeful, or reformative? (See Aristotle, Bentham, Owen, etc.) Incidentally great tracts of the science of Psychology are involved. And what right have we to interfere with our fellow-creatures at all? This opens up the vast domains of Law and Government, and requires the perusal of Montesquieu, Bodin, Rousseau, Mill, etc., etc. Sociology would also be called in to determine the beneficent or maleficent influence of the death-punishment upon the popular mind; and statistics would be required to trace the operation of the systems of punishment in various countries. History would be consulted to the same effect. The sanctity of human life being a religious dogma, the religions of the world would have to be studied, to see under what conditions it has been thought permissible to destroy life. One ought not to rely on translations: Confucius should be read in Chinese, the Koran in Arabic, and the few years spent in the acquisition of Persian would be rewarded by a first-hand familiarity with the Zend Avesta. The Old Testament enjoins capital punishment. On what grounds, then, if one is leaning the other way, may a text be set aside that seems to settle the matter positively? Here comes in the vast army of Bible commentators and theologians. But perhaps the text is of late origin, interpolated. The Dutch and German savants rise in their might, with their ingenious theories and microscopic scholarship. But there are other scientists who bid us not heed the Bible at all, because it contradicts the latest editions of their primers. Is, then, science strictly accurate? To answer this you must have a thorough acquaintance with biology, geology, astronomy, besides deciding for yourself between the conflicting views at nearly every point. By the time you have made up your mind as to whether capital punishment should be abolished, it has passed out of the statute-book, and you are dead, or mad, or murdered.

"But were this the only question a man has to settle in his short span of years, he might cheerfully engage in its solution. But life bristles with a hundred questions equally capital, and with a thousand-and-one minor problems on which he is expected to have an opinion, and about which he is asked at one time or other, if only at dinner."

At this moment the Poet who shares my chambers came in—later than he should have done—and interrupted my soliloquy. But I was still hot, and enlisted his interest in my vision and my apologia, and began drawing up a list of the questions, in which after a while he became so interested that he started adding to it. Hours flew like minutes, and only the splitting headache we both brought upon ourselves drove us to desist. Here is our first rough list of the questions that confront the modern man—a disorderly, deficient, and tautological list, no doubt, to which any reader can add many hundred more.

VEXED QUESTIONS

Queen Mary and Bothwell. Shakespeare and Bacon. Correct transliteration of Greek; pronunciation of Latin. Sunday opening of museums; of theatres. The English Sunday; Bank Holiday. Darwinism. Is there spontaneous creation? or spontaneous combustion? The germ theory; Pasteur's cures; Mattei's cures; Virchow's cell theory. Unity of Homer; of the Bible. Dickens v. Thackeray. Shall we ever fly? or steer balloons? The credit system; the discount system. Impressionism, decadence, Japanese art, the plein air school. Realism v. romance; Gothic v. Greek art. Russian fiction, Dutch, Bulgarian, Norwegian, American, etc., etc.: opinion of every novel ever written, of every school, in every language (you must read them in the original); ditto of every opera and piece of music, with supplementary opinions about every vocalist and performer; ditto of every play, with supplementary opinions about every actor, dancer, etc.; ditto of every poem; ditto of every picture ever painted, with estimates of every artist in every one of his manners at every stage of his development and decisions as to which pictures are not genuine; also of every critic of literature, drama, art, and music (in all of which departments certain names are equal to an appalling plexus of questions—Wagner, Ibsen, Meredith, Browning, Comte, Goethe, Shakespeare, Dante, Degas, Rousseau, Tolstoï, Maeterlinck, Strindberg, Zola, Whistler, Leopardi, Emerson, Carlyle, Swedenborg, Rabelais). Socialism, its various schools, its past and its future; Anarchism: bombs. Labour questions: the Eight Hours' Day, the Unemployed, the Living Wage, etc., etc. Mr. Gladstone's career. Shall members of Parliament be paid? Chamberlain's position; ditto for every statesman in every country, to-day and in all past ages. South Africa, Rhodes, Captain Jim. The English girl v. the French or the American. Invidious comparisons of every people from every point of view, physical, moral, intellectual, and aesthetic. Vizetelly. Vivisection. First love v. later love; French marriage system v. the English. The corrupt choruses in the Greek dramas (also in modern burlesque—with the question of the Church and Stage Guild, Zaeo's back, the County Council, etc.). How to make London beautiful. Fogs. Bi-metallism. Secondary Education. Volunteer or conscript? Anonymity in journalism. Christianity, Judaism, Buddhism, and Mohammedanism: their mutual superiorities, their past and their future. Plato, Spinoza, Kant, Hegel, and all philosophers and philosophies. The Independent Theatre. The origin of language, Where do the Aryans come from? Was Mrs. Maybrick guilty? Same question for every great murderer. The Tichborne case, and every other cause célèbre, including divorce cases. Crime and punishment. Music-hall songs. Heredity: are acquired qualities inherited? Is tobacco a mistake? Is drink? Is marriage? Is the high hat? Polygamy; the social evil. Are the planets inhabited? Is the English concert pitch too high? The divided skirt. The antiquity of man. Geology: is the story of the rocks short, or long, or true? Geology v. Genesis; Genesis v. Kuenen. Was Pope a poet? Was Whitman? Was Poe a drunkard, or Griswold a liar? Was Hamlet mad? Was Blake? Is waltzing immoral? Is humour declining? Is there a modern British drama? Corporal punishment in schools. Compulsory vaccination. What shall we do with our daughters? or our sons? or our criminals? or our paupers? or ourselves? Female franchise. Republicanism. Which is the best soap? or tooth-powder? Is Morris's printing really good? Is the race progressing? Is our navy fit? Should dynamite be used in war? or in peace? What persons should be buried in Westminster Abbey? Origin of every fairy-tale. Who made our proverbs and ballads? Cold baths v. hot or Turkish. Home Rule. Should the Royal Academy be abolished? and who should be the next R.A.? Should there be an Academy of Literature? or a Channel Tunnel? Was De Lesseps to blame? Should we not patronise English watering-places? Should there be pianos in board schools? or theology? Authors and publishers; artists and authors. Is literature a trade? Should pauper aliens be admitted? or pauper couples separated? Bank Holiday. Irving v. Tree. The world's politics, present, future, and even past—retrospective questions being constantly re-agitated: as, Should the American slaves have been emancipated? or Was the French Revolution a Folly? Apropos, which is the best history of it? Who is the rightful Queen of England? Is cycling injurious to the cyclist? or the public? Who was the Man in the Iron Mask? Is the Stock Exchange immoral? What is influenza? Ought we to give cabmen more than their fare? Tips generally. Should dogs be muzzled? Have we a right to extend our empire? or to keep it? Should we federate it? Are there ghosts? Is spiritualism a fraud? Is theosophy? Was Madame Blavatsky? Was Jezebel a wretch, or a Hellenist? The abuse of the quarantine. Should ladies ride astride? Amateurs v. professionals in sports. Is prize-fighting beneficial? Is trial by jury played out? The cost of law: Chancery. Abuses of the Universities. The Cambridge Spinning House. Compulsory Greek. The endowment of research. A teaching university in London. Is there a sea-serpent? Servants v. mistresses. Shall the Jews have Palestine? Classical v. modern side in schools. Should we abolish the censorship of plays? or fees? or found a dramatic academy? or a State theatre? Should gambling be legal? Should potatoes be boiled in their skins? should dynamiters? Should newspapers publish racing tips? or divorce cases? or comment? The New Journalism. What is the best ninth move in the Evans gambit? Would Morphy have been a first-class chess-player to-day? Is the Steinitz gambit sound? Do plants dream? Ought we to fill up income-tax papers accurately? Shelley and Harriet and Mary. Swift and Vanessa and Stella. Lord and Lady Byron. Did Mrs. Carlyle deserve it? The limits of biography; of photography in painting; of the spot-stroke in billiards. Did Shakespeare hold horses? Should girls be brought up like boys, or boys like girls, or both like one another? Are animals automata? Have they reason? or do they live without reason? Will Brighton A's fall? or Peruvians rise? Is it cruel to cage birds and animals? What is the best breed of horses? Did Wellington say "Up, Guards, and at 'em"? Cremation v. Burial. Should immoral men be allowed to retain office? Is suicide immoral? Opinion of the character of Elizabeth, Parnell, Catherine, Cleopatra, Rousseau, Jack the Ripper, Semiramis, Lucrezia Borgia, etc., etc. The present state of the Libel Law; and of the Game Laws. Is vegetarianism higher? or healthier? Do actors feel their parts? Should German type be abolished? or book-edges cut? or editions artificially limited? or organ-grinders? How about church-and-muffin-bells? Peasant proprietorship. Deer or Highlanders? Were our ancestors taller than we? Is fruit or market-gardening or cattle-farming more profitable? Dutch v. Italian gardening. What is an etching? Do dreams come true? Is freemasonry a fraud? or champagne? are Havanas? Best brand of whiskey? Ought Building and Friendly Societies to be supervised? Smoking in theatres. Should gentlemen pay ladies' cab-fares? Genius and insanity. Are cigarettes poisonous? Is luxury a boon? Thirteen at table, and all other superstitions—are they foolish? Why young men don't marry. Shall we ever reach the Pole? How soon will England and the States be at war? The real sites and people in Thackeray's novels. A universal penny post? Cheap telegrams and telephones? Is the Bank of England safe? Are the planets inhabited? Should girls have more liberty? Should they propose? or wear crinolines? Why not have an unlimited paper currency? or a decimal system and coinage? or a one-pound note? Should we abolish the Lords? or preserve the Commons? Why not euthanasia? Should dramatic critics write plays? Who built the Pyramids? Are the English the Lost Ten Tribes? Should we send missions to the heathen? How long will our coal hold out? Who executed Charles I.? Are the tablets of Tel-el-Amarna trustworthy? are hieroglyphic readers? Will war ever die? or people live to a hundred? The best moustache-forcer, bicycle, typewriter, and system of shorthand or of teaching the blind? Was Sam Weller possible? Who was the original of Becky Sharp? Of Dodo? Does tea hurt? Do gutta-percha shoes? or cork soles? Shall we disestablish the church? or tolerate a reredos in St. Paul's? Is Euclid played out? Is there a fourth dimension of space? Which is the real old Curiosity Shop? Is the Continental man better educated than the Briton? Why can't we square the circle? or solve equations to the nth degree? or colour-print in England? What is the use of South Kensington? Is paraffin good for baldness? or eucalyptus for influenza? How many elements are there? Should cousins marry? or the House be adjourned on Derby Day? Do water-colours fade? Will the ether theory live? or Stanley's reputation? Is Free Trade fair? Is a Free Press? Is fox-hunting cruel? or pigeon-shooting? How about the Queen's staghounds? Should not each railway station bear its name in big letters? and have better refreshments? Should we permit sky-signs? Limits of advertisement. Preservation of historic buildings and beautiful views v. utilitarianism. Is the coinage ugly? Should we not get letters on Sunday? Who really wrote the "Marseillaise"? Are examinations any real test? Promotion in the Army or the Civil Service. Is logic or mathematics the primal science? and what is the best system of symbolic logic? Should curates be paid more and archbishops less? Should postmen knock? or combine? Are they under military régime? or underpaid? Should Board School children be taught religion? The future of China and Japan. Is Anglo-Indian society immoral? Style or matter? Have we one personality or many?—with a hundred other questions of psychology and ethics. A graduated income tax—with a hundred other questions of political economy. Asphalt for horses. Will the French republic endure? Will America have an aristocracy? Shall Welsh perish? Is Platonic love possible? Did Shakespeare write "Coriolanus"? Is there a skull in Holbein's "Ambassadors"? What is the meaning of Dryden's line, "He was and is the Captain of the Test"? or of the horny projection under the left wing of the sub-parasite of the third leg of a black-beetle? Was Orme poisoned? Are there fresh-water jelly-fishes? Is physiognomy true? or phrenology? or graphology? or cheiromancy? If so, what are their laws? Opinions on Guelphs and Ghibellines, fasting displays, infanticide, the genealogy of the peerage, the origin of public-house signs, Siberia, the author of Junius, of the Sibylline Books, werewolves, dyeing one's hair, coffin-ships, standing armies, the mediaeval monasteries, Church Brotherhoods, state insurance of the poor, promiscuous almsgiving, the rights of animals, the C. D. Acts, the Kernoozer Club, emigration, book-plates, the Psychical Society, Kindergarten, Henry George, Positivism, Chevalier's Coster, colour-blindness, Total Abstinence, Arbitration, the best hundred books, Local Option, Women's Rights, the Wandering Jew, the Flying Dutchman, the Neanderthal skull, the Early Closing movement, the Prince of Wales, and the Tonic Sol-fa notation. Is there an English hexameter? Is a perfect translation impossible? Will the coloured races conquer? Is consumption curable? Is celibacy possible? Can novels be really dramatised? Is the French school of acting superior to ours? Should literary men be offered peerages? or refuse them? Should quack-doctors be prosecuted? Should critics practise without a license? Are the poor happier or unhappier than the rich? or is Paley right? Did Paley steal his celebrated watch? Did Milton steal from Vondel? Is the Salon dead in England? Should duelling be revived? What is the right thing in dados, hall-lamps, dressing-gowns, etc.? Should ladies smoke? Is there a Ghetto in England? Anti-Semitism. Why should London wait? or German waiters? Mr. Stead's revival of pilgrimages. Is Grimm's Law universal? The abuses of the Civil Service; of the Pension List. Dr. Barnardo. Grievances of match-girls; of elementary teachers. Are our police reliable? Is Stevenson's Scotch accurate? Is our lifeboat service efficient? The Eastern Question. What is an English fairy-tale? What are the spots on the sun? Have they anything to do with commercial crises? Should we spoil the Court if we spared the Black Rod? or the City if we spared the Lord Mayor? Is chloroforming dangerous? Should armorial bearings be taxed? or a tradesman's holiday use of his cart? Should classical texts be Bowdlerised for school-boys? Is the confessional of value? Is red the best colour for a soldier's uniform or for a target? Will it rain to-morrow? Ought any one to carry firearms? Do we permit the cancan on the English stage? or aërial flights without nets? Where are the lost Tales of Miletus? Should lawyers wear their own hair? Was the Silent System so bad? Should a novel have a purpose? Was the Victoria Fund rightly distributed? What is the origin of Egyptian civilisation? Is it allowable to say, "It's me"? Every other doubtful point of grammar and—worse still—of pronunciation; also of etymology. May we say "Give an ovation"? Is the German Emperor a genius, or a fool? Should bachelors be taxed? Will the family be abolished? Ensilage. Why was Ovid banished from Rome? Is the soul immortal? Is our art-pottery bad? Is the Revised Version of the Bible superior to the Old? Who stole Gainsborough's picture? Which are the rarest coins and stamps? Is there any sugar in the blood? Blondes or brunettes? Do monkeys talk? What should you lead at whist? Should directors of insolvent companies be prosecuted? Or classics be annotated? Was Boswell a fool? Do I exist? Does anybody else exist? Is England declining? Shall the costers stand in Farringdon Street? Do green wall-papers contain arsenic? Shall we adopt phonetic spelling? Is life worth living?

The last question at least I thought I could answer, as I bore to bed with me that headache which you have doubtless acquired if you have been foolish enough to read the list. If only one were a journalist, one would have definite opinions on all these points.

And to these questions every day brings a fresh quota. You are expected to have read the latest paragraph in the latest paper, and the newest novel, and not to have missed such and such an article in such and such a quarterly. And all the while you are fulfilling the duties of, and solving the problems of, son, brother, cousin, husband, father, friend, parishioner, citizen, patriot, all complicated by specific religious and social relations, and earning your living by some business that has its own hosts of special problems, and you are answering letters from everybody about everything, and deciding as to the genuineness of begging appeals, and wrestling with some form or forms of disease, pain, and sorrow.

"Truly, we are imperfect instruments for determining truth," I said to the Poet. "The sane person acts from impulse, and only pretends to give a reason. Reason is only called in to justify the verdict of prejudice. Sometimes the impulse is sentiment—which is prejudice touched with emotion. We cannot judge anything on pure, abstract grounds, because the balance is biassed. A human being is born a bundle of prejudices, a group of instincts and intuitions and emotions that precede judgment. Patriotism is prejudice touched with pride, and politics is prejudice touched with spite. Philosophy is prejudice put into propositions, and art is prejudice put into paint or sound, and religion is a pious opinion. Every man is born a Platonist or an Aristotelian, a Romanticist, or a Realist, or an Impressionist, and usually erects his own limitations into a creed. Every country, town, district, family, individual, has a special set of prejudices along the lines of which it moves, and which it mistakes for exclusive truths or reasoned conclusions. Touch human society anywhere, it is rotten, it crumbles into a myriad notes of interrogation; the acid of analysis dissolves every ideal. Humanity only keeps alive and sound by going on in faith and hope—solvitur ambulando—if it sat down to ask questions, it would freeze like the traveller in the Polar regions. The world is saved by bad logic."

"And by good feeling," added my friend the Poet.

"And in the face of all these questions," I cried, surveying the list ruefully again, "we go on accumulating researches and multiplying books without end, vituperating the benefactors who destroyed the library of Alexandria, and exhuming the civilisations that the earthquakes of Time have swallowed under. The Hamlet of centuries, 'sicklied o'er with the pale cast of thought,' the nineteenth of that ilk mouches along, soliloquising about more things in heaven and earth than were dreamt of in any of its predecessors' philosophies. Ah me! Analysis is paralysis and introspection is vivisection and culture drives one mad. What will be the end of it all?"

"The end will be," answered the Poet, "that the overstrung nerves of the century will give way, and that we shall fall into the simple old faith of Omar Khayyám:

"A Book of Verses underneath the Bough,
A Jug of Wine, a Loaf of Bread, and Thou
Beside me singing in the Wilderness—
O Wilderness were Paradise enow."

"Yes," said I, "the only wisdom is to live. Action is substance and thought shadow." And so—paradoxically enough—I began to think out

A WORKING PHILOSOPHY

The solar system turns without thine aid.
Live, die! The universe is not afraid.
What is is right! If aught seems wrong below,
Then wrong it is—of thee to leave it so.
Then wrong it first becomes for human thought,
Which else would die of dieting on naught.
Tied down by race and sex and creed and station,
Go, learn to find thy strength in limitation,
To do the little good that comes to hand,
Content to love and not to understand;
Faithful to friends and country, work and dreams,
Knowing the Real is the thing that seems.
While reverencing every nobleness,

In whatsoever tongue or shape or dress,
Speak out the word that to thy soul seems right,
Strike out thy path by individual light:
'Tis contradictory rays that give the White.

"The ideas are good. But what a pity you are not a poet!" said my friend the Poet.

But, though I recognise that prejudice in the deepest sense supplies the matter of judgment, while logic is only regulative of the form, yet in the more work-a-day sense of the word in which prejudice is taken to mean an opinion formed without reasoning and maintained in despite of it, I claim to write absolutely without prejudice. The syllogism is my lord and king. A kind-hearted lady said I had a cruel face. It is true. I am absolutely remorseless in tracking down a non sequitur, pitiless in forcing data to yield up their implicit conclusions. "Logic! Logic!" snorted my friend the Poet. "Life is not logical. We cannot be logical." "Of course not," said I; "I should not dream of asking men to live logically: all I ask is that they should argue logically."

But to be unprejudiced does not mean to have no convictions. The superficial confuse definiteness with prejudice, forgetting that definite opinions may be the result of careful judgment. Post-judiced I trust I am. But prejudiced? Heaven forfend! Why, 'tis because I do not wish to bind myself to anything that I may say in them that I mark these personal communications "Without Prejudice"! For I do not at all mind contradicting myself. If it were some one of reverend years or superior talents I might hesitate, but between equals—! Contradiction is the privilege of camaraderie and the essence of causerie. We agree to differ—I and myself. I am none of your dogmatic fellows with pigeon-holes for minds, and whatever I say I do not stick to. And I will tell you why. There is hardly a pretty woman of my acquaintance who has not asked for my hand. Owing to this passion for palmistry in polite circles, I have discovered that I possess as many characters as there are palmists. Do you wonder, therefore, if, with such a posse of personalities to pick from, I am never alike two days running? With so varied a psychological wardrobe at command, it would be mere self-denial to be faithful to one's self. I leave that to the one-I'd who can see only one side of a question. Said Tennyson to a friend (who printed it): "'In Memoriam' is more optimistic than I am"; and there is more of the real man in that little remark than in all the biographies. The published prophet has to live up to his public halo. So have I seen an actress on tour slip from a third-class railway carriage into a brougham. Tennyson was not mealy-mouthed, but then he did not bargain for an audience of phonographs. Nowadays it is difficult to distinguish your friends from your biographers. The worst of it is that the land is thick with fools who think nothing of a great man the moment they discover he was a man. Tennyson was all the greater for his honest doubt. The cocksure centuries are passed for ever. In these hard times we have to work for our opinions; we cannot rely on inheriting them from our fathers.

I write with a capital I at the risk of being accused of egotism. Apparently it is more modest to be conceited in the third person, like the child who says "Tommy is a good boy," or in the first person plural, like the leader-writer of "The Times," who bids the Continent tremble at his frown. By a singular fallacy, which ought scarcely to deceive children, it is forgotten that everything that has ever been written since the world began has been written by some person, by an "I," though that "I" might have been omitted from the composition or replaced by the journalistic "we." To some extent the journalist does sink his personality in that imaginary personality of his paper, a personality built up, like the human personality, by its past; and the result is a pompous, colourless, lifeless simulacrum. But in every other department of letters the trail of the "I" is over every page and every sentence. The most impersonal essays and poems are all in a sense egoistic. Everything should really be between inverted commas with an introductory Thus say I. But as these are omitted, as being understood, they come at last to be misunderstood.

In the days ere writing was invented, this elementary error was not possible. The words were heard issuing from the lips of a single man; every opinion, every law of conduct, must have been at first formulated through the lips of some one man. And to this day, in spite of the wilderness of tradition and authority by which we are overgrown, the voice of the one man is still our only living source of inspiration and help. Every new thought must pass through the brain, every moral ideal through the conscience, of an individual. Voices, voices, we want—not echoes. Better the mistaken voice of honest individuality than the soulless bleat of the flock. There are too many of Kipling's Tomlinsons in the world, whose consciences are wholly compact of on dits, on whom the devil himself, sinned they never so sadly, would refuse to waste his good pit-coal. "Bad taste"—that opprobrious phrase which, worse than the accusation of a crime, cannot be refuted, for it is the king of the question-beggars—"bad taste" is responsible for half the reticence that marks current writing, for the failure to prick the bladders of every species that bloat themselves all around us. "Good taste" is the staunchest ally of hypocrisy, and corruption is the obverse side of civilisation. I do not believe in these general truths that rule the market. What is "true for all" is false for each. It is the business of every man to speak out, to be himself, to contribute his own thought to the world's thinking—to be egoistic. To be egoistic is not to be egotistic. Egoism should be distinguished from egotism. The egoist thinks for himself, the egotist about himself. Mr. Meredith's Sir Willoughby should not have been styled the Egoist. The egoist offers his thought to his fellow-men, the egotist thinks it is the only thought worth their acceptance. These papers of mine joyously plead guilty to egoism, but not to egotism. If they, for instance, pretend to appraise the powers of my contemporaries, they do not pretend to be more than an individual appraisal. Whoever wants another opinion can go somewhere else. There is no lack of practitioners in criticism, more or less skilful. There must be a struggle for existence among opinions, as among all other things, and the egoist is content to send the children of his thought into the thick of the fray, confident that the fittest will survive. Only he is not so childish as to make-believe that an impersonal dignified something-not-himself that makes for the ink-pot is speaking—and not he himself, he "with his little I." The affectation of modesty is perhaps the most ludicrous of all human shams. I am reminded of the two Jews who quarrelled in synagogue, during the procession of palm-branches, because each wanted to be last, as befitted the humblest man in Israel, which each claimed to be. This is indeed "the pride that apes humility." There is a good deal of this sort of pride in the careful and conscientious suppression of the egoistic in books and speeches. I have nothing of this modesty to be proud of. I know that I am cleverer than the man in the street, though I take no credit to myself for it, as it is a mere accident of birth, and on the whole a regrettable one. It was this absence of modesty from my composition that recently enabled me to propose the toast of literature coupled with the name of Mr. Zangwill. I said that I could wish that some one more competent and distinguished than myself had been chosen to do justice to such a toast and to such a distinguished man of letters, but I did my best to pay him the tribute he deserved ere I sat down amid universal applause. When I rose amid renewed cheers to reply, I began by saying that I could wish that some one more competent and distinguished than myself had been chosen to respond to so important a toast—the last speaker had considerably overrated my humble achievements in the fields of literature. So that you see I could easily master the modest manner, if I took any pains or set any store by it. But in my articles of faith the "I" is just what I would accentuate most, the "I" through which for each of us the universe flows, by which any truth must be perceived in order to be true, and which is not to be replaced by that false abstraction, the communal mind. Here are a laughing philosopher's definitions of some cardinal things:

Philosophy—All my I. Art—All my Eye. Religion—All my Ay.

Also at the outset let it be distinctly understood that I write without any prejudice in favour of grammar. The fear of the critics is the beginning of pedantry. I detest your scholiast whose footnotes would take Thackeray to task for his "and whiches," and your professor who disdains the voice of the people, which is the voice of the god of grammar. I know all the scholiast has to say (surely he is the silly [Greek: scholastikos] of Greek anecdote), and indeed I owe all my own notions of diction to a work on "Style" written by him. It was from the style of this work that I learnt what to avoid. The book reminded me of my old schoolmaster, who grew very angry with me for using the word "ain't," and vociferated "Ain't! How often am I to tell you ain't ain't a word?" I suppose one may take it for granted that the greater the writer the worse the grammar. "Fools follow rules. Wise men precede them." (Query: this being a quotation from myself, was I bound to put the inverted commas?) Shakespeare has violated every rule of the schoolroom, and the more self-conscious stylist of our own day—Stevenson—would be caned for composition. I find him writing "They are not us," which is almost as blasphemous as "It's me." His reputation has closed the critics' eyes to such sentences as these in his essay on "Some Portraits by Raeburn": "Each of his portraits are not only a piece of history ..."; "Neither of the portraits of Sir Walter Scott were very agreeable to look upon." Stevenson is a master, but not a schoolmaster, of English. Of course bad grammar does not make a genius, any more than bad morals. (Note how much this sentence would lose in crispness if I made it grammatical by tacking on "do.") My friend the musician complained to me that when he studied harmony and form he was told he must not do this, that and the other; whereas, when he came to look into the works of the great composers he found they made a practice of all the three. "Am I a genius?" he queried pathetically. "If so, I could do as I please. I wish I knew." Every author who can read and write is in the same predicament: on the one hand his own instinct for a phrase or a sentence, on the other the contempt of every honest critic. The guardians of the laws of English have a stock of taboos; but unlike the guardians of the laws of England they credit every disregard of them to ignorance. They cannot conceive of malice aforethought. We are forbidden, for example, to use the word "phenomenal" in the sense of "extraordinary." But, with Mr. Crummles's Infant Phenomenon in everybody's mind, can we expect the adjective to shake off the old associations of its parent noun?

Last year I culled an amusing sentence from a "Standard" criticism of a tale of adventure: "The story is a well-told, and in spite of the word 'unreliable,' a well-written one." Now just as many foolish persons object to "a ... one" as to "unreliable." As for the first phrase, I am sure so great a writer as Tom Hood would have pronounced it A1, while "unreliable" is defended with unusual warmth by Webster's Dictionary. The contention that "reliable" should be "reli-on-able," is ridiculous, and Webster's argument is "laughable," which should obviously be "laugh-at-able." These remarks are made quite without prejudice, for personally I have little to complain of. (By the way, this sentence is as open to blame as that of the professor who told his pupils "You must not use a preposition to end a sentence with.") Though I have sat under an army of critics, I have but once been accused of inelegant English, and then it was only by a lady who wrote that my slipshod style "aggravated" her.

Finally it will be remarked that by dispensing with illustrations I preserve intact my egoism and the dignity of a rival art. Nothing can be more absurd than the conventional illustration which merely attempts to picture over again what the writer has already pictured in words. Not only is the effort superfluous, a waste of force, but the artist's picture is too often in flat contradiction of the text. Whom are you to believe, the author or the artist? the man who tells you that the heroine is ethereal, or the man who plainly demonstrates that she is podgy? How often, too, do the people dress differently in the words and in the picture, not to speak of the shifting backgrounds! Dickens had so much difficulty with his illustrations because he saw his characters so much more clearly than any other novelist; the sight of his inner eye was so good. And one can understand, too, how Cruikshank came to fancy he had created Oliver Twist, much as an actor imagines he "creates" a character. The true collaboration between author and artist requires that the work should be divided between them, not reduplicated. Those parts of the story which need the intervention of words should be allotted to the writer, while to the artist should be entrusted the parts better told by pencil. Neither need trench on the other's province. Description—which so many readers skip already—would be abolished. Even incidents—such as murder—could be caught by the artist in the act. And after the artist had killed a character, the author could preach over his corpse. Thus there would be an agreeable reversion to picture-language, the earliest way of writing, and the latest. The ends of the ages would meet in a romance written on these lines:—

"Sick at heart we watched till the grey dawn stole in through the diamond-paned casements of the Grange, and then, at last, when we had given up all hope, we saw coming up the gravel pathway—"

After which the author proceeds: "Fascinated by the blood that dripped from the edges of the eight umbrellas, we stood silent; then, throwing off our coats, we—

"So that was how I won the sweetest little bride I ever wedded. But if I live to wed a hundred, I shall never forget that terrible night in Grewsome Grange.

"THE END."

My friend the artist once collaborated with me in an experiment of this sort, but we did not pursue it, discovering how feeble an advance ours would be after all; for there were points at which both of us felt we ought to give way to the tone-poet. When the emotions became too intangible for intellectual expression I asked my friend the musician to insert paragraphs in a minor key. The love-scenes I was particularly anxious to have written in musical phrases. But he shrank from so unconventional a form, not being sure he was a genius. I was also disheartened by the disappointing behaviour of the diverse scents with which I had expressed myself on certain blank pages. They would not remain in their places.

II

TUNING UP

They were "tuning up" in a wooden hall, stupidly built on the pier to shut off the sea and the night (a penny to pay for the privation), and in that strange cacophony of desolate violin strings, tuneless trombones, and doleful double basses, in that homeless wail of forlorn brass and lost catgut, I found a music sweeter than a Beethoven symphony; for memory's tricksy finger touched of a sudden the source of tears, and flashed before the inner eye a rainbow-lit panorama of the early joys of the theatre—the joys that are no more. Was it even at a theatre—was it even more than an interlude in a diorama?—that divine singing of "The Last Rose of Summer" by a lady in evening dress, whose bust is, perhaps for me alone in all the world, still youthful? Was it from this hall of the siren, or was it from some later enchantment, that I, an infant Ulysses, struggled home by night along a sea road, athwart a gale that well-nigh blew me out to sea? How fierce that salt wind blew, a-yearn to drive me to the shore's edge and whirl me over! How fresh and tameless it beats against me yet, blowing the cobwebs from my brain as that real breeze outside the pier could never do! When my monitory friends gabble of change of air I inhale that wind and am strong. For the child is of the elements, elemental, and the man of the complexities, complex. And so that good salt wind blows across my childhood still, though it cannot sweep away the mist that hovers thereover.

For who shall say whether 't was I or my sister who was borne shrieking with fear from the theatre when the black man, "Othello," appeared on the boards! The first clear memory of things dramatic is of an amateur performance—alas! I have seen few others. 'T was a farce—when was an amateur performance other? There was much play of snuff-boxes passed punctiliously 'twixt irascible old gentlemen with coloured handkerchiefs. Also there was dinner beforehand—my first experience of chicken and champagne. And then there is a great break till the real theatre rises stately and splendid, like Britannia ruling the waves—nay, Britannia herself, or, as they call it lovingly down Shoreditch way, "the Brit."

When to my fashionable friends I have held forth on the glories and the humours of "the Brit.," they have taken it for granted, and I have lacked the courage or the energy to undeceive them, that my visits to this temple of the people were expeditions of Haroun Al Raschid in the back streets of Bagdad or adventures of Prince Florizel in Rupert Street; but of a truth I have climbed the gallery stairs in sober boyish earnestness, elbowed of the gods, and elbowing, and if I did not yield to the seductions of "ginger-beer and Banbury" that filled up clamantly the entr'actes, 't was that I had not the coppers. "Guy Fawkes" was my first piece, in the days when the drama's "fireworks" were not epigrams, and so the smell of the sulphur still purifies the air. All the long series of "London successes," with their array of genius and furniture, have faded like insubstantial pageants, but the rude vault piled with flour-barrels for the desperado's torch is fixed as by chemic process. Consider the preparation of the brain for that memory. What! I should actually go to a play—that far-off wonder! "The Miller and his Men" cut in cardboard should no longer stave off my longing for the living passion of the theatre. 'T was a very elongated young man who took me, a young cigar-maker fond of reciting, spouting Shakespeare from a sixpenny edition, playing Hamlet mentally as he rolled the tobacco-leaf. There was a halo about his head, for he was on speaking terms with the low comedian of the "Brit.," and, I understood, was permitted upon occasion to pay for a pint of half-and-half. Alas! all this did not avail to save him from an early tomb. Poor worshipper of the green room, perchance thy ghost still walks there. Or is there room in some other world for thy baffled aspirations?

In such clouds of glory did the drama first come to me, sulphurously splendid. In the "Brit." I made my first acquaintance with the limelit humanity that, magnificent in its crimes and in its virtues, sins or suffers in false eyebrows or white muslin to the sound of soft music. Here I met that strange creation, the villain—a being as mythic, meseems, as the centaur, and, like it, more beast than man. The "Brit." was a hot place for villains, the gallery accepting none but the highest principles of speech and conduct, and ginger-beer were not too weighty a form of expressing detestation of the more comprehensive breaches of the decalogue. Hisses the villain never escaped, and I was puzzled to know how the poor actor could discriminate betwixt the hiss ethical and the hiss aesthetic. But perhaps no player ever received the latter; the house was very loyal to its favourites, all of whom had their well-defined rôles in every play, which spared the playwrights the task of indicating character. Before the heroine had come on we knew that she was young and virtuous—had she not been so for the last five and twenty years?— the comic man had not to open his mouth for us to begin to laugh; a latent sibilance foreran the villain. Least mutable of all, the hero swaggered on, virtuous without mawkishness, pugnacious without brutality. How sublime a destiny, to stand for morals and muscle to the generations of Hoxton, to incarnate the copy-book crossed with the "Sporting Times!" Were they bearable in private life, these monsters of virtue?

J. B. Howe was long this paragon of men—affectionately curtailed to Jabey. Once, when the villain was about to club him, "Look out, Jabey!" cried an agonised female voice. It followed from the happy understanding on both sides of the curtain that—give ear, O envious lessees!—no play ever failed. How could it? It was always the same play.

Of like kidney was the Grecian Theatre, where one went out between the acts to dance, or to see the dancing, upon a great illuminated platform. 'T was the drama brought back to its primitive origins in the Bacchic dances—the Grecian Theatre, in good sooth! How they footed it under the stars, those regiments of romping couples, giggling, flirting, munching! Alas! Fuit Troja! The Grecian is "saved." Its dancing days are over, it is become the Headquarters of Salvation. But it is still gay with music, virtue triumphs on, and vice grovels at the penitent form. In such quaint wise hath the "Eagle" renewed its youth, for the Grecian began life as the Eagle, and was Satan's deadliest lure to the 'prentices of Clerkenwell and their lasses:

Up and down the City Road, In and out the Eagle;
That's the way the money goes! Pop goes the weasel.

Concerning which immortal lines one of your grammatical pedants has observed, "There ain't no rhyme to City Road, there ain't no rhyme to Eagle." Great pantomimes have I seen at the Grecian—a happy gallery boy at three pence—pantomimes compact of fun and fantasy, far surpassing, even to the man's eye, the gilded dullnesses of Drury Lane. The pantomimes of the Pavilion, too, were frolicsome and wondrous, marred only by the fact that I knew one of the fairies in real life, a good-natured girl who sewed carpet-slippers for a living. The Pavilion, by the way, is in the Whitechapel Road, not a mile from the People's Palace, in the region where, according to the late Mr. Walter Besant, nobody ever laughs. The Pavilion, like the "Brit.," had its stock company, and when the leading lady appeared for her Benefit as "Portia," she was not the less applauded for being drunk. The quality of mercy is not strained. And what more natural than that one should celebrate one's benefit by getting drunk? Sufficient that "Shylock" was sober!

In Music-Halls, the East-End was as rich as the West—was it not the same talent that appeared at both, like Sir Boyle Roche's bird, winging its way from one to t' other in cabs? Those were the days of the great Macdermott, who gave Jingoism to English history, of the great Vance, of the lion comiques, in impeccable shirt-fronts and crush hats. There was still a chairman with a hammer, who accepted champagne from favoured mortals, stout gentlemen with gold chains, who might even aspire to conversation with the comiques themselves. Sic itur ad astra. Now there is only a chairman of directors who may, perhaps, scorn to be seen in a music-hall: a grave and potent seignior whose relations with the footlights may be purely financial. There were still improvisatori who would turn you topical verses on any subject, and who, on the very evening of Derby-day, could rhyme the winner when unexpectedly asked by the audience to do so. A verse of Fred Coyne's—let me recall the name from the early oblivion which gathers over the graves of those who live amid the shouts of worshippers—still lingers in my memory, bearing in itself its own chronology:

And though we could wish, some beneficent fairy
Had preserved the life of the Prince so dear,
Yet we WON'T lay the blame on Lieutenant Carey;
And these are the latest events of the year.

With what an answering pandemonium we refused to hold the lieutenant accountable for the death of the victim of the African assegais! And the ladies! How ravishingly they flashed upon the boards, in frocks that, like Charles Lamb at the India Office, made up for beginning late by finishing early! How I used to agree with the bewitching creature who sang that lovely lyric strangely omitted from the Anthologies:

What a nice place to be in!
What a nice place, I 'm sure!
Such a very jolly place,
I've never seen before.
It gives me, oh! such pleasure,
And it fills my heart with bliss,
I could stay here for ever:
What a nice place is this!

Such eyes she made at me—at whom else?—aloft in the balcony; and oh, what arch smiles, what a play of white teeth! If we could only have met! Yester-year at a provincial town some one offered to introduce her to me. She was still playing principal boy in the pantomime—a gay, gallant Prince, in plumed cap and tights. But I declined. Another of the great comic singers of my childhood—a man—I met on a Margate steamboat. He told me of the lost glories of the ancient days quorum pars magna fuit, and of the after-histories of his great rivals. One, I recollect, had retired with a fortune, opened a magnificent Temperance Hotel at the seaside, and then broken his neck by falling down his own splendid staircase, drunk. "Ah," said the veteran, sighing at an overcrowded profession, "there were only two or three comic singers in those days." "There are only two or three now," quoth I. And the old man beamed. Another ancient hero of the halls, long since translated to the theatres, whom I first saw at a music-hall in St. Giles', buttonholed me the other night in St. James', in the halls of a Duchess: a curious meeting. That I should have ever reverenced him seemed as strange as that there should be still people to reverence the coronet of the Duchess. Yes, it is very far off, that magic time when the world was full of splendid things and splendid men and women, a great Fair, and I, like the child in Henley's poem, wandered about, enjoying, desiring, possessing. Now I know there is nothing worth wanting, and nothing but poor flesh and blood, despite all the costumes and accessories. For there is no sense in which I have not been "behind the scenes." And as for the literal theatric sense, I have flirted with the goddesses at the wings till they have missed their cues, I have supped at the Garrick Club of a Saturday night, when all the stars come out, I have toured with a travelling company, I have had words of my own spoken by dainty lips—nay, I have even played myself, en amateur, the irascible old gentleman with the snuff-box and the coloured handkerchief. And what is there to say of the human spectacle, but that perhaps the pains and the crimes are necessary to the show, and that without a blood-and-thunder plot human life would not run, drying up of its own dullness? "All the world's a stage," and we are all cast for stock rôles. Some of us have the luck to be heroes, the complacent centre of eternal plaudits, some are born for villainy and the brickbat. And while others have had to play goodness knows what—mediaeval Italian princesses, Cockney cabmen, old Greek hetairae, German cuirassiers, American presidents, burglars, South Sea Islanders—I find myself—for the first time on any stage—in the applauded rôle of man of letters, if with little option of throwing up the part. They have an optimistic phrase, those happy-go-lucky creatures of the footlights, when, on the very day of production, nobody knows his words or his business, the scene will not shape itself, and chaos is lord. "It will be all right at night," they say. And we, who play our parts gropingly on this confused and noisy scene, wondering what is the plot, and where is the manager, and straining our ears for the prompter's whisper, can but echo with another significance their cheery hope: "It will be all right at night." Perhaps, when the long day's work has drawn to its end, and the curtain, has fallen upon the plaudits and the hisses, we shall all sit down to supper after the play, complimented by the Author, smiling at the seriousness with which we took our rôles of hero or villain, and glad to be done with, the make-up and the paint. And in the music that shall hover about our table, we may perhaps find a celestial restfulness, compared to which the most exquisite orchestras of this earth shall sound but as "tuning up."

III

ART IN ENGLAND

My friend the Apostle was in hot haste, and would not stay to be contradicted. "Not going to-night!" he cried, in horror-struck accents. "Why, to-night is the turning-point in the history of the British drama! To-night is the test-battle of the old and the new; it is the shock of schools, the clash of nature against convention. This play will decide the fate of our drama for the rest of the century. Here you have a play by a leader of the old school produced at a leading theatre. If it succeeds, the old drama may linger on for a year or two more; but if it fails, it will be the death-blow of the old gang. They may pack up!" The Apostle was at the other end of the street ere I had taken in the full import of these brave words. What! there was a crisis in the drama, and I, living in the heart of art, had heard nothing about it! Fortunately it was not too late. I could still make amends for my ignorance. It was still open to me to assist at this historic contest, for the arena was to be the Haymarket, where I am a persona gratis. Visions of the great first night of "Hernani" thronged tumultuously before me; my blood pulsed with something of its ancient youthful ardour as I girded my loins with black trousers for the fray, and adjusted my white tie with faltering fingers. I had half a mind to don a gilet rouge, but the reflection that my wardrobe did not boast of coloured waistcoats gave the victory to the other half. I dashed up to the theatre. All was placid. The stalls were packed with a brilliant audience in correct and unemotional costume. There were classic faces, and romantic faces, and faces that were realistic, but each and all blank of the consciousness of a crisis. The talk was of everything save art and literature. The critics did not even sharpen their pencils. They looked bored to a man. In vain my eye roved the arm-chairs in search of a fighting figure. I could not even see the musical iconoclast who had carried his pepper-and-salt suit into the holy of holies of the Italian opera. My heart sank within me. When the orchestra ceased I gave one last despairing glance all round the theatre in search of my friend the Apostle. He was not there!

The play was "The Charlatan,"—the work of that other apostle, whose outspoken Epistles to the English chronically relieve the dull decorum of London journalism; the man of whom Tennyson came near writing—

Buchanan to right of him,
Buchanan to left of him,
Buchanan in front of him,
Volleyed and thundered.

But that night it was the audience that volleyed and thundered, in unanimous applause. Hisses or party-cries were not. During the intense episodes, when the house was wrapt in silence, and you could have heard a programme drop, no opposition partisan as much as laughed. The author was called at curtain-fall, and retired uninjured. Next morning the critics were scrupulously suave, with no sign of the battle they had been through. Most wonderful to relate, Mr. William Archer, the risen hope of the stern and unbending Radicals, launched into unwonted praise, and gave an airing to some of the eulogistic adjectives that had been mouldering in his dictionary; nor did he even appear to be aware that he had gone over to the enemy!

For one thing, Bard Buchanan had given us neither old school nor new, but a blend of both—nay, a blend of all forms of both—a structure at once modern and mediaeval, with a Norwegian wing. It combined the common-sense of England with the glamour of the East, the physiology of the hypnotist with the psychology of Ibsen. More! It was an epitome of all the Haymarket plays, a résumé of all Mr. Tree's successes. The heroine was a mixture of Ophelia and hysteria, the hero was a combination of Captain Swift, Hamlet, and the Tempter; the paradoxical pessimist was a reminder of Mr. Wilde's comedies, the bishop and scientist were in the manner of Mr. Jones. How clever! Social satire à la Savoy, séance à la salle Egyptienne, sleep-walking à la Bellini, moonlight poetry à la Christabel, a touch of spice à la Française, and copious confession à la Norvégienne, all baked into one pie. How characteristic! And characteristic, mark you, not only of Mr. Buchanan's chaotic cleverness, but of Mr. Tree's experimental eclecticism. Did I say an epitome of the Haymarket plays? This is but another way of saying an abstract and brief chronicle of the time, to whose age and body Mr. Tree so shrewdly holds up the mirror. For this dying century of ours is all things to all men. We are living in the most picturesque confusion of the old and new known to history—in a cross-road of chronology where all the ages meet. 'T is a confusion of tongues outbabbling Babel, a simultaneous chattering of the centuries. And, more troubled than the Tower-builders, we understand, one another better than we understand ourselves; again, like "The Charlatan," half odic force, half fraud, who is never so honest as when he confesses himself charlatan.

But this is not what I set out to say. There was a moral to the tale of my friend the absentee Apostle who was so cocksure about the crisis. This moral is that he has Continental blood in his veins. To these foreign corpuscles he owes the floridness of his outlook, his conception of the excited Englishman. The Englishman takes his authors placidly; he is never in a ferment or a frenzy about anything save politics, religion, or sport: these are the poles and the axis of his life's pivot; he is not an artistic person. Art has never yet taken the centre of the stage in his consciousness; it has never even been accepted as a serious factor of life. All the pother about plays, poems and pictures is made by small circles. Our art has never been national art: I cannot imagine our making the fuss about a great writer that is made about a second-rate journalist in Paris. It is Grace the cricketer for whom the hundred thousand subscribe their shilling: fancy a writer thus rewarded, even after scoring his century of popular novels. The winning of the Derby gives a new fillip to the monarchy itself. A Victor Hugo in London is a thought à faire rire. A Goethe at the court of Victoria, or directing Drury Lane Theatre, is of a comic-opera incongruity. Our neighbours across the border have a national celebration of Burns' birthday—they think as much of him as of the Battle of Bannockburn. We English, who have produced the man whom the whole world acknowledges its greatest poet, have not even a Shakespeare Day. Surely Shakespeare Sunday would do as much good to the nation as Hospital Saturday or Shrove Tuesday! Charles Lamb wanted to say grace before reading Shakespeare, but the Puritans who make England so great and so dull are only thankful for stomachic mercies.

I cannot easily conceive our working ourselves up to such enthusiasm as the Hungarians lately displayed over the jubilee of Jokaï, an enthusiasm that resounded even unto this country, and shook the lacunar aureum of the Holborn Restaurant with shouts of "Eljen."

The peculiarity of the Hungarian temperament does not, however, entirely explain their joy in Jokaï. He is so much more than a mere novelist, poet and dramatist, with three or four hundred volumes (one need not be particular to a hundred with this modern Lope de Vega) to his credit. He is also a soldier and a politician, skilful with the sword as well as the pen, and with the tongue as well as the sword. He has drawn blood with each and all of these weapons, and though nowadays he often votes in the House without inquiring what he is voting for till he has recorded his vote, this does not diminish his claims to practical wisdom. He married the leading actress of Hungary, who, without waiting for an introduction, rushed forward from the audience to present him with a bunch of flowers when a play of his made a hit. Fancy Ellen Terry rushing forward to present Pinero with a bunch of flowers at the conclusion of "The Second Mrs. Tanqueray"! No, the thing is as impossible in England as the combination of rôles in Jokaï himself. The idea of letting a man be at once man of letters and man of action! Why, we scarcely allow that a man of letters may occupy more than one pigeonhole! If he is a poet, we will not admit he can write prose—forgetting that is just what most poets do. If he is a novelist, he cannot write plays—the truth being, of course, that it is the playwrights who cannot write plays. If he is a humourist he can never be taken seriously, and if he is accepted seriously he must be careful to conceal his sense of the humour of the position. Not only so, but we insist on the sub-sub-specialisation which Adam Smith showed to be so profitable in the making of pins, and which, passing from the factory to the laboratory, now threatens to pass from science into literature. Having analysed away the infinitely great, we are now devoting ourselves to the apotheosis of the infinitely little.

A priori, one would think action the salvation of the literary man, the corrective of "the fallacies of the den," the provider of that experience which is the raw material of literature, and prevents it from being spun out of the emptiness of one's own entrails. But the practical Briton knows better. He has never forgiven John Morley for going into politics (though I doubt not "honest John" would now find much to revise in his essay on "Compromise"); and he finds Socialism ever so much more Utopian since William Morris went into it. Can you imagine a true-born Briton following the flag of Swinburne, or throwing up a barricade with George Meredith? To the last Beaconsfield was suspected of persiflage because he wrote novels and was witty. America makes her authors ministers and envoys, but England insists that brains are a disqualification for practical life. "Authors are so unpractical: we don't want them to act— we only want them to teach us how to act." A chemist or an astronomer must needs isolate himself from the world to supply the pure theory on which the practical arts are founded, and so the littérateur, too, is expected to live out of the world in order to teach it how to live. But the analogy is false.

You can work out your mathematical calculations by the week, and hand over the results to the navigator. But the navigation of the stream of time is another matter. There is no abstract theory of life that can be studied without living oneself. Life is always concrete; it is built up of emotions, and you cannot have the emotions brought into your study, as you can order in your hydrochloric acid or your frog's leg. As well expect anchorites to set the tune for men in the thick of the fight! They will chant Masses when they should be shouting Marseillaises. In despair our men of letters leave the country, and become politicians in little savage islands; or they leave the town and become invisible behind their haloes; or they take to golf in small Scotch cities, and pretend that this satisfies their thirst for activity. Sometimes they turn market-gardeners and fob off the interviewer with remarks about caterpillars. Browning was reduced to dining out. It may be contended that the writer must sequester himself to cultivate the Beautiful. But the Beautiful that has not its roots in the True is not the Good. Or it maybe urged that active life would limit the writer's output. Exactly: that is one of the reasons that make active life so advisable. Every writer would write less and feel more. The crop of literature should only be grown in alternate years. As it is, a writer is a barrel-organ who comes to the end of his tunes, clicks, and starts afresh, just as a scholar is a revolving bookcase. Consider, too, how a holiday of action would disenthral the writer from the pettiness of cliques and coteries, with their pedantic atmosphere and false perspectives. I would have every University don work in the docks six months a year (six months' idleness is surely quite enough for any man); every platonic essayist should attend a course of music-halls; and if I could afford it I would set up all the superfine critics in nice little grocers' shops, with the cosiest of back parlours. Why, bless my soul! it is your man of culture, your author, your leader of thought, who is parochial, suburban, borné, and the rest of it! It is a commonplace that the Londoner is the most provincial of all Englishmen, living in sublime ignorance of what is thought and done in the rest of the kingdom; and in similar wise, when a man sneers at the bourgeoisie, I never think of looking up his pedigree in Debrett. It is, no doubt, extremely exasperating that the world was not created for the convenience and to the taste of artistic persons, but unfortunately the thing had to be turned out before their advice could be obtained.

That young England—bless its stupid healthy soul—is more interested in life and football than in literature and art, was amply proved by the lethargy about the Laureateship. On the Continent the claims of the rivals would have set the students brawling and the journalists duelling; here it barely caused a ripple in the five o'clock teacup. My friend the Apostle was not wholly wrong; there is a development of native drama ahead of us; only it will come about peaceably—we shall not hear the noise of the captains and the shouting. And the old conventions have a long run yet before them. They cling even to the skirts of "The Second Mrs. Tanqueray." Indeed, the new school can scarcely be said to have appeared. The literary quality of our plays has improved, thanks to Jones and Pinero, and not forgetting Grundy. And that is all. The old school is as vigorous as ever. In the person of "Charley's Aunt" it is alive and kicking up its petticoats, and the audience rolls in helpless laughter at Mr. Penley's slightest movement. Talk of literature, indeed! Why, the fortunate comedian assured me that if he chose he could spin out "Charley's Aunt" from a two-hours' play to a four-hours' play, merely by eking out his own "business." Think of this, aspiring Sheridans, ye who polish the dialogue with midnight oil; realise the true inwardness of the drama, and go burn me your epigrams!

In literature, where the clash of new and old is more audible, it is still the same story. On the conservative side, the real fighting is done by Messrs. Smith, who refuse to sell the too daring publication. The radicals are crippled by the timidity of editors, and cajoled by the fatness of their purses. A gifted young story-teller has been lecturing on the Revolt of the Authors. But it seems to me our literature has already as wide a charter as is desirable. The two bulwarks of the British library are Shakespeare and the Bible, and both treat human life comprehensively, not with the onesidedness of self-styled Realism. I would advise my young literary friends to emblazon on their banner "Shakespeare and the Bible." Real Realism is what English literature needs. The one undoubted development in recent English literature is the short story. But this is less due to any advance in artistic aspiration than to the fact that there is a good serial market for short stories, and the turnover is quicker for the trader than if he turned out long novels. Small stories, quick returns! In verity, this much-vaunted efflorescence of the conte is due to the compte. It is quite characteristic of our nation to arrive at a new art-form through this practical channel. But if you want a proof of the half-heartedness of our literary battles, turn to the "Fogey's" article on "The Young Men" in a recent Contemporary Review. What a chance for a much-needed onslaught on our minor prophets! It might have been "English bards and Scotch reviewers" over again. But no! the Scotch reviewer's weapon is merely a rose-water squirt. The only thing that perturbates him (as Mr. Francis Thompson would say) is my assertion that a ray of hopefulness is stealing again into English poetry. Since the days of Jeffrey we have only had one really "first-class fighting man" (Henley); but even with him there is no real party fighting, for he is catholic in his antipathies, and those whom he chastises love him, and swear that his is the least jaded Pegasus of the day. You see, therefore, how well-balanced we are in this "happy isle, set in a silver sea." The Fogeys are respectful to the young men, and the young men actually admire the Fogeys. That the young men admire one another goes without saying. Here surely is "the atmosphere of praise" of Mr. Pinero's hortation.

And while I do not believe that art is best nourished in this "atmosphere of praise," preferring to read instead "an atmosphere of appraisal," I believe that of this appraisal the more important element is "praise." Criticism with the praise left out savours of the counsel for the prosecution rather than of the judge—and indeed some critics assume that every author is guilty till he is proved good: if he is popular the presumption of his guilt is almost irresistible. A Henley young man once explained to me that the function of the critic was to guard the gates of literature, keeping at bay the bulk of print, for it would surely not be literature. This last is true enough; yet the watch-dog attitude generates a delight to bark and bite, and turns critic literally into cynic. Should not the true critic be an interpreter? For bad work let him award the damnation of silence. "It is better to fight for the good than to rail at the ill."

It is a great privilege to praise. It is a great joy to give an artist the joy of being understood. Not every artist arrives at the divine standpoint: "And God saw all that He made, and behold it was very good." The human creator is not always content with the rapture of creation. He sits lonely amid his worlds. Neglect may be the nurse of strength, but as often it is the handmaid of idleness. The artist without an audience will smoke the enchanted cigarettes of Balzac. The rough labour of execution is largely the labour of conveying to others what the artist already feels and sees. Why should he toil thanklessly? It is sweeter to dream. Even the money that art produces may be a valuable incentive. Not, of course, if the artist aims at the money; but art wrought for love may bring in money, like a woman married for love. In so far as the lover has his eye on the dowry, in so far his love is vitiated; and in so far as the artist has his eye on the profits, in so far is he untrue to a mistress who demands undivided allegiance. Natheless, the auri sacra fames may be his salvation. What subtle sympathy connects fama with fames? The butcher's bill may drive him from the dreamland of luxurious meditation to the practical embodiment of his dreams. Only, while he is at work, the laws of art alone must be his masters; he must not alter or abate a jot by way of concession to the great cash question. When he has completed his work, then indeed he may sell it in the best market. But the least preliminary paltering with the spirit of commerce is a degradation. Does this seem an ideal demand? Let us remember, then, ideals are goads and goals, counsels of perfection. No one expects people to come quite up to them, but it is better for human nature that they should be there. For there is something in hero-worship, despite Carlyle's grandiosities, provided you choose your hero wisely. We do, in this valley of doubt and confusion, touched with false sparkles, follow men who speak from their souls sincerely, who work from their hearts. Instinctively we feel it degrading and disillusionising that inspiration shall be paid in hard cash, and genius entered on the credit side of a ledger. Does a man plead that he has to support his wife and children? Well, in the first place, he need not have got them. In the second, one may be admirable as a man, but as an artist abominable. Still it is better that a man should write Adelphi dramas than that his starving family should qualify for scenes in them. All honour to the artist who lives on bread and water in a garret rather than prostitute his art! but less honour to the man who lives on my bread, and adds somebody else's whisky to his water, rather than earn an honest living by dishonest books and plays. This was the question that split up the Bohemians of Murger. While the majority did odd jobs for the Philistines, to have the time for real art, the very poet consenting to write Alexandrines for a dentist at fifteen sous a dozen—vastly cheaper than oysters—there was an inner band of the faithful who preferred starvation to the desecration of their genius for the unsaleable. Even so among the vegetarians there is a holier circle that eats only nuts and fruits. The sensible artist will compromise. There is in political economy a region called "the margin of subsistence." It is a sort of purgatory. Above it, we enter the heaven of superfluities; below it, lies the dread Hades of hunger. It is here that the impecunious artist—with a family (and, alas! the artist is nearly always impecunious—with a family) should pitch his tent. He may be allowed to prostitute himself, if need be, sufficiently to pay the ground-rent. He must not be driven lower down by his devotion to the Muses: an artist who dies of starvation is simply a dead donkey.

Rather than play a false note, he stops his music for ever. It is sublime—but silly. He had better black boots. There is no reason on earth why a shoeblack should not read Schiller, or moralise as he does in Bret Harte's parody of Bulwer Lytton. A bachelor artist might do worse than get locked up for some simple offence, and thus throw himself upon the nation. Remember what Sir Walter Raleigh did in prison. The poet can rise superior to the sordidness of skilly. Only he must be careful to preserve his seclusion. Leigh Hunt made his cell the artistic centre of London, but I doubt if he got through much work; and more recently, when Jokaï was in gaol, he was compelled to insist on two hours' privacy and confinement per day. To be a "first-class misdemeanant" seems to me the height of happiness for a literary man.

Unfortunately there are few honest opportunities for going to gaol. The most honest way of all would be to write the truth about men and things; but this editors will not print. So one has to live at one's own expense. Nevertheless, the Hotel of the Black Maria remains an ideal.

IV

BOHEMIA AND VERLAINE

It is one of the pleasures of my life that I never saw Tennyson. Hence I am still able to think of him as a poet, for even his photograph is not disillusionising, and he dressed for the part almost as well as Beerbohm Tree would have done. Why one's idea of a poet is a fine frenzied being, I do not quite know. One seems to pick it up in the very nursery, and even the London gamin knows a poet when he doesn't see one. Probably it rests upon the ancient tradition of oracles and sibyls, foaming at the mouth like champagne bottles. Inspiration meant originally demoniac possession, and to "modern thought" prophecy and poetry are both epileptic. "Genius is a degenerate psychosis of the epileptoid order." A large experience of poets has convinced me as little of this as of the old view summed up in genus irritabile vatum. Poets seem to me the homeliest and most hardworking of mankind—'t is a man in possession, not a daimon nor a disease. Of course they have their mad moods, but they don't write in them. Writing demands serenity, steadiness, patience; and of all kinds of writing, poetry demands the steadiest pen. Complex metres and curious rhyme-schemes are not to be achieved without pain and patience. Prose is a path, but poetry is a tight-rope, and to walk on it demands the nicest dexterity. You may scribble off prose in the fieriest frenzy—who so fiery and frenzied as your journalist with the printer's devil at his elbow?—but if you would aspire to Parnassus, you must go slow and steady. Fancy inditing a sonnet with the compositors waiting for "copy"! Pegasus were more truly figured as a drayhorse than a steed with wings; he jogs along trot-trot, and occasionally he stands at an obstinate pause. The splendid and passionate lyrics of Swinburne, with their structural involutions and complicacies, must have been "a dem'd grind." The English language does not easily lend itself to so much "linked sweetness long drawn out." Even the manuscript of Pope's easy meandering verse is disfigured by ceaseless corrections. As he himself says:

True ease in writing comes from art, not chance,
As those move easiest who have learn'd to dance.

Probably these very lines run in the original manuscript.

Shelley is the ideal of a poet, a soul of white fire, fed by bread and raisins; yet Shelley's last manuscripts are full of lacunae and erasures, some of which have had to be reproduced perforce in the printed editions.

Clothed with the ... as with light,
And the shadows of the night,
Like ... next, Hypocrisy,
On a crocodile rode by.

It reads like a puzzle set by a Competition Editor. Here is another one, which begins as beautifully as Hedda Gabler could desire, and ends in blankness.

Within the surface of the fleeting river
The wrinkled image of the city lay,
Immovably unquiet, and for ever
It trembles, but it never fades away;
Go to the [   ]
You, being changed, will find it then as now.

The fact is, of course, that inspiration is no guarantee of perfection. The limitations of inspiration vary with the limitations of the writer—a proposition that may be commended to the theologians. Genius can no more safeguard a man against his own ignorance than it can find a rhyme to "silver." Inspiration could not save Keats from his Cockney rhymes nor Mrs. Browning from her rhymeless rhymes. I met a poet in a London suburb—it seemed odd to see one out of Fleet Street—but after a few bewildered instants I recognised him. There was on his brow the burden of a brooding sorrow. I sought delicately to probe the cause of his grief, and he confessed at last that in a much-praised poem just published he had made a monosyllable dissyllabic. He had never got over a youthful mispronunciation, and in an unguarded moment of inspiration it had slipped in.

This prosaic view of poetry is distasteful to many, who like to think that "Paradise Lost" came out in a jet. But all these grandiose conceptions belong to the obscurantist view of human life, which is popular with all who hate, in Matthew Arnold's phrase, "to think clear and see straight." People fancy that the dignity of human life demands that artists at least should be Ouidaesque, but the true dignity of the artist is to be sublimely simple rather than simply sublime. The finest art—be it literature, music, or painting—is, after all that inspiration can do has been done, a matter of painful pegging away; and the finest artists will be found quietly occupying themselves with their art without pose or fuss. That side of the business is largely monopolised by the little men. But even the big men sometimes fall victims to the popular conception, as when a Byron stagily takes the centre of the universe, and looms lurid like the spirit of the Brocken. We do not need biographical scandal-mongers to tell us what "the real Lord Byron" was like. He was like "Don Juan," his own poem; shrewd, cynical, worldly, with flashes of exquisite feeling. The poem which is cut out of young ladies' editions of Byron is the one that represents him most truly in his blend of sensualism and idealism, whereas the Brocken figure is but Byron as he appeared to himself in his stormiest and gloomiest moments, and even that phantasm artistically draped and limelit by a poet's imagination. If people realised how much Byron wrote in his pitiable span of thirty-six years, how much hard labour went to make those cleverly-rhymed stanzas of "Childe Harold" or "Don Juan," despite Swinburne's accusation of botchery, they would see that he really had very little time to be wicked. They would understand that art—even the most decadent—is based on strenuous labour.

Young, gay, Radiant, adorned outside; a hidden ground
Of thought and of austerity within.

Even in poetically declaring himself a decadent, the artist must take as many pains as fall to the prosiest bourgeois. This is the paradox of the position. Just as the pyrrhonist in maintaining that there is no truth asserts one, so the literary pessimist partly contradicts his contention of the futility of existence by his anxiety to express himself elegantly. Leopardi's Italian and Schopenhauer's German are far superior to those of the optimistic philosophers; and one of the most polished poems of our day is poor Thomson's "City of Dreadful Night." So, too, the poet who declares himself an idler and a vagabond gives the lie to his pretensions by the labour he takes to clothe them in unimpeachable verse. The other morning I looked out of my study window after breakfast and discovered that the weather was heavenly. I had lingered over the meal, reading the beautiful political speeches, from which I gathered there was a Crisis at hand. I knew that Crisis. I had heard about it ever since I learnt to hear. Nevertheless, the newspapers were still devoting as much space to it as if it were brand-new, and beguiling me to take interest in it. I felt quite annoyed when I looked at the blue sky after breakfast and took deep breaths of ambrosial air, and thought how I had wasted my time. Thrilled by the sunshine, a cosmic rapture seized me, and I wondered that men should fritter away their time in politics and other serious occupations. The inspiration grew and grew, and I felt that my lips had been touched by the sacred fire, and that I had been called to preach a great moral lesson to mankind. So I took up my pen and wrote:

Bright the sun this lovely May-day;
Youth and love should have their heyday;
Every day should be a play-day.

Yet mankind will work and worry,
Over trifles fuss and flurry,
Getting hot as Indian curry.

Orators, in such a season,
How unreasonable is reason!
'Gainst the sunshine't is a treason.

What care I for Gladstone's glories?
Hang the Radicals and Tories!
Give me hammocks, pipes and stories!

What's the use of all this wrangling,
Grammar and emotions mangling?
Up the river let's go angling.

Sweet are walks and swimming nice is,
Bring me lemon-squash and ices,
Bother that eternal Crisis!

I was called away to lunch in the middle of the attack of inspiration. Inspiration is of course very useful, but it has a way of suggesting words that won't rhyme, and luring you off into all sorts of false tracks. Moreover, it affords no help whatever in polishing. After lunch I set to work with renewed zeal, licking the lines into their present perfection. At last they were finished, and as I lit the gas to enable me to see to make a fair copy, I realised that the beautiful blue day was gone.

Yes, the busy bee is a fraud by the side of the irresponsible artistic butterfly.

Sims Reeves tells an amusing anecdote of Mario the singer. Being brought one Thursday night by an eminent composer to sing at a big fashionable party, he found so great a line of carriages in front of his own that it was past midnight ere he arrived at the door. The thought that it was already Friday, and that he was about to sing in a new house, whose hostess he did not even know, had already dismayed the superstitious singer. But when he saw the number on the door was 13, no power on earth and no amount of argument could induce him to enter. "Ah, yes," said the hostess, smiling pleasantly, when the composer explained, "a very ingenious excuse, for which Mario ought to be grateful to you. Of course he was intoxicated, and after a long argumentation you at last persuaded him to go home."

Poe was doubtless occasionally drunk; but think of the years of sober labour, of stooping over desks, that must have gone to make those wonderful tales! Which is the true Poe, the hard drinker or the hard worker? That the artist must get drunk is, indeed, the belief of certain schools of young men even to-day; but is it not based on the old eternal false-logic, that because some artists have got drunk, therefore to get drunk is to be artistic? It was Murger who invented the Bohemian artist, poor and gay and of an easy morality. "Musette and Mimi!" says Sarcey. "The image of those ideal beings shone on every man who was twenty-one about 1848. 'La Vie de Bohème' was youth's breviary—fifty years ago." The great dramatic critic goes on to complain of the onslaught made upon him because he wrote against this "idleness of disposition, this heedlessness for the morrow, this inclination to look for the day's tobacco and the quarter's rent from loans and debts rather than from honest work, this witty contempt for current morality." But this is scarcely the teaching of the ever delightful book, which catches the spirit of youth and gaiety and irresponsibility wedded to artistic ardour as no other book has done before or since, and for which one might put in the plea that Charles Lamb made for the dramatists of the Restoration. Its world is only a pleasing fiction, and the ordinary rules of morality do not carry over into it. It is the East of Suez of literature, "where there ain't no Ten Commandments, and a man may raise a thirst." The real Bohemia, as Jules Valdes showed in "Réfractaires," is a world of misery and discontent. Still more sordid is the English Bohemia expounded by Mr. Gissing in "New Grub Street." Mr. Robert Buchanan indeed writes as if there had been a Murgerian Bohemia in England in his young days. "Et ego fui in Bohemiâ. There were inky fellows and bouncing girls, then; now there are only fine ladies, and respectable God-fearing men of letters." Really! Surely there are plenty of bouncing girls and inky fellows still, just as there were respectable God-fearing men of letters and fine ladies even in the roaring forties. I doubt if Bohemia was ever so amusing as Mr. Buchanan imagines now, and I suspect the bouncing girls were "gey ill to live with." What is true in the immortal Bohemian myth, what appeals to the universal human instinct, is the eternal contrast between the dreams and aspirations of youth and the sobrieties of success and middle age. As Jeffery Prowse sang:

I dwelt in a city enchanted, And lonely, indeed, was my lot;
Two guineas a week, all I wanted, Was certainly all that I got.
Well, somehow I found it was plenty, Perhaps you may find it the same,
If—if you are just five-and-twenty, With industry, hope, and an aim;
Though the latitude's rather uncertain, And the longitude also is vague,
The persons I pity who know not the City, The beautiful City of Prague!

This Bohemia will never disappear, because every generation of youth reconstructs it afresh, to migrate from it into the world of respectability above or the world of shame below. "Qu'on est bien à vingt ans!" will always be a cry to fill the breast of portly respectability with tender regret. As Thackeray put it in that delightful poem, which is almost an improvement on Béranger:

With pensive eyes the little room I view,
Where, in my youth, I weathered it so long;
With a wild mistress, a staunch friend or two,
And a light heart still breaking into song;
Making a mock of life and all its cares,
Rich in the glory of my rising sun,
Lightly I vaulted up four pair of stairs
In the brave days when I was twenty-one.

What a pity that life is so stern and severe, that for the light morality of Bohemia somebody must pay, some life be wrecked! Nature fills us with youth and romance, but for her own purposes only. She is the great matrimonial agent, and heavy is the penalty she exacts from those who would escape her books, and extract from life more poetry than it holds. And so the beautiful roselight of Bohemia veils many a tragedy, many a treachery. Yet will the grisette be ever a gracious memory, and literature will always embalm the "Mimi Pinson" of De Musset.

She is dead now, la grisette, even in Paris, and "hic jacet" may be written over the bonnet she threw pardessus les moulins.

Ah, Clemence! When I saw thee last Trip down the rue de Seine,
And turning, when thy form had pass'd, I said, "We meet again,"
I dreamed not in that idle glance Thy latest image came,
And only left to Memory's trance A shadow and a name.

That is how she affected even the Puritan Oliver Wendell Holmes. Yes, there is something in the Bohemian tradition that touches the sternest of us—not the roystering, dissolute, dishonourable, shady Bohemia that is always with us, bounded by the greenroom, the racecourse, the gambling club, and the Bankruptcy Court, but the Bohemia that is as unreal as Shakespeare's "desert country near the sea," the land of light purses and light loves, set against the spiritual blight that sometimes follows on pecuniary and connubial blessedness. For, after all, morality is larger than a single virtue, and Charles Surface is always more agreeable than Joseph or Tom Jones than Blifil, even when Joseph or Blifil is as proper as he pretends. And if Tom or Charles is a poet to boot, what can we not forgive him? The poet must have his experiences—be sure that nine tenths of them are purely of the imagination. For the other tenth—well, if Burns had been strictly temperate, "the world had wanted many an idle song," and we should not have celebrated his centenary so enthusiastically. The poet expresses the joy and sorrow of the race whose silent emotions become vocal in him, and it is necessary that he should have a full and varied life, from which "nihil humanum" is alien. Mr. Barry Pain once wrote a subtle story, which only three persons understood, to show that a great poet might be an elegant egotist, of unruffled life and linen. If so, I should say that such a poet's genius would largely consist of hereditary experience; he would, in language that is not so unscientific as it sounds, be a reincarnation of a soul that had "sinned and suffered." But as a rule the poet does his own sinning and suffering, and catches for himself that haunting sense of the glory and futility of life which is the undertone of the modern poet's song, and which finds such magical expression in Heine's verses:

I have loved, oh, many a maiden kind,
And many a right good fellow—
Where are they all? So pipes the wind,
So foams and wanders the billow.

But the poet's morals are maligned. The fierce light which beats upon the throne of song reveals the nooks and crannies of the singers' lives, which for the rest they themselves expose rather than conceal. I should say that the average morality of the poet is much superior to the average morality of the man of the world who sins in well-bred silence. The poet gloats over his sins—is musically remorseful or swingingly defiant; he hints or exaggerates or invents. That is where the poet's imagination comes in—to give to airy nothings a local habitation and a name. The poet's imagination is often far more licentious than his life; the "poet's licence" is rightly understood to be limited to his language. To have written erotic verses is almost a certificate of respectability: the energy that might have been expended in action has run to rhyme. Qui ose tout dire arrive à tout faire, say the French. Arrives at, perhaps, though even this is doubtful, but certainly does not start from that platform. Much less questionable were it to say: Qui ose tout faire arrive à ne rien dire.

The late M. Verlaine will be cited as a substantiation of the popular idea of the vagabond poet. The Verlaine legend has now been consecrated by his death; and for all time, I suppose, Verlaine will rank with Villon as an impossible person. He may have been all that is said, all that is hinted, even in Mr. George Moore's famous description of him. "I once saw Verlaine. I shall not forget the bald prominent forehead (une tête glabre), the cavernous eyes, the macabre expression of burnt-out lust smouldering upon his face."

But there is another side to him, and it is perhaps because I do not go about the world with Mr. Moore's "macabresque" eye, which to-day happily sees things in a soberer colouring, that I saw this other side of Verlaine when, like Mr. George Moore, I hunted him up on his native heath. For one thing, I was not prepared to see anything very lurid and diabolique: life is really not so picturesque as all that. I knew besides that he had been a schoolmaster in England; and can you imagine anything more tedious and toilsome than to be the "French master," the poor, despised, "frog-eating Mounseer Jacques" of boys' stories, the butt of all their facetious brutality? If ever anything was calculated to make a man diabolique! I trust biographers will not forget to place all this depressing drudgery to our "vagabond's" credit. Think of it! The first poet of France correcting French exercises! The poet of the passions conjugating the verb aimer in its hideous grammatical reality!

Fumons philosophiquement,
Promenons-nous
Paisiblement: Rien faire est doux.

So might Verlaine write, though contradicting himself by doing something in so doing; but in the absurd actual he had to earn his bread and butter, and man cannot live by poetry alone, unless one sings the joys and sorrows of the middle classes. It was rather late at night before, having vainly hunted for him in his favourite restaurants, I found the narrow, poverty-stricken rue in which Verlaine was living a year or so ago. Passing through a dark courtyard, I had to mount interminable stone stairs, lighting foul French matches as I went, to relieve the blackness. At last I arrived outside his door, very near the sky. I knocked. A voice called out, "I've gone to bed." I explained my lateness and said I would call to-morrow.

"No, no! Attendez!" I heard him jump out of bed, stumble and grope about, and then strike a match; and in another instant the door opened, and in the interstice appeared a homely nightcapped bourgeois pulling on his trousers. There flashed on me incongruously the thought of our English laureate's stately home by the sea, in which, jealously guarded by hedges and flunkeys, the poet chiselled his calm stanzas; and all the vagabond in me leapt out to meet the unpretentious child of Paris. He greeted me with simple cordiality; and, ugly and coarse though his face was, it was lit up throughout by a pleasant smile. His notorious leg was bandaged, but not repulsively. No, "homely" is the only impression I shall ever have of Verlaine, the man. Even in that much maligned "macabresque" head of his, there was more of the bonhomme than of the poet or the satyr. The little garret was his all in all; a bed took up half the space. On the table stood the remains of supper. A few shelves of books, a sketch or two, and a bird-cage with a canary were the only attempts at ornament.

Such was Verlaine at the climax of his fame, when he had won a sure immortality; simple and childlike, and with a child's unshamed acceptance of any money one might leave behind on the mantelpiece. He seems to have made very little by his verses. He spoke English quite well, having probably acquired it when teaching French; and he was perhaps more proud of it than of his poems. Mr. Moore says he wished to translate Tennyson. He read aloud a poem he had just written in celebration of his own fiftieth birthday. There was an allusion to a "crystal goblet." "Ce verre-là!" he interpolated, with a humorous smile, pointing to a cheap glass with the dregs of absinthe that stood on the table. There was also an allusion to a "blue-bird," a sort of symbol of the magic of spring, I fancy, that flutters through many of his poems. (The "plumage bleutê de l'orgueil" figures in one of his very last verses.) When he arrived at this "blue-bird" he pointed to the cage with the same droll twinkle: "Cet oiseau-ci." When I left him he stood at the head of the gloomy stone stairs to light me down, and the image of him in his red cotton nightcap is still vivid. And now he is only an immortal name. Ah, well! after the English school-rooms, the French prisons, the Parisian garrets and hospitals, the tomb is not so bad. Rien faire est doux.

In giving him place with the immortals I feel no hesitation. An English clergyman found immortality by writing one poem—"The Burial of Sir John Moore,"—and, however posterity may appraise Verlaine's work as a whole, he has left three or four lyrics which can die only if the French language dies, or if mankind in its latter end undergoes a paralysis of the poetic sense such as Darwin suffered from in his old age. Much of his verse—especially his later verse—is to me, at least, as obscure as Mallarmé. But

Il pleut dans mon coeur
Comme il pleut dans la rue

can never be surpassed for the fidelity with which it renders the endless drip, drip of melancholia, unless it is by that other magical lyric:

Les sanglots longs
Des violons De l'automne
Blessent mon coeur
D'une langueur Monotone.

He is the poet of rhythm, of the nuance, of personal emotion. French poetry has always leant to the frigid, the academic, the rhetorical—in a word, to the prosaic. The spirit of Boileau has ruled it from his cold marble urn. It has always lacked "soul," the haunting, elusive magic of wistful words set to the music of their own rhythm, the "finer light in light," that are of the essence of poetry. This subtle and delicate echo of far-off celestial music, together with some of the most spiritual poems that Catholicism has ever inspired, have been added to French literature by the gross-souled, gross-bodied vagrant of the prisons and the hospitals! Which is a mystery to the Philistine. But did not our own artistic prisoner once sing:

Surely there was a time I might have trod
The sunlit heights, and from life's dissonance
Struck one clear chord to reach the ears of God?

Was ever more devout Catholic than Benvenuto Cellini, who murdered his enemies and counted his beads equal gusto?

V

THE INDESTRUCTIBLES

I wonder if you have ever been struck by the catholicity—not to say the self-contradictoriness—of the constant correspondent. The creature will enter with zest into any discussion; there is no topic too small for it, and certainly none too great. The following letters, carefully culled from the annual contributions of a lady whose epistolary career I have followed with interest, will indicate the delicious inconsequence that has made them for me such grateful reading:

1888.

SIR—There is nothing in life worth purchasing by pulsations and respirations. The world is a dank, malarious marsh, with fitful Will-o'-the-Wisp flashes of false radiance—a vast cemetery waiting for our corpses. There is no such thing as happiness.

Nature, red in tooth and claw
With ravin, shrieks against

the idea. Youth is an illusion, maturity a regret, and old age an apprehension. Fortunately Providence has sent us a panacea—Universal Suicide.

I am, Sir, Yours obediently, AGATHA P. ROBINS.

1889.

SIR—Surely "A Mad Englishman" and "Dorothy X.," who maintain so glibly that country life is more enjoyable than town life, fail to realise how much of our pleasure depends on human intercourse. It is given only to poets to talk with trees. Nor can ordinary mortals find

Sermons in stones,
Books in the running brooks.

We need the cathedrals and the libraries that are to be found only in the great centres of national life—yes, and also the art galleries and the theatres. Of course, if people will martyr themselves to keep up appearances, and want to live in a fashionable neighbourhood, they will not find town life either cheap or pleasant. But if they are content to live outside the aristocratic radius, they can find many a comfortable villa, with baths (hot and cold), and back gardens which may easily be converted into rustic retreats (I would especially recommend rhododendrons). If you are also not above omnibuses (taking a cab only when it rains, and selecting a driver who does not look as if he would swear), and are satisfied to go to the pit, then I feel sure London is not only as cheap as the obscurest village, but gives you a far greater return for your money. Newly-married couples in especial often make a great mistake in settling in the country for the sake of economy. It is only in the town that they can really lead a tranquil, happy life, enriched with all the resources of culture and civilisation.

I am, Sir, Yours obediently, AGATHA P. ROBINS.

1890.

SIR—The failure of marriage is too apparent to be glossed over any longer. "A.Y.Z." and "A Woman of No Importance" deserve the thanks of every honest heart for their brave outspokenness. Too long has this mediaeval monstrosity cramped our lives. The beautiful word "Home" conceals a doll's house or whitewashes a sepulchre. Marriage is misery in two syllables. How can people be happy chained together like galley-slaves? It contradicts all we know of human nature.

Love, free as air, at sight of human ties
Spreads his light wings and in a moment flies.

Away with this effete Pharisaism! Let us realise the infinite possibilities of happiness latent in the blessing of existence. The world is longing for freedom to love truly, nobly, wisely, many.

I am, Sir, Yours obediently, AGATHA P. ROBINS.

1891.

SIR—I can testify by personal experience to the fact that the manners of our children are deteriorating. Coming up to the Metropolis for a day's excursion last Bank Holiday, I could not walk anywhere without overhearing ribald remarks—and, what was worse, at my own expense—even from respectably dressed children. Let those look to it who

Teach the young idea how to shoot.

I thank Heaven my lot has always been cast in a sweet Devonshire village, where the contagion of ill-conduct has not yet spread among the juvenile population.

I am, Sir, Yours obediently, AGATHA P. ROBINS.

1892.

SIR—Have your flippant correspondents, "Polygamist" and "Illegal Brother-in-Law," any conception of the thousands (ay, tens of thousands) of hearts that are, languishing in misery because they cannot marry their deceased sisters' husbands? And all because of a text which is not to be found in the Bible! Fie upon you, ye so-called Bishops,

Dressed in a little brief authority.

Abolish this unrighteous law, I say, and let floods of sunshine and happiness into a million darkened homes.

I am, Sir, Yours obediently, AGATHA P. ROBINS.

But, after all, is it fair to juxtaposit Agatha's letters? What if one were to collect the leaders of any newspaper on any given subject, before or after any event? I have met Agatha P. Robins in many other places at many other times. Sometimes she is interested in the best substitute for shirt-buttons or for Christianity, sometimes in the problem of living on a thousand a year, sometimes in the abolition of stag-hunting.

SIGNS OF THE SILLY SEASON.

A gooseberry that groweth green and great,
A serpent round the sea serenely curled,
A lonely soul that fails to find a mate,
A boy redundant in a teeming world,

A sister yearning for dead sisters' shoes,
A life that longs for death, or after-life,
A ghost, a mistress whom her maids abuse,
An erring judge, a French or German wife,

A child's long ear or holiday, a slum,
A man gone bald, or drunk, a coin's design—
Should things like these across your paper come,
Conclude the Silly Season will be fine.

It is difficult to trace exactly when "The Season" ends and "The Silly Season" begins. It needs the finest discrimination to know when the adjective comes in—without a worldly training, indeed, you cannot tell the one from the other. But the past masters of the social art proclaim that "The Season" is dead, and we bow our heads in reverence. Yes, it is vanished, that focus of futilities, that wonderful Season, that phantasmagoria of absurdities, of abortive ambitions, over which a hundred humourists have made merry: it is dead, with its splendours and jubilations and processions—dead as the ropes of roses in St. James's street. Often have I debated the potency of satire, again and again have I suggested to learned friends a scientific and historical investigation of the popular belief that satire moves mountains or even molehills. But they agree only in shrinking from the task. To take only the last half-century: we have had one supreme satirist who harped eternally on the failings of fashion and the vanity of things. In his novels society saw itself reflected in all its attitudes and postures and posings. Not one meanness or folly escaped. What Professor Huxley has done for the crayfish, that Thackeray did for the Snob. He studied him lovingly, he dissected him, he classified every variety of him. A thousand disciples, less gifted but equally remorseless, followed in the Master's footsteps. "Punch" took up the tale, and week by week repeated the joke. It was heard in drawing-room recitations to the accompaniment of pianos; it even went on the stage. Ladies rushed into print to expose foibles men never guessed, and to say of the sex at large what less gifted women say only of their personal friends. For years we have never ceased for a moment to hear the lash of the whip, the swish of the birch, the whizz of the arrow, the ping of the bullet, the thwack of the flail, the thud of the hammer, the buzzing of the hornet. And what does it all amount to? How much execution has been done? Is society purer or nobler? Have less daughters been sold at Vanity Fair, or more invitations been sent to poor relatives? Has Jones got better manners or champagne? Is Mrs. Ponsonby de Tomkins more distant to duchesses? Did my Lady Clara Vere de Vere consider whether Hood's seamstress was at work on her court gown? Is any one wiser or kinder or honester for all the literary pother? Are the diplomatic corps less maculate than in the days of Grenville Murray? Have we not, on the contrary, cast on our own imperfections the complaisance of an eye educated in the superior imperfections of our neighbours?

Lo, here is a new satirist arisen, Sarah Jeannette Duncan, who, in "The Simple Adventures of a Memsahib," sketches Anglo-Indian society in a manner that would not discredit Thackeray—and with something, too, of Thackeray's haunting sense of the pathos of the dead Past and the flying Present. But will the memsahib of to-morrow take warning by the fate of Helen Peachey, who went out to India in all her bridal bravery, in all her youth and freshness? Will she escape exchanging the placidity of Fra Angelico's piping cherubim for the petulance and ring-shadowed eyes of the seasoned matron? Will she be on her guard against shrinking to the prejudices and flirtations of a coterie, dying to all finer and higher issues? Will she worship virtue more and viceroys less? Alas, I fear me not—no more than Pagett, M. P., will leave off talking solar myths, or foolish things cease to be done under the deodars. Will Hogarth keep wine-bibbers from the bottle, or can you make men sober by acts of "L'Assommoir"? Will "Madame Bovary" stay a sister's fall, or "Sapho" repel an eligible young man? Will "The Dunciad" keep one dunce from scribbling, or "Le Tartufe" elevate a single ecclesiastic? As well expect "long firms" to run short, and the moths to avoid the footlights, and the fool to cease from the land. "How gay they were, and how luxurious, and how important in their little day! How gorgeous were the attendants of their circumstances, on the box with a crest upon their turbans!—there is a firm in Calcutta that supplies beautiful crests. And now, let me think! some of them in the Circular Road Cemetery—cholera, fever, heat-apoplexy; some of them under the Christian daisies of England—probably abscess of the liver." Yes, madam, we know it all, we recognize the Thackeray touch. "And soon, very soon, our brief day, too, will have died in a red sunset behind clustering palms, and all its little doings and graspings and pushings, all its petty scandals and surmises and sensations, will echo further and further back into the night." True, most true, and pity 't is 't is true. But meantime we will go on with our little doings and graspings and pushings—yes, madam, even you and I who have realised the vanity of all things; for the knowledge thereof—this, too, is vanity. "And it was all a striving and a striving, and an ending in nothing, and no one knew what they had lived and worked for." Yea, so it is, Frau Schreiner. And still we are living on—and oh! how hard we work (on African farms or otherwise) to express artistically our sense of the futility of life!

VANITAS VANITATUM.

A rich voluptuous languor of dim pain,
A dreamy sense of passionate regret,
Delicious tears and some sweet, sad refrain,
Some throbbing, vague, and tender canzonet,
That mourns for life so real and so vain,
Wherein we glory while our eyes are wet.

I am afraid, if I pursue this investigation, I shall end by believing that satire is simply an aesthetic satisfaction—the last luxury of the sinful. Ridicule, we are always told, is a tremendous destructive—an atmosphere in which nothing can live. But is it? Christianity, Kings, and War are little the worse for the jets of mockery that have been playing on them for two centuries. In Swift's day the wits at the coffee-houses regarded religion as a farce that even the Augurs could not keep up any longer without public winking; yet Diderot and the Encyclopaedia are dead, and the bishops we have always with us! It was thought War could not survive Voltaire's remark that a monarch picks up a parcel of men who have nothing to do, dresses them in blue cloth at two shillings a yard, and marches away with them to glory—but here is our Henley singing a song of the sword, while all our novelists are looking to their weapons. Despite Heine's sarcasm, the collection of English kings is as incomplete as ever. A passing fad can, perhaps, be made to pass along a little faster, but it only makes room for another. True, "Punch" killed the craze for sunflowers and long necks; but then "Punch" invented it. It was merely made to be destroyed brilliantly, like a Chinese cracker or a Roman candle. Folly is older than "Punch's" jokes, and will survive them. Snobbery and self-seeking, pettiness and stupidity, envy, hate, and all uncharitableness, were no secret to the mummies in the British Museum. "Unto the place whither the rivers go, thither they go again." Are there not a hundred sayings in Ecclesiastes and Menander, in Horace and Molière, as apt to-day as though fresh from the typewriter? One of the learned friends to whom I proposed the thesis contended that Perseus and Juvenal at least are out of date. But this was merely my learned friend's ignorance. Is it not the truest piety to conclude that those things which the ridicule of the ages cannot kill deserve their immortality—that Kings, War, and Christianity play a part in the scheme of creation, and that even snobbery and jobbery, folly and fraud, rouge and respectability, and horse-racing, bounders and politicians, the prize-ring and the marriage market, are all necessary to the fun of Vanity Fair! They are thrown up by the flux of things for Honesty to set his heel on. So houp-la! On with the dance! louder, ye fiddlers! faster, O merry-go-round! Nay, not so glum, ye moralists and satirists, philanthropists and preachers; link hands all—ducdame, ducdame!—and thank the gods for keeping you in occupation. What should we do without our fools? The question seems pat for a Silly Season correspondence. Come, gather, fools all. Ye could not be better employed than in answering it. For, mark, brother-satirists mine, you cannot kill the Silly Season correspondence.

And you cannot kill Ghosts. Perhaps because they do not exist. No other dead thing is so tenacious of life as your ghost. If ridicule were really fatal, we should have given up the ghost long since. Consider the fires of burlesque through which he has passed unscathed. What indignity has been spared him? Now at last he is to encounter the supreme test—he is to be taken seriously. The Psychical Society has the matter in hand—or should one say, the spirit? And Mr. Stead, who believes in himself in a way that is refreshing in these atheistic times, proposes either to rehabilitate the ghost or to lay him for ever. But this latter is beyond the might of man or society.

And you cannot kill Grouse. At least I can't. I sometimes suspect there are others of the population equally incompetent, and perhaps still less interested in battues; though the Twelfth figures in everybody's calendar like a Church festival, and the newspapers devote leaders to it, and the comic papers have pictures, and sometimes even jokes about it, and you would think the whole population of these islands struck work and went a-shooting with gillies and dogs and appropriate costume. But that is the craftiness of the editors, from Mr. Buckle and Mr. Yates down to the editor of the Halfpenny Democrat—they make the humblest of us feel we are in the best sets, so we all come up to town for the season, and are seen at three parties a night, and we ride in the Park, and we go to Henley and Goodwood to a man; and we yacht at Cowes, and pot grouse in Scotland—still with the same wonderful unanimity; and we hunt with the hounds, and run with the salmon, and keep our Christmas in country houses, and come up smiling for the New Year, ready to recommence the same old Sisyphean round. I suppose the people who really do these things could be exhibited in the National Gallery, but the space their doings fill is incalculable.

And you cannot kill Adelphi Melodrama. But I have a piece of advice to offer to the Italian gentlemen who have done so much for our stage. It is, that they run their theatre on a principal of duality befitting their joint management. Let it be the home of Melodrama and Burlesque, the same play serving for both genres. Let, say, Mr. Sims—who is so clever in either species—write the pieces—each melodrama being its own burlesque. An extra dash of colour here, an ambiguous line there, with a serious meaning in the melodrama and a droll in the burlesque, will secure the brothers two audiences, and after eight o'clock I guarantee standing room only. The simple will come to weep and thrill, the cynics to laugh and chuckle. And everybody will be happy.

In sooth, is not the world divided into those who take the great cosmic drama seriously, and those who treat it as farce? On the one hand the workers and the fighters, on the other the journalists, politicians, and men about town. Yet have the workers and the fighters the nobler part. A genuine emotion, an earnest conviction, vitalises life. The day-dreams of hungry youth are better than the dinners of prosaic maturity, and a simple maiden in her flower is worth a hundred epigrams. I had rather be an Adelphi god than a smoking-room satyr.

Who shall blame the melodramatist? He writes for those to whom literature makes no appeal. Literature is a freemasonry of the highest minds, and that poetry is Greek to the masses I should scarcely have thought a "Question at Issue" demanding substantiation from Mr. George Gissing. Mr. Gosse must know that the eclipse which darkened England at the passing of Alfred Tennyson was invented by the newspapers and the poets who outraced one another to weep upon his tomb. Look upon Mr. Booth's map of East London, with its coloured lines showing the swarms of human beings who live ignobly and die obscurely, and realise for yourself of what import the cult of beautiful form is to these human ant-heaps. Walk down the populous Whitechapel Road of a Saturday night, or traverse the long slimy alleys of Rotherhithe among the timber wharves, and discover how many of your countrymen and contemporaries are living neither in your country nor in your century. To Mr. Henry James, the dull undertone of pain and sorrow is part of the music of London—such harmony is in aesthetic souls. But the dull and the gross, who only suffer and endure, the muddy vesture of decay closes them in and they cannot hear it.

What shall literature do for these? In a great smoky Midland town, on dreary pavements, under sloppy skies, I saw a girl who was a greater argument for melodrama than all the cheques of all the managers. She was going to her work in the raw dawn, her lunch in a package under her arm; the back was bent and the face was pale and pinched, but there was a slumbering fire of romance in the deep-fringed eyes, and suggestions of poetry lurked in the shadows of her hair; and at once my breast was full of stirrings to write for her—only for her—a book full of beauty and happiness and sunshine, and, oh! such false views of life, such inaccurate pictures of the pleasures of a society she would never know. The hero should be handsome and brave and good, with a curling moustache; and the heroine should be beautiful and true, with an extensive wardrobe; and the clouds would come only to roll by, and the story should die away in an odour of orange-blossom, and in a music of marriage-bells. And there should be lots of money for everybody, and any amount of laughter and gaiety, and I would give dances twice a volume, and see that all the girls had partners, delightful waltzers with good conversation. And there would be garden-parties (weather permitting invariably), and picnics without green spiders, and sails without sea-sickness. And as for truth and realism—fie on them! We can create a much nicer world than nature's. Why be plagiarists, when we can make universes of our own?

VI

CONCERNING GENERAL ELECTIONS

Twice in succession has it befallen me to be privately busy in a backwater when the main stream was spuming and ramping with the great bore of a general election. I have been able to hear the swallows twitter at sunrise in serene unconsciousness of the crisis, to watch the rooks homing at twilight, as though the course of Nature were still the same, and to see the moonlight rippling over the sombre water at midnight in unaffected tranquillity. Myself was scarcely better informed of the tidal flood: stray echoes of speech, odd fragments of newspaper floated down to me, and at intervals some visitant from the greater deep held, like a sea-shell, the rumour of its sounding waters.

And, indeed, where shall we find a better metaphor for party-government than this of the tide, of the ebb and flow of political power—remorseless, inevitable, regardless of those who, tossed high on the stream, imagine they direct it? And in this metaphor the People must play Moon, like the clown in "A Midsummer Night's Dream." But, as Juliet says:

O swear not by the moon, th' inconstant moon.

The cause of this inconstancy has not escaped even the philosophers. The Whig and the Tory, rival lovers of Luna—moonstruck ravers—woo her with honeyed words and dulcet promises, and she inclines her coquettish ear—most of the month she is all ear—to the highest bidder. But when she comes to her full—and is all eye—then she perceives her swain faithless and empty-handed, and straightway she plights her troth to his clamorous and expostulant fellow, who dangles his untried promises before her disappointed vision. And the days pass, and she rises and sets; but lo! the bridal gifts linger still, and the horn of plenty is an empty trumpet, and, forgetful of her first lover's failure, she turns to him again. And so for ever, in a fickle quest of fidelity, pathetic enough. Perhaps she—with the two strings to her bow—shares the just fate of coquettes, happy with neither; perhaps she were wiser to give herself to a single lover, and be rid for ever of these hesitancies. And yet, would she profit by the change? Endymion, the one youth whose beauty drew her from heaven, remained perpetually asleep. Is there not some profound significance in the ancient myth, some truth that would have pleased Francis Bacon, Baron Verulam (as the pedants will have us call the man who did not write Shakespeare).

But the philosophers, who have understood the levity of mind that underlies changes of Cabinets, have not always understood the numerical pettiness of the voting power by which the change is effected. Just as every philosopher is born a Platonist or an Aristotelian, so, as Mr. Gilbert sings, is every Englishman born a little Liberal or a little Conservative: even if his politics be not original sin, it is early acquired. Thus, then, the nation consists of two great camps—the Liberals and the Conservatives—which are practically fixed; standing armies that may be relied upon. A born Liberal may wax fat and kick at his ancient principles: a born Conservative may change his coat and turn Whig. But these exceptions are rare. For the most part men stick to their party and die as foolish as they were born—which is called consistency. Convinced sometimes against their will, they are of the same opinion still. Loyalty and obstinacy will look facts in the face and never blench, and every one remains truer to his social circle than to his private judgments. People's politics are their prejudices at a masked ball, and the Conservatives will vote Conservative and the Liberals Liberal, through a cannonade of unanswerable cartoons. Apart from these two great standing armies, there is a shifting body of free-lances, guerrillas, Jacks-o'-both-sides, call them what you will—waverers who have too much conscience or too little, who are swayed by their reason or their pocket, or who are gullible enough to believe that the opposition will do better, or sportsmen enough to desire fair play and a chance for the other side, and who are found fighting now in this camp, now in that. The camps themselves are fairly matched: Rads and Tories—the sexes of politics—are as evenly created as men and women. They are like ten-pound weights standing on either scale of a balance. What, then, determines the oscillation this way or that? Evidently the miserable little half-ounce weight placed sometimes on one side, sometimes on the other. In fine,'tisthe tiny squadron of free-lances that wins general elections, the voters who think or who don't think, or who veer to be with the majority. The Jacks-o'-both-sides rule England, even as the Parnell brigade ruled Parliament. To this floating population is it given to make or unmake Cabinets; theirs is the righteous indignation that sweeps the country like a new broom, and sweeps Ministries into limbo; to them is made the magniloquent "appeal to the country!" L'état, c'est nous! might be the motto of this third party, were it but conscious of itself as a party.

"The majority is never right," cries Dr. Stockmann in "The Enemy of the People." "Never, I say. That is one of those conventional lies against which a free, thoughtful man must rebel. Who are they that make up the majority of a country? Is it the wise men or the foolish? I think we must agree that the foolish folk are, at present, in a terribly overwhelming majority all around and about us the wide world over. But, devil take it, it can surely never be right that the foolish should rule over the wise.... The majority has might—unhappily—but right it has not. I and a few others are right." But how if "I and a few others" organised themselves after the fashion of the Parnellites? how if the wise men made up their minds that the world should no longer be governed with the proverbial minimum of wisdom, and, taking advantage of the natural balance of parties, resolved that they should be the ones to supply the principle of movement to the equilibrated social machine? Surely the Millennium could not long resist the Philosophers' party. But, alas! would the wise men agree? Would not they also split up into two factions? And even if philosophers were kings and kings philosophers, would the kingdom of Plato be at hand?

Popular suffrage is much maligned. "Think," says Bouvard, one of the tragi-comic twain who serve for title to that saddest of all humorous books, Flaubert's "Bouvard et Pécuchet," "think of all those who buy pomades and patent medicines. These blockheads form the electorate and we submit to their will. Why can't one make three thousand a year by breeding rabbits? Because too much crowding together is fatal to them. In like manner, by the mere coming together of a crowd the germs of stupidity which it contains get developed and the consequences are incalculable." But popular suffrage does not operate like this at all. One might almost say that half the stupidity contradicts and annihilates the other half: in practice the franchise carries its own antidote—the "germs of stupidity" do not get developed, but destroyed. The metaphor of germs would be more appropriate if applied to the ideas of the party-programmes, for these ideas are introduced by a few wise or foolish men and disseminated epidemically throughout their respective parties. Democracy never escapes aristocracy, for the people never invents ideas; its whole power is that of choice between the ideas offered by its would-be leaders, and even these ideas it accepts less as a philosopher than as a patient, rather as "germs" than as thoughts. And when once it has accepted its leaders or its representatives, the beautiful parliamentary system deprives it of all further rights of interference for a term of years, and the policy of the country is far more dependent on the intestine rivalries and manoeuvrings of the representatives than on the desires and demands of the represented. In a really democratic system there would be a central bureau of statesmen not necessarily elected by the voice of the people, and this bureau should have for object not the wrangling over measures, but the mere proposition of them. These trained thinkers and diplomatists—accepting advice freely from the great newspapers and the chiefs of factions—would propose whatever measures seemed necessary from time to time for the preservation, the elevation, and the dignity of the commonweal, and these propositions would be submitted officially to every franchise-holder, just as the inquisitive census-paper or the parochial voting-paper is to-day. The "Ayes" or "Noes" of the people would have it, not of those who represent them, save the mark! The details could be drafted by specialists, as to-day. That this would be a better or even a feasible system I do not say; but I do maintain that any other democracy than this is a fraud. To have the ten-thousandth part of a voice in selecting among the varying policies of sundry ambitious gentlemen, all of whom have been foisted on me by committees, and of whom the successful one—whose professed views may be quite antithetical to mine and can at best only roughly represent them—will have, when he is not absent or manoeuvred into silence, the six-hundred-and-seventieth part of a voice in accepting or rejecting the ideas of half a dozen very ambitious gentlemen, whose measures are themselves liable to be quashed at the eleventh hour by an Upper House that sits without my will or consent, and which is in its turn legally liable to be superseded by the Sovereign, whose government is all the while being really carried on in silence by permanent officials whose very names I do not know and who have no connection with me beyond accepting, in ignorance of my existence, my dole towards their salaries—this is not a form of democracy that appeals very attractively to me as an individual member of Demos.

And, moreover, the position of my Member of Parliament is scarcely less paradoxical than my own rôle of free and independent elector. He is the mouthpiece of his constituents, and yet he is expected to have a will and conscience of his own. Why? Why should he be any more honest than a lawyer or a journalist? Each of these classes is paid to maintain certain propositions, and the most successful in these lines are those with the highest powers of persuasion. The constituency wishes certain opinions and desires put forward in Parliament—why should the man who offers to execute the job be presumed to share those opinions and desires? The point is, can he represent them more forcibly than the rival candidates? I do not for a moment imagine that the M. P. invariably agrees with the politics of his electors; I only inquire why he should have to profess to—why should he pay this homage of hypocrisy to an illogical ideal? Theoretically we do not elect our M. P. because he wants to get on, but because we want to get on or the country to get on; because we want certain measures carried, not because he wants certain measures carried. Therefore it is to our interest to get the most skilled advocate at our command; his personal opinions are no concern of ours. A fig for his ambitions and aspirations! This may not be a dignified position for the M. P., but it is the one logically implicated in the democratic notion of universal suffrage; and when the gentleman honestly asserts himself and his private ambitions and his private conscience, he is deucedly dishonest to his constituents.

To be strictly logical, indeed, M. P.'s should confine themselves to stating the wishes of the people they represent: they might as well be mechanical dolls, moved through the lobbies by the respective wire-pullers and fitted with inarticulate noises. Or, for the matter of that, they might be superseded altogether by written summaries of the opinions of the winning majority in each constituency on all the points at issue in the current session. The chiefs of the party could play the game with markers. But indeed what is the use of dealing the cards at all, when the Prime Minister holds all the trumps in advance, not up his sleeve, but openly on the table? As for the speeches in the House, they have as much effect upon the issue as the conversations at the card-table. They are an obsolete survival from the times when members were liable to come to the House with open minds, instead of having them closed by their constituencies. Indeed, I can suggest a simple device by which, without any departure from the ancient forms of the House, most of the evils of Party Government could be swept away. By the system of "pairing" a Tory may neutralize a Radical, and both go on together without interfering with the good of the country. Let therefore the entire minority pair off with members of the opposite party, leaving the bare majority in possession of the floor. Being agreed on their policy, these would not want to make speeches, but would simply spend their time walking through the "Ayes" lobby. A few afternoons of pleasant promenading would provide the country with enough legislation for a lifetime. Solvitur ambulando. The party leaders would be enabled to husband their energies for the hustings, since like all the agreeable members they would easily find "partners." It is only the bores who would be left to walk the House. It will be observed that this incalculable gain of time, temper, money, and Acts of Parliament would be secured without revolution, on constitutional lines, and by a mere extension of an existing practice. I am convinced the salvation of the country depends on the universal adoption of the system of Parliamentary "pairing," or legislation by walking "wall-flowers."

A further advantage of this system deserves to be noted. As it takes forty members to make a House, should the Governmental majority fall below this number no business could be transacted. Thus it would become impossible, when the country was almost equally divided, for one party to impose its will on the nation by force of a bare majority. Again, therefore, a very necessary reform would be achieved on strictly constitutional lines.

In so confused a constitution, or so constitutional a confusion, it ill becomes one to inquire why pre-eminence in Parliament is attained by dexterity in the word-duel, and why a John Stuart Mill, who gave his life to the study of sociological questions, is a failure in the House, while a Randolph Churchill, who confessedly found politics more exciting than any other form of sport, including even horse-racing, should be a success. As in Athens of old, the rhetorician is master of the field. Does it not seem ridiculous that a man shall be allowed to legislate who has not passed an examination in political philosophy, political economy, and universal history? As absurd as that men should be able to set up as critics merely by purchasing reviews, that they should be permitted to ply without a license. Still, monstrous as is the mischief wrought by the quack critic, his sphere of influence is limited. But this question of government touches us all. No one ought to be allowed in the House who has not satisfactorily grappled with papers like the following.

1. Explain the use of the following phrases: "Home Rule," "Liberty," "Well-being of the Masses," "G. O. M.," "Good of the State," "The Constitution." What meaning do you attach to them, if any?

2. "The Function of an Opposition Is To Oppose." Criticise this statement from the point of view of the Party in Power, and trace carefully the modification in its view produced by a change of government.

3. What is a good electoral address? Is there any relation between it and its owner's votes in the House?

4. (a) Prove that Female Franchise is demanded not only by the women of England, but by every consideration of reason and justice.

(b) Disprove the same.

5. The leader of your party suddenly reverses his policy.

(a) What would you think?

(b) What would you say?

(c) How would you vote?

Give no reasons for your answer.

6. If C represents Conscience, and C1 the Constituency, show that C1 will always be represented by C2[*].

[Transcriber's note: So in original.]

7. What is a working-man? Explain why professional men who work sixteen hours a day are excluded from this category.

8. Define a political victory, and distinguish between a political victory and a moral victory.

But perhaps the discrepancy is less than meets the eye. The House of Commons is a Representative Assembly; the rhetoricians and fencers represent the unreason and the pugnacity of the partisans. A country has the politicians it deserves. I have heard the most ignorant girls rage against Mr. Gladstone; damsels in their teens who knew nothing of life or its problems, nor could have studied any question for themselves; pretty girls withal, but who at the mention of the veteran statesman took on the avenging aspect of the Eumenides.

It was a girl of quite another temper who replied to me when, talking over old times and old discussions, I said I had not yet become a Socialist: "I don't think you ever knew what you were." I winced as at a just reproach, yet when I had left her the retort occurred to me (as retorts will, when too late) that there was no particular merit in being a "what," that men were not necessarily "'ists" or "'ites," that thoughts did not fit into pigeonholes, and that if there was any merit in the matter it consisted rather in preserving free play and elasticity of mind. Because certain men had put certain ideas into the world it did not follow that every other man had definitely to accept or reject each and all of them, and to become an "'ite" or an "anti-'ite" in so doing. Plague take great men! What right had they to force one into the jury-box? Still less was it compulsory to return a verdict if, as the vulgar were apt to think, the acceptance of any one "'ism" precluded the acceptance of another, so that to be an Ibsenite was synonymous with detesting the dramas of Sardou, and to be a Wagnerite involved a horror of Mendelssohn. It was only the uncultured who held their artistic and political creeds with the narrowness of Little Bethel, importing into thought and aesthetics the zealotry they had lost in religion. The book of Experience, thought I, is not an Encyclopaedia, with every possible topic neatly ranged in alphabetical order; 'tis no A B C Time Table, with the trains docketed for the enlightenment of the simple,'t is rather an Encyclopaedia torn into a million million fragments by kittens and pasted together again by infants, so that all possible things are inextricably interfused, every one with every other; 't is a Bradshaw edited by a maniac, where the trains that start but don't arrive are not even distinguished from the trains that arrive but don't start. Wherever persons are conscious of the infinite complexities of things, they will be found cautious of creed and timid of assertion. You have probably noted that at Waterloo Station, in London, no porter will ever bind himself to a definite statement concerning any train. It is only the inartistic who hold that black is black and white is white, unconditionally, irretrievably; and who have invented the proverb "He'd say black's white" to express the Sophist in excelsis. It must be true, as Ruskin contends, that not one man in fifteen thousand has ever observed anything, else how account for this wide-spread fallacy? The "wit of one," instead of crystallising this "wisdom of the many," should have flatly contradicted it. For, take two blackboards and place them at right angles to each other: let a ray of bright sunlight fall upon them, so that one cast a shadow on the other. The portion of blackboard overshadowed will indeed be blackish, but the portion illuminated by full sunlight will be comparatively white, although it is still thought of as a "black-board." So, too, ask the man in the street for the colour of trees, and he will reply "green." If I may permit myself a vulgar locution, the green is in his eye. Trees are, of course, all colours of the rainbow, according to kind and season; and grass, too, is by no means always so green as people think it. We start in our childhood with prejudices on these subjects—what is education but the systematic imparting of prejudice?—and we rarely recover. Even the primitive rhymes of childhood fix ideas unalterably in our minds:

The rose is red, the violet's blue,
Sugar is sweet and so are you.

Tea-roses are not red nor Neapolitan violets blue; sugar is only sweet to those unversed in metaphysics, and sugar of lead not even to them. As for the compliment to the juvenile petticoat, let it remain. But the blackness of black is a superstition that deserves no such courteous concessions. There is, in fact, no black and no white at all, as any black-and-white artist will tell you. Black is not a colour: it is merely the negation of light. By day nothing is ever black—it always contains reflected light from some surrounding object or objects: if you look at a "black" thing by day, you see its details, which convincingly proves that light is not absent. If there were such a thing as a black object, it could only prove its existence by being seen; but if it is seen it is no longer black, and if it is black it is no longer seen. The mourners at a funeral no more wear black than the bridesmaids at a wedding wear white. To be white, a thing would have to escape all reflected light; and even if this were possible, the sunlight itself, the source of all light and colour, would tinge it with yellow, or red, or pink, according to the time of day. "What!" the injudicious reader will cry, "is not snow white? Does not the Dictionary boast even a double-barreled epithet 'snow-white'! How about the 'great white sea' that stretches round the Pole?" I cannot help it: these adjectives, these expressions were invented before artists had taught men to see: hastily, as by men falling in love at first sight, who are destined to make many discoveries concerning their idol later on. Snow is never white, any more than the beloved is absolutely blameless. For snow to be "snow-white," the sky would have to be white, whereas in those arctic circles it should be either blue or grey. Moreover, the snow being only semi-opaque must be tinctured by the shadow of the darkness of its own depths; as for icebergs, well, you may see green, brown, and even deep-grey ice, whilst the whitest have pinnacles and crags that must break the light like prisms into all the colours of the spectrum, and all these hues, again, do not fail to tint the snow. Nor will the white bear improve the situation, for, to judge by the specimen in our London Zoological Gardens, white bears are dirty yellow, just as black bears are dirty brown.

But, so far from realising that black may be white, your average voter seems to imagine that neither is ever even tempered: that his party is purest white, and the opposition party impurest black. That the other side reverses this colouring does not trouble him: it is merely due to the aforesaid sophistical faculty of proving black white. I once knew a man—no average voter he—who owned two comic papers, the one Radical, the other Conservative. How he must have chuckled as he planned the cartoons and settled the chiaroscuro! What blacks for the Tories to be answered by counter-blacks for the Radicals! Beaconsfield as a sweep, Gladstone as an Angel of Light; Beaconsfield as Ormuzd, Gladstone as Ahriman; each in turn Lucifer, Son of the Morning, and Satan, the discomfited demon. I tremble to think what would have happened if, by one of those contretemps which sometimes occur even in real life, the cartoons had got interchanged. And caricatures such as these influence the elections! The most childish nonsense, written in the picture-language so dear to children! And on such ineptitudes the destinies of the nation are supposed to turn! 'T is a comforting reflection, then, that the whole thing is so largely a farce, that the real axis of events is elsewhere—by no means a thing to grieve over. If the British Constitution is a paradox not to be fathomed by human intellect, why, that is a quality which it shares with Space and Time and all deep and elemental things. Your deep thinker is invariably a paradox-monger, because everything when probed to its bottom proves illusive, and is found to contain its own contradiction. Truth is not a dead butterfly, to be transfixed with a pin and labelled, but a living, airy, evasive butterfly. Perhaps that is the inner meaning of the Whistlerian motto. The Hegelian self-contradictoriness of the British Constitution will not, therefore, affright us. To Tennyson the fact that it is a "crowned republic" seemed a source of security. The English have abolished the Crown, though they are too loyal to inform the Sovereign of his deposition; in like manner they have evaded Democracy by conceding universal suffrage. The strength of the British Constitution lies in its inherent absurdity, its audacious paradoxicalness. It exists by force of not being carried out. And the reason of this illogicality is clear: our Constitution, like Topsy, was not made but "growed," and that which grows is never logically perfect; it is like an old tree, strangely gnarled, with countless abrasions and mutilations, and sometimes even curious grafts. Here the lightning struck it, and yonder branch was snapped in the great gale. Machine-made schemes may be theoretically perfect, but they will never suit human nature, which is a soil for living growths, not a concrete foundation for elegant architecture. This is the truth which trips up Comte, and Fourier, and St. Simon, and all the system-makers and utopia-builders. Perfect things are dead things: the law of life is imperfection and movement. Life is never logical, it is only alive. If man had been made by machinery his body would not have been erratically hairy; his toes would long since have been improved away or welded together by an American patentee; nor would there have remained, for our humiliation, those traces of a caudal appendage which some osteologists have thought to perceive in our distinguished anatomy; our brotherhood to the beasts would have been betrayed only by our behaviour.

So that, though Politics be as absurd as the Constitution, God bless her, it may yet fulfil as useful a function. Who would deprive the hosts of working-men of their generous enthusiasms, even though these be to the profit of the professional politician? Who would narrow their horizon back to the public-house and the workshop or the clerical desk and the music-hall, by assuring them that all these great national and international questions will be no penny the worse or the better for their interest in them? For it is they, not the State, that will be benefited. Politics is a great educative force: it teaches history, geography, and the art of debate, and is not without relation to Shakespeare and the musical glasses. The flies on the wheel are not moving the wheel, but they are travelling and seeing the world, whereas they might otherwise be buzzing around the dust-bin. Politics sets the humblest at the centre of great cross-roads of history: it promotes clubs and all manner of fellowship, and enables the poorest—on polling-day at least—to know himself the equal of the greatest. Even the most illiterate is spared the mortification of being reminded that he cannot sign his name. And finally, and most of all, it preserves among us the lost art of fighting. The long and oft-vaunted immunity of England from the foot of a foreign foe has its drawbacks: we have forgotten what war really means, we have delegated our courage and patriotism to an army of mercenaries, who represent us in the field as a nobleman's carriage represents him at a funeral; we are valiant vicariously and sublime by deputy; we take the war-fever in its pleasant heats, and contract out the chills and the blood-letting. And so the blood-letting fails to purge us as before: the evil humours are still in the system. All those seething, restless spirits which generate in the blood of a once warlike race clog us up and turn to bile and dyspeptic distempers. Our militant instincts, suppressed by a too-secure civilization, break out in sordid maladies of the social organism. As a vent-hole for the envy, hatred and uncharitableness of mankind, politics cannot be overestimated. In the absence of real battles on our soil these sham fights of the polling-booth—sham because they determine nothing, because the great silent forces are working behind all the noises—are the national purge for "our present discontents"; no more truly efficacious than that ancient therapeutics of the lancet, a General Election yet comforts the patient, he takes a lease of fresh hope, the sun leaps out, the clouds pack, the sky is blue, the grass is dew-pearled, God's in his heaven, and all's right with the world. Even the beaten party feels that it has won a moral victory, and confidently looks forward to victory without morality at the next turn of the wheel. And so all these diseased humours of the body politic pass harmlessly off.

No one but a confirmed cynic would wish to do away with all this harmless dissipation, all the innocent fun of electioneering, the speeches, riotings, mud-throwings, everybody happy as sandboys or mudlarks. What a great day that was—Plancus being M. P. and I a boy in a provincial town—when the Blues and the Reds meant broken heads, and the flowing tide of beer, and spruce carriages with beribboned horses, and jocund waggonettes, and bands and banners, and "hoorays," and shuttered shops, and an outpour of citizens; a day festive, yet solemn, pregnant with mysterious dooms and destinies, fatal, ineluctable, if victory fell to the wrong-coloured ribbons. I remember when my father went to poll his vote—a strange, weird article that had to be carried carefully concealed on the person, lest the roughs of the opposition should catch a glimpse of the tip of it and bash in the holder's head—with what awed imagination we followed his course, as of a hero gone to storm a redoubt or lead a forlorn hope! with what anxiety we waited at home with the bandages! For the civil war, which our constitution foments, was less of a sham then than now, and the polling-booths vied with the playing-fields of Eton as the nursery of England's heroes. Ah, the brave old times! An anaemic age languishes for want of you, and finds its solace in "bluggy" tales. For just as politics supplies the shadow, the simulacrum of fighting, so art supplies the shadows of life to those who lack the substance. We herd in towns, and take the country in dashes of water-colour framed in gilt. We marry for money, and satiate our baulked sense of romance with concoctions from Mudie's. We lie and haggle and cheat only the better to apprehend the subtleties of spiritual discourse in fashionable churches, and our generous appreciation of the consummate chivalry of the hero of melodrama is the reward we owe ourselves for the pain it gave us to kick our wives. Practical joking is banished from reputable circles—even Bob Sawyer is ranging himself; and so this primitive appetite seeks its satisfaction in farcical comedies. Poetic tragedies owe their attraction to the dominance in real life of the drab and the unlovely, and the overstrain of the intellect in modern life gives a peculiar flavour to the ineptitudes of Gaiety burlesque. All the primal instincts and passions are still in us, though distorted, exaggerated, diminished, modified, applied to different objects and purposes. The man with vagabond instincts becomes an explorer, Ishmael writes social dramas, the happier son of a defalcating cashier rises to be a minister of finance, the born liar turns novelist, the man with murder in his soul hunts big game in foreign lands or settles down at home as a critic. And so, too, the born warrior becomes a political leader; and politics, if it does not do any of the things it professes to do, plays yet an invaluable part in modern life, bridging over, perchance, the transition from the bellicose ages to those belauded days when the war-drum shall throb no longer, "and the kindly earth shall slumber, lapt in universal law."

That this is confusedly and sub-consciously understood, even by politicians, is shown by their very vocabulary. The Salvation Army itself boasts no more militant a phraseology than the profession whose business it is to administer peacefully the affairs of the realm. That which should be, and sometimes is, expressed by nautical metaphors—the ship of state, guiding the helm, and the rest of it—is much more frequently expressed by military metaphors. Even the posts of duty are the "spoils" of office. The State which to Plato was a deliberately harmonised music is to us a deliberate discord, and the acme of politics, whose crowning glory should be a peaceful measure, is by the vulgar not so inaccurately regarded as attained at a General Election, the nomenclature of which positively bristles with bayonets. Seats are won as towns were of old, and, as in the days of Joshua, victory is achieved by walking round the town and blowing your own trumpets. Great organs shamelessly lament that their side has no good grievance to go to the country with—as if the absence of grievances were not the very object of government! A stirring war-cry—that is the indispensable. If good government were really the object of a General Election, it would all be over and done with in a day. Election day would everywhere be as simultaneous as Christmas, and votes would be polled with the punctuality with which puddings are eaten. But this would be to contract a campaign into a battle—to make a short story out of a great military serial, peppered with exciting incidents, to be continued in our next. We want our vicissitudes, our sharpshooting, our skirmishing, our days of triumph for the Whigs, and our days of triumph for the Tories. What we like best of all is when the fighting is so level that the Election progresses as breathlessly as a good University boat race. Failing that, we like to see one side swamping the other, like a great flood, the stream rising daily higher and higher, with a crescendo roar, till the vanquished are swept away in a thunderous mountain of waters. So for a full moon the waters rage, the noise of battle roars, till our suppressed fighting instincts have been deluded into repose and satisfaction, till the champing war-horses have been quieted by being allowed to snort and cry "Ha! ha!" to see the glitter of stage spears, and to hear the noise of the supers and the shouting. This is the real end masked beneath all those interminable phrases. And it is achieved at any and every cost. For does not everybody complain that a General Election upsets everything? The publishers groan, the theatrical managers tear their wigs. Englishmen cannot think of two things at once; they are like heavy, solid craft, sound of timber but slow of turning. "One thing at a time" is a national proverb. They cannot even read two books at once, and if two classics should be published on the same day one would be a failure. There is the book of the week, and the book of the season, and the book of the year. This applies even to our appreciation of past periods, and because Shakespeare is the first of the Elizabethan dramatists, the rest are nowhere. Wherefore one would suppose that everybody would make haste to get the Election out of the way; but, on the contrary, it is allowed to linger on, till sometimes our overstrained suspense snaps, and the Election dribbles out in unregarded issues. No, the fight's the thing! War, if not dead, is banished from our shores; the duello has been laughed to death; cock-fighting and bull-baiting have ceased to charm: politics alone remains to gratify the pugnacity and cruelty that civilisation has robbed of their due objects. How we brighten up again at a bye-election, when duels which passed unregarded in the big battle, when towns scarcely noted at the fag-end of the great campaign, become the cynosure of every eye. Through Slocum or Eatonswill the hub of the universe temporarily passes: to its population of four thousand, mostly fools, are entrusted the destinies of the Empire; it is theirs to make or mar. The duel is watched by a breathless nation. The party leaders on each side cheer on their men; their careers and claims and countenances fill up the papers, and they cross swords in a shower of telegrams. Advice to those about to enter Parliament: Elect for a bye-election. Why be a nonentity, a mere M.P., when by a little patience you may hold the centre of the stage, if only for a week? Better almost to be beaten at a bye-election than to be successful at a General.

In case I should ever seek the suffrages of electors myself, I would venture to remind opposition agents and private secretaries that these random criticisms of the glorious constitution (hear, hear!) of that great Empire on which the sun never sets (cheers), over which the Union Jack waves (loud cheers)—a thousand years the battle and the breeze—hem!—I—I—ahem!—Lord Salisbury (loud and prolonged cheers)—I mean that I trust they will not forget that all this is set down without prejudice.

VII

THE REALISTIC NOVEL

The realistic novel, we know from Zola, that apostle of insufficient insight, is based on "human documents," and "human documents" are made up of "facts." But in human life there are no facts.

This is not a paradox, but a "fact." Life is in the eye of the observer. The humour or the pity of it belongs entirely to the spectator, and depends upon the gift of vision he brings. There are no facts, like bricks, to build stories with. What, pray, in the realm of human life is a fact? By no means a stubborn thing, as the proverb pretends. On the contrary, a most pliant, shifting, chameleon-coloured thing, as flexible as figures in the hands of the statistician. What is commonly called a fact is merely a one-sided piece of information, a dead thing, not the series of complex, mutually inter-working relations that constitutes a fact as it exhibits itself to the literary vivisectionist. I walked with a friend in a shabby district of central London, a region that had once been genteel, but was now broken up into apartments. Squalid babies, with wan, pathetic faces, pullulated on the doorsteps; they showed from behind dingy windows at the breasts of haggard women. The fronts of the houses were black, the plaster had crumbled away, the paint had peeled off. It was the ruins of a minor Carthage, and, like Marius, I was lost in mournful reverie; my companion remarked, "These houses are going up; they now pay 7 per cent." He was perfectly justified. There are a hundred ways of looking at any fact. The historian, the scientist, the economist, the poet, the philanthropist, the novelist, the anarchist, the intelligent foreigner—each would take away a different impression from the street, and all these impressions would be facts, all equally valid, all equally true, and all equally false. Life, I repeat, is in the eye of the observer. What is farce to you is often tragedy to the actual performer. The man who slips over a piece of orange peel, or chases his hat along the muddy pavement, is rarely conscious of the humour of the situation. On the other hand, you shall see persons involved in heartrending tragedies to whom the thing shows as farce, like little children playing in churchyards or riding tombstones astride. To the little imps of comedy, who, according to Mr. Meredith, sit up aloft, holding their sides at the spectacle of mankind, to the

Spirit of the world,
Beholding the absurdities of men,
Their vaunts, their feats, ...

human life must be a very different matter from what we poor players on the scene imagine it; we are cutting a very different figure, not only from that which faces us from the mirror of vanity, but from that which is "as ithers see us." Not only, then, may our tragedy be comedy; our comedy may be tragedy. The play of humour at least suggests these alternatives. Life is Janus-faced, and the humourist invests his characters with a double mask; they stand for comedy as well as for tragedy; Don Quixote wears the buskin as well as the sock. Humour, whose definition has always eluded analysis, may, perhaps (to attempt a definition currente calamo), be that subtle flashing from one aspect to another, that turning the coin so rapidly that one seems to see simultaneously the face and the reverse, the pity and the humour of life, and knows not whether to laugh or weep. Humour is, then, the simultaneous revelation of the dual aspects of life; the synthetical fusion of opposites; the gift of writing with a double pen, of saying two things in one, of showing shine and shadow together. This is why the humourist has always the gift of pathos; though the gift of pathos does not equally imply the gift of humour. The tragic writer must always produce one-sided work, so must the "funnyman" who were only a "funny man" and not a humourist (though this is rarer). Each can only show one side of life at a time; the humourist alone can show both. Great novels of romance and adventure, great works of imagination, great poems, may be written by persons without humour; but only the humourist can reproduce life. Milton is great; but the poet of life is Shakespeare. Thus the whole case of "realism" falls to the ground. There being no "facts," Zola's laborious series is futile; it may be true to art, but it is not true to life. His vision is incomplete, is inexhaustive; it lacks humour, and to the scientific novelist the lack of humour is fatal. He is the one novelist who cannot succeed without it. Leave out humour, and you may get art and many other fine things, but you do not get the lights and shadows or the "values" of life.

All novels are written from the novelist's point of view. They are his vision of the world. They are not life, but individual refractions of it. The ironical pessimism of Thomas Hardy is as false as the sentimental optimism of Walter Besant or the miso-androus meliorism of Sarah Grand. What Hall Caine happily calls "the scenic view of life" of Dickens is no more true than the philosophic view of Mrs. Humphry Ward. Each is existence viewing itself through a single medium. "Tess of the D'Urbervilles" is as false as "Lorna Doone" or "Plain Tales from the Hills." Life, large, chaotic, inexpressible, not to be bound down by a formula, peeps at itself through the brain of each artist, but eludes photography. This is the true inwardness of the Proteus myth. The humourist alone, by presenting life in its own eternal contradictoriness, by not being tied down to one point of view, like his less gifted brother, comes nearest to expressing its elusive essence. The great novelists are Fielding, Cervantes, Flaubert, Thackeray. But all the novelists supplement one another, and relatively-true single impressions of life go to make up a true picture of

Life, like a dome of many coloured glass.

It is because there are all novels and every aspect of existence in Shakespeare that he sits supreme, the throned sovereign of the literature of life.

All this is writ to console those who suffer too poignantly from book-tragedies and "pictures of life." The artist selects, he studies tone and composition, whereas in real life tragedies are often accompanied by "extenuating circumstances." The unloved girl temporarily forgets her sorrow in the last new novel, or a picnic up the river; the broken-hearted hero betakes himself to billiards and brandy-and-soda, or toys with a beefsteak. Again, many pathetic tales are the outcome of imperfect insight. The novelist imagines how he would feel in the shoes of his characters, and cries out with the pain of hypothetic bunions. This mistake better deserves the name of "the pathetic fallacy" than the poetic misreading of Nature to which Buskin has annexed it. A good novel may be made of bad psychology; indeed, this is what most novels are made of. Yet the gentle reader, misled by the simulation of life, makes himself miserable over dabs of black ink on white paper. The failure of two imaginary beings to unite their lives in wedlock brings unhappiness into myriad homes. How delicious is that story of the German novelist who, having failed to unite his leading couple at the conclusion of a newspaper serial, saw no way of appeasing the grief and indignation of his vast audience save by inserting in the advertisement columns of a later issue of the journal an announcement of their union under the usual head of "Marriages"!

VIII

IN DEFENCE OF GAMBLING

Without gambling life would lose its salt in many a humble household. The humdrum, deadening routine of monotonous daily toil finds relief by this creation of an outside interest; to have a shilling on the favourite enlarges and colours existence, gives it a wider and vaguer horizon. Imagine the delicious anguish of suspense, the excitement of hearing the result, the exultation of winning. And the beauty of gambling is that you cannot lose. Gambling is really a disguised system of purchase. One buys excitement, a most valuable emotion, for which even the members of the Anti-Gambling League are prepared to pay heavily in other forms! And the advantage of gambling over all these other forms is the possibility that you may not be called upon to pay for your purchase after all—nay, that you may even be paid instead! You get not only excitement, but a possible bonus. Is there any earthly transaction that offers such advantages? Why, 't is always "heads I win, tails you lose." Who speaks of losing at cards? As well speak of losing at play-going or novel-reading; what is called loss is simply payment for excitement. You cannot lose at cards, though you may win; unless it be in games where skill preponderates, and then loss means penalty for lack of skill. The mere transfer of money from hand to hand leaves the wealth of the world what it was before. 'T is redistribution, not destruction. It is scarcely relevant to look for the evils of gambling in its effects—to point to ruined reputations and ruined homes. Everything is capable of abuse, from love to religion. The evil of gambling lies in the fact that it is an unworthy form of excitement—that it is possible to colour life more intellectually. The Anti-Gambling League, for all its recent prospectus, will not put down gambling among the poorer classes, except by widening their outlook otherwise, by creating other interests outside the dull daily groove. For the well-to-do classes there is less excuse. With all the arts and amenities of life at their command, it is degrading to use up time and nervous energy in so brainless a pursuit. The gambling that is inherent in the constitution of modern civilization is another affair: that is pursued for the sake of gain; or for a livelihood. The Stock Exchange is an unhappy consequence of the joint-stock company; credit in business is an equally inevitable outcome of the ramified mechanism of exchange. We are all gamblers to-day, insomuch as there is no stable relation between work and reward, and the failure of a bank in Calcutta may impoverish a shopkeeper in Camden Town. Our investments may rise or fall in value through the obscure machinations of unknown millionaires. And even the Anti-Gambling League has no word to say against those great gambling concerns, Life and Fire Assurance Societies, which bet you that you will not die or be burnt out within a certain number of years, or those journals which offer you large odds that you won't be smashed up while reading them. The prudential considerations behind these forms of gambling seem quite to moralise them: indeed, to refuse to accept the bet of the Life Assurance Companies is now considered immoral; a man is expected to amend on his marriage at the very latest.

There is a form of gambling to which I must myself plead guilty. A forlorn, shabby creature, pathetically spruced up, arrives from a ten-mile tramp. He has been a journalist or a poet, but owing to this or that he is on his beam-ends. He has eaten nothing for two days. His wife is dying, his children are weeping for food. His voice breaks beautifully as he tells me I am his last hope. What is to be done? According to Charles Lamb, the solution is to give, to give always. For either the man is in need and speaks truth, or he is a liar and therefore a consummate actor. We pay for stage representations: why deny our obolus to the histrionics of the beggar? So artistic a make up, an elocution with such moving notes of pathos, surely deserve our tribute. Nay (and this Elia forgot to note), the beggar-actor is frequently the author of his own piece; that consistent argument, those tragical episodes, those touches of nature, that minute detail, all are his. For my part, this view does not touch me; I scarcely ever pay for the play, so I expect even the beggar to perform to me as to one of "the press." If I give to beggars, it is purely from the gambling spirit. What are the odds against the man being a scamp? If they are short, or if the betting is level, I incline to the side of mercy. The money is of so much more consequence to him than to me, if the beggar is genuine, that the speculation is well warranted. I know how wrong it is from the point of view of the Charity Organization Society, but I am a man, not a bureau of beneficence. Few of us, I fancy, escape this godly gambling.

How ill Society is ordered! We pay poor rates and support hospitals and orphan asylums; but is there any thinking man who can banquet with the assurance that nobody is starving? It spoils the dinner of Dives to meditate on the longings of Lazarus, and this is the true skeleton at the feast. The business of philanthropy seems but a mockery, and Government takes charitable toll from us without pacifying our consciences. There is something rotten in the state of Denmark. Cannot the intellect of man devise a means of guaranteeing the deserving poor against starvation?

Novel-reading is the woman's substitute for gambling—the thing that takes her outside her narrow circle of interests. Her ravenous appetite for new novels is amazing; children are not so gluttonous of cream-tarts. To supply this demand sequestered spinsters in suburban or rustic bowens sit spinning the woof and warp of life as it never was on sea or land. Bound goes the wheel, to and fro glides the shuttle, and the long, endless pattern unwinds itself in all its wealth of imaginative device and all its glory of fanciful colour. Poor things! What are they to do? They have not the means to study the life they depict; they cannot mix in the circles they describe. Fortunately their ignorance is their salvation; the pretty patterns please the young ladies, the brave notes of colour set them a-dreaming. And now in the revolt against the three-volume novel these simple scribblers are to be swept away; the country parcels will know them no more, and the three-deckers they built of yore will be dismantled in the dry dock of the fourpenny box. Poor creatures! Some will take to typewriting and some to drink, some will be driven to the workhouse and some to literature.

IX

TRULY RURAL

"ENGINEER AND SURVEYOR'S DEPARTMENT.

"5 & 6 Wm. IV., cap. 50, sect. 65.

"SIR,

"I am directed to call your attention to the present condition of trees within your premises, which now overhang the public footpath adjoining, and thereby cause considerable inconvenience to the public. I shall be glad if you will kindly give the matter your best attention, with a view to lopping or cutting the trees in such a manner as to obviate the inconvenience at present complained of.

"Yours obediently, "P. LEONARDO MACREADY, "Engineer to the Board."

Amid the cosmopolitan medley of letters on my metropolitan breakfast-table—the long and formal-looking, the fat and foreign, and the over-scrawled and the underpaid (the last mainly requests for autographs)—this delightful home-grown epistle came with refreshing piquancy. It brought a breath of summer into the grey chillness of a London winter, a suggestion of rustling foliage about the chandelier, and the scent of the hay over the gaslights. "My dear!" I exclaimed to the partner of my bosom (a tame white rat that likes to perch there), "Have we any trees?"

My partner gave a little plaintive squeak. That is her idea of conversation. She screams at everything. She would scream at the sight of a mouse.

I pushed away my plate. I had sat down hungry as a hunter, and had had two helpings of everything; but now I could eat no more. Excitement had taken away my appetite. The prospect of rural discoveries agitated me. I hastened to the window and looked at the front garden. To my astonishment and joy there was vegetation in it. There was a dwarf evergreen bush and a fragment of vine stretching itself sleepily, and a tall thin tree—they might all have got comfortably into one bed, but they had been planted in three far apart, and this gave the garden a desolate Ramsgate-in-winter air of "Beds to let." The tall thin tree was absolutely naked, without an inch of foliage to cover its wooden limbs; a mere mass of dry sticks. I looked hard at the tree to see where it offended, determined to pluck it out. But it returned my gaze with the stolidity of conscious innocence—it held up its wooden arms in deprecation. I re-read Mr. P. Leonardo Macready's letter. "Which now overhang the public footpath"! Ah! that was what was the matter with my trees. It was raining, but I am an Englishman and the law is sacred, and I went outside into the public highway and looked at the tall thin tree from the new point of view. Sure enough—very far up—there was a bough overhanging the public footpath.

I looked up at it and shook my fist menacingly, but it waved its twigs in response with an irritating amiability. I began to understand what an annoyance it must be to have a bough up there that you couldn't flick at with your stick as you passed by, and that even when weighed down by its summer greenery would bemock you if you made a casual clutch at its foliage, and laugh at you in its leaves. I went inside and returned with a step-ladder and an umbrella and a carving-knife, and I stood on the summit of the ladder and made abortive slashes at space with my right hand, while the open umbrella in my left made equally abortive efforts to soar with me skywards. After nearly stabbing the partner of my bosom I went in, both of us wet like drowned rats, and as I settled myself again to coffee and correspondence, I could not help wishing that Chang, the Chinese giant, had remained alive to triumph over my tantalising trees. Nor could I help wishing that the activity of the local engineers and surveyors had been directed by His Gracious Majesty King William IV. into quite a contrary channel.

William, spare that tree,
Touch not a single bough;
If you had planted three,
They would protect me now.

If, instead of being requested to amputate a beautiful overhanging arm of foliage, every citizen of London were served with a notice to plant a tree in front of his demesne, the face of the great stony city would be transformed. It would become a rus in urbe. Why not? Everybody knows what the late Duke of Devonshire made of Eastbourne; and the beauty of Bournemouth is mainly an affair of trees. Why should we not walk under the boughs of Oxford Street? What law of nature or William IV. ordains an eternal divorce between shops and trees? Why should one not hear the birds sing in the Strand as well as in the Inns of Court? Let us have trees instead of lamp-posts—with electric lights twinkling from their leaves. Already there are London streets quite well-wooded. Even in the Whitechapel Road it is possible to read—

A book of verses underneath a bough;

but I shall not be content till Matthew Arnold's exquisite quatrain comes literally true of London—

Roses that down the alleys shine afar,
And open jasmine-muffled lattices,
And groups under the dreaming garden-trees,
 And the full moon and the white evening star.

It might be well if we could transplant to our more prosaic city ways the beautiful old custom of planting a tree on the birth of a child. It is true that ladies might object to having their age recorded by the growth of rings on the trunk; but then they could easily pass the tree on to an elder sister when they got beyond the average wedding-ring age. Besides, people would quickly forget whose birth it marked, and the town trees would soon become anonymous. I would therefore suggest the formation of a tree-planting party, pledged not to support any candidate for Parliament who would not vote for the ruralisation of the Metropolis. To the Home Rule of Mr. Gladstone, with his weakness for cutting down trees, must be opposed Home Ruralisation. What a fine platform cry—"a truly rural London!"—with the unique advantage of being unpronounceable by demagogues in drink. The poor would welcome the policy as a boon. They are not by any means so unpoetical as Gissing would make out. Only the other day a baby was found buried in a window flower-box; which is practically the idea of Keats' "Isabella, or the Pot of Basil," an idea which was itself a graft from the stock of Boccaccio.

If the parish dignitaries became thus associated in our minds with the Beautiful instead of with bills and blue papers, one might be able to whip up some enthusiasm for the civic life, and contemplate even income-tax schedules with a Platonic or Aristotelian rapture. It is not everybody who can rhapsodise with Mr. Bernard Shaw or the Fabian Society over sewer rates, and find in the contemplation of communal gas and water something of the inspiration and ecstasy that the late Professor Tyndall found in the thought of the conservation of energy.

In firing us to local patriotism by the example of provincial cities, the enthusiast does not allow sufficiently for the size of London. It swallows us all up; there are twenty provincial cities in its maw: it is not a city, but a province. We cannot rouse ourselves to an interest in Brixton and Camberwell, in Poplar and Highbury. There is no glory in being a dweller in so amorphous a city, whose motley floating population is alone sufficient to stock a town; there can be no sense of brotherhood in meeting a Londoner abroad, still less a Middlesex or Surrey man. Devonians may feast off junkets and cream, in touching fellowship, and the hearts of Edinburgh men stir with common memories of Princes Street; but a Cockney, who has far more to be proud of, is overwhelmed into apathy. It is only in a compact city that one can develop that sense of special belonging which George Eliot contends is at the root of so many virtues. I might just as well be taxed to beautify Dublin as Canonbury, for all the difference it would make in my grumblings. And if our city is too large to inspire us, our parish is too small. And so to most of us, I fear, parochialism is a bore. Theoretically, we know that the parish we live in is greater than many a provincial town. We know that we ought to take an interest in its history, and be proud of its great men. But somehow, despite Mr. Frederic Harrison, our suburb leaves us cold. Our real life does not centre about our own parish at all. We circle about the great thoroughfares that radiate from Charing Cross, and the pivot of our lives is Piccadilly. Born to the Metropolis, we cannot narrow our minds to a district, nor to parish give up what was meant for London. We refuse to become provincials. We do not even know that we boast of a Town Hall, till we are compelled to attend and show cause why we have not paid the rates, or any part thereof, the same having been lawfully demanded. If there are any other great men in the neighbourhood, we do not know their addresses. They are shy and retiring. It is only the retired who are not shy. That sort of great man comes forth in his tens. He has been a butcher, a baker, or a candlestick maker, and he is—a bore. Once he solicited your patronage, to-day he solicits your vote. Having given up making profits, he now wishes to make by-laws, and finds a gleam of his old delight in sending out heavy bills to the neighbourhood. You get a list of him, which policemen announce their intention of calling for. You are asked to decide among a column of him, uniformly obscure, but divided invidiously enough into tradesmen and gentlemen. Who compiled this list or nominated these gentlemen and tradesmen, you have not the ghost of a notion. They are sprung upon you as imperiously and mysteriously as their own demand-notes. You look down the column and make random crosses by the wayside. You select a sanitary engineer in preference to an undertaker, forgetting that he is the deadlier of the two, and you vote for your retired wine-dealer to prevent him going back into business. But most of the names convey nothing to you, and give you the sensation of a donkey between two heaps of straw, or of a straw between two heaps of donkeys. And having thus exercised that high English privilege, for which you would shed your blood if it were taken away, you are content for the rest of the year to grumble at the doings of your representatives. It does not occur to you that public duty calls upon you to comprehend the parochial mysteries and solicit the parochial dignities. They seem too petty for a man of any stature—a sort of small beer for babes and sucklings.

May it not be that the voice of public duty, when it calls upon you to be a citizen and a parishioner, calls with too piping a voice? There is no rousing note, nothing of the resonance of a clarion call. A suggestion of poverty and the workhouse clings to everything parochial, something of drab and joyless. Is there no way of infusing colour into this depressing greyness, a martial timbre into this anaemic note? If we are to pay the piper let us hear him. Let the tax-collector go his rounds at the head of a brass band, playing patriotic airs. Let brocaded standard-bearers raise aloft a banner with the soul-stirring insignia, "England expects every man to pay his duty." Let the hollow roll of the drum thrill the dull suburban street, and animate the areas of semi-detached villas. No longer shall the devil and General Booth have all the good tunes, and the ragged rearguard of urchins keeping time with their bare feet shall follow the drum to the surer and saner goal of civic salvation. The music of the streets will become a joy instead of a terror, and English performers will find a new market. See paterfamilias prick up his ears as the distant strains of national music impinge upon his tympanum, see his heart heaving his shirt-front with patriotic ardour, while, with a joyous cry "The Collectors are coming, hurrah, hurrah!" he rushes to his cheque-book as the soldier rushes to arms. Is he not serving his country as much as the soldier, and without pay—or even discount? Nay, why should the idea of patriotic duty be so emphatically connected with the shedding of blood, and all the pomp and pageantry reserved for the profession of Destruction? Why should not the lifeboat be launched, or the coal dug, or the drain-pipe laid, or the taxes paid, to a musical accompaniment, and under the shadow of the national flag? Great is the power of the Symbol: for a few inches of rag at elevenpence three-farthings a yard (warranted not to shrink) men will give their lives. And greater still is the power of music.

Dear to the London housemaid,
The fife of fusilier,
And to the Cockney urchin
The drum of Booth is dear;
Sweet sounds the barrel-organ
Where'er the cits parade;
But the dearest of all music
The Tax-Collectors played.

You will be glad to hear that scarcely had this grumble appeared in print when I saw a procession that made me think Birnam wood had come to Dunsinane. Soon either pavement was planted with ready-made trees, all a-blowing and a-growing. If it had happened in the night, I should have rubbed my eyes and imagined some good genius had transported me to the Boulevards. I hastened to place a little guéridon outside the garden gate, and to decorate it with glasses of absinthe and vermouth; but a gendarme came along and asked me to move on.

X

OPINIONS OF THE YOUNG FOGEY

When I first met the Young Fogey I thought him very brilliant. His philosophical pose, too, of combining the caution of age with the daring of youth was fascinating. "I have evolved," he used to say. "Once I would not attach sanctity to ideas because they were old: now I attach no sanctity to ideas because they are new." But I soon discovered that the Young Fogey was one of that large class of persons who do not evolve but revolve, whose brilliancy is that of the fixed star. They give out arrestive thoughts, and you are vastly impressed, but on longer acquaintance, or on returning to them after an interval, you find that it is they who have been arrested by their thoughts. Such persons do not last you more than one or two years: they require a succession of new audiences to keep up their reputation, like a witty play, which all the world goes to see in turn, but which it would be deucedly dull to see night after night, year in, year out. The cleverest of them know this need of new ears, and of making provincial and foreign tours when they have exhausted London. But when the Young Fogey chanced upon me drinking lager beer at the Austrian Derby, during a tedious interval between the races, he was probably confused by the distance from Piccadilly into a sense of originality, and perceiving a couple of books on my table: "What! do you read the books you review?" he asked in feigned astonishment; adding, with an impromptu air, "I always write the books I review. Criticism of other people is waste of time. An artist who is worth his salt knows his value better than anybody else; and an artist who is not worth his salt is not worth your criticism, and will learn nothing from it in any case. There is immeasurably too much book-making, as it is."

"But criticism tends to keep down book-making," I observed meekly.

"Quite the contrary. Criticism encourages it. Most books are not read. Who can possibly read ninety-nine of the worst hundred books published every week? If they were not even criticised, the writers would shut up their inkstands. Publicity is their aim, but publication does not supply it. Most publishers are rather privateers. It is the critics who supply fame to fools. It's even worse with plays. Why should every trumpery farce that can get itself badly produced by a moneyless manager who decamps the day after, be allotted a space in every morning, evening, and weekly newspaper, Fame blowing simultaneously a hundred trumps? My greatest book never got half as much notice as a wretched little curtain-raiser which took me a morning to knock off, and the news of which was flashed from China to Peru immediately, whereas the eulogies of my book were dribbled out in monthly instalments, and belated testimonials kept straggling in long after its successor had been published. In those days I belonged to a Press-cutting Agency, and I discovered that—to measure Fame by the square inch—you may get many more yards of reputation by the most flippant playlet than by your literary magnum opus; to say nothing of the pictures and interviews of your actors and actresses. That your silliest player—especially if it be a pretty she—gets photographed in the papers sixteen times to your once, goes without saying. The only real recipe for Fame nowadays is to be a pretty girl and exhibit yourself publicly. The modern editor has got it into the paste-brush he calls his head that the public is infinitely greedy for the minutest theatrical details. It is really too idiotic, this fuss over our parrots. If there were only plays for them to talk! The decline of the British drama—"

"By which you mean that they decline your plays," I interrupted.

"Granted," said the Young Fogey; "but even when they give us Shakespeare, they play the patron, and literary critics argue deferentially with them as to the treatment of the text, and beg them not to put William's head under the pump. Did you see that monumental headline in the 'Daily Chronicle,' the paper that poses as the organ of sweetness and light?—

'MR. TREE'S NEW PLAY. 'Henry IV. At The Haymarket.'

"So Mr. Tree 'created' Falstaff in more than the conventional sense of that arrogant stage-verb! Act? Anybody can act! We're all acting, always, in every phase of our social life. Every back drawing-room is a theatre royal. A child can act, and the 'infant phenomenon' cannot be distinguished from the leading lady or gentleman except by size. But no child ever wrote a play. Acting is the lowest of the arts. And even if it were the highest, it would be brought low again by its infinite self-repetition. Imagine playing one part for a season, a year, a decade. Actors are not even parrots—they are automatic puppets that move their limbs in fixed fashions, and make squeaking sounds at prescribed moments. There was a French Minister of Education who drew up a most rigid Time-Code, which hung in his bureau; and it was the joy of his life to take out his watch and say 'Half-past three! Ha! every boy in France is now learning geography'; or, 'A quarter to twelve! Ha! every French schoolgirl is now writing in a copy-book.' I have the same sort of feeling about my actor-acquaintances. 'Half-past nine? Ah! What is Herbert doing? He is taking poison.' 'A quarter to eleven! Dear me! Rose is crawling under a table.'

"And these creatures want every privilege, forsooth! Fame, gold, champagne, the best society and the worst. To be of Bohemia and Belgravia, to make the best of both worlds. If things don't mend, to sit in a stall will soon become an index of imbecility. It will be like being seen at the Academy.

"And, talking of the Academy, did ever any more infantile idea enter the human brain than that a couple of thousand pictures worth seeing can be painted every year? Why, since the beginning of the world there haven't been two thousand pictures painted worth seeing! Imagine two thousand manuscript novels being scattered around on two thousand desks, a shilling admission! Do we get one good novel a year? Scarcely. One good symphony or opera? Of course not. Then why expect to get a picture worth hanging? And every picture should hang by itself—it's an artistic entity, self-complete. To crowd it among a lot of others is like conducting an orchestra every instrument of which is playing a different tune. 'T isn't even as if the poor painters got anything out of the show. People won't buy pictures— prices are monstrously inflated to an artificial point: the artists would take less, only they don't like to come down from their pedestal, and so they starve up there in dignity. Artists have played a foolish game. They have gone nap on gentility and high prices, and gentility has failed them.

"When great prices are given for pictures, it is generally with a view to selling them again: a dubious compliment to the artist. No man gets a thousand pounds' worth of pure art joy out of any picture. He can spend his thousand pounds to much more of aesthetic advantage. But there is no inherent sacredness in prices. A picture is worth only what it will fetch. Let our artists be satisfied with a fair day's wage for a fair day's work, like any other species of craftsman. After all, they were all craftsmen— Michael Angelo, Titian, Donatello, Canova—wall-decorators, door-painters, ceiling-colourers, tomb- builders, stone-masons, working to contract and to measure. When our artists are content with the pay of manual labourers and the joy of art, taste may be stimulated in the masses, and original work be going at the price of lithographs. Why shouldn't artists even paint public-house signs? Beer being the national religion, why shouldn't it find adequate expression in Art?

"Not that it matters much whether our artists live or die—Art seems about over. It seems to be an accident that happened once or twice in the Past—among the Greeks, at the Renaissance, in Spain, in Holland—which no amount of art-schools and art-publications can coax back. To found Academies and R.A.-ships is to spur a dead horse. Look at the Greek sculptures, look at the Italian pictures, and ask yourself what we have to put beside them after all our endless exhibitions! Modern improvements! Plein air! Bah! Where can you show me more 'atmosphere' than in Carpaccio, or in Jacques d'Arthois.

Impressionism? Look at that snow-effect by old Van Valckenborch here! But we do the modern, the contemporary, you cry—"

"No, I don't," I interrupted feebly, more to let him take breath than for the jest's sake. But he ignored the opportunity.

"But they've all done the contemporary! Only their contemporary, not yours. The fallacy almost amounts to an Irish bull. The ancients were the moderns—to themselves—just as we shall be the ancients to our successors. The Renaissance people all did contemporary work, under pretence of doing historical: contemporary types for Madonnas, local landscapes for Oriental scenery, up-to-date dresses for New Testament episodes, portraits of their patrons for patron-saints and apostles. Did you ever see a more modern figure than Tintoretto's portrait of himself, the elderly man in a frock-coat who looks on at his own wonderful picture of St. Mark descending to rescue a Christian slave? An Academician or a new English Art Clubbite who had done only one tiny corner of this picture would so swell as to the head that his laurel-wreath wouldn't fit him any longer. There's no ambition nowadays—Degas, Whistler, yes. But for the rest—dwarfs. Modern improvements indeed! Science may improve, but not art. Art, like religion, is an absolute in life—nobody will ever paint better than Velasquez, write better than Shakespeare, or pray better than the Psalmist. Science is the variable—always on the go; and when we think of progress it is just as well that we foolishly keep our eye on the machine-room."

"Won't you have a drink?" I broke in, seizing the first opportunity.

"Thanks! What's that book?"

"'Olympia's Journal'! It's all about Olympia's husband, she married him to write about him—he was such 'good copy.'"

I had unchained a torrent. "Novelists ought never to be introduced into novels," burst forth the Young Fogey. "The subject-matter of novelists is real normal life, and novelists are neither real nor normal. They are monsters whose function in life is to observe other people's lives. For one novelist to make copy of another is like cannibalism.

"If the psychology of the novelist, who is the student of other people's psychology, is to be studied, where are you to stop? Why not study the peculiarities of the novelist who studies the novelist, of the reflector of life who reflects the reflector of life—nay, of the critic who reflects upon the reflection of the reflector? This modern mania for picking ourselves to pieces is only the old childish desire 'to see the wheels go wound.' People were much better in the old days when they didn't bother so much how their wheels went round. I always sympathised with the indignant old lady who came to my schoolmaster when our class began to take up physiology, and protested that she wasn't going to have her boy learn what was in his inside—it was indecent. People are not made healthier by knowing how their functions work; animals never study physiology, and plants blossom without knowing anything at all about anything. Knowledge only generates a morbid fussiness, as with Mr. Jerome's celebrated Cockney who discovered himself to be possessed of every ailment in the medical dictionary except housemaid's knee. And to learn what is in your mental inside is equally indecent and equally discomposing. 'I have never thought about thinking,' said the wise Goethe. No one can go through a treatise on insanity and come out as sane as he started. And there is an even more insidious way in which this human vivisection operates for evil. People now forgive their friends—they call their eccentricities 'pathological,' and endure instead of discouraging them. I had two letters this very morning. 'Poor A!' said B.: 'his vanity has ceased to offend me—I feel it is pathological.' 'Poor B!' said A.: 'it is impossible to resent his egotism—it is simply pathological.'

"This scientific Christianity wouldn't be so bad if people didn't condone their own faults, too. They can't get up early—it's heredity. The early bird who caught the worm must have had a grandparent who stayed out late. Are they lazy? Their uncle was a country parson. They are like the man who refused to give charity because he had such expensive tastes. To acquiesce in your own weaknesses because they are hereditary, without making an effort to eradicate them, is bad science as well as bad morals. Among the items given you by heredity do not forget the potentiality of self-improvement by inward struggle. No one says, 'I can't speak French, and I sha'n't try, because my father was an illiterate Irishman.' Self-knowledge tends to weaken self-discipline, foster self-indulgence, and corrode character."

"But what of the old Greek maxim 'Know thyself'?"

"Old Greek sophistry! Knowing requires a subject to know and an object to be known. You can't be subject and object too—introspection is a self-contradiction. Hasn't every one noticed that everybody else fails to discover himself in a novel or a sermon, though his lineaments are painted down to the minutest details of wart and mole? And it's quite natural. Every soul is to itself the centre of the universe—through which the infinite panorama passes; nothing exists but in relation to it: to its standards of beauty, of right and wrong, of humour, of admiration, everything is brought. There's no man so low or so ridiculous but he finds somebody else more so, and the London street-boy who sneers at the long-haired poet is exalted to a sense of superiority. I once met a human monstrosity—hunch-backed, cross-eyed, palsied, and wooden-legged. My soul sickened with pity, but his face brightened in a smile of contempt and his cross-eyes danced with glee. I appealed to his sense of the ridiculous. Listen to the comments of people upon one another after a party, and confess that a coterie is often but a mutual contempt society. That is what makes life livable—every living creature is an amused eye upon the universe. Terence said as much long ago. We amuse one another, and exist to gratify one another's sense of superiority, like the islanders who live by taking in one another's washing. It will be a thousand pities if the spread of travelling removes the mutual superiorities of Englishmen and Frenchmen, Chinamen and Hindoos. I went to a dinner-party the other day. The host and hostess were impossible—like spiteful studies by Thackeray caricatured by Dickens. Yet there were they arrogating to themselves every privilege of judgment and jurisdiction that the most fashionable peers or the sublimest souls could claim; to their own minds the arbiters of elegance, the patrons of the arts, the flagellators of vice and snobbery, the gracious laudators of virtue, the easy fomenters of scandal.

"Prithee, was ever one of us capable of not lecturing on ethics or not preaching a sermon? Did not Sir Barnes Newcome lecture on the Family? Do we not all hold forth on the condition of the poor, the morality of the mining-market; the inferior ethics of the coloured races, and a hundred other lofty topics, warming our coat-tails at the glow of our own virtue? 'T is the fault of language which enables arrant scoundrels to use fine words that they have never felt. Humility, self-sacrifice, noble-mindedness, are phrases easily picked up by people for whom their only meaning is in the dictionary, and who know it is the correct thing to admire them. They are like students of chemistry who babble of H_2SO_4 and NH_3 by book without ever having seen a laboratory or a retort, or tone-deaf people raving over Beethoven. And these lip-servants of virtue are unconscious that they have never known the real thing. Every discussion between civilised persons presupposes moral perfection all round—a common elevated platform from which one surveys the age and its problems, and considers how to bring the world at large up to one's own level. You cannot discuss anything with a person who has ever been publicly imperfect—at any point you may tread on his corns. Has he been bankrupt? The slightest reference to honesty, finance, or business may seem an insult. Has he figured in the Divorce Court? How are you to talk about the last new play without seeming personal? This explains why exposed persons are cut: they have made conversation impossible by cutting away the common ground of it, the hypothesis of perfection. Even with persons who have merely lost relatives one has to be careful to avoid references to mortality. The complete diner-out has to be equipped with a knowledge of his fellows to the third and fourth generation, so as to avoid giving offence. To say that late marriages are a mistake or second marriages a folly may be to make enemies for life. Which, by the way, is absurd: all conversation should be regarded as privileged and impersonal. 'T is brain meeting brain, not foot treading gingerly among irrelevant personal considerations. And just as we are all willing to preach, we are all willing to be preached at—it gives us such an opportunity of gauging the preacher's morality and ability. The Scotch peasants who denounce their meenister's orthodoxy are an extreme case, but if we were not really judging our judges we should go to opposition churches. What we demand from preaching—as from newspapers—is an echo of our own voices, and when the preacher or the newspaper leads it is only by pretending to follow. Opportunity makes the politician. Watch the crowd streaming out of church after a sermon. Do they wear an air of edification or humiliation? Are they bowed down with the consciousness of their backslidings? No: they are aesthetes come from a literary and oratorical performance. They are not thinking of themselves at all, but of the quality of the sermon. Yes, around each of us the world turns, and each soul is the hub of the universe. Popular suffrage is the recognition of this great fact: not one of us but is competent to arrange the affairs of the country. Every man Jack and woman Jill is a standard, a test, an imperial weight and measure, and the universe must endure our verdict as it goes round us. To expect this central standard to turn back on itself and become aware of its own defects and distortions is like expecting a pair of scales to weigh itself; or—more absurd still—expecting a false pair of scales to weigh itself truly. 'All men think all men mortal but themselves,' and so all men find all men wanting except themselves. If they ever for a moment suspect that they are not perfect—whether the suspicion leak in through reflection or reprobation—'t is but for a moment. We cannot live on bad terms with ourselves, nor with a consciousness which doubts and despises us—whether it be our own consciousness or a friend's. Our nature throws up earthworks against a contemptuous opinion. Just as a bodily wound is repaired by the wonderful normal processes of circulation and nutrition, so our self-love tends to repair the wounds of the soul. We feel that even if we are not perfect, we are as perfect as possible under the circumstances. If so-and-so and so-and-so had had to go through our sufferings or our temptations, he or she would have acted no better. And even in our wildest remorse we are self-satisfied with our self-dissatisfaction. Nor is this need of our nature for self-reconcilement wholly without spiritual significance. It points to an incurable morality in the human soul, and to the truth that if we mainly use our ideals to condemn other people by, we are bound to condemn ourselves by them if we can once be got to perceive that we have violated them ourselves, though we at once seek peace in extenuating circumstances. Peace of mind is the homage which vice pays to virtue. Nor, though it matters immensely to society what ideals people have, and that they have the right ones, to the people themselves it matters only that they have ideals, right or wrong. Where there is honour among thieves, a thief may have a fine sense of self-respect."

"Plato agrees with you," said I. "He points out that if thieves were utter scoundrels they could not act in concert."

"Ah!" said the Young Fogey, "Plato was a great thinker. In truth, the only incorrigible rogue is he who is devoid of ideals, who has allowed his ethical nature to disintegrate. Such a one ceases to be a person. He has lost the integrating factor—the moral—which binds human personality together. He is a mere aggregation of random impulses. The last stage of moral decay is impersonality. Impersonality sums up 'the daughters of joy,' with their indifference to aught but the moment.

"But it is wonderful what shreds of personality, what tags and rags of the ideal, the most degraded may retain. Was there ever a soul that did not think some one action beneath its dignity? An absolutely unscrupulous person is a contradiction in terms. To be unscrupulous were to cease to be a person, to have become a bundle of instincts and impulses. But no one is so good or so bad as he appears. The chronicler of the 'Book of Snobs' was himself a bit of a snob, and the poet who sought for the spiritual where Thackeray had looked for the snobbish, who bade us note

"All the world's coarse thumb
And finger failed to plumb,
So passed in making up the main account;
All instincts immature,
All purposes unsure,
That weighed not as his work,
Yet swelled the man's amount,

was almost as weak as the satirist in that respect for titles and riches which is the veritable 'last infirmity of noble minds.'

"Still, Browning's is the truer view of human life, and till we see our neighbours as Omniscience sees them, our kindest and cruellest estimates will be equally wide of the mark.

"And conversely, unless you develop a personality, you cannot be moral, or even immoral. You can be social or anti-social—that is, your actions can make for the good or the ill of society. But moral or immoral it is not given to everybody to be. For I do not agree with those who would substitute social and anti-social for those ancient adjectives. We are concerned with the quality of acts as well as with their effects, with the soul as well as its environment. And it takes a real live soul to do good or evil. That is the point of Mr. Kipling's Tomlinson—a mere bundle of hearsays—who could win neither hell nor heaven. It is also the teaching of Ibsen. You must not shrink from wrong because you are told it is wrong, but because you see it is wrong. But few people can expect to develop a personality of their own. Current morality is the automatic application of misunderstood principles. And so it must always be. For the function of the average man is to obey. Was it not Napoleon who said that men are meant either to lead or to obey, and those who can do neither should be killed off? Ethics is the conscience of the best regulating the conduct of the worst. Hence there are no immutable rules of morality:

"For the wildest dreams of Kew are the facts of Khatmandoo,
And the crimes of Clapham chaste at Martaban.

But there are immutable principles. To spit in a guest's face is with some savage tribes a mark of respect. But this does not invalidate the principle that to guests should be shown courtesy. Rules vary with time and place, principles are eternal; and even if unmentionable things are done in Africa and Polynesia, if 'the dark places of the earth are full of cruelty,' that does not invalidate the principles of morality, as our modern blood-and-thunder young man affects to believe. For that the principles of right and justice have not yet been discovered in barbarous countries no more destroys their universality and legitimacy than the principles of the differential calculus are affected by the primitive practice of counting on the fingers. And while the ethical geniuses—the senior wranglers of the soul—are groping towards further truths and finer shades of feeling, deeper reaches of pity and subtler perceptions of justice, the rank and file and the wooden spoons must needs apply the old ethics, even against the new teachers themselves.

Every truth has to fight for recognition, to prove itself not a lie. The brilliant and impatient young men who scoff at conventions because the people who hold them are unreal—not persons, feeling and passing moral truths through their own soul, but parrots—forget that just because the people are unreal, their maxims are real; that they do not represent the people who mouth them, but the great moralists and thinkers behind. Against the brilliant rushlights of contemporary cleverness shine the stars of the ages. 'T is the immemorial mistake of iconoclasts—even granted they are taller than their fellow-men—to be ever conscious of the extra inches, instead of the common feet. Nevertheless" (and here the Young Fogey put on his most judicial manner) "the extra inches must tell. For because real ethics resides not in rules but in principles, obedience to the letter may mean falsity to the spirit, if the circumstances that dictated the rules have changed. This is not casuistry. 'T is a concept not to be found in Panaetius or Cicero or the Jesuit Fathers. It means that we are not to wear our boyhood's waistcoats, but to be measured for manhood's. Tight-lacing is bad for the spiritual circulation. 'Get rid of the Hebrew old clo', cried that curious Carlyle, the chief dealer in them. Amen, say I: but do not let us therefore go naked. And since we have stumbled upon 'Sartor Resartus,' permit me a comparison in keeping. I once saw a tailor measuring the boys in a charity school. He drew a chalk line five feet up a wall, and dividing the upper part of the line by horizontal chalk-marks, stood the boys beside it, one after another, and according to the chalk-mark which the crown of the unfortunate creature's head grazed, Master Snip called out 'Fours,' 'Ones,' 'Fives.' Fat boys or lean boys, big-bodied or big-legged, narrow-chested or broad-shouldered, 't was all ones—or twos—to him. Did they agree in height, the same clothes—tight or loose—for all! Thus is it with our moral maxims. Genius or goose, saint or sinner—your head to the chalk-mark! And rightly. When one has to deal with great masses one cannot consider little details. The principles of morality must be broad and simple, and the world is right to apply them sternly and undiscriminatingly. The general cannot consider the peculiarities of a particular soldier, though the corporal of the regiment may make allowances for him. And so with breaches of morals. The world at large should condemn; but the private friends, who know the circumstances in every petty involution, who know the temptations and the extenuating factors, should form as it were a court of appeal. If they elected to stand by the offender, the world at large should reconsider its verdict. This is what practically took place in the George Eliot and Lewes instance. Weighed, not by the steelyard of general principle, but by the delicate chemical balance of special detail, they were not found wanting. The Magna Charta is still only a pious aspiration. 'Every man shall be tried by a jury of his peers.' How profound! For only our equals can know our travails and temptations. How, now, if we had to try Shakespeare! which of us would dare sit on the panel? Yet we 'chatter about Shelley.' He did wrong—granted. But was it wrong of him to do it? That is another question altogether. Subjective morality and objective morality are two different things. But the whole subject of the sexes is wrapped in hypocrisy, and the breaches of morality are committed less by the celebrated than by the obscure. The savage sarcasm of Schopenhauer's refusal to discuss monogamy because it had never yet come within the range of practical politics is still justified. I remember once reading an anecdote about a besieged town. The defenders resolved to make a sortie on a certain day, only, in dread of their plan somehow leaking out beyond the gates, or of their womankind dissuading some from the perilous enterprise, they administered a solemn oath to one another that none of them should tell his wife, nor speak of it again even to another man, till the moment arrived. But each individual man told the partner of his bosom, only binding her by most fearsome oaths to say nothing to any other woman or man. All the women kept their oaths, each going about with the proud sense of being the only woman in the great secret. And so the women all met in the market-place, chattering about every subject on earth but that which was nearest their hearts, and the men moved among them, mutually silent. The whole community knew the secret whereof no one spoke. You perceive the parallel? Sex is the secret we are all in. Why shouldn't we talk openly? Why shouldn't we face facts? The marriage laws should be made as flexible, not as inflexible, as possible. Why? Because the bad people will evade everything and the good people endure anything. The bad people will break the best laws and the good people will respect the worst laws. Hence, stringency squeezes the saint and lets the sinner slip. Harsh legislation puts a penalty on virtue: the vicious skirt round it surreptitiously, or are openly happy in despite of it. The only thing immutable in sexual morality is the principle of regulating it with a view to the highest ends of the soul and the state: the regulations themselves are mutable, and we should not sacrifice too many human beings to gratify the idealism of the happily married. At the same time do not suspect me of Hilltopsy-turveydom, which seems to me based on bad physiology and worse psychology. Mr. Grant Allen, man of science as he is in his spare moments, is more like Matthew Arnold's Shelley, a beautiful and ineffectual angel beating in the void his luminous wings in vain. So complex is the problem which seems to him so simple, that it is not improbable that the present monogamy (tempered by polygamy) is the best of all possible arrangements. This is not to belaud the present system, any more than it is optimistic to say this is the best of all possible worlds. It may be so, but it remains a pity that no better was possible. And Mrs. Grundy herself seems to me as over-abused as marriage. The celerity with which she became a byword, from the moment she made her accidental appearance in Tom Morton's 'Speed the Plough,' shows how the popular instinct needed some such incarnation of our neighbours' opinions. She stands, the representative of the ethical level of the age, not of fixed pruderies. She is by no means the staid old soul her maligners imagine—never was there creature more changeable. As we move on, so will she move on with us. Once she allowed our squires to get drunk after dinner, now she is shocked at a one-bottle man. You will never shake her off, you brilliant young gentlemen. For as you established your own ethics, she would still be there to see that your ideas were carried out. Granted she is a scandal-monger. But scandal is the sewer-system of society: the dirty work must be done somehow. Mrs. Grundy is your scavenger. Americans don't talk scandal, but I fail to see how they will keep their homes clean without it. The scandal-mongers may be inspired by no lofty motives, but they make a wonderful unpaid detective force. Sheridan was not a philosopher. Ubiquitous and omniscient, Mrs. Grundy is always with you. Once you might have escaped her by making the grand tour, but now she has a Cook's circular ticket and watches you from the Pyramids or the temples of Japan—especially if, like myself, you have the misfortune to be a celebrity. The only way to escape her is to be photographed widely. Wasn't it Adam Smith who said that conscience was only the reflection in ourselves of our neighbours' opinions? If we didn't value their opinions there would be no morality. Foreign travel makes you feel there is something in the idea. Who cares what a parcel of jabbering strangers think about his actions? The moment you lose touch with your environment, the moment you cease to vibrate to its nuances, your morality is in a parlous condition. Better go home and sit down on the well-known couch of Catullus, and feel once more that people are real and life is earnest and the horizon is not its goal. What is this mania for movement? If you travel unintelligently you see nothing that you couldn't have seen more comfortably in a panorama—the world going round you. If you travel intelligently, you discover the relativity of all customs and ideas, you distrust your own beliefs, your backbone is relaxed, your vitality snapped, and you come home a molluscous cosmopolitan. It is the same thing that happens if you travel mentally instead of by mileage—if you go in for that modern curse, 'Culture.' You are not meant to absorb the art and literature of foreigners and dead peoples, fluttering like a bee from flower to flower. These things were made by men for their own race and age; they never thought of you—you are an eavesdropper. Cathedrals were built for Christians to pray in, not for connoisseurs to gloat over. You should develop along your own lines, strong and simple, not be a many-sided nullity. The true Englishmen are ploughmen and sailors and shopkeepers, not culture-snobs.

"The greatest poets in every language are those who know only their own language. Shakespeare and Keats handled English as a million Professors of Poetry cooperating could never handle it. The greatest Art has always sprung from the direct pressure of the real world upon the souls of the artists. To be cultured is to lose that vivid sense of the reality of the life around you, to see it intellectually rather than to feel it intuitively. Hence art that is too self-conscious misses the throb of life. George Eliot failed as soon as she began to substitute intellectual concepts for the vivid impressions of early memories. The moment people begin to prate about Art, the day of Art is over, and decadence is set in. Art should be the natural semi-unconscious enhancement of other things. The speaker wishing to convince becomes artistically oratorical, the prophet becomes artistically poetic, the church-builder artistically architectural, the painter of Madonnas artistically picturesque, the composer of prayer-chants artistically musical. Art was the child of Religion, but it has long since abandoned its mother. Portrait and landscape painting arose as accessories to sacred pictures; the origin of the opera is to be sought in the Mass; literature developed from religious writings. But gradually it was discovered that you might paint noblemen as well as sages, and that scenery could be dissociated from the backgrounds of Crucifixions and Marriages at Cana. And from seeing that Art needn't have a religious meaning or content, men came to see that it needn't have any meaning or content at all. Art, indeed, presents possibilities of a divorce from intellect and morals of which artists have eagerly availed themselves. But Art for Art's sake is Dead-Sea fruit—rosy without, ashes within. Socrates was not perhaps quite right in saying that the Beautiful was the Useful, but it doesn't follow that the Beautiful should be the Useless. Even crockery, cutlery, and furniture should never be Beautiful at the cost of utility. Their Beauty should be implicated with their natural shapes, inblent with and inseparable from their uses, not a monstrous accretion from without. The most artistic knife is the quintessence of knifehood."

"But that is my idea of Art for Art's sake," I interrupted, for he had now got his second wind. "Art has always to express the quintessence of something—be it a street, a life, a national movement, a—"

"Art for Art's sake means making beautiful knives that won't cut and beautiful glasses that won't hold water, and beautiful pictures and poems that say nothing. The people who want their Art dissociated from their morals are in danger of spiritual blight, and inhabiting a universe of empty nothings. Too much self-consciousness is as sterile as too little. Look at these modern Renaissances! They all—"

"Yes, I know: I have written about that," I said. "And now there is another one, the Jewish. Have you read the plan for 'A Jewish State,' by Dr. Herzl, of Vienna? No dreamer he, but wonderfully sane, despite his lofty conception of a moralised, rationalised, modern State. Too 'modern,' indeed, this idea of Messiah as a joint-stock company! I predicted years ago we should come to that. But methinks the Doctor—"

"They are starting the Grand Prix," hastily interrupted the Young Fogey. "Good-bye! Such a delightful talk!" And turning his back on the horses, he hurried off the field to lose himself and perhaps find a new pair of English ears among the parasols and equipages of the sunlit Prater.

XI

CRITICS AND PEOPLE

What is the critic's duty at the play? Does he represent Art, or does he represent the Public? If he represent Art, then he is but a refracting medium between the purveyor and the public, which will therefore be wofully mistaken if it seek in his critiques a guide to its play-going, as it to some extent does. For while people do not always like a play because they are told it is good, they often refrain from going to see one because they are told it is bad. When I was a dramatic critic—a phrase that merely means I did not pay for my seat—nothing struck me more forcibly than the frequent discrepancy between the opinions of the audience at a première and the opinions of the papers. Again and again have I seen an audience moved to laughter and cheers and tears by a play which the great outside public would be informed the next morning was indifferent or worse. The discrepancy was sometimes explicable by claques, which are almost as discreditable to managements as the keeping of tame critics, who eat food out of their hand. Sometimes it was not professional claques, but amateurs come to see a friend's play en masse, and applauding out of all proportion to its merits, not so much perhaps from friendship as from simple astonishment at finding any merits. But putting aside claques, it remains true that an audience will often heartily enjoy what a critic will heartily damn—sometimes in half a dozen papers, your capable critic being like a six-barrelled revolver. And so—often enough—the piece, after futile efforts to masquerade in the advertisement columns in a turned garment of favourable phrases, dies in an odour of burnt paper; the treasury is robbed of its due returns; and numerous worthy persons to whom it would have given boundless pleasure are deprived of their just enjoyment. The obvious truth is that the public and the critics—the people who pay to see plays and the people who are paid to see plays—have different canons of criticism. Sometimes their judgments coincide, but quite as frequently they disagree. It is the same with popular books. And the reason of this is not far to seek. The critic is not only more cultured than the average playgoer, he is more blasé. He knows the stock situations, the stage tricks, the farcical misunderstandings, the machine-made pathos, the dull mechanic round of repartee, the innocent infant who intervenes in a divorce suit (like the Queen's Proctor), the misprised mother-in-law, the bearded spinster sighing like a furnace, the ingenuous and slangy young person of fifteen with the well-known cheek, and the even more stereotyped personages preserved in Mr. Jerome's "Stage-land." They all come, if not from Sheffield, from a perpetual tour in the provinces. The critic knows, too, which plays are taken from the French and which from the English, where the actor is gagging and when he is "fluffy." A good deal of the disillusionment of the scene is also his: he knows that the hero is not young nor the heroine beautiful, nor the villain as vicious as either.

How different the attitude of the occasional playgoer! Seeing only a tithe of the plays of the day, he neither knows nor cares whether they repeat one another. The most hackneyed device may seem brilliantly original to him, the stalest stage trick as fresh as if just hot from the brain; and jokes that deterred the dove from returning to the ark arride him vastly. Per contra, for his unjaded imagination absolutely new scenes and dialogues have no more novelty than the comparatively aged. Probability or truth to life he demands not, perfection of form were thrown away upon him. His soul melts before the simplest pathos, he is made happy by a happy ending, and when Momus sits on a hat "he openeth his mouth and saith Ha! ha!" He is a flute upon which you may play what false notes you will. In some versions of "Uncle Tom's Cabin" he placidly accepts two Topsies. I s'pec's one growed out of t' other. He hath a passion for the real as well as the ideal, and in order to see a fire-engine, or Westminster Bridge, or a snow-storm, he will perspire you two hours at the pit's mouth. He could see them any day in the street, but it gives him wondrous joy to see them in their wrong places. How absurd, then, for the average critic to be play-taster to the occasional playgoer! He no more represents him than an M. P. represents the baby he kisses. As well might one ask a connoisseur to choose the claret for a back-parlour supper-party. Thus the critic cannot honestly represent the Public. That he cannot represent Art without injuring the Theatre as well as the Public, has already been shown. The conclusion one is driven to is that the critic has no raison d'être at all in the topical press. There he should be replaced by the reporter. The influence of cultivated criticism should be brought to bear on the drama only from the columns of high-class magazines or books.

Nor am I more certain of the use of the art critic. He is far too conflicting to be of any practical value, and he as often contradicts himself as his fellows. He hides his ignorance in elegant English, sometimes illuminated by epigram, and from his dogmatic verdicts there is no appeal. Not infrequently he is resolved to be a critic "in spite of nature," as Sir Joshua has it in a delicious phrase which was possibly given him by his friend "the great lexicographer." In a letter to the "Idler," the painter recommends those devoid of eye or taste, and with no great disposition to reading and study, to "assume the character of a connoisseur, which may be purchased at a much cheaper rate than that of a critic in poetry." "The remembrance of a few names of painters, with their general characters," says Sir Joshua, "and a few rules of the Academy, which they may pick up among the Painters, will go a great way towards making a very notable Connoisseur." He goes on to describe a gentleman of this cast, whose mouth was full of the cant of Criticism, "which he emitted with that volubility which generally those orators have who annex no ideas to their words."

When I once expressed to Mr. Whistler my conviction that, with the single exception of religion, more nonsense was talked on the subject of art than on any other topic in the world, that great authority refused to allow religion any such precedence. Certainly during the season when, for the middle-class Londoner, art "happens," the claims of art to that proud pre-eminence become overwhelming, if only temporarily so. Everybody gives his opinion freely, and it is worth the price. To criticise painting is only less difficult than to execute it. Fifty per cent. of art is sheer science, the rigid, accurate science of form and perspective, I do not say that accuracy is necessary to art. Still it is what most people presume to judge. But does one person in a hundred know the true proportions of things, or possess the eye to gauge the anatomy of a figure? Owing to the neglect in schools of the rudiments of drawing, our eyes barely note the commonest objects; we remark just enough of their characteristics to identify them. "Consider!" as Mr. John Davidson writes in his "Random Itinerary": "did you ever see a sparrow? You have heard and read about sparrows. The streets are full of them; you know they exist. But you could not describe one, or say what like is its note. You have never seen a sparrow, any more than you have seen the thousand-and-one men and women you passed in Fleet street the last time you walked through it. Did you ever see a sparrow?" And then there is colour. Do you really know what the colour of that landscape is, or what complex hues mantle the surface of yonder all-mirroring pool? Do you know that, the appearance of nature is constantly varying with every change of light and every passing cloud? Do you know how Primrose Hill looks at night? Perhaps you think you know how a haystack looks in the sunlight; yet across the Channel the illustrious Monet devoted months to painting one haystack, making fresh discoveries daily. I do not believe you know how many Roman figures there are on your watch-dial. You probably think there are twelve. But what is far more important, you may be quite devoid of artistic sensibility. Yet you would not hesitate to criticise the Academy or even to be paid for it. I had occasion to buy a doll the other day. It was a she-doll. There seems, by the way, a tremendous preponderance of the fair sex in dolls: what difficult social problems must agitate the Dolls' Houses! This was a pretty doll, with wide blue eyes, and a wealth of golden tow, and an expression of aristocratic innocence on its waxen cheek, faintly flushed with paint, and I bore it home with pride. But when I came to examine it, I found it was but a sawdust abomination. Oh the modelling of the arm, oh the anatomy of the leg, oh the patella proximate to the ankle! I felt that if I gave that doll to the expectant infant, she might grow up to be an art critic. Thus, then, mused I sorrowfully, is the nation's taste made in Germany. We are corrupted from the cradle, even as upon our tombs badly carved angels balance themselves dolefully. Let me make a nation's dolls: I care not who makes its pictures. Was it of these dolls a late President of the Royal Academy was thinking, when he said that the German genius did not find its best expression in plastic art? The Academy will not be permanently improved until we improve our dolls.

Now that the world is so full of free dinners for the well-fed, it behoves hostesses to reconsider their methods. With so many dinner-tables open to the lion, or even to the cub, they must do their spiriting dexterously if they would feed him. In these days when seven hostesses pluck hold of the swallow-tails of one man, and the form of grace before meals must be, "For those we are about to receive, Lord make us truly thankful," something more than the average attraction is needed to induce the noble animal to dine at your expense. There is one improvement in the great dinner function for which I would respectfully solicit the attention of ladies who entertain but do not amuse. "It is a great point in a gallery how you hang your pictures," says the sage of Concord, "and not less in society how you seat your party. When a man meets his accurate mate, Society begins and life is delicious." Yes, but how rarely does a man meet his accurate mate in these minor marriages of the dinner-table! How often is he chained for hours to an unsympathetic soul he has not even made the mistake of selecting. The terrible length of the modern dinner makes the grievance very real, and in a society already vibrant with the demand for easier divorce it is curious that there has arisen no Sarah Grand of the dining-room to protest against this diurnal evil. Suppose that at a dance you were told off to one perpetual partner, who would ever don pumps? Is it not obvious that at a dinner you should have the same privilege as at a dance—the privilege of choosing your partner for each course? It could be done during the drawing-room wait. I give an example of an ordinary menu, marked after the fashion of a gentleman's dance programme, from which it will the seen at a glance how much more delightful a dinner would become if you could change your partner as often as your plate.

MENU, JUNE 15th, 1894.

Plats.   Engagements.
1. Hors d'oeuvres . . . . S. S.
2. Soup . . . . A. P. S.
3. Poisson . . . . Pinky.
4. Poisson . . . . L. R.
5. Entrée . . . . Blue Bow.
6. Entrée . . . . Red Hair.
7. Joint . . . . W.
8. Sweet . . . . Minnie. 9.
Sweet . . . . Minnie.
10. Cheese . . . . Long Arms.
11. Dessert . . . . I. V.

(Interval before ladies rise.)

Extra Entrée . . . . . . Agnes.
Extra Joint . . . . Eyeglasses.
Extra Sweet . . . . Minnie.

You perceive at once that you would always put your idol pro tem, down for the sweets, which would become as fertile a source of flirtation as "love" in tennis. Of course the same tact and discretion would be needed in filling your menu as in filling your programme. Some ladies who are excellent at the entrée may be inadvisable for the joint, which they may sit out, expecting to monopolise your attention to the detriment of your meal. Others who are dull at the soup may be agreeably vivacious towards the later items. A new series of formulae would be added to the language:

"May I have the pleasure of seeing your menu?"

"Will you give me one sweet?"

"Can you spare me the joint?"

"I am so sorry: I have just given it away."

"See me eat the poisson, as Grossmith says."

"Will you put me down for a fish?"

"This is our entrée, I think."

"May I have my dessert, Minnie?"

"Are you engaged for the cheese?"

"Yes; but you can have the second entrée."

"Don't forget to keep the soup for me!"

"If you don't mind sitting it out!"

"Are you open for the extra joint?"

"Thank you: I am full up."

For hostesses who shrink from such a revolution, a beginning might be made by an automatic change of seats by the gentlemen, say one to the right as in the chassé-croisé of the Caledonians. Failing this, the only remaining method of avoiding monotony and the chilling separation of the extremes of the board is to follow the example of King Arthur and employ a round table. The round dinner-table is the only way of making both ends meet.

Having got your round table, what are you to eat upon it? There is hardly any edible known to the menu which some sect or other would not banish from the kitchen, while if you were to follow the "Lancet" you would eat nothing at all, starving like Tantalus amid a wealth of provisions. Of these sects of the stomach I was aware of many. But it is only recently that the claims of "natural food" have been brought within my heathen ken. The apostle of the new creed is an American lady doctor, whose gospel, however, is somewhat vitiated by her championship of Mrs. Maybrick, so that one cannot resist the temptation of suspecting that she thinks the jury would never have found that interesting lady guilty if they had fed upon starchless food. For this is the creed of the new teaching. All starch foods are chiefly digested in the intestines instead of in the main stomach, and hence are unnatural and morbiferous, and the chief cause of the nervous prostration and broken-down health that abound on all sides. (Herr Nordau gives quite a different explanation of the general breakdown, but no matter.) "The 'Natural Food

Society,'" says its official organ, "is founded in the belief that the food of primeval man consisted of fruit and nuts of sub-tropical climes, spontaneously produced; that on these foods man was, and may again become, at least as free from disease as the animals are in a state of nature." How curiously apposite seem Dryden's lines, written in a very different connection!

This was the fruit the private spirit brought,
Occasioned by great zeal and little thought.
While crowds unlearned, with rude devotion warm,
About the sacred viands buzz and swarm.

And this couplet of his, too, might be commended to the devotees:

A thousand daily sects rise up and die;
A thousand more the perished race supply.

What does it matter what primeval man ate? It is not even certain that he was a member of the Natural Food Society. The savage, as we know him, lives on the game he hunts and shoots, and prefers his fellow-man to vegetarianism. No one ever accused the red Indian of nervous prostration, "when wild in woods the noble savage ran"; nor are leopards and tigers usually in broken-down health. But, in justice to the Natural Food Society, I must admit that it displays a pleasant absence of fanaticism, for there is a proviso in italics: "All persons about to experiment with the non-starch food system are urged at first not to use nuts, but to use instead whatever animal food they have been accustomed to." The central feature of the system is abstention from bread, cereals, pulses, and starchy vegetables, for which food fruits are to be substituted. All this seems a mighty poor excuse for the formation of a new sect. Fortunately the Society uses up its superfluous energies "in working for the higher life," and in its coupling of health and holiness is sound in its psychology, whatever it may be in its physiology.

You never heard of Peterkin's pudding, by the way, but there is a fine moral baked in it. Johannes came to his wife one day and said, "Liebes Gretchen, could you not make me a pudding such as Peterkin is always boasting his wife makes him? I am dying of envy to taste it. Every time he talks of it my chops water." "It is not impossible I could make you one," said Gretchen good-naturedly; "I will go and ask Frau Peterkin how she makes it." When Johannes returned that evening from the workshop, where Peterkin had been raving more than ever over his wife's pudding, Gretchen said gleefully, "I have been to Frau Peterkin: she has a good heart, and she gave me the whole recipe for Peterkin's pudding." Johannes rubbed his hands, and his mouth watered already in anticipation. "It is made with raisins," began Gretchen. Johannes's jaw fell. "We can scarcely afford raisins," he interrupted: "couldn't you manage without raisins?" "Oh, I dare say," said Gretchen, doubtfully. "There is also candied lemon-peel." Johannes whistled. "Ach, we can't run to that," he said. "No, indeed," assented Gretchen; "but we must have suet and yeast." "I don't see the necessity," quoth Johannes. "A good cook like you"—here he gave her a sounding kiss—"can get along without such trifles as those." "Well, I will try," said the good Gretchen, as cheerfully as she could; and so next morning Johannes went to work light-hearted and gay. When he returned home, lo! the long-desired dainty stood on the supper-table, beautifully brown. He ran to embrace his wife in gratitude and joy; then he tremblingly broke off a hunch of pudding and took a huge bite. His wife, anxiously watching his face, saw it assume a look of perplexity, followed by one of disgust. Johannes gave a great snort of contempt. "Lieber Gott!" he cried, "and this is what Peterkin is always bragging about!"

XIII

THE ABOLITION OF MONEY

The Cynic was very old and very wise and very unpopular. I was the only person at his "At Home" that afternoon. I gave him my views on Bi-metallism, having just read the leader in the "Times." He yawned obtrusively, and growled, "Bi-metallism, indeed! The only remedy for modern civilisation is A-metallism. Money must be abolished. The root of all evil must be pulled up."

"Money abolished!" I echoed in amaze. "Why, any student of political economy will tell you we could not live without it. Lacking a common measure of value, we—"

"So it has always been held by students when answering political-economy papers," he interrupted impatiently. "Yet I dreamt once of a land where the currency was called in, and the morning stars sang together."

"But the exchange of commodities—" I began.

"Was effected by the sublime simplicity of barter. At one sweep were swept away all that monstrous credit system which had created an army of accountants and a Court of bankruptcy; all that chaos of single and double-faced entry—all that sleight-of-hand abracadabra of signatures—all those paper phantoms of capital. The Stock Exchange and other gambling-hells shrivelled up. There was a vast saving of clerical labour, and there were few loopholes for fraud. Everything was too simple. Swift retribution overtook the man who shirked his obligations to his fellows. Nobody could juggle with bits of paper at the North Pole and ruin people at the South. The windows of human Society were cleared of the gigantic complex cobweb full of dead flies. One could look inside and see what was going on. 'Gentlemen' could not flourish in the light. They were like the fungi that grew in cellars. Every man became both a worker and a trader."

"Not an unmixed gain, that," I protested.

"I grant you," said the Cynic. "Some of the finer shades of fine gentlemanliness were lost: the honourable feeling of cheating one's tradesmen, the noble scorn of tailors, the lofty despisal of duns. When all men were tradesmen, these higher class distinctions fused into one another. There arose a clannish feeling which prevented the tradesman from defrauding one of his own class. But there was an even graver evil to be placed to the debit side of the new system. For the professors of political economy (who had thrown up their posts as a conscientious protest against the abolition of money and of salaries) proved to be right. So clumsy was the mechanism of exchange that men were actually driven to doing more than one kind of work. All those advantages of specialisation which Adam Smith, supplemented by Babbage, had so laboriously pointed out were completely lost to a wasteful world. Rather than be without certain luxuries and necessaries men gave up moving their legs all day up and down in time with iron treadles, or feeding machines with bits of material exactly alike, or remaining doubled up underground, or making marks from hour to hour and from year to year on pieces of ruled paper. The waste by friction became enormous. Some of the least thrifty even made their own furniture, and wove their own clothes, and carved out rude ornaments for themselves. Whether from a natural want of economy, or from an unwillingness to encounter the difficulties of traffic, or from a mere spirit of independence, these men deliberately reverted to the condition from which mankind had so painfully emerged.

"Some even pretended to enjoy it, and, rather paradoxically, asserted that the abolition of gold had brought about the golden age of primitive legend. Others who felt keenly the falling-off in production, and the absence of those huge stores of unsold commodities which glutted the ancient markets, and gave a nation a sense of wealth in the midst of poverty; the aesthetic spirits who lamented the disappearance of the ancient mansions and palaces, which, although they were empty three parts of the year, yet afforded men the consolation of knowing that they were ample enough to shelter the majority of the homeless—men of this stamp were chagrined by the cumbersome mechanism of exchange, which made these glories of the past impracticable, and they were for introducing counters. But counters, although they had the advantage of lacking intrinsic value, would be quite as bad as actual coins if men could entirely trust one another never to repudiate their obligations. Unfortunately Society had grown so honest under the new régime that this condition was fulfilled, and the operation of counters would have been identical with that of money. Moreover, counters would have brought back card-playing, horse-racing, fire and life assurance, and other forms of gambling, which without them involved such complex calculations and valuations of loaves and fishes that all the pleasure was spoilt. When these things were pointed out to the aesthetic and the economical, they were convinced and remained of the same opinion.

"But even with all these deficits, the balance in favour of the status quo was eminently satisfactory. It was rediscovered that man really wanted very little here below, and that it was better for all to get it than for some to continue to want it; and, taking into account also the general freedom from war, newspapers, and other evils of a moneyed civilisation, it must be conceded that the common people had very little to grumble at."

"But what of the uncommon people?" I interrupted at last. "They must have been martyred."

"Certainly, for the good of the common people. You see, everything was topsy-turvey. Besides, they suffered only during the earlier stages of transition. There was, for instance, the poet who went round among the workmen to chaffer verses. But there were few willing to barter solid goods for poetry. Here and there an intelligent artisan in love purchased a serenade, and an occasional lunatic (for Nature hath her aberrations under any system) became the proprietor of an epic. But the sons of toil drove few bargains or hard with the sons of the Muses. The best poets fared worst, for the crowd sympathised not with their temper, nor with their diction, and they were like to die of starvation and so achieve speedy recognition. But the minor poets, too, were in sore strait. The market was exceedingly limited. Sellers were many and buyers few. Rondeaux were hawked about from butcher to baker, at ten to the joint, or three to the four-pound loaf, and triolets were going at a hollow-toothful of brandy. A ballade-worth of butter would hardly cover a luncheon biscuit, while a five-act blank-verse tragedy was given away for a pound of tea, and that only when the characters were incestuous and the caesuras irreproachable. A famous female poet was reduced to pawning her best sonnet for a glass of lemonade and a bun.

"Times were no less hard for the comic writer. Hitherto he had only to outrage his mother-tongue, or to debase the moral currency, to find the land ready to accord him of the fat thereof. He used to sit in a room in Fleet street and make or steal jokes in return for gold. By the wonderful mechanism of the old Society other men and women, in whatever part of the world he might stray, would rush to feed and clothe and house him, and play and sing and dance to him, and physic him, and drive him about in carriages, and tell him the news and shave him, and press upon him aromatic mixtures to smoke, and love him, and kowtow to him, and beg of him, and even laugh at his jokes, all in return for making or stealing jokes in Fleet street. Some of these men and women would detest jokes, or have a blindness to their points; nevertheless, not one but would be eager to express in the most practical form his or her sense of the services rendered to Society by the joker. But now that people saw with open eyes through the transparent mechanism of exchange, they were extremely loth to part with their tangible commodities in return for mere flashes of wit or vulgarity. Previously they had only half realised that they were soberly and seriously making coats, or working machines, or smelting iron, while these jesters were merely cudgelling their brains or consulting back files. The complexity of the thing had disguised the facts. But now that they saw exactly what was going on, they became suddenly callous to numerous vested interests, and their new-found desire to know why they should give up the fruits of their labour pressed very cruelly upon innocent individuals. The comic writer found it no joke to live with 'I'd Rajah not's' going at seventy-five to the cigarette, or mockeries of the mother-in-law yielding but a ton of coals to the thousand. Puns were barely vendible, and even comic pictures could only be sold at a great sacrifice of decency.

"The heir was a type of sufferer. When he came around asking for champagne and chicken, the working-man said, 'What are you offering us in exchange?' and he replied, 'My relationship to my father.' But they would not buy.

"Antiquarians and scholars, too, found it a hard task to live. No one needed the things they raked up from the dust-heap of the past. Critics were in an exceptionally critical condition. No one cared to exchange his productions with a man who in return had to offer only his opinion of somebody else's! As this opinion was usually worthless even under the old régime, people soon began to turn up their noses at it, and nobody would give a rusk for the information that Turner was a better artist than Nature, or that hanging was too good for Whistler. Remarks about the Italian Renaissance were accounted paltry equivalents for green peas, invidious comparisons among the Lake poets were not easily negotiable for alpaca umbrellas, and the subtlest misreadings of Shakespeare were considered trivial substitutes for small-clothes. The artists were reduced to borrowing half-rolls from their models, partly because people had gone back to Nature and liked their scenery free from oil, and drank in the Spirit of Beauty without water, and partly because it was so difficult to assess the value of a picture now that critics had been starved out and speculation had died away. Allegorical painters continued a much-misunderstood race, and the fusion of classes had reacted fatally on the brisk trade in 'Portraits of a Gentleman.' People who, in their celestial aspirations after the True, the Good, and the Beautiful, had forgotten that they ate and drank and required food, warmth, and shelter to hatch all these sublime things with Capital Letters—people who had heretofore poured lofty scorn on those who could not forget that a man was a being with a body—these were now the most clamant demanders of the material. Only by the withdrawal of physical necessaries and luxuries did they come to realise how much they had depended on such, or to perceive the impossibility of the Worship of Truth on an empty stomach. Alas! under this crude system of barter the most ardent expression of their sentiments concerning the ideal and the Kalokagathon would not keep them in cigars. The professional paradoxist went about with holes in his boots. Epigrams in hand, sickness at heart, and emptiness at stomach, he crawled through the town in search of a buyer. He offered a dozen of the choicest apothegms for a pair of hob-nailed boots, conjuring the cobbler like the veriest 'commercial' to note the superiority of the manufacture. He pointed out that he travelled with the latest novelties in Impressionist Ethics, perfect unfitness guaranteed. He even offered to make a reduction if the cobbler would take a quantity. The worthy craftsman, stung by the prospect of a cheap job lot of epigrams, was prevailed upon to look at the goods. But when he read that 'Vice is the foundation of all virtue,' that 'Self-sacrifice is the quintessence of selfishness,' and that 'The Good of Evil outweighs the Evil of Good,' he felt that he could do much better with his boots, even if he only employed them to kick the epigrammatist. The poor wretch thought himself lucky when he succeeded in purchasing two epigrams worth of tobacco and a paradox worth of potatoes. To cap his misfortunes, the nation suffered from a sudden invasion of immigrant epigrammatists, so that cynicisms went a-begging at ten for a sausage-roll. Nor was the dull but moral maxim at less discount than the witty but improper epigram. Essays inculcating the most superior virtues failed to counterbalance a day's charing, and the finest spiritualistic soft soap would not wash clothes. Even the washerwoman deemed her work more real and valuable than the manufacture of moralities too fine for use, and the deliberate effusion of sentiments too good to be true.

"In those days, too, a complete political platform, comprising a score of first-class articles of faith, sold at a pair of second-hand slop-trousers, and a speech of three hours and three hundred parentheses could not fetch more than a pot of jam in the open market. The workhouses were crowded with politicians, critics, poets, novelists, bishops, sporting tipsters, scholars, heirs, soldiers, dudes, painters, journalists, peers, bookmakers, landlords, punsters, idealists, and other incorrigible persons. Nothing was more curious and heartrending in the history of this transition to a new stage than the rapidity with which those who had been most exigent towards life bated their terms. Men who, in their aspirations after the Good and the Beautiful and the True, had unwittingly wasted an intolerable deal of the world's substance in riotous idealising—men who had so long breathed the atmosphere of ottomans and rose-leaves that they were barely conscious of their privileges—now found themselves clamouring for bread wherewith to stay the cravings of their inner selves, and accounted themselves happy if they found a roof to shelter them. The pathos of it was that they felt it all too intensely to see the pathos of it, or to express it in poem, picture, or song.

"It was, of course, the current political economy to which was due this immense depreciation in the exchange value of the higher kinds of intellectual and artistic work. In the old Socialistic system which had been swept away by the abolition of money, men had purchased literary and musical commodities in common, each consumer paying his quota for his share of an unconsumable and infinitely divisible whole. But now few individuals cared or could afford to purchase whole works for their private edification; and so it came to pass that men of talent suffered as much as men of genius in the olden days. And when it began to be understood of the people that the times were other, and that Art and Letters and Apostleship would not pay, men turned in resignation to work with their hands, and they made all kinds of useful things.

"And the bookmakers returned not to their pens, nor the pot-boiling painters to their palettes, nor the apostles to their prophesying, being otherwise engaged and not thereto driven by inward necessity.

"And the Society of Authors perished!

"But the great poets, and the prophets, and the workers in colour and form, upon whom the spirit rested, these wrought on when their daily labour for a livelihood was at an end, for joy of their art and for the religious fire that was in them, giving freely of their best to their fellow-men, and exempt for evermore from all taint of trade."

The Cynic paused, and I sat silent, deeply impressed by what he had said, and striving to imprint every word of it upon my memory, so that I might sell it to a magazine.

XIV

MODERN MYTH-MAKING

So far as I can gather from the publications of the Folklore Society, the science of Folklore is in a promising condition. The doctors seem to be agreed neither about the facts nor the methods nor the conclusions, but otherwise their unanimity is wonderful. Originally the science was made in Germany, where it still flourishes, like all sciences that require infinite pains and inexhaustible dulness. All that can be done with any fruitfulness is apparently the collection and classification of stories, songs and superstitions. Hypotheses and theories are mainly bricks without straw, and the only certain conclusion that may be drawn from the prevalence of folk-tales all over the world is that all men are liars. This was the first contribution to the science, and the Psalmist may be regarded as the founder of Folklore. Herder made an advance when he collected the folk-songs of many nations; and Grimm as a collector was truly scientific, but when he brought in his mythological explanations he brought in mythology. Benfey's celebrated theory that European folk-tales are Oriental in origin and comparatively recent in date seems to be bearing up well.

But no one seems to study the mythopoetic instinct as it manifests itself in modern life, in the daily refraction of fact through the medium of imagination (a medium whose power of refraction is far greater than that of water). Because we no longer create gods and goddesses, or people the woods and brooks with fairies and nymphs, and the forest with gnomes and the hills with hobgoblins—because we do not soften our lives with an atmosphere of gracious supernaturalism, and fresco our azure ceiling with angels—it is assumed that the mythopoetic instinct is dead. Far from it! It is as lively as ever, and we may watch it at play in the building up of legends, in the creation of mythical figures; in the shaping of the Boulanger legend, the Napoleonic legend, the Beaconsfield legend with its poetical machinery of the primrose, the Booth legend, the Blavatsky legend; in the fathering of epigrams upon typical wits like Sheridan, or the attribution of all jokes to "Punch"; in the creation of non-existent bodies like the Æsthetes, and in the private circulation of scandals about public personages; in the perpetual revival of the Blood Accusation against the Jews, or the pathetic clinging to the miracles of exposed Spiritualists and Theosophists; in the Gladstone of Tory imaginations and the Balfour of Radical; in the Irish patriot of oratory; in the big-footed Englishwoman of French fancy, and the English conception of the Scotchman who cannot see a joke; in the persistence of traditional beliefs or prejudices that would be destroyed by one inspection.

Apotheosis is still with us, and diabolification (if I may coin a word). We canonise as prodigally as in the mediaeval ages, and are as keen as ever about relics. We are still looking out for dead King Arthur: he will return by way of the County Council. Plus ça change plus c'est la méme chose—probably the profoundest observation ever made by a Frenchman. Our mythopoetic instinct is as active as of yore, only the mode of its expression is changed. It works on modern lines, has taken to prose instead of poetry, and only occasionally unfurls wings. Why does not the Folklore Society investigate the origin of our modern myths? Why not seize on the instinct as it is seen at play in our midst, moulding movements and fashioning faiths? Why not catch it in the act—employ vivisection, so to speak, instead of dissecting dead remains? Why not try to extract from the living present the laws of the creation and development of myths and the conditions of their persistence, so that by applying these laws retrospectively we may come to understand our heritage of tradition? Ah! but this would require insight into life, which your scientist has no mind for. Besides, dry-as-dust work—collation and classification—may be distributed among the members of a society; but how require of them fresh vision? There is dispute as to how folklore arose: one school talks vaguely of creation by the clan, the community, the race; another insists that the germ at least must always have sprung from some one individual mind, just as a proverb may be the wisdom of many but must be the wit of one; that ideas that are "in the air," like a tree whose branches are everywhere and whose trunk nowhere, had a single root once; and that every on dit was literally "one says" originally. But if we watch the process of mythopoetising in our daily life, we shall see both theories illustrated. Consider the myth of Lord Randolph's small stature: it may be traced easily enough to Mr. Furaiss's pencil. Many people who have the impression forget whence they derived it; and many who never saw Punch had the idea conveyed to them by London letter-writing journalists who never saw Churchill. Yet there is no doubt that the myth is the creation of a single man. In this instance the genesis is clear, and it makes for the one-man theory. In other instances, I can quite imagine myths arising from a spectacle witnessed in common by a multitude, or an incident developing itself under the eyes of many. No single reporter of the doings in Sherwood Forest built up the Robin Hood legend.

Doubtless every ballad was the work of an individual; crowds do not spontaneously burst out into identical remarks, except on the stage. But the crowd was ready for the individual's ballad; it furnished him with his theme and his inspiration, so that he "gave back in rain what he received in mist." Thus, most folklore would owe its birth to the co-operation of the individual and the community—the former the creative or male factor, the latter the receptive or feminine factor. The one man launches his jest, his caricature, his story, his melody, into a sympathetic but inarticulate environment. Then it is taken up, it is transformed, it grows mighty. The "Times" is something very different from the total of the contributors' manuscripts.

Perhaps the most interesting field of folklore work, from the point of view of mere literature, was that opened up by Von Hahn's classification of the stories of the world according to their original elements, their bare plots. There are about seventy main types of stories to which all the wandering tales of the world may be reduced. As thus:

GRATEFUL BEASTS' TYPE

1. A man saves some beasts and a man from a pit.

2. The beasts somehow make him rich, and the man somehow tries to ruin him.

I have little doubt that these might be fined down to seventeen on a very broad basis of classification. I should like to see an analysis of the world's novels similar to that which Polti has made for the drama. Probably it would need a Society to do it, though it would be easy enough to keep pace with the output when once the arrears were cleared off. There are only twenty novels published every week in England, omitting serials, and probably only two or three hundred in the whole world. By a division of labour these could be easily taken to pieces and their plots dissected. In time this might lead to a copyright in incidents as well as in words and titles, and the stock situations would be stocked no more, and the conventional novelists would be killed off. Even if Parliament did not see its way to copyrighting incidents, for fear good ideas spoiled by weak writers should be lost to use by the strong, the publication of a catalogue of the motives of fiction already treated would deter all but the most shameless from changing infants at nurse, or rescuing young ladies from bulls, or mistaking brother and sister for lovers, or having to do with wills lost, stolen, or strayed. Colossal as the task looks, a first rough analysis would sweep away half the new novels of the month and include three-fourths of the fiction of the past. Here is the broadest and most general formula of English fiction as she is wrote for the young person: A young man meets a young woman under unpropitious conditions which delay their union.

Nine-tenths of the novels of the day may be dissected under the following heads: (a) Description of Hero; (b) Of Heroine; (c) How they first met; (d) Why they did not marry till the last chapter.

There! Quite unintentionally I have given away the secret of novel-writing. It is, for all the world, like the parlour game of Consequences, wherein each person fills up a form unknown to the others. The muscular John Jones met the beautiful Princess of Portman Square in the Old Kent Road, and said to her, "Oh, 'Arriet, I'm waitin' for you," and she replied, "You must wait till the end of the third volume," and the consequences were that they got married, and the world said, "We must get this from Mudie's." After this lesson in fiction any one may rival the masters, provided he can hold a pen and doesn't mind leaving the spelling to the compositors. You may perhaps think that the real value of a book lies in the accessories before the marriage, in the pictures of life and character; but I can assure you, unless you turn everything round this axis, the critics will tell you you can't construct. For my part, I would rather have "The Story of an African Farm," two-storied as it really is, than a hundred bungalow romances. Better genius without art than art without genius.

For French fiction the formula would have to be varied. It would run: (a)Hero; (b)Heroine; (c)How they first loved; (d)What the hero's wife or the heroine's husband did; (e)Who died?

Another piece of work I should like to see done is a census of the population of novels. Then we should see clearly how far they are a reflection of life. In England I warrant the professional men would outnumber all others; the aristocracy would come next, and the urban working-man would be swamped by the villagers. The nation of shopkeepers would be poorly represented, and artisans would be few in the land. There would be more perfectly beautiful English girls than there are girls in England, more American millionaires than even the States can raise, and more penniless lords than if Debrett were a charity list of paupers; more satanic guardsmen than ever wore "the widow's uniform," more briefless barristers than all the men who have eaten dinners in vegetarian restaurants, and more murderers than have ever been caught since the days of Jonathan Wild. Indeed, I am not certain but what the population of English novels would come out thirteen millions, mostly criminals. The relative proportions of blondes and brunettes would also be brought out, and whether there is a run on any especial colour of hair. Plain heroines came in with Jane Eyre. It would be interesting to ascertain if they are still worn or still weary.

XV

THE PHILOSOPHY OF TOPSY-TURVEYDOM

My friends, topsy-turveydom is not so easy as it looks. The trouble is not in inverting, but in finding what to invert. Our language is full of ancient saws, but it takes wit to discover which to turn upside down. Anybody can stand anything on its head, but it is only the real humourist who knows which thing can stand on its head without falling or looking foolish. 'T is the same in stage dialogue. Many a man of moderate wit can find a repartee when the joke is unconsciously led up to by another speaker. It is the preparation for the joke that is the dramatist's difficulty. To borrow a term from the Greek grammars, the protasis of the repartee is more troublesome than the apodosis. The puzzle is, therefore, find the protasis. When Barry Pain says that sometimes the glowing fire in the grate stares at you from behind its bars, as if it could read pictures in you, you cannot help laughing. If he had given you the protasis, "You gaze into the fire as if you could read pictures in it," even you could have invented the inversion. Topsy-turveydom is, I repeat, no laughing matter. It is an art—and must be studied. When Besant's School of Literature is founded, there will be

EXERCISES IN TOPSY-TURVEYDOM

1. Invert the following commonplaces humorously:

Honesty is the best policy. The cup that cheers but not inebriates. Fools rush in where angels fear to tread. Like a child in its mother's arms. (Not so easy, you see!)

2. Invert the following motifs humorously:

(a) A parted husband and wife reconciled by their little child. (Stock Poetry.)

(b) A patient marrying his nurse on recovery. (Stock Story.)

(c) A mother-in-law who comes to stay six months. (The Old Humour.)

Inversion may be applied, you see, both to ideas and to phrases. Let me contribute a specimen of either sort to the literary primer of the future:

THE ECONOMY OF SMOKING

I must really give up not smoking, at least till the American Copyright Act works smoothly, and I am in a position to afford luxuries. At present this habit of not smoking is a drain upon my resources which I can ill support. Whenever a man comes to my house, I have to give him cigars, or else gain the reputation of a churly and ill-mannered host. In the olden days, when I was economical and smoked all day long, I could go to that man's house and get those cigars back. Very often, too, I used to get the best of the bargain, and thus effect considerable economies in the purchase of good tobacco. Nowadays, not only have I got to give away cigars for nothing, but they must be good ones. Formerly if I gave my friends bad cigars, it was from a box I was obviously smoking myself, and therefore they had at least the consolation of knowing I was a companion in misfortune. But to give others "evils from which you are yourself exempt" (to quote Lucretius) would be a terrible blend of bad taste and inhospitality. Under such circumstances a man looks on a bad cigar as an insult, and the greater insult because it is a gratuitous one. But my losses from these sources are trivial compared with the item for theatres. In the pure, innocent days, when I could not bear to let my pipe out of my mouth even for a moment, I was unable to go to theatres; but now that I have taken to not smoking, I have fallen a victim to my other craving—the passion for the play. Three stalls a week tot up frightfully in a year. No, decidedly I must check this extravagant habit of not smoking before I am irretrievably ruined.

This is forced, but Truth often dwells the bottom of a paradox.

THE DANGER OF LEARNING TO SWIM

The danger of drowning arises mainly from being able to swim. The ability to swim is of little use as a safeguard against drowning, for it is only in a minority of cases that the accident thoughtfully allows you every facility for displaying your powers of natation; you are not conceded calm stream, a calm mind, and a bathing-costume; usually you are disorganised, ab initio, by the unexpectedness of the thing, you are weighed down by your clothes and your purse, you are entangled with sails, or clutched at by fellow-passengers, or sucked into vortices. In a big steamer accident, what chance is there for those who can swim? Only an occasional Hercules can keep afloat in a heavy sea, and he not for long. The most that swimming can do for you is to enable you to save yourself in circumstances where you would very probably be saved by somebody else. On the other hand, the ability to swim exposes you to many risks you w|uld never have run had you been helpless in the water. You swim in perilous places, you go out too far and cannot get back, you expose yourself to the possibilities of cramp, you try to save other people's lives and lose your own. There is also the temptation to go to the Bath Club in Piccadilly and die of a too luxurious lunch. On the whole, I believe as many swimmers are drowned as non-swimmers when a general accident occurs, while the swimmers invite special accidents of their own. Do you deduce from this that I advise you not to learn to swim? Quite the contrary: it is a delightful and invigorating exercise. Only you must not imagine you are thereby armed against fate. Swimming for amusement is as different from swimming for life as yachting on the Thames is from crossing the Atlantic.

For my example of phrase-inversion I cannot do better than reprint the open letter addressed by me—in the height of his success, and in parody of his manner—to the great phraseur and farunix of his little day; especially as some have thought to see in it proof that prophecy has not yet died out of Israel.

MY DEAR SIR: I have never for one moment doubted that you are a thinker, a poet, an art critic, a dramatist, a novelist, a wit, an Athenian, and whatever else you say you are. You are all these things—I confess it to your shame. I have always looked down upon you with admiration. As an epigrammatist I consider you only second to myself, though I admit that in the sentiment, "to be intelligible is to be found out," I had the disadvantage of prior publication. When you point out that Art is infinitely superior to Nature, I feel that you are cribbing from my unpublished poems, and I am quite at one with you in regarding the sunset as a plagiarism. Nature is undoubtedly a trespasser, and should be warned off without the option of a fine. I say these things to make it quite clear that I speak to you more in anger than in sorrow. You are much too important to be discussed seriously, and if I take the trouble to give you advice, it is only because I am so much younger than you. I am certain you are ruining yourself by cigarette cynicism; far better the rough, clay-pipe cynicism of a Swift. There is no smoke without fire, but it requires very little fire to keep a cigarette going. The art of advertising oneself by playful puffs is not superior to Nature. But you are not really playful and innocent; it would be ungracious to deny that you have all the corruption which the Stage has so truly connected with the cigarette. Still, isn't it about time you got divorced and settled down? At present there are only two good plays in the world—"The Second Book of Samuel" and "Lady Windermere's Fan"; surely you have power to add to their number. Try a quiet life of artistic production, and don't talk so much about Art. We are tired of missionaries, whether they wear the white tie of the Church or of Society, and it is a great pity we have not the simple remedy of the savages, who eat theirs. These few words of admonition would be incomplete if I did not impress upon you that policy is the only honesty. Art is short and life is long, and a stitch in time debars one from having a new coat. You can take a drink to the horse, but you can't make him well; and nothing succeeds like failure. Vice is the only perfect form of virtue, and virtue— Easy there! Steady! Avast! Belay! Which!

The Boeotians are dull folk, no doubt, but life would be dull without them. Imagine a wilderness of Wildes! It would be like a sky all rainbows. Then what beautiful whetstones the Boeotians are! Abuse them, by all means, so long as they will pay for it. But what a blessing that the minds capable of taking the artistic view of life are rare enough to keep the race sane! The coarser forms of egotism seem less baneful to the brain-tissue. You claim to be an Athenian, but the Athenians did not smoke cigarettes. It is true that tobacco had not been invented, but this is a sordid detail If Athens stands for anything in the history of culture, it is for sanity, balance, strength. Aristotle, at least as much an Athenian as any native of Ireland, meditated about aesthetics, but he meditated also about politics, logic, philosophy, political economy, ethics—everything. Socrates was a causeur, but he was also a martyr. No, after all the Beautiful is not so important as you imagine you are. No doubt for a few billion years painters and musicians and epigrammatists will remain the centre cf creation; but when the sun grows cold it is conceivable that invaluable canvases may be used up as fuel, and that humanity may sacrifice even your printed paradoxes to keep warmth a little longer in its decrepit bones. The fact is, you are too borné, too one-sided, to be accepted as as a "king of men." You take such broad views that you grow narrow. What you want is a little knowledge of life, and twelve months' hard labour.

But though topsy-turveydom may be attained with comparative ease, it performs a lofty philosophical function. Everything rusts by use. Our moral ideals grow mouldy if preached too much; our stories stale if told too often. Conventionality is but a living death. The other side of everything must be shown, the reverse of the medal, the silver side of the shield as well as the golden. Convex things are equally concave, and concave things convex. The world was made round so that one man's "up" should be another man's "down." The world is the Earthly Paradox, with four cardinal points of mutual contradiction, all equally N., S., E., and W. 'T is thus a symbol of all paradoxes, of all propositions in which mutually contradictory things are true. Nay, paradox is the only truth, for it cannot be denied; including, like the world, its own contradiction. Topsy-turveydom unfolds our musty ideas to the sun and spreads them out the other way. The man who reverses the Fifth Commandment and says that parents should honour their children is not a flippant jester, but a philosophic thinker. This is the true inwardness of the topsy-turvey humourist.

Topsy-turveydom has played a prodigious part in the progress of thought. The history of philosophy and science is merely a tale of development by topsy-turveydom, every new thinker simply contradicting his predecessor. Thales said water was the primitive principle of all things; so Anaximander said it was air, whereupon Anaximenes said it was matter. This made Pythagoras maintain it was not concrete matter but abstract number; whereupon Xenophanes would have it that it was not number but pure monistic being, and his disciple Zeno invented some delightful and immortal paradoxes to prove that time and motion and number and change have no existence, and only existence exists. Up comes Heraclitus, proving that existence doesn't exist, and there is nothing in the world but becoming: that so far from change not existing, nothing exists but change. It was now about time to return to earth, and so Empedocles and Democritus came along with their Atoms; thereby provoking Anaxagoras into bringing in Soul to explain things. Things were going on thus satisfactorily when the Sophists appeared on the scene to say that we didn't really know anything, because all our knowledge was subjective, so Socrates insisted that it didn't matter, because conduct was three-fourths of life. Plato retorted that it did matter, and he invented an archetypal universe of which this was a faint and distorted copy. Naturally Aristotle must contradict him by founding empirical science, which concerns itself only with this world. On his heels came the Stoics, who would have nothing to do with science except in so far as it made men virtuous, and who wanted to live soberly and severely. This provoked the neo-Platonists into craving for ecstatic union with the supernatural. The transition period from ancient philosophy to modern was one long fight between Nominalists and Realises, the one school teaching the exact opposite of the other.

But it is in the history of Modern Philosophy and Modern Science that one finds the strongest examples of this progress by paradox. The triumph of topsy-turveydom was when Galileo, the Oscar Wilde of Astronomy, declared that the earth went round the sun—a sheer piece of inversion. Darwin, the Barry Pain of Biology, asserted that man rose from the brutes, and that, instead of creatures being adapted to conditions, conditions adapted creatures. Berkeley, the Lewis Carroll of Metaphysics, demonstrated that our bodies are in our minds, and Kant, the W. S. Gilbert of Philosophy, showed that space and time live in us. In Literature it is the same story. To credit the scholars, Homer is no longer a man, nor the Bible a book. As for Zechariah, it was written before Genesis. This topsy-turveydom is a valuable organon of scientific discovery. Take any accepted proposition, invert it, and you get a New Truth. Any historian who wishes to make a name has but to state that Ahab was a saint and Elijah a Philistine—that Ananias was a realist and George Washington a liar—that Charles I. was a Republican hampered by his official position, and that the Armada defeated Drake—that Socrates died of drinking, and that hemlock was what he gave Xantippe. In fact, there is no domain of intellect in which a judicious cultivation of topsy-turveydom may not be recommended. Ask why R. A.'s are invariably colour-blind, and you become a great art critic, while a random regret that Mendelssohn had no ear for music will bring you to the very front in musical circles. For the tail shall always wag the dog in the end, and Aristides will never be able to remain in Athens if men will call him "the Just." Tout passe, tout casse, tout lasse. We are bored—and then comes the topsy-turveyist's opportunity. "To every action there is an equal and contrary reaction" is a sure law of motion, and in the seesaw of speculation the "down" of to-day is the "up" of to-morrow. Next century we shall be sick of science; and indeed the spooks are already returning for the funeral of this. I shall end with

AN APOLOGY TO A CELEBRATED CHARACTER

As a synonym for sin, Jezebel, I 'll no longer drag you in, Jezebel.
Now I know your glorious mission was to spread the truths Phoenician, Metaphoric life anew you shall begin, Jezebel; Metaphoric life anew you shall begin,

Cultured Baalite, loyal wife, Jezebel, Martyr in a noble strife, Jezebel; Protestant for light and sweetness 'gainst the narrow incompleteness Of Elijah and Elisha's view of life, Jezebel; Of Elijah and Elisha's view of life.

XVI

GHOST-STORIES

Why do ghosts walk at Christmas? What seduction hath Yule Tide for these phantastic fellows, that it lures them from their warm fireplaces? Is it that the cool snow is grateful after the fervours of their torrid zone, where even the pyrometer would fail to record the temperature? Is it that Dickens is responsible for the season, and that Marley's ghost has set the fashion among the younger spooks? The ghost of Hamlet's father was not so timed: he walked in all weathers. Perhaps it is the supernatural associations of Christmas that create the atmosphere in which ghosts live and move and have their being. Or perchance it is at the season of family reunion that the thoughts turn most naturally to vacant chairs and the presences that once filled them. Or is it that the ghosts walk for me alone, by reason that Christmas always brings me haunting thoughts of them? For my youth was nursed upon the "penny dreadfuls" of an age that knew not "Chums," nor the "Boys' Own Paper." They were not so very dreadful, those "penny dreadfuls," though dreadfully disrespectful to schoolmasters, who were wont to rend them in pieces in revenge. The heroes of the stories began to urge on their wild career in the school-room, where they executed practical jokes that would have gladdened the heart of Mr. Gilbert's merry Governor; the jokers were never found out unless they confessed to spare another boy's feelings, and then the schoolmaster was so touched that he spared theirs. After passing through five forms and upsetting them all, they arrived at the sixth form, which demanded a new volume to itself, called, let us say, "Tom Tiddler's School-days Continued," and mainly devoted to cigars and flirtation. "Tom Tiddler at College" followed—all "wines" and proctor-baiting, with Tom Tiddler as stroke in the victorious 'Varsity eight. "Tom Tiddler Abroad" was the next title, for the chronicle of a popular hero would run on for years and years; and in this section red Indians and wild beasts were rampant. 'T were long to trace the fortunes of Tom Tiddler in all their thrilling involutions; but when he had painted the globe red he married and settled down. And then began "Young Tom Tiddler's School-days," "Young Tom Tiddler's Schooldays Continued," "Young Tom Tiddler Abroad," and all the weekly round of breathlessness; and never was proverb truer than that the young cock cackles as the old cock crows. By the time interest palled in the son a new generation of readers had arisen, and the unblushing paper commenced to run "Tom Tiddler's School-days" again. So went the whirligig. But at Christmas, when the blue-nosed waifs carol in the cold and boys have extra pennies, Tom Tiddler himself slunk into the background, lost in the ample folds of a "Double Number," the same blazoned impudently, as though it did not demand double money. But the extra pennyworth was all ghosts: ghosts, ghosts, ghosts; full measure, pressed down and running over; not your Ibsenian shadows of heredity, but real live ghosts, handsomely appointed, with chains and groans and wavy wardrobes. They lived in moated granges and ivy-wreathed castles, and paced snowy terraces or dark, desolate corridors. There was no talk then of psychic manifestations, or auras, or telepathy, or spiritual aether. Ghosts were solid realities in those days of the double number.

"To every man upon this earth death cometh soon or late," as Macaulay sings, and it is no less impossible to escape spirit-rapping and all the fascinating menu of the Psychical Society. The epidemic, which is contagious to the last degree, seizes its victims when they are off guard, under pretense of amusing an idle hour, and ends by robbing them of sleep and health; some it drives into lunatic asylums and some into newspaper correspondence. That thought-reading is not necessarily delusion or collusion is now generally recognised; a protégée of Mr. F. W. Myers convinced me of the possibility of simple feats, though not of her explanation of them. She credited them to spirits, and wicked spirits to boot. In vain, I pointed out that spirits who occupied themselves so docilely about matters so trivial must be harmless creatures with no more guile than the village idiot: she would concede no grain of goodness in their composition. Table-turning I had never seen. Ghosts I had never met, though I had met plenty of persons who had their acquaintance. Like Lady Mary Wortley Montagu—or is it Madame de Stäel?—I did not believe in them, but I was afraid of them. Premonitions I had often had, but they had scarcely ever come true. But now I am prepared to believe anything and everything, and to come up to the Penitent Form—if there be one—of the Psychical Society and to declare myself saved. I am already preparing a waxen image of a notorious critic, to stick pins thereinto. Not that I did not always believe the Spook Society was doing necessary work in supplementing the crude treatises of our psychologists, who are the most fatuous and self-complacent scientists going.

My conversion to a deeper interest in the obscurer psychic phenomena befell through encountering a theatrical touring company in a dull provincial town. The barber told me about it—a dapper young Englishman of twenty-five, with an unimpeachable necktie.

BARBER
"They're playing 'Macbeth' to-night, sir."

AUTHOR (growling)
"Indeed?"

B

"Yes, sir; I'm told it's pretty thick."

A

"What's pretty thick?"

B

"'Macbeth.'"

A

"What do you mean by 'thick'?"

B

"Full of gore, sir. I don't like those sort o' pieces. I like opera—'Utopia' and that sort o' thing. You can see plenty o' thick things in real life. I don't want to go to the theatre to get the creeps and horrors. But I've seen 'Othello' and 'Virginius.'"

A

"Ha! Do you know who wrote 'Othello'?"

B

"No, that I don't."

A

"Do you know who wrote 'Macbeth'?"

B

"Now you ask me something!"

A (speculating sadly on the vanity of fame and the absurdity of being a national bard, but determined to vindicate a brother author)
"'Othello' and 'Macbeth' were written by Shakespeare."

B (unmoved)
"Ah! that's the man that wrote 'Taming of the Shrew,' isn't it?"

A (astonished)
"Yes."

So the Author went to see the thick play, and found he knew Lady Macbeth, nay, had—by an odd episode—first seen her in dressing-gown and curl-papers; so, presuming upon this intimate acquaintanceship, he got himself bidden to the Banquet—in less Shakespearian language, he went to supper. The Banquet was uninterrupted by Banquos or other bogies. Lady Macbeth—in a Parisian art-gown—sipped milk after her bloody exertions, and listened graciously, her fair young head haloed in smoke, to her guest's comparison of herself with Mrs. Siddons. But Lady Macbeth's Chaperon was a Medium, self-made, and when the compliments and the supper had been cleared away, the Medium kindly proposed to exhibit her newly-discovered prowess with the Planchette. The Planchette, as everybody knows, and as I didn't know myself till I saw it, is a wooden heart that runs on two hind wheels, and has a pencil stuck through the centre of its apex. The Medium gracefully places her hand upon the heart, which after an interval of Quaker-like meditation begins to write, as abruptly as a Quaker is moved by the Spirit, and as abruptly finishes.

AUTHOR
"What do I want to do early to-morrow morning?"

What was in his mind was: "Send a wire to Manchester." The Planchette almost instantly scribbled: "Send a telegram to your brother." Now, his brother was connected with the matter; and although at the time he considered the Planchette half wrong, yet in the morning, after reconsidering the question, the Author actually did send the wire to his brother instead. Sundry other things did the Planchette write, mostly wise, but sometimes foolish. It did not hesitate, for example, over the publisher of a certain anonymous book, but failed to give the title, though it wrote glibly, "Children of Night." These results were sufficiently startling to invite further investigation, so the trio next proceeded to "call spirits from the vasty deep" by making a circle of their thirty fingers upon a wooden table. Very soon the table gave signs of upheaval, while some cobbling sprite fell to tapping merrily at his trade within its ligneous recesses. Lady Macbeth said that these taps denoted its readiness to hold communion with the grosser earth, and constituted its sole vocabulary. As in the game of Animal, Vegetable, and Mineral, its information was to be extracted by a series of queries admitting of "yes" or "no" in answer. One tap denoted "no," three "yes," and two "doubtful." It could also give numerical replies. The table or the sprite, having indicated its acquiescence in this code, proceeded to give a most satisfactory account of itself. It told the Author his age, the time of day, the date of the month, carefully allowing for its being past midnight (which none of the human trio had thought of); it was excellently posted on his private concerns, knowing the date of his projected visit to America, and the name of his past work and his future wife. Its orthography was impeccable, though its method was somewhat todious, for the Author had to run through the alphabet to provoke the sprite into tapping at any particular letter. But one soon grew reconciled to its cumbrous methods, as though holding converse with a foreigner; and its remarks made up in emphasis what they lacked in brevity, and were given with exemplary promptitude. Interrogated as to its own personality, it declared it was an unborn spirit, destined to be born in ten years. "Do you know what makes you be born?" inquired the Author. "Yes," it replied. "Will you tell us?" "Yes." "Tell us, then." "F-O-R-C-E." "Is it God's force?" "No." "Is He not omnipotent, then?" "No." "What is the true religion?" "Buddhism." "Do you mean Madame Blavatsky was right?" "Yes." "Is there a heaven?" "Yes." "A Hell?" "No." To hear a small still voice rapping, rapping in the silence of the small hours, rapping out the secrets of the universe, was weird enough. It was as though Milton's words were indeed inspired, and—

Millions of spiritual creatures walk the earth
Unseen.

"What!" thought the Author, "shall the Great Secret which has puzzled so many heads—heads in caps and heads in turbans, heads in bonnets and heads in berettas, as Heine hath it—shall the explanation of the Universe, which baffled Aristotle, and puzzled Hegel, and still more his readers, be the property of this wretched little unborn babe, this infant rapping in the night, and with no language but a rap? Was, then, Wordsworth right, and is our birth 'but a sleep and a forgetting'?" And, mingled with these questionings, a sort of compassion for the poor orphan spirit, inarticulate and misunderstood, beating humbly at the gates of speech. Natheless was the Author quite incredulous, and even while he was listening reverently to these voices from Steadland, his cold cynic brain was revolving a scientific theory to account for the striking manifestations.

In the course of two or three séances, with lights turned low, but honesty burning high—for Lady Macbeth was guileless, and her Chaperon above suspicion—various other "spirits" hastened to be interviewed. There was "Ma," who afterwards turned out to be the Chaperon's "Pa," whose name—a queer French name—it gave in full. The Chaperon's "Pa," who was dead, announced he was no longer a widower, for his relief had just rejoined him on Wednesday—the 10th. This news of her mother's death was unknown to the Chaperon. In truth, "Pa" is still a widower.

Another "spirit"—a woman (who refused to give her age)—predicted that the amount of money taken at the theatre the next night would be £44. The actual returns on the morrow were £44 0s. 6d. But when, elated by its success, it prophesied £43, the returns were only £34. But this same creature, that gave only an inverted truth—perhaps it was momentarily controlled by the spirit of Oscar Wilde—displayed remarkable knowledge in other directions. Asked if it knew what piece had been played the week before in the theatre—a question that none of the three could have answered—it replied, "'The Road to —'" "Do you mean 'The Road to Ruin'?" the Author interrupted eagerly, tired of its tedious letter-by-letter methods. "No," it responded vehemently; and finished, "'F-o-r-t-u-n-e.'" Lady Macbeth consulted the "Era," and sure enough "The Road to Fortune" had preceded her own company. "Can you tell us the piece to follow?" the author asked; and the "spirit" responded readily "'The Pro—'" "Do you mean 'The Professor's Love Story'?" the Author again interrupted. "No; 'The Prodigal,'" answered the table. "Ah! 'The Prodigal,'" echoed the Author, confounding it temporarily with "The Profligate"; but the spirit dissented, and added, "'Daughter.'" There being no means of verifying this for the moment, the Author proceeded to inquire for the piece to follow that, and was unhesitatingly informed that it was "The Bauble Shop." "Where is 'The Bauble Shop' now?" he inquired. The spirit amiably rapped out "Eastbourne." This was correct according to the "Era." Consulting the hoardings after leaving the house, the Author discovered that the other replies were quite exact, save for the fact that "The Bauble Shop" was to come first and "The Prodigal Daughter" second. Here was the paradoxical humour of this Oscar Wilde-ish "spirit" again.

Endless was the information vouchsafed by these disembodied intelligences, in any language one pleased; and, although they at times displayed remarkable obstinacy, refusing to answer, or breaking off abruptly in the middle of a most interesting communication, as though they had been betrayed into indiscretion: yet, to speak generally, there was scarcely any topic on which they were not ready to discourse—past, present, or to come—and their remarks, whether accurate or not, were invariably logical, bearing an intelligible relation to the question. Even sporting tips were obtainable without a fee, and Avington was given as the winner of the Liverpool Cup, though the Author had never heard of him, and the other two were not aware he was booked for the race, still less that he was the favourite. In the sequel he only came second. Real tips did the "spirits" give, tipping the table vehemently. They were also very obedient to commands, moving or lifting the table in whatsoever direction the Author ordered, much as though they were men from Maple's; and when he willed them to raise it, the united forces of Lady Macbeth and Lady Macbeth's Chaperon could not easily depress its spirits. Nor did they contradict one another. There was a cheerful unanimity about the Author's dying at fifty-seven. But this did not perturb the Author, whose questions were all cunningly contrived to test his theory of the "spiritual world." For instance, he set them naming cards, placed on the table with faces downwards and unknown to anybody; arguing that with their bloated omniscience they could scarcely fail to name a card shoved under their very noses. Nor did they—altogether. Most began well, but were spoiled by success. However, here is the record performance—eight consecutive attempts of the table to give the "correct card" under the imposition of the hands of the Chaperon and the Author only, neither knowing the card till it was turned up to verify the table's assertion:

TABLE'S CARD.   ACTUAL CARD.

1. Jack of Diamonds . . . Queen of Spades.

2. Jack of Diamonds . . . Jack of Diamonds.

3. Three of Clubs . . . Jack of Spades.

4. Jack of Diamonds . . . Jack of Diamonds.

5. Seven of Clubs . . . Five of Diamonds.

6. Three of Spades . . . Three of Spades.

7. Ten of Hearts . . . Ten of Hearts.

8. Nine of Clubs . . . Nine of Clubs.

Here are five bull's-eyes out of eight shots! The name of the performer deserves record. It was the spirit of a German woman, named Gretehen, who died three years ago, but refused to say at what age. She was wrong sometimes, but then it may have been her feminine instinct for fibbing. "The spirits play tricks," say the spiritualists. "Sometimes they are wicked spirits, who tell lies." The Planchette also wrote out the names of unseen cards placed upon it face downwards. The artistic spirit of the Author now bids him pause: the narrative has now reached a point of interest at which recollections of "Tom Tiddler's Schooldays" urge him to pen the breathless motto: "To be continued in our next."

XVII

A THEORY OF TABLE-TURNING

The yearning of humanity for the supernatural, even for the pseudo-supernatural, is as pathetic as it is profound. Wherefore I regret that I can make no concessions to it. The following theory of table-turning came to me as I experimented, from my general knowledge of psychology. I have not compared it with the theories of the Psychical Society, which I have never read, preferring to jot down the impressions of an independent observer, which, if they should at all coincide with the explanations of the spook-hunters, will irrefutably demonstrate that their Society was founded in vain. If, moreover, as Mr. Andrew Lang has since pointed out, it coincides largely with the theory of Dr. Carpenter, so much the better.

What are the facts? If two or more people (according to the size of the table) place their hands in circular contact around a table, and possess their souls in patience for a delightfully uncertain period, sundry strange manifestations will occur. Even after the first few moments the more imaginative will feel the table throbbing, unsuspicious of the fact that it is the blood at their finger-tips. Presently, too, an uncanny wave of cold air will pass underneath the arch of their palms. This is, according to the professional witches of Endor, the frigid flitting of the spirits, but the most superficial meteorologist will expound it you learnedly. Your hand, passive and in a fixed position, heats the air under it, which, becoming lighter, is constantly displaced by the colder circumambient air. Finally, when everybody is wrought up to an exalted expectation of the supernatural, the table begins to oscillate, to move slowly to and fro, to waltz, and even to raise itself partially or wholly off the ground. Sometimes it taps instead of moving. Nor are these motions and these taps merely the intoxicated irregularities of an exuberant energy. They are coherent responses (according to a code agreed upon with the "spirit" in possession) to questions asked by one of the sitters. They are the expression of infinite and ungrudging information on almost every subject. Through this wooden language, through this music of the tables and this dancing movement of their legs, tabular information respecting your past or other people's past and future lives, together with full details of the doings of the departed in those other spheres of heaven or hell which they adorn or illumine respectively, may be obtained at the lowest rates, and with only that reasonable delay which results from the exigencies of a letter-code. For the "spirits" of the table, be it understood, are unable to communicate with earth except by taps and movements for "yes" or "no," or by rapping out numbers; so that they have to signify their meaning, snailwise, letter by letter. The "spirit" of the Planchette will indeed write you out sentences; but to that, like the actor in melodrama, I will return anon. In the stock séances, I know, spirits materialise themselves and glide white-sheeted through darkened rooms. But as my own séances and "spirits" were personally conducted by myself, the optical illusions of Messrs. Maskelyne & Cook, the Pepper's Ghost of the dear old Polytechnic, had no opportunity of putting in an appearance. My spooks did nothing but answer questions, so that the very suggestion that they were spirits came entirely from me. In fact, they do but dance to the "medium's" piping; and should he suggest that they are methylated, the chances are that not a few would cheerfully acquiesce in this description of themselves. In short, it is only the prepossession, the pathetic prejudice, in favour of visitors from other worlds that leads at all to the thought of "spirits," drawing such a red herring across the track that the average observer, who is nothing if not unobservant, has all his partisan faculties of mis-observation brought into full play on behalf of the spirit-world. Doubtless the actual presence of "spirits" is the cheapest way of accounting for the phenomena. But one might as well call in "spirits" to explain the dancing of a kettle-lid. Not till every natural hypothesis has been exhausted is the scientific observer entitled to call in the supernatural. And in reality all that has to be explained is the mechanical movements of tables under certain specified conditions, the said movements having an apparent relation to will and intelligence.

First of all, what moves the table?

Well, the slightest exercise of the finger or wrist muscles is sufficient to move the small, light round table which is usually the subject of experiment; and when once the slightest movement is established—by the involuntary contraction of a single muscle—all the other persons' muscles, in accommodating themselves to the movement of the table, cannot help helping it, either by pulling or pushing in the direction in which it is going. It is, in fact, almost impossible to follow the movement of a moving table and yet keep your superimposed hands perfectly passive; and with ninety-nine persons out of a hundred the startled interest in the movement even begets an unconscious desire to help it, which at times almost rises to a curious semi-conscious self-deception, a voluntary exaggeration of the marvellous. Yet nothing makes the ordinary sitter angrier than to be told he has helped to move the table. It is as though he were accused of cheating at whist, or worse, of playing a foolish card. Take half a dozen persons at random, and there are sure to be one or two so impressionable and emotional that they cannot help contributing the slight initial impulse which gathers force as it goes. These nervous subjects cannot sit a quarter of an hour perfectly still without a twitching of the muscles, while the tense state of expectation which subtly transforms itself into a wish to see the table move and not have the experiment in vain, finally compels them, despite themselves, to start the "manifestations." Indeed, to think of a thing is half to do it. Every idea has a tendency to project itself in action. If you think strongly, for instance, of lifting your hand, it is difficult not to do it, for the idea of motion is motion in embryo. The wish is father to the thought, and the thought to the deed. The wish to see the table move is the grandfather of its motion. Even with the most sceptical, when the table is requested to go in a particular direction the muscles involuntarily tend thither. All the deepest analyses of scientific psychology are involved in this wretched little episode of table-turning, and it is not marvellous that the ordinary observer should perceive only the marvellous.

So much for the movements. But how about the raps? How about those mysterious tappings which come from the very heart of the table, as eloquent of the preternatural as those immortal taps heard by Poe ere the raven stepped into his chamber? I should be more impressed by these taps if I were not capable of manufacturing them myself ad lib. without detection, by secretly manipulating the ball of my thumb. One is therefore justified in assuming that, where these raps are not produced by conscious fraud, they are the involuntary result of the same motions that produced them voluntarily. Even wood has a certain elasticity, and an imperceptible increase followed by an imperceptible relaxation of pressure on the surface of the table will alter the tension of the wood, the molecules of which in springing back to their prior position will emit a creak or a tap, just as a piece of extended elastic will when let go again. Both the raps and the movements, then, are in essence phenomena of the same order: simple results of muscular pressure, conscious, sub-conscious, or unconscious.

It now only remains to explain the answers themselves, to account not only for their almost invariably logical form, but also for their occasionally astonishing content. For the table is not infrequently wiser than anybody in the room; also it knows the past and is ready to predict the future.

The whole thing is really an excellent object-lesson in Psychology. For the solution is obvious. The table being unconscious, you answer yourself—you not only produce the raps and movements, but you regulate them.

The connection between mind and body is, it seems to me, admirably illustrated by table-turning. According to the latest philosophic view, the connection itself defies human comprehension. It is simply a case of non possumus intelligere. But the connection itself may be expressed thus: No idea or feeling without physical disturbance, no physical disturbance without feeling or idea. Mind and body are as related as the tune to the violin-string. Every state of mind tends to set up nervous vibration, and every nervous vibration tends to set up a state of mind. In either case the tendency may be, and usually is, counteracted. The average member of a spiritualistic circle cannot prevent the thought in his brain taking on bodily expression to the extent of a muscular contraction stimulating the very sensitive tips of the fingers. You cannot think of a joke or see the humour of anything without wanting to smile, though you may suppress your smile in obedience to other considerations. Nor can you put your features into smiling position, without experiencing a latent sense of amusement, though you would not know what you were smiling at. But if six cool scientific intellects, acquainted with the tricks of their own organisms and determined to dissever thought from motion, were to sit round a table, they might sit till doomsday without the "spirit" turning up. This is what the spiritualists mean by unsympathetic persons, persons obnoxious to the spirits, persons with antipathetic auras, and all the rest of the jargon. But six intellects taken at random, being anything but cool and scientific, are not able to prevent their ideas passing over into action in the shape of muscular twitches; though if even the unscientific were to look up at the ceiling and forget all about the table, the table would probably forget to move. Now the majority of the replies of the table deal with matters actively present to the consciousness of at least one of the six owners of the superimposed hands. When the table raps out something known only to this one person, and the startled person admits that the table is right, an uncanny feeling is produced; the table seems at least to be a thought-reader, and on this wave of astonishment the hypothesis of "spirits" rides up triumphantly. When the topic is one of which nobody knows anything—e.g., whether the supposed spirit is a man or woman—chance, or a vague idea floating up in the mind of one of the party, determines the reply.

But what of those replies in which some striking truth is told of which none of the party was conscious, as for instance in the examples I gave in my last, when the table informed us that Mr. Jones's "Bauble Shop" was then playing at Eastbourne, or that "The Road to Fortune" had been playing in the town in which we were the week before we arrived? To clear up this most remarkable aspect of the whole matter we must go still deeper into Psychology.

What we are pleased to call our Mind is made up of two parts—our Consciousness and—what I shall call loosely yet sufficingly and without prejudice to Metaphysics—our Sub-Consciousness. The latter is immeasurably the vaster portion. It is a tossing ocean of thoughts which feeds the narrow little fountain of Consciousness. It holds all our memories. We cannot be conscious of all ourselves and all our past at once—that way madness lies, or divinity. We may know ten languages, but we can only think in the mould of one at a time. Our thoughts and memories can only come up into clear Consciousness by ones or twos—to be dealt with and then dismissed. They spirit from the great deep of Sub-Consciousness into the thin fountain-stream of Consciousness, and fall back again into the great deep. And this great deep is never still, though we know nothing of its churning save by its tossing up through the fountain some new mental combination of which it had received only the elements—as when the mathematician has the solution of a problem flashed upon him at the moment of waking, or as the author has the development of his plot thrust upon him when he is playing billiards, or as the wit finds repartees invented for him by his brilliant but unknown collaborator. This is what the crowd calls "inspiration," the late Mr. Stevenson "Brownies," and the scientist "unconscious cerebration." A man of talent has a good Working Consciousness, a man of genius a good Working Sub-Consciousness. Hence the frequent mental instability of genius. The Infant Prodigy's feats are done by his Sub-Consciousness. Instinct is Racial Genius, Genius is Individual Instinct. The highest Genius is sane. A Shakespeare or a Goethe has both a good Working Consciousness and a good Working Sub-Consciousness, with the former so self-balanced that it regulates the products of the latter. The cultivation of the Working Consciousness may either improve or impair the products of its bigger brother. Education, the cultivation of the critical faculty, would be fatal to some writers, actors, painters, and musicians; it would but spoil the Working Sub-Consciousness. Others—more sanely balanced—would gain in art more than they lost in nature.

Now, what are the elements with which our Sub-Consciousness works?—what does this ocean contain? It would be easier to discover what it does not contain. Wrecks and argosies and dead faces, mermaidens and subterranean palaces, and the traces of vanished generations; these are but a millionth part of its treasures: the Sub-Consciousness were perhaps better likened to the property-room and scene-dock of the Great Cosmic Theatre, holding infinite wardrobes and scenes ready-painted, parks and seas and libraries, and ruined cottages and whitewashed attics, to say naught of an army of supers ready to put on all the faces we have ever seen. In our Sub-Consciousness, moreover, are stored up all the voices and sounds and scents we have ever perceived, and to all these reminiscences of our own sensations are perhaps added the shadows of our ancestors' sensations—episodes that perchance we re-experience only in dreamland—so that part of the vivid vision of genius, of the poet's eye bodying forth the shapes of things unknown, may be inherited Memory. And thus Imagination, when it is not a mere fresh combination of elements experienced, may be only a peculiar variety of atavism.

From this boundless reservoir, then, which holds our heredity and our experience, go forth the battalions of dreams—the infinitely possible permutations and combinations of its elements, wrought by the Working Sub-Consciousness when the poor Working Consciousness cannot get sound asleep, but must watch perforce with half an eye the procession of thoughts and images over which it has lost control. For it is the duty of Consciousness to control the stream sent up by Sub-Consciousness. When it is awake but unable to do this, we have Insanity; when asleep, Dreams. In Somnambulism the Working Sub-Consciousness is seen in an accentuated phase. It does all the work of its little brother, even to exercising its owner's muscles. To be "possessed" by a popular song is a species of insanity— Consciousness ridden by a singing Sub-Consciousness.

Between our Consciousness and our Sub-Consciousness there is more or less easy communication. It is not perfect. You cannot draw up what you will from the ocean: you cannot always directly remember a name or a date that you know—you can only set an indirect train of thought at work. Per contra, it is not easy to transfer certain conscious states to the storehouse of Sub-Consciousness—to learn a page of prose, or deposit the memory of a piece of music, which you are forced to play slowly and thoughtfully before the digital dexterity is added to the treasures of your Sub-Consciousness. Under exceptional conditions, exceptional flotsam and jetsam is tossed up into Consciousness, as in the case of that servant girl who spoke Latin, Greek, and Hebrew in her delirium, having unconsciously absorbed the same from overhearing the studies of her learned master many years before.

Now, just as a conscious thought has an accompaniment of physical motion, so has a sub-conscious thought. Thus, then, a thought which does not pass through the thin fountain-stream of Consciousness may yet produce the same muscular twitches as if it were clearly present to the presiding Ego. In the case of the "Road to Fortune," the name must have really sunk into my brain, although I was unaware of it, and probably could not have consciously recalled it to save my life. The stage-manager subsequently reminded me that he had in my presence regretted that the "Road to Fortune" had done such good business, since there would probably be a reaction. I have only a recollection of his telling me that the success of the preceding piece would hurt his—my Consciousness had grasped at the intellectual side of his remark, my Sub-Consciousness had absorbed the irrelevant fact of the name of the piece. In examining the "Era," to verify this item, Lady Macbeth's eye must have unconsciously noted that "The Bauble Shop" was at Eastbourne; but the information was not registered in her Consciousness, for there is a struggle of thoughts to catch the thinker's I—that is to say the Central Consciousness—and only the fittest can survive. We are indeed wiser than we know. Our Sub-Consciousness knows all we know, and all we have forgotten, and all that our mental sponge sucked in without spirting it through Consciousness. In fact, attention or inattention often determines whether a thought or a feeling shall come up into clear Consciousness or not. You can feel a pain in your big toe if you want to. Conversely, in the excitement of battle soldiers do not always feel their wounds.

When the table prophesies or delivers "a message from the other world," the result is a compound of fluke with expectation or with apprehension. Fears or hopes dimly in the mind get accentuated, or transmuted, or distorted as in dreams; and when the "spirits" are proved wrong, as in the matter of the Chaperon's mother, the spiritualists tell you that you have got hold of a "lying spirit." Verily a cheap explanation! "They play tricks sometimes," say their apologists. The true explanation is that your Sub-Consciousness was ignorant of the reply your Consciousness asked for. Endless as its contents seem, there are limits; and when it does not know, your Sub-Consciousness will rarely confess it. It makes a brazen guess, keeping the logical form of the answer, because your Sub-Consciousness knows that, but blundering deplorably in the matter. Sometimes it will not speak at all, but when it does it is cocksure to the last degree. Its humour is the humour of the stock joke, the Old Humour—as when it will not tell a woman's age. Its sulkiness and eccentricity and occasional indecency are just what one would expect from a Sub-Consciousness, whose thoughts have no central I to keep them in order. (Compare Goethe's explanation of the obscenities of Ophelia.) Sometimes, too, there are Obstructive Associations, which account for its inability to make up its want of mind; and as there are usually several persons at table, the result is complicated by their separate Sub-Consciousnesses. In brief, table-turning is a method of interrogating your Sub-Consciousness. It is, so to speak, objective introspection. The table enables you to peep at your Sub-Consciousness, to know your larger self. It is an external medium on which you may see registered visibly and audibly (through the vibrations you sub-consciously communicate to it) that Sub-Consciousness which ex hypothesi you cannot peep at directly. The moving table may be considered the objectification of Sub-Consciousness, or a mirror in which Sub-Consciousness is reflected to the gaze of Consciousness (to the great benefit of the science of Psychology, which may be revolutionised by table-turning). By humouring your Sub-Consciousness, by addressing it as though it were a separate identity utterly unconnected with you, by asking a "spirit" to answer you, you help to break your Mind in two, to detach the Sub-Consciousness from the Consciousness, and so to get results which astonish yourself. So divided is mind against itself that (as when I thought "The Pro—" was to be "The Professor's Love Story") even a conscious expectation of something different does not turn the Sub-Consciousness from its first dogged determination; or it may be that somebody else's Sub-Consciousness was in the ascendant. The "mediums" who excuse the "spirits" on the ground of their mendacity are not necessarily frauds: they are themselves deceived; they do not know that if the "spirits" lie, it is because a true reply was not latent in any one of the human Consciousnesses or Sub-Consciousnesses present. But the conclusion of the whole matter seems to be this: there is a germ of scientific truth which the professional spiritualists doctor and wrap round with complex trickery in order to extract backsheesh from poor old women of both sexes anxious for information about deceased relatives. Circles are formed with pretentious mysticism, and no self-respecting "spirit" will appear without being received in state with extinguished lights and creepy accompaniments. The unconscious revelations made by the sitters are the sole genuine foundation of the spiritualists' influence. Consciousness holds converse with deceased relatives, and Sub-Consciousness, which knows all about them, answers for them. "I can call spirits from the vasty deep" myself, and they will come when I call them, but the "vasty deep" is the deep of my own Sub-Consciousness. We seem to hear voices from spirit-land; but as when we hold a sea-shell to our ear and seem to hear the ocean it is only the blood in our own veins, so—to continue Eugene Lee-Hamilton's fine sonnet—

Lo! in my heart I hear, as in a shell,
The murmur of a world beyond the grave,
Distinct, distinct, though faint and far it be.
Thou fool! this echo is a cheat as well—
The hum of earthly instincts—and we crave
A world unreal as the shell-heard sea.

Tables might be "turned" to various purposes. Criminals might be compelled to yield up their secrets to them in uncontrollable muscular vibrations, their Sub-Consciousness being tapped. For students under examination table-turning would be very useful for recalling forgotten knowledge. The Planchette would be the most convenient form. For obviously the modus operandi of the Planchette is exactly the same as the table's. The medium's Sub-Consciousness arrives at an answer by guesswork, reminiscence, etc., and produces the muscular movements of writing without first passing the message through the writer's Consciousness. Mr. Stead has, I believe, a familiar spirit called Julia. This is merely a projection of his own Sub-Consciousness, the Planchette being the artificial instrument for enabling him to give pseudo-objectivity to his thought, to detach a shred of his mind. Even so, many a dramatist marshals toy figures on a mimic stage. The external image is a help to weak imaginations. The process of novel-writing involves breaking up your mind into bits—one for each character. And when the characters are said to take the reins into their own hands, it means that the bits are developing an independent existence. If Mr. Stead is not careful, Julia will get the upper hand of him, his Sub-Consciousness will dominate his Consciousness, and then he will be mad. This detachment of bits of mind is dangerous; the monster may overpower Frankenstein. Julia is literally a child of Mr. Stead's brain, a psychical daughter embodied in a Planchette. Double Consciousness, Double Identity, are well-known forms of insanity. In a mild degree they consist with sanity. Landseer could paint different heads simultaneously with both hands.

Hypnotism, on this theory, would be the lulling of the patient's Consciousness, the closing of his central I, and the setting of his Sub-Consciousness to work in accordance with suggestions. Thought-transference seems a superfluous hypothesis here. Death is the cessation of both Consciousness and Sub-Consciousness; and when a drowned man is resuscitated his Sub-Consciousness can never have ceased. Do you fail to understand Sub-Consciousness? So do I—as much as that our digestion operates and our blood circulates without asking our permission. It is not unreasonable to suppose that Sub-Consciousness is simply the psychical side of the molecular changes that are going on in our nervous system. There is more than "metaphysical conceit" in that elegy of Donne's:

Her pure and eloquent blood
Spoke in her cheeks, and so distinctly wrought
That one might almost say her body thought.

Sub-Consciousness is a greater marvel in itself than any that it explains, and beats the spooks hollower than they are. Just consider the phenomena of dreams, what things we do, what sights we see. It is only the commonness of dreams that blinds us to the fact that they are more marvellous than ghost-stories. Mr. Lang thinks the theory of the sub-conscious self that uses our muscles for its own ends is "the most startling thing ever offered to the public; and that it should be regarded as true by a sceptic is staggering to our judicial faculties." But why? Our noble selves—are they not already exposed to the indignity of dreams? What matters another insult? We need not be greatly put out if Sub-Consciousness is busy in the day-time too. And what about Somnambulism? What about musical or literary creation? Are not our ideas made for us in the kitchen of our Sub-Consciousness? Our Consciousness is only a small part of ourselves. What produced De Quincey's opium dreams was certainly not Consciousness. I can see visions, myself, without opium. In certain excited states of the brain I can travel in my chair, or bed, perfectly awake, through an endless and variegated series of scenes—domestic interiors with people talking or eating or playing cards, battle-fields with glittering phalanxes, beautiful tossing seas, gorgeous forests, melancholy hospitals, busy newspaper offices, etc., etc. These are almost entirely detached from my will, and the chief interest of the spectacle is the unexpectedness of its episodes. The scenes and the people have all the concreteness and detail of actuality, although I never forget that I am observing my own hallucinations. Just fancy what ghosts I could see in the dark if I lost my central control and let my Sub-Consciousness get the upper hand! Sociologists say, the seeing of dead people in dreams gave rise to the idea of ghosts. I would suggest that the same process as that of dreaming gives rise to the ghosts themselves. Great is the Sub-Consciousness! Who shall say what it does not contain, either in esse or in posse! Till we have exhausted the Sub-Consciousness let us not talk of spooks.

Two things alone remain to be considered. One is how the Planchette or the table is able to read cards placed face downwards upon it; the second is, is telepathy or thought-transference a possibility? As to the first point I have never yet been able to satisfy myself whether the results are more than Chance would account for; for Chance has strange vagaries—themselves part of the doctrine of Chances—and in order to decide, one would have to make a far more extended induction than I have had time for. But if the mathematical probabilities are really exceeded, one would be driven to the suspicion that there resides in the Sub-Consciousness a sense of which we are unaware, perhaps an extra way of perceiving by the tips of the fingers, which may be either a new embryonic sense, not yet developed by the struggle for existence, or the rudimentary survival of an old sense eliminated in the struggle, perhaps a relic from those primeval homogeneous organisms in which every part of the body did every kind of work. After all, the senses are all developments of the sense of touch. This suspicion is strengthened by the fact that the correct card is often given at the first trial, and not after, as if this unused sense were soon exhausted. By the way, though the "spirits" mostly failed to tell a card placed face down, and unknown to any one in the room, they were invariably successful when it was placed face up: a sufficient proof—is it not?—that there could be nothing in the replies which was not already in some one's mind.

With regard to the question of telepathy, though I am tempted to believe in it, I have not yet met with any convincing instance of it. Thought-reading à la Stuart Cumberland almost any one could do who practised it. The thought-reader merely takes the place of the table as a receiver of muscular vibrations. What tempts me to believe in the transfer of thought without physical connection is that, given telepathy, all the mysterious phenomena that have persisted in popular belief through the centuries could be swept away at one fell swoop. By telepathy, working mainly through the Sub-Consciousness, I will explain you Clairvoyance (that is, not the mere seeing of pictures, which is a phenomenon akin to dreaming, but the vision of other people's Sub-Consciousnesses), ghosts, witchcraft, possession, wraiths, Mahatmas, astral bodies, etc., etc. But it is rather absurd to call in a new mystery to explain what may not even be facts. And so, till I am convinced either of ghosts or of telepathy, I must accord an impartial incredulousness to both. Credat Christianus, F. W. Myers or W. T. Stead! For I gather that the Psychical Society assert that they must exist. But as yet—je n'en vois pas la nécessité. If it is indeed possible to telegraph without fees and to put a psychical girdle round the earth in twenty seconds, by all means let the noses of those extortionate cable companies be put out of joint. To me it is just as wonderful that mind can communicate with mind by letter or even by speech. One more puzzle adds no light to our darkness. And as for ghosts, I have more than a lurking sympathy with the farrier in "Silas Marner."

"'If ghos'es want me to believe in 'em, let 'em leave off skulking i' the dark and i' lone places—let 'em come where there's company and candles!'

"'As if ghos'es 'u'd want to be believed in by anybody so ignorant!' said Mr. Macey, in deep disgust at the farrier's crass incompetence to apprehend the conditions of ghostly phenomena."

And supposing "ghos'es" do exist—the moment the Supernatural is attested and classified it becomes as natural as anything else. Such spooks would add nothing to the dignity and sanctity of the scheme of creation, and are no friends to religion. The world would only be made to look more ridiculous if our deceased friends really rapped tables and pulled off bedclothes, as Miss Florence Marryat's do. Mrs. Besant (who up to the moment of going to press is still a Theosophist), in her latest reading of the riddle of this painful earth, does but explain obscurum per obscurius. Where is the point of a progression through stages, if there is no continuous consciousness? What does it matter if I am not myself, but somebody else in his fifth plane or her nineteenth incarnation? Decidedly it is better to bear the religions we have, than fly to others that we know not of. If Mr. F. W. Myers hears that some ill-trained observers have seen ghosts, he becomes Dantesque and dithyrambic about "the love that rules the world and all the stars." For my part, I fail to draw the moral. I am content to look nearer home—at coal-heavers and costermongers, poets and engineers—and to found my theory of life on less deniable data.

A fig for your ghosts! What! Here have I been living and working and thinking nigh half a lifetime, and only now these gentry should deign to give me cognisance of their existence. Dame Nature would have indeed treated me scurvily had she reduced me to such absurd oracles. The phenomena seem so rare and so irregular, the vast majority of mankind having to go through life only afraid of ghosts, but never seeing them, that no general law of posthumous existence could be based on these obscure and erratic accidents. There may be only a survival of the fittest. It is not in the aberrations, but in the constant factors of human life that we must seek for light, and the attitude of these smellers after immortality is precisely that of the mediaevals who sought for the workings of divinity in eccentric variations from its own habits, till miracles became so commonplace that, as Charles Reade deliciously sums it up, a man in "The Cloister and the Hearth" could reply to his fellow, who was anxious to know why the market-place was black with groups, "Ye born fool! it is only a miracle." If I am to seek for "intimations of immortality," let me find them not in the haphazard freaks of disembodied intelligence, but where Wordsworth found them, and where Mr. Myers was once content to find them, in

Those obstinate questionings
Of sense and outward things,
Fallings from us, vanishings!
Blank misgivings of a creature
Moving about in worlds not realised,
High instincts before which our mortal nature
Did tremble like a guilty thing surprised.

If Moses came to London he would be very disgusted with Mr. Stead and the correspondents of "Borderland" who collect "facts" for him. For that supremely sane and sage legislator made one clean sweep of all the festering superstitions that fascinate the silly and the sentimental to-day as much as they did three thousand years ago. Mr. Stead is a Puritan, and the Old Testament should be his impregnable rock. Yet Deuteronomy is most definite about "Julia." "There shall not be found with thee ... a consulter with a familiar spirit. For whosoever doeth these things is an abomination unto the Lord." His organisation of research is a delusion; science is not to be thus syndicated. The ordinary observer has no idea of scientific sifting, and in ten minutes I exposed a gentleman who impressed a large London club as "the most wonderful thought-reader in Europe."

"Nature has many methods of producing the same effect," says Henry James's greater brother. "She may make our ears ring by the sound of a bell, or by a dose of quinine; make us see yellow by spreading a field of buttercups before our eyes, or by mixing a little Santonine powder with our food." Probably not ten per cent. of the correspondents of "orderland" are aware of the existence of such "subjective sensations," or realize, despite their nightly experience of dreams, that it does not take an actual external object to give you the sensation of something outside yourself. And passing optical illusions may have all the substantiality of ghosts. When Benvenuto Cellini went to consult a wizard, as he relates in his "Memoirs," countless spirits were raised for his behoof, dancing amid the voluminous smoke of a kindled fire. He actually saw them: it was a splendid case for "Borderland." Yet the probabilities are that the cunning magician merely projected magic-lantern pictures on the background of the vapour. My brother woke up one morning, and accidentally directing his eyes to the ceiling, beheld there a couple of monsters—uncouth, amorphous creatures with ramifying conformations and deep purple veins. After a few moments they passed away; but the next morning, lo! they were there again, and the next, and the next, till at last, in alarm, off he goes to a specialist in eyes and unfolds his tale of woe. Is he, perhaps, going blind? "So you've discovered them at last!" laughs the eminent oculist. "These things are Purkinje's Figures—the shadows of the network of blood-vessels of the retina microscopically magnified on the ceiling: everybody ought to see them—it's a sign the eye is a good working lens. But they don't notice them except by accident, when the light slants sideways, and when there's a specially good background for them to be projected and magnified upon." And, taking him into his mystic chamber, and reconstituting the conditions, "Look!" says he, "there are your old friends again!" And there they were, sure enough, in all their amorphous horror. It is, in fact, not so much the actual external object that determines our perception, as attention or inattention; and with wise unconsciousness we ignore all that it is not necessary for us to see at the moment. If our organism were always in perfect health, if our senses were not deceivers ever, if we did not dream as solid a world as that which we inhabit by day, then, indeed, a single appearance of a ghost would settle the question; but as things are, our own eyes are just what we mustn't believe.

As Helmholtz pointed out, we ought to see everything double, except the few objects in the centre of vision; and as a matter of fact we do get double images, but the prejudiced intelligence perceives them as one. The drunken man is thus your only true seer. Genius, which has always been suspected of affinity with drunkenness, is really a faculty for seeing abnormally—that is to say, veraciously. Andrew Lang, who thinks that all children have genius, is thus partially justified; for till they have been taught to see conventionally, they see with fresh insight. Hence the awkwardness of their questions. Mr. Bernard Shaw recently wrote an article on "How to Become a Genius," but he omitted to supply the recipe. It is simply this: see what you do see, and not what everybody tells you you see. To think what everybody says is to be a Philistine, and to say what everybody thinks is to be a genius. Every healthy eye sees Purkinje's Figures when the conditions are present; but only a rare eye perceives them consciously. That is the eye of genius, but the Philistines cry, "Disease! Degeneration!"

XVIII

SOCIETIES TO FOUND

I have noted in my Sancho Panza moments a number of deficiencies in the commonweal which can only be remedied—in our modern manner—by societies. Let me start with a few of the most needed.

1. SOCIETY FOR PROVIDING NEW OATHS

The present currency is badly worn and was always nasty. Swear-words are a necessity. They are the safety-valves of the soul. Why not have them nice and innocent—the kind of oath a girl can use to her mother? It is unfair men should monopolise the bad language. I wonder the Women's Rights women have not sworn about it. I have already suggested that Wellington's "twopenny damn" be replaced by "I don't care a double-blank domino." This gives a compound or twopenny sensation of the unspeakable, combined with absolute innocuity, like a vegetarian chop or a temperance champagne. A milder form (the penny plain) would be "a blank cheque." The society ought to offer prizes for the best suggestions.

2. SOCIETY FOR PROMOTING READINGS AMONG REVIEWERS

It is a notorious fact that critics are the most ill-read class in the community. There are few occupations so laborious, exhaustive, and inadequately remunerated, as reviewing; and who can wonder if the wretched reviewer never finds time to read a book from one week's end to the other. It is a cruel anomaly that men, some of whom may have souls as much as we have, should be shut out from all the pleasures of literature, and all the possibilities of self-culture that books contain. The poor critic goes to his grave, picking up a smattering of cant phrases that are in the air—"Zolaism,"—"Ibsenites," "Décadents," "Symbolism," "the new humour," "the strong-man poetry," and what not—but to become acquainted at first hand with the meaning or meaninglessness of these phrases is denied him by the hard conditions of his life. Publishers would greatly help the proposed society by sending out books cut.

3. SOCIETY FOR THE SUPPRESSION OF CELEBRITIES

"Mankind's available stock of admiration is not large enough for all the demands made upon it," wrote Professor Bain, with the one flash of humour I have noticed in his big treatises. If, as Wordsworth contends,

We live by Admiration, Hope, and Love,

a certain number of objects of admiration is indispensable. But the surplusage of celebrities in this age is simply overwhelming. Celebrity is cheap to-day. You may arrive at it by a million avenues. It is almost impossible to keep your name out of the papers. Culture is so catholic that celebrities who in the old days would have been monopolised by esoteric cliques are common property. The paleographer and the coleopterist claim a share of our admiration equally with the serpentine dancer and the record-breaking cyclist, and the judicious editor prints their "interviews" at equal length. We have an impartial acquaintance with the tastes and views of cardinals and comic singers; and the future of the papacy is given almost as much space as Little Tich's talent for water-colour, and his fondness for the 'cello and his baby. Moreover, that coil of cable which makes the whole world kin has burdened us with the celebrities of the universe. When to these are added the celebrities of the past, of every period, country, and variety, the brain reels. Too many cooks spoil the broth, and too many celebrities numb our faculty of wonder. The vivid feeling that is possible when heroes are few fades into a faint reflection of emotion. The celebrity's name calls up not admiration, but only a shadowy consciousness that admiration is due. We never pause to get the emotion. I am afraid the first proceeding of the society will have to be the suppression of the illustrated weeklies, which manufacture celebrities artificially to fill up their pages, and, in order to have pretty pictures, give every actress that makes a little hit a prominence which Shakespeare did not deserve. If there is no celebrity of the week it is necessary to create one, is the editorial motto. If a man is a celebrity you interview him, and if you interview him he is a celebrity.

You will not believe me (though I don't care a double-blank domino if you don't, for it is true) when I tell you that an opposition society already exists—a society for the manufacture of celebrities. Self-puffery has always gone on in a sporadic fashion, most people sending their own puffs to the papers, and rolling their own logs, on the principle that if you want a thing done well you must do it yourself. But the idea of the society is the organisation of self-puffery. It is done through an association which undertakes (for a fee) to insert anything you choose to send it about yourself in a hundred native papers, and a hundred Colonial, Indian, and American papers, as well as to get special articles written thereon, and to organise press receptions, luncheons, journeys, dinners, etc., etc. O tempora! O mores! What an exposure of the lower journalism! Oh the crush of celebrities there will be when the society has been at work a few years!

4. THE CHARITY OF CHARITIES

The begging-letters and circulars are enough to light your fires the whole year, and it is a pity they are not sent to the poor, to whom they would be of more value. Still, not to have the worry of receiving and discriminating among these appeals is another of the many compensations of poverty. There are a thousand varieties of Charity (some beginning at a Home and others going abroad), and the most munificent can support only a few, and perhaps will select the wrong few. And most of these Charities are struggling along painfully, their resources taxed to the utmost by the severe winter and the coal strike; many can scarcely make both ends meet. There is nothing to prevent the weaker dying of want, and our Charities suffering from a heavy mortality. And of course it will be the best and most retiring Charities that will starve to death rather than beg of the first comer, while the brazen Charities will perambulate the streets with strident clamour, rattling full money-boxes.

Do we not therefore need another Charity? Nay, blaspheme not, nor clench thy purse-strings. One other Charity—just one more—is a social necessity. I would call it "The Charity of Charities." 'T is a central bureau of beneficence, to which each doubting philanthropist should send such sums as he knows not how to dispense. The bureau should inquire into the circumstances of each Charity, and grant or refuse relief strictly in accordance with its needs or merits. The Charity Organisation Society is another affair altogether. Perhaps people are afraid of pauperising the Charities assisted, but there is no reason why these should not continue to be self-supporting as far as possible. Such as could not manage to exist in this country could be assisted to emigrate, while every help would be given to exiled or persecuted Charities to gain a sphere of activity in this country. Fortunately, there are always large-minded men among us who will receive any Charity, however despised, with open arms! There would be visitation committees to call at the offices of the Charities, to see that they were not pleading poverty when the officials were drawing big salaries; a loan society to help them over bad times, so as not to destroy their self-respect by doles in aid; while a cookery school for accounts and a sanatorium for those that failed to keep their balance might also be annexes of this grand institution.

XIX

INDECENCY ON THE ENGLISH STAGE

[This protest was dated Jan. 1, 1891. Things are rather better now.]

I am not a young person. Nothing ever brings a blush to my cheek except the rouge-pencil or the exposure of my stealthy deeds of good I can read the Elizabethan dramatists or Rabelais with equanimity, and the only thing that mars my enjoyment of Juvenal is the occasional obscurity of the Latin. I like the immoral passages in "Mademoiselle de Maupin," even if I do not go so far as Swinburne and call it "the holy book of beauty." Ibsen refreshes me like a tonic, and I even believe in Zola. And yet, if I were State censor of the English stage—which fortunately I am not—I should suppress half of our plays for their indecency. The other half I should suppress for their fatuity. But that is another story.

That vice loses half its evil by losing all its grossness, is a maxim for which the world cannot be too thankful to Burke; for though the point of view be not true, an important aspect of the truth is undoubtedly exhibited. Now, what we get on the English stage is the grossness without the vice—or, to put it more accurately, the vulgarity without the open presentation of the vice. You may mean anything, so long as you say something else. Almost every farcical comedy or comic opera—to leave the music-hall alone—is vitiated by a vein of vulgar indecency which is simply despicable. The aim of the artist is not to conceal art—there is none to conceal—but to conceal his indecencies decently, and yet in the most readily discoverable manner. The successful stage-piece is too often but a symphony in blue. What the

English, with their fashion of spoiling French importations, incorrectly term doubles entendres, are almost indispensable items in the fare of some London theatres of good repute. And the references to things sexual are usually as stupid as they are superfluous to the development of the plot or the characters. There is not the shadow of an excuse for their introduction. They are simply silly accretions on the play, quite unimplicated with the spirit of the scene, and losing all meaning in their effort to have two. One can enjoy the sparkle of wit and the rich halo of comedy playing around situations unaffectedly "improper"; even the farces of the Palais Royal amuse with the broad foolery of their esprit gaulois; but the English endeavour to make the best of both worlds, the English author who combines the prude and the pimp—for these one can have nothing but contempt. And the measure of one's longing for a sane and virile view and presentation of life will be the measure of one's abhorrence of immorality which has not even the decency to be indecent.

The French dramatist gives us characters living in "a state of sin" (one of the United States not recognised at the Court of St. James's). The English dramatist conveys the plot, conveys the situations which spring out of the "state of sin," but leaves out the basis on which the whole rests. Thus, instead of situations intelligibly indecent, we get situations unintelligibly indecent. Eros, like an Indian conjuror, is left suspended from nothing. As the English playgoer does not ask for intelligible situations, he is satisfied with the residuum. The dramatist's uneasy striving to account for the behaviour of his personages only renders the latent character of the residuum more glaring.

The truth is, that everything depends on treatment and atmosphere. Lord Houghton has treated the difficult theme of a mother's and daughter's love for the same man with tenderness and grace; a foreign writer would lay bare and anatomise with more of scalpel and less of sentiment. The former satisfies our aesthetic instincts; the latter would, in addition, appeal to our intellectual curiosity. To the English dramatist the whole story would be tabu; but if the Continental man had got some striking situations out of it, the Briton's soul would hanker after those situations. So he would make the mother a maiden aunt, and give us the familiar spectacle of the aged spinster languishing for matrimony, as incarnated for the nonce in the person of her niece's lover. Miss Sophie Larkin would play the part, and it would be intended to be a comic one. There is more suggestiveness in the conventional stage figure of the amorous old maid than in all Congreve's comedies. And yet what figure is more certain to please, in the whole gallery of puppets? Scenes and characters of this sort you may have by the dozen; but to build a moral play upon an "immoral" basis is to court damnation. To construct a noble piece of work on the basis of "improper" relations between your chief characters is to show the cloven hoof. Once the initial scheme granted, the rest may be as bracing as an Alpine breeze; but the critics will scent brimstone. But to build an immoral play upon a "moral" basis—that way gladness lies. Critics, who would rage at the delineation of a character remotely resembling a human being's, will pat you on the back with a good-humoured smile, and at most a laughing word of reprobation for your azure audacities. Ladies, who, whether they are married or unmarried, are in England presumed to be agnostics in sexual matters, will roar themselves hoarse over farces whose stories could only be told to the ultramarines. Ibsen may not untie a shoe-latchet in the interest of truth, while English burlesque managers may put an army of girls into tights. One dramatist may steal a horse-laugh by a tawdry vulgarity, while another may not look over an ankle. It is the same with literature. We look askance at "The Kreutzer Sonata," but tolerate the vulgar anecdotal indecencies of the sporting journal. The artist's eye may not see life steadily, and see it whole; but it is licensed to wink and ogle at will from behind its blinker. If the artist's "immorality" is the artistic embodiment of a frank Paganism, or is inspired by an ethical or a scientific purpose, he is a filthy-minded fellow. Seriousness is the unpardonable sin. Coarseness can be condoned, if it is only flippant and frivolous enough. In short, the only excuse for indecency is to have none.

Unfortunately, practical considerations are so involved with artistic that it may be imprudent to accord the artist as wide a charter as he would wish. The ideals of sincerity and honesty may in the present social environment be so potential for harm that it is for the common interest that they should not be gratified. This may be so, though I do not believe it. But whether it be so or not, of one thing I am certain—and that is that the half-hearted dallying with things sexual is wholly an evil; that the prurient sniffing and sniggering round the subject is more fraught with peril to a community, more debasing to the emotional currency, more blighting to the higher sexual feelings of the race, than the most shameless public repudiation of all moral restraints. Evil cures itself in the sunlight; it grows and flourishes in the darkness. Vice looks fascinating in the gloaming; the morning shows up the tawdriness and the paint.

XX

LOVE IN LIFE AND LITERATURE

Love! Love! Love! The air is full of it as I write, though the autumn leaves are falling. Shakespeare's immortal love-poem is playing amid the cynicism of modern London, like that famous fountain of Dickens's in the Temple gardens. The "largest circulation" has barely ceased to flutter the middle-class breakfast-table with discussions on "the Age of Love" and Little Billee and Trilby—America's "Romeo and Juliet"—loom large at the Haymarket. Mr. T. P. O'Connor, forgetting even Napoleon, his King Charles's head, is ruling high at the libraries with réchauffés of "Some Old Love Stories," and the "way of a man with a maid" is still the unfailing topic of books and plays. One would almost think that Coleridge was to be taken "at the foot of the letter"—

All thoughts, all passions, all delights
Whatever stirs this mortal frame,
All are but ministers of Love,
And feed his sacred flame.

But alas! suffer me to be as sceptical as Stevenson in "Virginibus Puerisque." In how many lives does Love really play a dominant part? The average taxpayer is no more capable of a "grand passion" than of a grand opera. "Man's love is of man's life a thing apart." Ay, my Lord Byron, but 'tis not "woman's whole existence," neither. Focused in books or plays to a factitious unity, the rays are sadly scattered in life. Natheless Love remains an interest, an ideal, to all but the hopeless Gradgrinds. Many a sedate citizen's pulse will leap with Romeo's when Forbes-Robertson's eye first lights upon the Southern child "whose beauty hangs upon the cheek of night like a rich jewel in an Ethiop's ear." Many a fashionable maid, with an eye for an establishment, will shed tears when Mrs. Patrick Campbell, martyr to unchaffering love, makes her quietus with a bare dagger.

For the traces left by Love in life are so numerous and diverse that even the cynic—which is often bad language for the unprejudiced observer—cannot quite doubt it away. There seems to be no other way of accounting for the facts. When you start learning a new language you always find yourself confronted with the verb "to love"—invariably the normal type of the first conjugation. In every language on earth the student may be heard declaring, with more zeal than discretion, that he and you and they and every other person, singular or plural, have loved, and do love, and will love. "To love" is the model verb, expressing the archetype of activity. Once you can love grammatically there is a world of things you may do without stumbling. For, strange to say, "to love," which in real life is associated with so much that is bizarre and violent, is always "regular" in grammar. Ancient and modern tongues tell the same tale—from Hebrew to street-Arabic, from Greek to the elephantine language that was "made in Germany." Not only is "to love" deficient in no language (as home is deficient in French, and Geist in English), but it is never even "defective." No mood or tense is ever wanting—a proof of how it has been conjugated in every mood and tense of life, in association with every variety of proper and improper noun, and every pronoun at all personal. Not merely have people loved unconditionally in every language, but there is none in which they would not have loved, or might not have loved, had circumstances permitted; none in which they have not been loved, or (for hope springs eternal in the human breast) have been about to be loved. Even woman has an Active Voice in the matter; indeed, "to love" is so perfect that, compared with it, "to marry" is quite irregular. For, while "to love" is sufficient for both sexes, directly you get to marriage you find in some languages that division has crept in, and that there is one word for the use of ladies and another for gentlemen only. Turning from the evidence enshrined in language to the records of history, the same truth meets us at any date we appoint. Everywhere "'T is love that makes the world go round." It is dizzying to think what would have happened if Eve had not accepted Adam. What could have attracted her if it was not love? Surely not his money, nor his family. For these she couldn't have cared a fig-leaf. Unfortunately, the daughters of Eve have not always taken after their mother. The statistics of crime and insanity testify eloquently to the reality of love, arithmetic teaching the same lesson as history and grammar. Consider, too, the piles of love at Mudie's! A million story-tellers in all periods and at all places cannot have all told stories, though they have all, alas! told the same story. They must have had mole-hills for their mountains, if not straw for their bricks. There are those who, with Bacon, consider love a variety of insanity; but it is more often merely a form of misunderstanding. When the misunderstanding is mutual, it may even lead to marriage. As a rule Beauty begets man's love, Power woman's. At least, so women tell me. But then, I am not beautiful. It must be said for the man that every lover is a species of Platonist—he identifies the Beautiful with the Good and the True. The woman's admiration has less of the ethical quality; she is dazzled, and too often feels, "If he be but true to me, what care I how false he be."

"The Stage is more beholding to Love than the life of man," says Bacon. The "Daily Telegraph" is perhaps even more "beholding" to it. The ingenuity with which this great organ raises the cloyless topic every silly season under another name, is beyond all praise. No conclusion will ever be arrived at, of course, because "Love" means a different thing with each correspondent, and it is difficult to lay down general truths about a relation that varies with each of the countless couples that have ever experienced it, or have fancied they experienced it. The set theme of a newspaper correspondence always reminds me of a nervous old lady crossing the roadway: she runs this way and that way, gets splashed by every passing wheel, jumps back, jumps forward again, finds temporary harbour on a crossing-stage under a lamp, darts sideways, and ends by arriving in another street altogether. So that the heading of a correspondence is scant guide as to what is being discussed under it; and no one would be surprised to find a recipe against baldness under the title of "The Age of Love." But then "The Age of Love" is an absurd and answerless question. Experience shows that all ages fall in love—and out again; so that, to quote the pithy Bacon again, "a man may have a quarrel to marry when he will." Octogenarians elope, and Mr. Gilbert's elderly baby died a blasé old roué of five.

Romeo's passion was a second, not a first, love: he had already loved Rosaline. Juliet's first—and only—love came to her only eleven years after she had been weaned, "come Lammas." Save that the "Age of Love" may be said to be "Youth"—for Love aye rejuvenates—there is nothing to be said. Wherefore the German gentleman who protested against the clichés of novel-writers in the matter of the eternity of passion was well within the wilderness of the subject. The cliché metaphor, by the way, is itself becoming a cliché, so stereotyped do we grow in protesting against the stereotyped. Germans are, perhaps, not the best authorities on passion: they are too sentimental for love and too domestic for romance. Still, our German is justified in his complaint: the love-scenes in our novels and dramas correspond very little to human nature. In works of pure romance this is no drawback to artistic beauty; but in much modern work purporting to mirror contemporary life, the love-making has neither the beauty that springs from idealisation, nor that which springs from reality. Property-speeches and stock-sentiments still do duty for what really takes place in modern love-making. We have played with the traditional puppets so long that we have come to believe they are alive. They may have been alive once—when life was more elemental; they still exist, perchance, in those primitive conditions which are really the past surviving into the present. But in no field of human life is there greater need of fresh observation than in this of love. The ever-increasing subtlety and complexity of modern love have not yet found adequate registration and interpretation in art. Art always seems to me a magic mirror in which the shapes of the past are held long after they have passed away. The author of to-day looks not into his heart—but into the mirror—and writes. Primitive Love found its poet in Longus the Greek, with his "Daphnis and Chloe"; but who has given us Modern Love? Not Meredith himself, despite his sonnets; though "The Egoist" is a terrible analysis of a modern lover, as saddening as the "Modern Lover" of George Moore. The poets are ill guides to love. Their passions are half-fantastic, if not of imagination all compact. Shelley's "Epipsychidion" was the expression of a passing mood; Tennyson's "Come into the Garden, Maud," a lyric exaltation that must have died down when Maud appeared, and could in any case scarce have survived its fiftieth rewriting; Rossetti's interpretation of "The House of Life" is as purely individual as Patmore's "Angel in the House"; Swinburne sings of phantasms; we can no more take our poets for types of modern lovers than we can accept Dante or Petrarch as representatives of the mediaeval lover. These poets used their goddesses as mystic inspirers. Dante was not in love with Beatrice, the daughter of Portinari, but with his own imagination: she married Simone as he Gemma, and thus he was still able to worship her. The devotion of Petrarch to Laura did not prevent his having children by another lady. If we turn to modern prose-writers, we fail to find any really subtle treatment of Modern Love. Henry James himself shrinks from analysing it, even allusively and insinuatingly. Zola's handling of the love-theme is as primary as Pierre Loti's, for Zola has the eye for masses, not for individual subtleties. Tolstoï, informed by something of the rage of the old ascetics, is too iconoclast; Maupassant's stories sometimes suggest a cynicism as profound as Chamfort's or that old French poet's who wrote:

Femme, plaisir de demye heure,
Et ennuy qui sans fin demeure.

Ibsen is as idealistic as Strindberg is materialist. Shall we seek light in the modern lady-novelist, with her demand for phases of passion suited to every stage of existence? Shall we fall in with the agnosticism of John Davidson, and admit that no man has ever understood a woman, a man, or himself, and vice versa? 'T is seemingly the opinion of Nordau that, after the first flush of youth, we do but play "The Comedy of Sentiment," feigning and making believe to recapture

That first lyric rapture.

And his friend Auguste Dietrich writes:

Se faire vivement désirer et paraître refuser alors ce qu'elle brûle d'accorder ... voilà la comédie que de tout temps ont jouée les femmes.

Not quite a fair analysis, this: like all cynicism, it is crude. Juliet for one did not play this comedy, though she was aware of the rôle.

Or, if thou think'st I am too quickly won,
I'll frown and be perverse and say thee nay,
So thou wilt woo.

Nor is it always comedy, even when played. Darwin, in his "Descent of Man," recognizes a real innate coyness, and that not merely of the female sex, which has been a great factor in improving the race. And, since we are come to the scientific standpoint, let it be admitted that marriage is a racial safeguard which does not exhaust the possibilities of romantic passion. Nature, as Schopenhauer would say, has over-baited the hook. Our capacities for romance are far in excess of the needs of the race: we have a surplus of emotion, and Satan finds mischievous vent for it. We are confronted with a curious dualism of soul and body, with two streams of tendency that will not always run parallel: hinc illae lachrymae. This it is that makes M. Bourget's "Cruel Enigme." Perhaps the ancients were wiser, with whom the woman had no right of choice, passing without will from father to husband. When the Romans evolved their concept of the marriage-contract between man and woman instead of between father and son-in-law, the trouble began. Emancipated woman developed soul and sentiment, and when Roman Law conquered the world, it spread everywhere the seeds of romance. Romance—the very etymology carries its history, for 't is only natural that the first love-stories should have been written in the language of Rome. Nor is it inapt that the typical lover should recall Rome by his name:

O, Romeo, Romeo! wherefore art thou.
Romeo?

Romantic Love is the rose Evolution has grown on earthly soil. Floreat! Strange that Nordau, in his "Conventional Lies of Civilisation," should echo this aspiration and gush over the Goethean Wahlverwandtschaft—the elective affinity of souls—almost with the rapture of a Platonist, conceiving love as the soul finding its pre-natal half. Surely, to his way of thinking, scientific selection were better for the race than such natural selection, especially as natural selection cannot operate in our complicated civilisation, where at every turn the poetry of life dashes itself against the dead wall of prose. The miracle has happened. Edwin loves Angelina, and by a strange coincidence Angelina also loves Edwin. But then come the countless questions of income, position, family. Adam and Eve were the only couple that started free from relatives. Else, perhaps, had their garden not been "Paradise." All later lovers have had to consult other people's tastes as well as their own, and there has probably never been a marriage that has pleased all parties unconcerned. And even when the course of true love runs smooth, do the lovers marry whom they were in love with? Alas! marriage is a parlous business: one loves one's ideal, but the beloved is always real. The wiser sort take a leaf out of Dante's book or Petrarch's, and retain their illusions. "The poets call it love—we doctors give it another name," says a kindly old character in one of Echegaray's comedies: "How is it cured? This very day with the aid of the priest; and so excellent a specific is this, that after a month's appliance, neither of the wedded pair retains a vestige of remembrance of the fatal sickness."

There is a kind of scientific selection in the intermarriage of persons of quality, which is at the bottom of their supposed superciliousness and disdain of trade, though blood does not infallibly produce breeding. There is the same tribal instinct in the aversion of Jews from exogamy, and it is this sort of scientific selection which is subconsciously going on when parents and guardians, sisters, cousins, and aunts, interfere with the "elective affinities." Money, too, is really a security for the due rearing of offspring. It is to be hoped there is a tear beneath the sneers of Sudermann's comedy, "Die Schmetterlingschlacht," for the sorrows of moneyless mothers with unmarriageable girls.

Doän't thou marry for munny, but goä wheer munny is,

said Tennyson's Northern Farmer—a sentiment which was anticipated or plagiarised by Wendell Holmes as "Don't marry for money, but take care the girl you love has money." Few people may marry directly for money, or even for position, but few marriages are uncomplicated by considerations of money and position. Little wonder if

Love, light as air, at sight of human ties
Spreads his light wings and in a moment flies.

Lovers may thrust such thoughts into the background, but is not this wilful blindness as much "The Comedy of Sentiment" as that which supplies the theme of Nordau's novel? It weighed upon Walter Bagehot that "immortal souls" should have to think of tare and tret and the price of butter; but "sich is life"—prose and poetry intertangled. The cloud may have a silver lining, but clouds are not all silver. Wherefore Nordau's glorification of the love-match is curiously unscientific; it belongs to silver-cloudland; it might work among the birds of [Greek: Nephelo-kokkugia]. Loveless marriages may beget happiness, if not ecstacy; and love-matches may be neither for the interest of the individuals nor of the race. They serve, however, to feed Art, and one real love-match will justify a hundred novels and plays, just as one good ghost will supply a hundred ghost-stories. Considering how many dead people there are, the percentage of those permitted to play ghost is so infinitesimal as to be incredible a priori; nevertheless, how we snatch at the possibility of ghosts! Even so we like to connect love and marriage, two things naturally divorced, and to fancy that wedding bells are rung by Cupid. But, after all, what is love? In lawn-tennis it counts for nothing. In the dictionary it figures, inter alia, as "a kind of light silken stuff." And, as Dumas fils sagely sums it up in "Le Demi-Monde": "Dans le mariage, quand l'amour existe, l'habitude le tue, et quand il n'existe pas elle le fait naître."

XXI

DEATH AND MARRIAGE

It was with melancholy amusement that I read in the scientific journals that sewer-gas was comparatively innocuous. After the hundreds of sanitary tracts in which the deadliness of sewer-gas has been an axiom of faith, after the thousand-and-one deaths from it in the contemporary novel, it is grimly diverting to learn that sewer-gas may be welcomed without fear to our hearths and homes. The same process appears to be overtaking science with which we are familiar in the sphere of history—all the bad gases are getting purified and the good spirits vilified. The invincible solids are being liquefied, and the aëry nothings are being given solid habitations. The Professor tells me that liquid oxygen is obtainable only under great pressure, and at a colossal cost. I beg respectfully to suggest to the millionaires the advisability of laying in quarts of it for their dinner-parties. This sparkling beverage— essence of oxygen, mark you—would not need to be iced, for the North Pole is as a red-hot poker compared with it. Such a beverage would make a sensation and provide paragraphs for the society journals and the "Times" obituary. It is true the guests would not like it, but they would be anxious to quaff it. Have you never noticed the innocent joy which the pop and froth of cheap champagne gives to suburban souls? There is a magic halo about champagne—an aroma of aristocracy—which sanctifies it for people who would be happier with lemonade. Wherefore I doubt not there would be a public to adventure on liquid oxygen, though it were congealed in the attempt. The imbibition thereof might indeed replace suicide and cremation—it would both kill and cure, and our frozen bodies might be preserved in family ice-safes for the edification of scientific posterity. I should not marvel if liquid air or oxygen became an article of the euthanasian creed. As for sewer-gas, we may yet live to see it manufactured artificially for the improvement of the public health, and conveyed to our overcrowded drawing-rooms with all the paraphernalia of pipes and the mendacious meter. Science has turned so many somersaults even in my short lifetime that I am prepared for anything. I have even serious doubts as to the stability of Darwinism, I have seen so many immortal truths die young. I verily believe that the cocksureness of our century is destined to be the amusement of the next, which may not impossibly believe that the ape is descended from man by retrogression.

Our little systems have their day,
They have their day—and come again.

The science of medicine in particular seems to be always in a critical condition, and the bacillus bobs up and down in a manner that is "painful and free." Like Hamlet's father's ghost, it eludes our question: we know not if it is "a spirit of health or goblin damned," angel or demon or delusion. The microbe of to-day is the myth of to-morrow. Surgery is the only department of medicine which has made real advances in our century. The rest is guesswork and experiment on vile bodies. I do not know why the Peculiar People should be persecuted for refusing vivi-injection. Tolstoï, a friend of his told me, breathes fire and fury against the doctors, and will have none of their drugs or their doctrines, and he is not alone in believing that every tombstone is a monument to some doctor's skill. "When doctors disagree," says the proverb. But do they ever agree—unless they consult? I went to an eminent oculist once, who anointed my eyes with cocaine in order to make the pupils dilate. But my pupils refused to obey. He was dumfoundered, and said that such a refusal was unheard of: it contradicted all experience and all the books. I felt quite conscience-stricken. He tried again and again, but my pupils remained obdurately small. I apologised for my originality, and he peered at my eyes minutely, evidently expecting to find the new humour. So I suggested he might try Horror, which I understood from the novelists made the pupils dilate; but he replied that that would not be professional. He told me, however, a fact which I thought well worth his fee. An erudite scientist had devoted a monograph to cocaine, but failed to discover the one fact about it which was worth knowing, and which had raised cocaine to the first rank—to wit, that applied externally it was an anaesthetic, so that if you put a drop on your tongue you might bite your tongue without hurting yourself. Doubtless the poor man was ready enough to bite his tongue when his book was spoilt by the discovery. But I cannot help thinking that his case was typical of science—which is appallingly exhaustive and self-satisfied, but seems just to miss the one essential thing.

Have you heard the legend of the Marriage of the Angel of Death with a mortal woman? He was aweary of his cheerless professional round, and longed for domestic joys to brighten his scanty leisure. It did not strike him to "domesticate the Recording Angel"; but one day, being sent to despatch a beautiful woman, he fell in love with her instead, and married her. But dire was the punishment of his disobedience. The beautiful woman turned out a shrew, who made Death's life not worth living, and as he had refused to kill her when her hour sounded, she was now immortal. In despair he deserted her and her child, and would never go near her, so that her neighbourhood was always healthy, and she unconsciously made the fortune of several insanitary watering-places. In course of time Death's son grew up, and with that curious filial perversity (which has been especially remarked in the children of clergymen) he became a physician. And his fame as a physician spread far and wide, inasmuch as he knew the secret of Death, that uxorious and henpecked Angel having revealed it to his wife in a weak moment. If the Angel stood at the foot of the bed, he was only terrifying the patient; if, however, he took up his position at the head of the bed, he was in deadly earnest, and hope was vain. Inheriting sufficient of his father's nature to see him when he was invisible to others, the physician was naturally able to prophesy with undeviating accuracy, though the cunning rascal made great play with stethoscopes and syringes and what not, and felt pulses and thumped chests before he gave judgment, and was solicitous in administering drugs when he foresaw the patient was destined to recover. Now, it befell one day that the Princess of Paphlagonia (of whom I have told elsewhere) fell grievously sick, and none of the physicians could do aught to relieve her. So the king issued a proclamation that whosoever could cure her could have her to wife. Now, the fame of the beauty of the princess had travelled as far as the renown of the mighty physician, so that desire was kindled in his heart to try for the grand prize. And so Death's son set out and travelled over land and sea, comforting the sick everywhere as he passed by, and curing all those that were fated not to die. And at last he arrived in the capital of Paphlagonia, and was received with great joy by the king and all his court, and ushered into the sick-chamber. A great warmth gathered at his heart as his eyes fell upon the marvellous fairness of the princess; but the next moment his heart was turned to ice, for lo! he perceived the Angel of Death standing at the head of the bed. After a moment of agony the physician commanded all present to leave the chamber; then for the first time he broke the silence his mother had imposed upon him. "Father," he said, "have you no pity upon me—you who once loved a woman yourself?" Then Death answered, in a hollow voice: "I must do my duty. I disobeyed once, and my punishment was greater than I could bear." "Father," pleaded the physician again, "will you not move to the foot of the bed?" "Nay, I cannot," answered Death harshly: "I was commanded to stay here, and here I must stay." "And thou wilt stay there whatever I say or do?" asked the physician plaintively. "Yea," answered Death stoutly. Then, wrought up to desperation, the physician called the attendants in again and bade them turn the bed round, so that Death was left standing at the foot. But the Angel, seeing himself outwitted, rushed back to the head. The physician thereupon dismissed the attendants and upbraided him with his broken promise, but Death stood firm. At last the physician lost his temper and all his good bedside manner, and cried furiously: "If you're not gone instantly, I'll send for mother!" And the Angel of Death vanished in the twinkling of the bedpost.

Till we can marry off Azrael to a termagant, I do not believe we shall ever really turn the tables upon him. Nothing is more surprising to a reader of advertisement columns than that people still continue to die. An army of alchemists has discovered the Elixir of Life, and retails it at one-and-three-halfpence a phial. Paracelsus has turned pill-maker, and prospers exceedingly, and sells out to a joint-stock company. But the great procession gravewards goes on, the "thin black lines" creeping along all day long, and there is no falling off in the consumption of sherry and biscuits. The scythe of the Black Angel shines—opus fervet—and it is always the mowing season. Sometimes he stands at the foot of the bed, and then there is triumph for the pharmacopoeia; sometimes he stands at the head, and then the bed becomes a grave and he a tombstone. Alas! his marriage is but a pleasant myth, and his infallible son a dream. Azrael is still a bachelor, and science is not shrew enough to drive him away. Perhaps 't is as well the leeches cannot avert him; perhaps 't is a blessing that they blunder, and the kindly grass grows over their mistakes. As it is, too many people are an unconscionable long time in dying. Their habit of procrastination is with them to the last. They linger on—a misery to themselves, and a thorn to those anxious to mourn their loss. They do not know how to retire gracefully. The art of leaving a world should be taught as a branch of deportment.

An American philanthropist who died recently was in the habit of girding at the arrangements of the universe, which did not seem to him organised after the fashion of a bureau of beneficence. He was wont to regret that he had not been present at the creation, so as to give a few hints. "Well, what would you have advised?" a friend once challenged him to say. "I would have advised," he retorted, "that health be made catching instead of disease." At first hearing, this sounds taking, but its plausibility diminishes under investigation. Health is the normal state of an organism, the perfect working of its parts—it is not something superadded, as disease is. You might as well expect one watch to catch the right time from another. The philanthropist would have been more within the bounds of the reasonable if he had demanded that disease should be more egotistic and less epidemic. Every organism ought to consume its own smoke, and not communicate its misfortunes to its neighbours. And this it does satisfactorily enough in organic disease; it is only when those impish germs, microbes and bacilli, mix themselves up with the matter that we get pathological socialism. I confess that the whole germ business seems to me an illogical element in the scheme of destruction, though 't is of a piece with the structure of things. And yet there is a sense in which health is catching. There is a contagion of confidence as well as of panic, and the surest way to escape epidemics is to disbelieve them. Radiant people radiate health. The mind is a big factor in things hygienic. 'T is a poor medicine that takes no account of the soul. We are not earthen receptacles for drugs, but breathing clay vivified by thoughts and passions. And in the universe of morals, at any rate, health is catching just as much as disease. We are ennobled by noble souls, and uplifted by righteousness. We pattern ourselves unconsciously upon our friends. Character is contagious, and emotion epidemic, and good-humour has its germs; copy-book maxims are null and void: packets of propositions leave us cold. Morality can only be taught by object-lessons; they err egregiously who would teach it by the card. A fine character in a play or a novel outweighs a sermon; and in real life the preacher pales before the practiser. It is a great day when a man discovers for himself that honesty is the best policy. Morality is a matter of feeling and will, not of intellect. Handbooks of ethics may edify the intellect, and "Cicero de Officiis" be the favourite reading of rogues. I knew a university student who at his examination cribbed Kant's panegyric of the moral law from a concealed text-book.

The legend of Death's marriage recalls to me that of John L. Sullivan's. It is said that the famous bruiser was in like grievous plight. His wife beat him, and he had to sue for a divorce on the ground of cruelty! There is something deliciously pathetic about the insignificance of a great man to his wife—his valet feels small at least on pay-day. "The Schoolmaster Abroad" is a rampant divinity with a ferocious ferule; at home he is a meek person in slippers. The policeman who stands majestically at the cross-roads, waving the white glove of authority, nods in the chimney-corner without a helmet. Bishop Proudie was not much of a hero to Mrs. Proudie, and even a beadle is, I fear, but moderately imposing in the domestic sanctum. That a prophet is not without honour save in his own country, we know; but even if he travel abroad, he must leave his wife behind him—else will he never continuously contemplate his own greatness. This is why so many great men remain bachelors. It perhaps also explains why the others are so unhappy in their marriages. Perhaps there ought to be a training-school for the supply of great men's wives.

XXII

THE CHOICE OF PARENTS

"Yes," said Marindin quietly, "they may say they write for Posterity, but what living author besides myself does write for Posterity?"

This sounded so unlike Marindin's modesty that I wondered if the port and the paradoxes of our Christmas dinner had got into his head at last. The veteran man of letters had talked brilliantly more suo of many things, most of all perhaps of his dead friend, Charles Dickens. Who seemed more surely to have been writing Christmas stories for Posterity? we had asked ourselves musingly, as we discussed the change of temper since the days when Dickens or Father Christmas might have stood for the Time-Spirit. Many good things had Marindin said of Ibsen and Nietzsche and the modern apostles of self-development who sneered at the Gospel of self-sacrifice, and at all the amiable virtues our infancy had drawn from "The Fairchild Family" with its engaging references to Jeremiah xvii. 9. But now he was breaking out in a new way, and I missed the reassuring twinkle in his eye.

"I think I may without arrogance claim to be the one author who really has considerable influence with Posterity," he went on, drawing serenely at his cigar and adjusting his right leg more comfortably across the arm of his easy-chair. "Is there any one else whom Posterity listens to?"

I shifted uneasily in my own arm-chair. "What do you mean?" I inquired baldly.

"Don't you know I write for the unborn?" he counter-queried.

"But they don't read you—yet," I said, trying to smile.

"My dear fellow! Why, I'm the best-read man in Ante-land. The unborn swear by me! My publishers, Fore and Futurus, are simply rolling in promissory notes."

"You've become a Theosophist!" I cried in alarm, for that familiar twinkle in his eye had been replaced by a strange exaltation.

"And what if I have?"

"Theosophy!" I cried scornfully—"Theology for Atheists! The main contemporary form of the Higher Foolishness."

"The Higher Foolishness!" echoed Marindin indignantly.

"Yes, the Foolishness of the fool with brains. The brainless fool fulfils himself in low ways—in alcoholic saturnalia, in salvation carnivals, in freethought hysterics, in political bombs. The Higher Foolishness expresses itself in aberrations of poetry and art, in table-rapping and theosophy, in vegetarianism, and in mystic calculations about the Beast."

"It is you who are the fool," he replied shortly. "Theosophy is true—that is, my form of it. Birth is but the name for the entry upon this particular form of existence.

"Our birth is but a sleep and a forgetting.
The soul that rises with us, our life's star,
Hath had elsewhere its setting,
And cometh from afar.

"The unborn pre-exist, even as the dead persist; and instead of addressing Posterity posthumously and circuitously, I have anticipated its verdict. I have written for the unborn, direct. I have been the apostle of the New Ethics among the pre-natal populations, the prophet of individualism among the unborn."

"What! You have propagated the teaching that free choice must be the battle-cry of the future, that the only genuine morality is that which is the spontaneous outcome of an emancipated individuality!"

"Precisely."

"But what has free choice to do with the unborn?"

"What has it to do? Great heavens! Everything. The battle-cry of the future will be Free Birth."

"Free Birth!" I echoed.

"Yes—this is what I have been preaching to the unborn—the choice of their parents before consenting to be born! Compulsory birth must be swept away. What! would you sweep away all checks upon the individuality of the individual—once he is born would you tear asunder all the swaddling-bands of our baby civilisation; would you replace the rules of the nursery by the orderly anarchy of manhood and womanhood, and yet retain such an incoherent anachronism as compulsory birth—a disability which often cripples a man upon the very threshold of his career? Without this initial reform the individualism of your Ibsens and Auberon Herberts becomes a mere simulacrum, a hollow mockery. If you are to develop your individuality, it must be your own individuality that you develop, not an individuality thrust upon you by a couple of outsiders."

"And you have preached this with success?"

"With unheard-of success."

"Unheard-of, indeed!" I muttered sarcastically.

"In your plane of existence!" he retorted. "In Ante-land the movement has spread widely; scarcely a soul but has become convinced of the evils of compulsion in this most personal matter, and of the necessity of having a voice in its own incarnation. And it is I, moi qui vous parle, who have sown the seeds of the revolt against our present social arrangements. Too long had parents presumed upon the ignorance and helplessness of the unborn and upon their failure to combine. But now the great wave of emancipation which is lifting us all off our feet has reached the coming race. And soon the old ideal will be nothing but a strangled snake by the cradle of Hercules."

"Why, I never heard of such a thing in all my born days!" I cried helplessly.

"Of course not; you are more ignorant than the babe unborn. You trouble yourself about the next world, but as to what may be going on in the last world, that never enters your head. But for the tyranny of outward social forms you and I might have deferred our birth till a serener century. Henceforth the dreamer of dreams will have only himself to blame if he is born out of his due time and called upon to set the crooked straight. Job himself would have escaped his misfortunes if he had only had the patience to wait. In future any one who is born in a hurry will be a born idiot."

"What! Will the unborn choose the time of birth as well as their parents?"

"One is implicated in the other. Suppose the soul wished to be the son of an American Duke, naturally it would have to wait till aristocracy was developed across the Atlantic, say some time in the next century."

"I see. And is there a public opinion in Ante-land that regulates private action?"

"Yes, but I have now educated it to the higher ethics. It used to be the respectable thing to be born of strangers without one's own consent, though at the bottom of their souls many persons believed this to be sheer immorality, and cursed the day they were led to the cradle, and became the mere playthings of the parents who acquired them—pretty toys to be dandled and caressed, just a larger variety of doll. But all this is almost over. Henceforth birth will be considered immoral unless it is spontaneous—the outcome of an intelligent selection of parents, based on love."

"On love?"

"Yes; should not a child love its father and mother? and how can we expect it to love people it has never seen, to whom it is tied in the most brutal way, without a voice in the control of its destinies at the absolutely most important turning-point of its whole existence?"

"True, a child should love its parents," I conceded. "But is not the quiet, sober affection that springs up after birth, an affection founded on mutual association and mutual esteem, better than all the tempestuous ardours of pre-natal passion that may not survive the christening?"

"Ah, that is the good old orthodox cant!" cried Marindin, puffing out a great cloud of smoke. "What certainty is there this post-natal love would spring up? And, at any rate, a man would no longer be able to blame Providence if he found himself tied for life to a couple for whom he had nothing but loathing and contempt. Even the adherents of the old conception of compulsory childship begin to see that the stringency of the filial tie needs relaxation. Already it is recognised that in cases of cruelty the child may be divorced from the parent. But there is a hopeless incompatibility of temper and temperament which is not necessarily attended with cruelty. Drunkenness, lunacy, and criminality should also be regarded as valid grounds for divorce, the parent being no longer allowed to bear the name of the child it has dishonoured."

"But who shall say," I asked sceptically, "that the new self-appointed generation will be happier than the old? What guarantee is there that the choice of parents will be made with taste and discretion?"

Marindin shrugged his shoulders impatiently.

"Come and interview the unborn," he said, and fixed his unsmiling eye on mine, as though to hypnotise me. What happened then I shall never be able to explain. I was translated into another scale of being, into the last world in fact; and just as it is impossible to describe a symphony to a deaf mute or a sunset to a man born blind, so it is impossible for me to put down in terms of our present consciousness the experiences I went through in that earlier pre-natal stage of existence. What I perceived in Ante-land must needs be expressed through the language of this world, to which in effect it bears as true and constant a relation as the vibration of a violin string to its music. I soon gathered that, as Marindin had claimed, his doctrines had made considerable incursions in the last world, and, what was more surprising, in this. There seemed to be quite a considerable sect of parents spread all through Europe and America, pledged to respect the rights of the unborn, and it was in co-operation with this enlightened minority—destined, no doubt, in time to become the Universal Church—that the unborn worked. The sect embraced many couples of wealth and position, and, as was to be expected, at the start there had been a rush among the unborn for millionaire parents. But it was soon discovered that birth for money was a mistake, that it too often led to a spendthrift youth and a bankrupt age, and that there was not seldom a legacy duty to pay in the shape of hereditary diseases, sometimes amounting to as much as two pains in the pound; the gold rush was therefore abating. Birth for beauty had also been popular till experience demonstrated the insubstantiality of good looks as a panoply throughout life. Gradually the real conditions of earthly happiness were coming to be understood. Unborn preachers in their unbuilt churches tried in their unspoken sermons to lead souls to the higher bodies or to save souls from precipitate incarnation. Marindin's own unwritten books sustained Paley's thesis of the essentially equal distribution of happiness among all classes, and left it for the individual soul to decide between the realities of toil and the unrealities of prosperity, Marindin took the opportunity of our presence in Ante-land to pay a visit to his publishers, Fore and Futurus, of whose honesty and generosity he spoke in glowing terms. Fore received us; he seemed to be a thorough gentleman, this unborn publisher. He showed us the design for a cover to a new "Guide to the Selection of Parents," which he was about to bring out, and which he hoped would become the standard work on the subject. I gathered that these "Guides" were very popular as birthday presents, enabling, as they did, those just about to be born to think once more before making the final plunge. The feature of the Fore and Futurus "Guide" was the appendix of contributions from souls already born, whose mistakes might serve to benefit those still unattached.

"But how can there be a guide to such a frightful labyrinth?" I inquired curiously. "Japhet in search of a father had a light task before him compared with the selection of one. And it is not only the selection of a father, but of a mother! To take the outside variations only: the father may be handsome, good-looking, plain or ugly; the mother may be beautiful, pretty, plain or ugly. Any of these types of fathers may be paired with any of these types of mothers, which makes sixteen complications. Then there is complexion—fair or dark—which makes sixty-four, for you know how, by algebraic calculations, every new possibility multiplies into all the others. If one turns to mental and moral characteristics, one's brain swims to think of the new complications incalculably numerous and all multiplying into the old physical combinations. Multiply furthermore by all the combinations arising from considerations of health, money, position, nationality, religion, order of birth—whether as first, second, or thirteenth child—and the strongest intellect reels and breaks down. Even now I have not enumerated all the possibilities; for the total would have to be doubled for the contingency of sex, since I presume birth would not be absolutely free, unless it included the right of choosing one's sex.

"To take a concrete instance of the embarrassment which Free Birth would bring, and of the invidious distinctions that would have to be made: which is the better lot?—to be the third daughter of a nineteenth-century, healthy, ugly, penniless, clever, middle-aged, moral, free-thinking German Baron by a beautiful, rich, stupid, plebeian Spanish dancer, with one child by a previous marriage, and a tendency to consumption; or the second son of a twentieth-century American Duke, unhealthy, uncultured, handsome, chaste, Ritualist, elderly and poor, by an English heiress, ugly, low-born, Low Church, ill-bred, intellectual, with a silly and only semi-detached mother? But this would be a problem of unreal simplicity, bearing as much relation to actuality as the first law of motion to the flight of a bird, for your choice would lie not between one pair and another, but among all possible pairs."

"All existing pairs possible to you," corrected Marindin. "People manage to choose husbands and wives, though according to your computation the whole of the opposite sex would have to be examined and selected from. In practice the choice is narrowed down to a few individuals. So with the choice of parents—most are already snapped up, monopolised or mortgaged, or contracted for, and you have either to choose from the leavings or postpone your birth, and bide your time a century or two. But the problem is greatly simplified by the P. C."

"What is the P. C.?" I murmured.

"The Parental Certificate, of course. Throughout the terrestrial branch of our sect no one is eligible for parentage who does not possess it. It is given only to those who have passed the P. D. or Parents' Degree examination, and supplements the old P. L. or Parents' Licence, which was openly bought and sold."

"And the qualifications?"

"Oh, very elementary. The candidate is required to pass an exam, (both written and oral) in the training of the young, and to be certified of sound mind in sound body. The P. L. itself has been transformed into a licence to keep one, two or more children, according to means."

"You see our 'Guide' deals merely with the great typical pairs," explained the publisher. "What Aristotle did for Logic our author has done for Birth. He only pretends to give general categories. Aristotle could not guarantee a man shall properly reason, nor can any individual be infallibly inspired to the wisest choice of parentage. Of course the photographs of parents are of great service to the unborn who are thinking of settling down."

"How do they get to see them?"

"Oh, as soon as a couple passes the P. D. and receives the P. C. they appear in the illustrated papers—especially the ladies' papers. 'Graduates of the Week' is the heading. And then there is the P. T.—the Pathological Tree."

I looked at the publisher in perplexity.

"Gracious! I forget this is your first visit to Ante-land," he said, apologetically. "Look! Here are some P. Ts. my lawyer has just been looking over for me, the property of parents whose advertisements for children I have been answering. My friends are rather anxious I should incarnate."

I surveyed the parchment roll with curiosity. It was a tree, on the model of a genealogical tree, but tracing the hygienic record of the family.

"In our sect," said Marindin impressively, "it will become the pride of the family to have an unblemished pedigree, and any child who gets himself born into such a family will do so with the responsibility of carrying on the noble tradition of the house and living up to the sanitary scutcheon—santé oblige. When children begin to be fastidious about the families they are born into, parents will have to improve, or die childless. And, as the love of offspring springs eternal in the human breast, this will have an immense influence upon the evolution of the race to higher goals. I do not know any force of the future on which we can count more hopefully than on the refinement resulting from the struggle for offspring and the survival of the fittest to be parents. Undesirable families will become extinct. The unborn will subtly mould the born to higher things. Childlessness will become again what it was in the Orient—a shame and a reproach."

"Yes," asserted the publisher, smoothing out the P. Ts.; "the old unreasoned instinct and repugnance will be put on a true basis when it is seen that childlessness is a proof of unworthiness—a brand of failure."

"As old-maidenhood is, less justly, to-day," I put in.

"Quite so," said Marindin eagerly. "In their anxiety to be worthy of selection by Posterity, parents will rise to heights of health and holiness of which our sick generation does not dream. If they do not, woe to them! They will be remorselessly left to die out without issue.

"The change has begun; our sect is spreading fast. In the course of a century or two physical and mental deformities will vanish from the earth." His eye flashed prophetic fire.

"So soon?" I said, with a sceptical smile.

"How could they survive?" Marindin inquired scathingly.

"Is it likely any of us would consent to be born hunchbacks?" broke in the publisher; "or to enter families with hereditary gout? Would any sane Antelander put himself under the yoke of animal instincts or tendencies to drink? Ah, here is a bibulous grandfather!" and he tossed one of the P. Ts. disdainfully aside, though I observed that the old gentleman in question had been an English Earl.

"But, Mr. Fore," I protested, "will all the unborn attach such importance to the pathological pedigree as you do? What power will make them train up their parents in the way they should go?"

"The greatest power on earth," broke in Marindin; "the power of selfishness, backed by education. Enlightened selfishness is all that is needed to bring about the millennium. The selfishness of to-day is so stupid. Let the unborn care only for their own skins, and they will improve the parents, and be well brought up themselves by the good parents they have selected."

"But come now, Mr. Fore," I said; "the new system has been partially at work, I understand, for some time. Do you assure me, on your word of honor as an unborn publisher, that the filial franchise has been invariably exercised wisely and well?"

"Of course not," interrupted Marindin. "Haven't I already told you there has been much fumbling and experimentation, some souls being born for money and some for beauty and some for position? But pioneers must always suffer—for the benefit of those who come after."

"Certainly there have been rash and improvident births," admitted the publisher. "Hasty births, premature births, secret births, morganatic births, illegitimate births, and every variety of infelicitous intrusion upon your planet. The rash are born too early, the cautious too late; some even repent on the very brink of birth and elect to be stillborn. But in the majority of cases birth is the outcome of mature deliberation; a contract entered into with a full sense of the responsibilities of the situation."

"But what do you understand by illegitimate birth?" I asked.

"The selection of parents not possessing the P. C. There are always eccentric spirits who would defy the dearest and most sacred institutions organised by society for its own protection. We are gradually creating a public opinion to discountenance such breaches of the law, and such perils to the commonweal, subversive as they are of all our efforts to promote the general happiness and holiness. Even in your uncivilised communities," continued the publisher, "these unlicensed and illegitimate immigrants are stamped with life-long opprobrium and subjected to degrading disabilities; how much infamy should then attach to them when the sin they are born in is their own!"

"A lesser degree of illegitimacy," added Marindin, "is to be born into a family already containing the full number it is licensed for. This happens particularly in rich families, introductions into which are naturally most sought after. It is still a moot point whether the birth should be legitimatised on the death of one of the other children."

"But it is the indirect results that I look forward to most," he went on after a pause. "For example, the solution of Nihilism in Russia."

"What has that to do with the unborn?" I asked, quite puzzled.

"Don't you see that the czarship will die out?"

"How so?"

"No one will risk being born into the Imperial family. I should say that birth within four degrees of consanguinity of the Czar would be so rare that it would come to be regarded as criminal."

"Yes, that and many another question will be solved quite peaceably," said the publisher. "You saw me reject a noble grandfather; the growth of democratic ideals among us must ultimately abolish hereditary aristocracy. So, too, the question of second marriages and the deceased wife's sister may be left to the taste and ethical standards of the unborn, who can easily, if they choose, set their faces against such unions."

"You see the centre of gravity would be shifted to the pre-natal period," explained Marindin, "when the soul is more liable to noble influences. The moment the human being is born it is definitely moulded; all your training can only modify the congenital cast. But the real potentialities are in the unborn. While there is not life there is hope. When you commence to educate the child it is already too late. But if the great forces of education are brought to bear upon the unformed, you may bring all Itigh qualities to birth. Think, for instance, how this will contribute to the cause of religion. The unborn will simply eliminate the false religions by refusing to be born into them. Persuade the unborn, touch them, convert them! You, I am sure, Mr. Fore," he said, turning to the worthy publisher, "would never consent to be born into the wrong religion!"

"Not if hell-fire was the penalty of an unhappy selection," replied Mr. Fore.

"Of course not," said Marindin. "Missionaries have always flown in the face of psychology. Henceforward, moreover, Jews will be converted at a period more convenient for baptism."

"We hope to mould politics, too," added the publisher, "by boycotting certain races and replenishing others."

"Yes," cried Marindin; "it is my hope that by impregnating the unborn with a specific set of prejudices, they might be induced to settle in particular countries, and I cannot help thinking that patriotism would be more intelligent when it was voluntary; self-imposed from admiration of the ideals and history of a particular people. Indeed this seems to me absolutely the only way in which, reason can be brought to bear on the great war question, for in lieu of that loud eloquence of Woolwich infants there would be exercised the silent pressure of the unborn, who could simply annihilate an undesirable nation, or decimate an offensive district by refusing to be born in it. Surely this would be the most rational way of settling the ever-menacing Franco-Prussian quarrel."

"I observe already a certain anti-Gallic feeling in Ante-land," put in the publisher. "A growing disinclination to be born in France, if not a preference for being made in Germany. But these things belong to la haute politique"

"My own suspicion is," I ventured to suggest, "that there is a growing disinclination to be born anywhere, and this new privilege of free choice will simply bring matters to a climax. Your folks, confronted by the endless problem of choosing their own country and century, their own family and their own religion, will dilly-dally and shilly-shally and put off birth so long that they will never change their condition at all. They will come to the conviction that it is better not to be born; better to bear the evils that they know than fly to others that they know not of. What if the immigration of destitute little aliens into our planet ceased altogether?"

Marindin shrugged his shoulders, and there came into his face that indescribable look of the hopeless mystic.

"Then humanity would have reached its goal: it would come naturally and gently to an end. The euthanasia of the race would be accomplished, and the glorified planet, cleansed of wickedness at last, would take up its part again in the chorus of the spheres. But like most ideals, I fear this is but a pleasant dream." Then, as the publisher turned away to replace the P. Ts. in a safe, he added softly: "Intelligence is never likely to be so widely diffused in Ante-land that the masses would fight shy of birth. There would always be a sufficient proportion of unborn fools left who would prefer the palpabilities of bodily form to the insubstantialities of pre-natal existence. Between you and me, our friend the publisher is extremely anxious to be published."

"And yet he seems intelligent enough," I argued.

"Ah, well, it cannot be denied that there are some lives decidedly worth living, and our friend Fore will probably bring up his parents to the same profession as himself."

"No doubt there would always be competition for the best births," I observed, smiling.

"Yes," replied Marindin sadly; "the struggle for existence will always continue among the unborn."

Suddenly a thought set me a-grin. "Why, what difference can the choice of parents make after all?" I cried. "Suppose you had picked my parents—you would have been I, and I should be somebody else, and somebody else would be you. And there would be the three of us, just the same as now," and I chuckled aloud.

"You seem to have had pleasant dreams, old man," replied Marindin. But his voice sounded strange and far away.

I opened my eyes wide in astonishment, and saw him buried in an easy-chair, with a book in his hand and two tears rolling down his cheeks.

"I've been reading of Tiny Tim while you snoozed," he said apologetically.

XXIII

PATER AND PROSE

It seems only yesterday—and it is only yesteryear—since Walter Pater sat by my side in a Club garden, and listened eloquently to my after-lunch causerie, and now he is gone

To where, beyond the Voices, there is Peace.

You grasp that his eloquence was oracular, silent. He had an air. There was in him—as in his work—a suggestion of aloofness from the homespun world. I suspect he had never heard Chevalier. I should not wonder if he had never even heard of him. He was wrapped in the atmosphere of Oxford, and though "the last enchantments of the Middle Ages" in no wise threw their glamour over his thought, there was a cloistral distinction in his attitude. He reminded me of my friend the Cambridge professor, who, when the O'Shea business was filling eight columns daily of the papers that deprecate honest art, innocently asked me if there was anything new about Parnell. Pater did not probably carry detachment from the contemporary so far as that, but he was in harmony with his hedonistic creed in permitting only a select fraction of the cosmos to have the entry to his consciousness. A delightful, elegantly-furnished consciousness it was, with the latest improvements, and with every justification for exclusiveness. But there is in men of Mr. Pater's stamp something of what might be termed the higher Pod-snappery. They put things aside with the wave of a white-gloved hand: this and that do not exist, Mr. Podsnap himself— O the irony of it!—among them. Like Mr. Podsnap, though on a different plane, they take themselves and their view of life too seriously. When I told Mr. Pater that there was a pun in his "Plato and Platonism," he asked anxiously for its precise locality, so that he might remove it. This I could not remember, but I told him I did not see why he should remove one of the best things in the book. But my assurances that the pun was excellent did not seem to tranquillise him. Now, why should not a philosopher make a pun? Shakespeare was an incorrigible punster. Why should a man's life be divided into little artificial sections, like the labelled heads in the phrenologist's window? I do not want to see a man put on his Sunday clothes to talk about religion. But a congenital inelasticity is fostered in the atmosphere of common-rooms, there where solemn-footed serving-men present the port with sacerdotal ceremonies, and where, if the dons are no longer (in the classic phrase of Gibbon) "sunk in port and superstition," the port is still a superstition. This absence of humour, this superhuman seriousness bred of heavy traditions peculiarly English, this sobriety nourished by sacerdotal port, give the victim quite a wrong sense of values and proportions. He mistakes University for Universe. His tastes become the measure of a creation of which he is the centre. Hence an abiding gravity that is ever on the brink of dulness. The Englishman cannot afford to be grave, the bore is so close at hand.

And yet, if one did not take oneself seriously, I suppose nothing would ever be done. A kindly illusion about their importance in the scheme of things is Nature's instrument for getting work out of men. "Don't you think Flaubert took himself too seriously?" I heard a lady novelist ask a gentleman practitioner. Certainly his correspondence with George Sand reveals an anchorite of letters, who tortured the phrase and sacrificed sleep to the adjective, and the brothers De Goncourt—themselves very serious gentlemen—have recorded how he considered his book as good as finished because he had invented the "dying falls" of the music of his periods. But if Flaubert had sufficiently contemplated the infinities, the immense indifference of things, if, like the astronomer in search of a creed, he had concentrated his vision on the point to which the whole solar system is drifting, French prose would have lost some of its most wonderful pages; and had the late Mr. Pater been less troubled by the rose-leaf of style and more by the thorns of the time, English prose would have been the poorer by harmonies and felicities unsurpassed and unsurpassable. This is to ignore Pater the Philosopher and Pater the Critic. Of these persons there will be varying estimates. They have even in a sense, through the extravagances of a disciple, been subjected to the verdict of a British jury—a sufficiently ironic revenge upon the fastidious shrinker from the Philistines; and though, of course, it was not theories of art and philosophy that were being "tried by jury," yet these side-issues contributed to prejudice the twelve good men and true. But it is only congruous with the trend of democratic thought that everything should come under the censorship of the crowd, and the only wonder is that long ere this the vexed questions of our troubled time have not been solved by plébiscite.

A leading New York paper is commended for its patronage of literature, because it offers large prizes for stories, the prizes to be awarded by the votes of its readers. If the crowd is capable of appraising literature, there is no reason why it should not take science and art similarly into its hands, nor why the counting of heads should not replace the marshalling of arguments in philosophy and ethics. In politics the mob has a right to be heard, because it has a right to express its grievances. Could an aristocracy be trusted to do justly by Demos, democracy would have no reason to be. But this right of the many-headed monster to a control of the governmental agencies that affect its own happiness, does not involve the ability to decide less selfish problems; and when, as rarely happens, abstract problems find themselves in the witness-box, then the "Palladium of British liberty" becomes a mockery of justice. "Legal judgment of his peers," says Magna Charta; but when an exceptional man blunders into the dock, is he ever accorded a panel of his equals? Things are no better in France. When Flaubert was arraigned for his "Madame Bovary," he did not get a box of men of letters, though there is so much more sense of art in the citizens of Paris, that even by the bourgeois jury he was acquitted without a stain on the character of his book. The central figure of our English episode had nothing so creditable as an immoral book to his charge, but indirectly the relations of art and morality came into question, and he declared that he followed Pater, the one critic he recognised, in believing that there were no relations between art and morality, that a book could not be immoral, but might be something worse—badly written. Now, this is the favourite doctrine of Chelsea, and doubtless something may be said for it; but to put it forth, as the doctrine of Pater is a libel—almost a criminal libel—on that great writer. These young men who live for the Beautiful have only understood as much of Pater as would justify epicurean existence.

Let us examine this pretension of the prophet of the importance of being flippant, to be a disciple of Pater.

No doubt Pater was something of an Impressionist in his philosophy of life. An eloquent expounder of the Heracletian flux, [Greek: panta rei], of the relativity of systems of thought and conduct, and of the duty of seizing the flying moments—"failure in life is to form habits,"—he did not omit, like his one-sided disciples, to consider the quality of those moments. It was the highest quality you were to give to your moments as they passed; to fail to do this was "on this short day of frost and sun to sleep before evening." ("The Renaissance.") "Marius the Epicurean" was not an Epicurean in the sense in which the doctrines of Epicurus have been travestied through the ages: he turned away sickened from the barbarities of the gladiatorial combats, longing for the time when the forces of the future would create a heart that would make it impossible to be thus pleasured. If "Carpe diem" is Pater's motto, the hour is not to be plucked ignobly; if style is his watchword in art, style alone cannot make great Art, though it may make good Art. The distinction, between good Art and great Art depends immediately not on its form but on its matter. "It is on the quality of the matter it informs or controls, its compass, its variety, its alliance to great ends, or the depth of the note of revolt, or the largeness of hope in it, that the greatness of literary art depends, as 'The Divine Comedy,' 'Paradise Lost,' 'Les Misérables,' the English Bible, are great art." ("Essay on Style.") Your Chelsea manikin would never dream of these things as great art: his whole soul is expressed in ballads and canzonets, in strange esoteric contes, in nocturnes and colour-symphonies, in the bric-à-brac of aesthetics. Furthermore let the soi-disant disciples ponder this explicit statement of the Master: "Given the conditions I have tried to explain as constituting good art—then, if it be devoted further to the increase of men's happiness, to the redemption of the oppressed, or the enlargement of our sympathies with each other, or to such presentment of new or old truth about ourselves and our relation to the world as may ennoble and fortify us in our sojourn here, or immediately, as with Dante, to the glory of God, it will also be great Art." Yes, if Pater protested against "the vulgarity which is dead to form," he was no less contemptuous of "the stupidity which is dead to the substance." ("Postscript to Appreciations.") If he fought shy of the Absolute, if he denied "fixed principles," and repudiated "every formula less living and flexible than life" ("Essay on Coleridge"), he could still sympathise passionately with Coleridge's hunger for the Eternal.

So much for the literary art. But even in painting, where the self-sufficiency of style is proclaimed somewhat more speciously, the purveyor of Chelsea ware will find scant countenance in the adored Master. Nowhere can I find him preaching "Art for Art's sake," in the jejune sense of the empty-headed acolytes of the aesthetic. With him the formula was for the spectator of art; it has been misapplied to the maker of art. Pater's studies of the great pictures of the Renaissance are, if anything, rather too much taken up with their intellectual content, and their latent revelation of the temper of the time and the artist. No, these young men are no disciples of Pater. In their resoluteness to live in the Beautiful (which is not always distinguishable from the Bestial), they have forgotten the other items of the trinity of Goethe, they have lost sight of the True and the Whole. It is Whistler who is the prophet of the divorce of Art from Life, of the antithesis of Art and Nature. When Whistler said, "Another foolish sunset," he spake the word that called into being all these "degenerate" paradoxes, though I am not sure but what Mr. Sydney Grundy was before him in creating a stage-manager who thinks meanly of the moons and the scenic backgrounds of real life. It is a good joke, this of Nature paling before Art, or reduced to plagiarising Art—"Where, if not from the Impressionists, do we get those wonderful brown fogs that come creeping down our streets, blurring the gas lamps and changing the houses into monstrous shadows?"—but as the basis of a philosophy of Art it palls. The germ of truth in it is that metaphysically these effects may be said not to have existed till artists taught us to see and to look for them. But, after all, wise old Shakespeare has the last word:

Nature is made better by no mean
But Nature makes that mean: so o'er that Art,

Which you say adds to Nature, is an Art
That Nature makes.

But these things are not for the British jury. Pater, the literary artist, however, one is more driven to praise than to appraise. This exquisite care for words has something of moral purity—as well as physical daintiness in it. There is indeed something priestly in this consecration of language, in this reverent ablution of the counters of thought, those poor counters so overcrusted with the dirt of travel, so loosely interchangeable among the vulgar; the figure of the stooping devotee shows sublime in a garrulous world. What a heap of mischief M. Jourdain has done by his discovery that he was talking prose all his life! Prose, indeed! Moliere has much to answer for. The rough, shuffling, slipshod, down-at-heel, clipped, frayed talk of every-day life bears as much relation to prose as a music-hall ditty to poetry. The name "prose" must be reserved for the fine art of language—that fine art whose other branch is poetry. It is a grammarians' term, "prose," and belongs not to the herd. They do not need it, and it would never have come into M. Jourdain's head or out of his mouth, had he not taken a tutor. And yet the delusion is common enough—even with those to whom Moliere is Greek—that prose is anything which is not poetry. As well say that poetry is anything which is not prose. Of the two branches of the art of language, prose is the more difficult. This is not the opinion of those who know nothing about it. They fancy a difficulty about rhymes and metres. 'T is all the other way. Rhymes are the rudders of thought; they steer the poet's bark. He cannot get to Heaven itself without striking "seven," or mixing up his meaning with foreign "leaven." His shifts to avoid these shifts are pathetic to a degree. He flounders about twixt "given" and "levin," and has been known to snatch desperately at "reaven." Of all fraudulent crafts commend me to the poet's. He is a paragon of deceit and quackery, a jingling knave. 'T is a game of bouts rimés, and he calls it "inspiration." No wonder Plato would have none of him in his Republic, even though Plato's poets were guiltless of rhyme and slaves only to metre. But the metre of verse, too, is a friend to thought, and its enemy. It is like wheels to a cart; not unsagaciously is Pegasus figured with wings. He flies away with you, and you are lulled by the regular flap, flap of his pinions, and his goal concerns you little. The swing and the rush of the verse compensate for reason, and it is wonderful how far a little sense will fly when tricked out with fine feathers. Even in stately, rhymeless decasyllabics the march and music of the verse help a limping thought along like a sore-footed soldier striding to the band. But the prose-writer has none of these advantages. He is like an actor without properties. His thoughts do not go along with a flutter of flags and a blare of trombones. Nor do they glide upon castors. They must needs lumber on after a fashion of their own, and if there is a music to their ambulation it must be individual, neither in common nor in three-eight time, but winding and quickening at will, with no strait symmetry of antiphonal bars. There is nothing to tell you the writer has made "prose"—as the spacing and the capital letters invite you to look for poetry. He has to depend only upon himself. This is why blank verse—which approaches prose most nearly—is so much more difficult to write than rhymed verse, though it looks so much easier and more tempting to the amateur. Are we not justified, then, in taking the logical step further, and saying that prose, which strips itself of the last rags of adventitious ornament, and which tempts the amateur most of all, is the highest of all literary forms, the most difficult of all to handle triumphantly? May we not compare the music of it—that music which we get in Ruskin and in Pater—to the larger rhythms to which the savage drum-beat has developed? Rhythm is undoubtedly an instinct, but civilisation brings complexity. From the tom-tom to the tune, from the tune to the symphony. In the vaster reaches and sweeps of the rhythm of prose there is a massive music as of Wagnerian orchestras. Anybody can enjoy the castanet-play of rhymes; half your popular proverbs clash at the ends; "the jigging of our rhyming mother-wits" is on everybody's lips. But for the blank verse of "Paradise Lost" there is only "audience fit, though few"; and as for the music of prose, so little is it understood that critics vaguely aware of it had to invent the term "prose poet" when they found the stress of passion and imagination effervescing into resonant utterance. On the other hand, there are those who do not acknowledge Pope as a poet. The essence of the long-standing quarrel is a confusion. From the point of view of form there is only one kind of writer to be recognised—the artist in words. Of him there are two varieties: the artist who uses rhyme and metre, and the artist who—wilfully or through impotence—dispenses with them. From the point of view of matter there is the artist with "soul" and the artist without "soul." "Soul" is shorthand for that mysterious something the absence of which urges people to deny Pope the title of poet. They feel the intangible something is not there, "the consecration and the poet's dream." But with the conventional distinctions, there is no name left for Pope, if he is not a poet. The truth is that he was an artist in words—as masterly as the Mantuan himself, though without that golden cadence and charm which keep Virgil a poet by any classification. On the other hand, Carlyle, who had such scorn of the rhyming crew, was himself a poet to the popular imagination, though to us he will be an artist in prose plus soul. There are, thus, really two classes of writers:

I. Prose-Artists. II. Verse-Artists.

Each of these splits up into two kinds, according as the writer has or lacks "soul." Or, if you think "soul" the more important differentia, we will say there are artists with "soul" and artists without "soul," and that some of each sort work in prose and some in verse. But the classification is a crass one, and the English language unfortunately does not possess words to express the distinctions, while the ambiguous associations of the word "prose" increase the difficulty of inventing them. We do not even possess any equivalent of the French "prosateur," though I see no reason why "prosator" should not be used. Without neologisms, and avoiding the ambiguous adjective "prosaic," and using "poetic" to express "soulfulness" and not the handling of metres, we get

1. Poetic Verse-Artists. (Poets.)

2. Non-Poetic Verse-Artists. (Verse-Writers.)

3. Poetic Prose-Artists. (Prose Poets.)

4. Non-Poetic Prose-Artists. (Prose Writers.)

Keats is a verse poet, Pope a verse writer, Buskin a prose poet, and Hallam a prose writer.

The two great writers of our day who have sinned most against the laws of writing are Browning and Meredith, the one in verse, the other in prose. I speak not merely of obscurities, to perpetrate which is in every sense to stand in one's own light, but of sheer fatuities, tweakings-of-the-nose to our reverend mother-tongue, as either might have expressed it. But what I am most concerned to suggest here is that the distinction between prose and poetry (using prose to mean artistically wrought language) will not survive investigation. The popular instinct has long ago seen that the vital thing is the matter—that it is profanity to call that "poetry" which is only verse; it remains to be recognised that even the distinction of form rests only on the non-recognition of the rhythm of "prose,"—a rhythm that is not metre in so far as metre has the sense of regular measure, but may for all that have laws of its own, which await the discoverer and the systematiser.

The affinity of prose-rhythms is, I have hinted, with the higher developments of music, which, compared with the simple tunes of the street, are as apparently lawless and unlicensed as is prose compared to verse. And as it is not poets who follow laws, but precede them—as trochee and iambic, alcaic and hexameter, are the inventions of grammarians following on the trail of genius—so it behoves the Aristotle who would discover the laws of the rhythm of prose to study the masters of the art, masters by instinct and a faultless ear and the grace of God, and endeavour by patient induction to wrest from their sentences the secrets of their harmonies. Who will write the prosody of prose?

It is sad to have to declare that the bulk of contemporary writers lie outside all these classifications. They are artists neither in prose nor verse, and though they may have "soul," they cannot make it visible. For "soul" may be expressed equally through painting and sculpture and music and acting, audits dimly discerned presence can scarcely convert slipshod writing into literature. No one would accept as art a picture in which a gleam of imagination struggled against the draughtsmanship of the schoolboy to whom arms are toasting-forks, or applaud an actor who might be brimming over with sensibility but could command neither his voice nor his face. No one has any business to come before the public who has not studied the medium through which he proposes to exhibit his "soul": unfortunately this is the age and England is the country of the amateur, and in every department we are deluged with the crude. The fault lies less with the amateur than with the public before which he presents himself, and which, incompetent to distinguish art from amateurishness, is as likely to bless the one as the other. Of all forms of art literature suffers most; for the pity is, and pity'tis't is true, everybody learns to talk and write at an early age. This makes the transition to literature so fatally easy. Facilis descensus Averni! To paint, one must at least know how to mix colours and handle a brush; to compose, one must be familiar with the meaning of strayed spiders' legs on curious parallel bars, and there are strange disconcerting rumours of "orchestration." But to produce literature you have simply to dip pen in ink or open your mouth and see what God will give you. Hence particularly the flood of novels, hence the low position of the novel; although, as Theodore Watts has pointed out, it is practically the modern Epic. I have met distinguished students of Greek texts who have never conceived of the novel as a work of art, or as anything beyond the amusement of an idle hour—something for the women and the children. One such told me he would not read "The Mill on the Floss" because it ended unhappily. I must conclude he has only read Aeschylus for his examinations. Acting stands next to literature in its seductiveness. The actor's instrument is his body, and everybody has a body. If, in addition to a "body," the creature conceives himself to possess a "soul," the odds are there will be laughter for the "gods." I tremble for the time when the popular educationist shall have had his way and every child be seised of the rudiments of drawing. We shall see sights then. At present, despite the horrors of the galleries and the widespread ignorance of art, painting cannot compete with literature as a misunderstood art. For the public—which is the only critic that counts in the long run—does not demand grammar, much less style; and the novel of the season may bristle with passages that could be set for correction at examinations in English. It is a little thing, but it seems to me significant, that the announcement of terms of the local branch of Mudie's, in the little town at which I am writing these lines, runs thus:

The subscription for one set entitles the subscriber to one complete work at a time, whether in one, two, or three volumes, and can be exchanged as often as desired.

XXIV

THE INFLUENCE OF NAMES

Far-fetched as the idea seems that names and characters have any interconnection, yet no great writer but has felt that one name, and one alone, would suit each particular creation. The tortures and travels that Balzac went through till he found "Z. Marcas" are well known. So is the agony of Flaubert on hearing that Zola was anticipating him in the name of Bouvard, which it had cost Flaubert six years' search to find. Zola's magnanimity in parting with it deserves a fauteuil. Somebody in the provinces told me that his minister had preached upon the subject of names, laying it down that in every name lurked a subtle virtue—or vice; the former the bearer of the name was in duty bound to cultivate, the latter to root out. Fantastic as this speculation be, even for a minister, no one doubts that people's names may have an influence upon their lives; and, in the case of the Christian name at least, children ought to be protected by the State against the bad taste and the cruelty of their parents. More certainly than the stars our names control our destinies, for they are no meaningless collocation of syllables, but have deep-rooted relations with the history and manner of life of our ancestors. The Smiths were once smiths, the Browns dark in complexion; and so, if we could only trace it, every name would reveal some inner significance, from Adam (red earth) downwards. Why do publishers tend to "n" in their names'? Some of the chief London publishers run to a final "n"—Macmillan, Longman, Chapman; Hodder & Stoughton; Hutchinson & Co.; Sampson Low, Marston & Co.; Lawrence & Bullen; Fisher Unwin; Heinemann. The last, indeed, is nothing but "n" sounds; such a name could not escape taking to publishing. I find also in the publishers' lists T. Nelson & Co.; Eden, Remington & Co.; Henry Sotheran; John Lane; Effingham Wilson; Innes & Co. (as fatal as Heinemann); George Allen & Co.; Osgood, McIlvaine & Co.; Gardner, Darton & Co. Sometimes the "n" is prominent at the beginning or in the middle, as in Henry & Co.; Ward & Downey; Constable & Co.; Digby, Long & Co.; Arnold; G. P. Putnam's Sons; Kegan Paul, Trench, Trübner & Co. (wherein each partner boasts his separate "n"); Oliphant, Anderson & Ferrier (wherein there are at least three "n"s); John C. Nimmo; Edward Stanford; Gibbings & Co.; Chatto & Windus; Nisbet & Co. When the "n" is not in the surname, at least the Christian contains the indispensable letter, as John Murray, Elkin Matthew.

Even when it can find refuge nowhere else the "n" creeps into the "and" of the firm or into the "Sons." The very Clarendon Press has the trademark. Who is the stock publisher of the eighteenth century? Tonson! Who were the first publishers of Shakespeare? Condell & Heminge.

And while publishers run mysteriously to "n," authors run with equal persistency to "r"—in their surnames for the most part, but at least somehow or somewhere.

Who are our professors of fiction to-day? Hardy, Meredith, Blackmore, Barrie, Rudyard Kipling, Walter Besant (and James Rice), George Moore, Frankfort Moore, Olive Schreiner, George Fleming, Henry James, Hamlin Garland, Henry B. Fuller, Harold Frederic, Frank Harris, Marion Crawford, Arthur Conan Doyle, Rider Haggard, Miss Braddon, Sarah Grand, Mrs. Parr, George Egerton, Rhoda Broughton, H. D. Traill, Jerome K. Jerome, Barry Pain, W. E. Norris, Crockett, Ian Maclaren, Robert Barr, Ashby Sterry, Morley Roberts, Mabel Robinson, F. W. Robinson, John Strange Winter, Du Maurier (late but not least to follow his lucky "r"), Helen Mathers, Henry Seton Merriman, etc., etc.

Who were the giants of the last generation? Thackeray, Charles Dickens, Charles Reade, George Eliot, Bulwer Lytton, Charlotte Brontë, Trollope, Disraeli.

Who are our prophets and thinkers? Carlyle, Ruskin, Emerson, Darwin, John Stuart Mill, Herbert Spencer, Froude, Freeman.

Who are the poets of the Victorian era? Robert Browning, Alfred Tennyson, Algernon Charles Swinburne ("r"-ed throughout), D. Gabriel Rossetti, Christina Rossetti, Matthew Arnold, William Morris, Robert

Buchanan, Andrew Lang, Robert Bridges, Lewis Morris, Edwin Arnold, Alfred Austin, Norman Gale, Richard Le Gallienne, Philip Bourke Marston, Mary F. Robinson, Theodore Watts, etc., etc.

Who are the dramatists of to-day? Grundy, Pinero, Henry Arthur Jones, W. S. Gilbert, Haddon Chambers, Comyns Carr, Carton, Raleigh, George E. Sims (mark the virtue of that long-mysterious "r").

And who in the past have done anything for our prose dramatic literature? Sheridan and Oliver Goldsmith, and, earlier still, Congreve, Wycherley, Farquhar, and Vanbrugh. Nay, which are the mighty names in our literature? Chaucer, Spenser, Marlowe, Shakespeare, Herrick, Dryden, Alexander Pope, Butler, Sterne, Byron, Wordsworth, Coleridge, Walter Scott, Robert Burns.

You may even look at the greatest names in the world's literature. Homer, Virgil (Maro), Horace, Firdusi, Omar Khayyam, Cervantes, Calderon, Petrarch, Rabelais, Dante Alighieri, Schiller, Voltaire, Rousseau, Moliere, Corneille, Racine, Honore de Balzac, Flaubert, Victor Hugo, Verlaine, Heinrich Heine.

Of course there are not a few minus the "r," as Milton, Keats, Goethe, Swift, etc., etc.

There seems indeed to be a sub-species of "sons"—Ben Jonson, Dr. Johnson, William Watson, John Davidson, Austin Dobson. Nevertheless there is an overwhelming preponderance of "r" sounds in the names of the world's authors. What is the underlying reason? Is there a certain rugged virility in the letter, which made it somehow expressive of the nature of the original owners? "N" is certainly suave and plausible in comparison, and might well produce a posterity of publishers. What adds some colour to the suspicion is that, when writers have chosen noms de guerre, they have frequently—though all unconsciously—taken names in "r." This explains why all the lady novelists run to "George." Publisher versus author may now be expressed symbolically as N/R, N over R, the N of money over the R of art.

With our artists I find a less strong tendency to "l's" as well as to "r's," and it is therefore only appropriate that a Leighton should long preside over the Royal Academy, a Millais be its chief ornament, and finally its head, and a Whistler its chief omission; that constable and Walker should be the glory of English art, that Reynolds should be our national portrait-painter, and Landseer our animal-painter, and Wilkie our domestic painter. Turner made up for his surname by the superfluity of "l's" in his William Mallord, Raphael starts as an R. A., while Michael Angelo, with his predominance in "l's," is rightly king of art. The absence of "l" in Hogarth's name and the strong presence of "r" of course denotes that the satirist was more of a literary man than an artist. The "r" in Whistler, on the other hand, clearly indicates the literary faculty of the author of "The Gentle Art of Making Enemies." And if Du Maurier's real future was hinted in his orthography, Leech and Tenniel and Phil May and Linley Sambourne have vindicated their "l's." So have Luke Fildes, Alma Tadema, H. T. Wells, G. D. Leslie, John Collier, Val Prinsep, Solomon J. Solomon, Frank Bramley, Phil Morris, Calderon, Leader, Nettleship, Seymour Lucas, Waterlow, William Strutt, Albert Moore, W. W. Ouless, C. W. Wyllie, Sir John Gilbert, Louise Jopling, Onslow Ford, and even W. C. Horsley. There are only three foreign Academicians at the time of writing, but they all boast the "l."

With musicians there is a tendency to "m's" and "n's," which sounds harmonious enough, Mendelssohn, Massenet, Mascagni, Mackenzie, Schumann, have both letters; Mozart but one. Haydn, Beethoven, Chopin, Saint-Saëns, Sullivan, Charles Salaman, Edward Solomon, Frederic Cowen, run "n"-wards with the unanimity of publishers, while Gounod, Stanford, Audran, Sebastian Bach, Donizetti, work in the "n" otherwise, and Wagner has the librettist's "r" in addition. Would you play the piano? You must have the "n" of the piano, like Pachmann, Rubinstein, Rosenthal, Hofmann, Frederick Dawson, Madame

Schumann, Fanny Davies, Agnes Zimmermann, Leonard Borwick, Nathalie Janotha, Sapellnikoff, Sophie Menter. Even for other instruments, including the human voice divine, the "n" is advisable. Paganini, Jenny Lind, Norman Néruda, Christine Nilsson—all patronized it largely. Adelina Patti, Johannes Wolf, and many others make a "Christian" use of it. If, on the other hand, you wish to manufacture pianos your chance of founding a first-class firm will be largely enhanced if your name begins with "b."

Actors, like authors, roll their "r's"; and if their names are pseudonyms, so much the greater proof that some occult instinct makes them elect for that virile letter. Who are our leading actors and actor-managers? The double-r's: Henry Irving, Herbert Beerbohm Tree (two pairs), Forbes-Robertson, George Alexander, Arthur Roberts, Edward S. Willard, Edward Terry, Charles Brookfield, Wilson Barrett, Fred Terry, Fred Kerr, Charles Warner, W. Terriss, George Grossmith, Charles Hawtrey, Arthur Bourchier (two pairs). Scarcely any leading actor lacks one "r," as Charles Wyndham, Cyril Maude, Louis Waller, etc., etc. Those without any "r's" may console themselves with the memory of Edmund Kean, though Garrick—a name almost wholly compact of "r"—is the patron saint of the stage.

The ladies follow the gentlemen. From Ellen Terry and Winifred Emery to Ada Rehan and Mrs. Patrick Campbell, from Rose Leclercq and Marie Bancroft to Marion Terry and Irene Vanbrugh, few dare dispense with the "r."

But I have said enough. I have opened up new perspectives for the curious and the philosophic, which they may follow up for themselves. Here is a fresh field for faddists and mystagogues. Already I have proved as much as many systems of mediaeval philosophy which strove to extract the essence of things from the study of words and letters. Already I have collected more evidence than the sectarians of the Shakespeare-Bacon. Bacon write Shakespeare, indeed! A man without an "r" to his name, pointed out by his "n" for a publisher, and, indeed, not without some of the characteristics of the class. Seriously, the truth is that l, m, n, and r are the leading letters in name-making; but still there does seem to be more in the coincidence to which I have drawn attention than mere accident explains.

XXV

AUTHORS AND PUBLISHERS

It is done. The publishers have formed a League. The poor sweated victims of the author's greed have at last turned upon the oppressor. Mr. Gosse, on a memorable occasion, confusedly blending the tones of the prophet of righteousness with the accents of the political economist, admonished the greedy author that he was killing the goose with the golden eggs. And now the goose has resolved to be a goose no longer. The Authors' Society, a sort of trade union, has been answered by the creation of a Publishers' Union, with all the delightful potentialities of a literary lock-out. It is time, therefore, for a person without prejudice to say a word to both sides.

With the spirit which prompted the creation of the Authors' Society, Literature has nothing to do. To define Literature exactly is not easy. To say at what point words become or cease to be literature is a problem similar in kind to the sophistical Greek puzzle of saying at what point the few become many. Perhaps we shall find a solution by looking at the genesis and history of written words. Literature, we find, began as religion. The earliest books of every nation are sacred books. Herbert Spencer dwells on the veneration which the average person feels for the printed word, his almost touching belief in books and newspapers. "I read it in a book" is equivalent to saying "It is certainly true." The great philosopher has failed to see that this instinct is a survival from the times when the only books were holy books. The first book published in Europe, as soon as printing was invented, was the Latin Bible—the Mazarin Bible as it is called; and it is the Bible which is responsible for the belief in print. Despite the degradation of the printed word to-day, there is something fine in this tenacious popular instinct, as there is something ignoble in all Literature which palters with it. The Literature of every country is still sacred. The books of its sages and seers should still be holy books to it. The true man of letters always was and must always be a lay priest, even though he seem neither to preach nor to be religious in the popular sense of those terms. The qualities to be sought for in Literature are therefore inspiration and sincerity. The man of letters is born, not made. His place is in the Temple, and it is not his fault that the moneychangers have set up their stalls there. But, in addition to these few chosen spirits, born in every age to be its teachers, there is an overwhelming multitude of writers called into being by the conditions of the time. These are the artists whom Stevenson likened to the "Daughters of Joy." They are cunning craftsmen, turning out what the public demands, without any priestly consciousness, and sometimes even without conscience, mere tradesmen with—at bottom—the souls of tradesmen. Their work has charm, but lacks significance. They write essays which are merely amusing, histories which are only facts, and stories which are only lies.

The capacity of the world for reading the uninspired is truly astonishing, and the hundred worst books may be found in every bookseller's window. Would that it were of books that Occam had written: "Non sunt multiplicandi praeter necessitatem"! The men who produce these unnecessary books perform a necessary function, as things are. Why should they be less well treated than bootmakers or tailors, butchers or bakers or candlestick makers? Why should they not get as much as possible for their labours? Why should they not, like every other kind of working-man, found a Labour Union? Indeed, instead of censuring these authors for trying to obtain a fair wage, I feel rather inclined to reproach them for not having more closely imitated the methods of Trades-Unionism, for not having welded the whole writing body into a strong association for the enforcement of fair prices and the suppression of sweating, which is more monstrous and wide-spread in the literary than in any other profession whatever. Such an organisation would be met by many difficulties, for writing differs from other species of skilled labour by the immense differences of individual talent, while from professions in which there are parallel variations of skill, e.g., law and medicine, it differs by the fact that there is no initial qualification (by examination) attesting a minimum amount of skill. Not even grammar is necessary for authorship, or even for successful authorship. Besides which, writing is done by innumerable persons in their spare time—Literature is a world of inky-fingered blacklegs. Thus, writing admits neither of the union-fixed minimum wage of the manual labourer, nor of the etiquette-fixed fee of the professional; so that the methods of the trade union are only partially applicable to the ink-horny-handed sons of toil. But even the possible has not yet been achieved, so that the current idea of an organization of the writing classes, against which publishers have had to gird up their loins to fight, has very little foundation. There is nothing but a registered disorganisation. What the publishers are really afraid of is not a Society, but a man, and that man a middle-man? no other than that terrible bogey, the agent, who drinks champagne out of their skulls.

So much for the author-craftsman. But what of the author-priest? Do the commercial conditions apply to him? Certainly they do—with this important modification, that, while with the author-craftsman the commercial conditions may justly regulate the matter and manner of his work, with the author-priest the commercial conditions do not begin until he has completed his work. The state of the market, the condition of the public mind—these will have no influence on the work itself. Not a comma nor a syllable will he alter for all the gold of Afric. But, the manuscript once finished, the commercial considerations begin. The prophet has written his message, but the world has yet to hear it. Now, we cannot easily conceive Isaiah or Jeremiah hawking round his prophecies at the houses of publishers, or permitting a smart Yankee to syndicate them through the world, or even allowing popular magazines to dribble them out by monthly instalments. But the modern prophet has no housetop, and it is as difficult to imagine him moving his nation by voice alone as arranging with a local brother-seer to trumpet forth the great tidings simultaneously at New York in order to obtain the American copyright. Even if he should try to teach the people by word of mouth, there will be bare benches unless he charges for admission, as all lecturers will tell you. People value at nothing what they can get for nothing; and, as Stevenson suggested, "if we were charged so much a head for sunsets, or if God sent round a drum before the hawthorns came in flower, what a work should we not make about their beauty!" No, the prophet cannot escape the commercial question. For, in order that his message may reach his age, it must be published, and publication cannot be achieved without expense.

Tolstoï himself, who gives his books freely to the world, cannot really save the public the expense of buying them. All he sacrifices is that comparatively small proportion of the returns which is claimed by the author in royalties; he cannot eliminate the profits of the publisher, the bookseller, etc., etc. For between the message and its hearers come a great number of intermediaries, many of them inevitable. We will assume for the purposes of our analysis that our prophet is already popular. The hearers are waiting eagerly. Here is the manuscript, there are the readers. Problem—to bring them together. This is the task of the publisher. Incidentally, the publisher employs the printer, bookbinder, etc.; but this part of the business, though usually undertaken by the publisher, does not necessarily belong to him. He is essentially only the distributor. In return for this function of distribution, whether it includes supervising mechanical production or not, the publisher is entitled to his payment. How much? Evidently, exactly as much as is made by capital and personal service in business generally. The shillings of the public are the gross returns for the book. These have to be divided between all the agents employed in producing the book—author, printer, binder, publisher, bookseller, etc. This is not literally what happens, but it is arithmetically true in the long run. How much for each? Evidently just as much as they can each get, for there is no right but might and nothing but tug-of-war. There is nothing absolute in the partition of profits: infinite action and reaction. While the costs of the mechanical part are comparatively stable, the relation of author and publisher oscillates ceaselessly; and while the cautious publisher by the multiplicity of his transactions may rely upon an average of profits, like all business men plucking stability out of the heart of vicissitude, the author has no such surety. Between merit and reward there is in literature no relation. Just as the music-hall singer may earn a larger income than the statesman, so may the tawdry tale-teller drive the thinker and artist out of the market.

The artistic value of a book is therefore absolutely unrelated to the commercial value; but such commercial value as there is—to whom should it fall if not to the author? Like the other parties, he has a right to all he can get. You will say it is very sordid to think of money; you will speak of divine inspiration; you would rather see him go on the rates; to save him from base reward you even borrow his books instead of buying them; you cannot understand why he should prefer an honest Copyright Act to a halo. Good! Put it that I agree with you. It is sordid to sell one's muse. One should be like Mr. Harold Skimpole, and let the butcher and the baker go howl. The thought of money sullies the fairest manuscript. The touch of a cheque taints. Good again! Only, when the great poem is written, when the great novel is done, there is money in it! Who is to have this money? The author? Certainly not. We are agreed his soul must be kept virgin. But why the publisher? (Above all, why the American publisher?) Why not the printer? Why not the binder or the bookseller? Why not the deserving poor? None of these will be defiled by the profits. Why should the money not be used to found a Lying-in Hospital, or an Asylum for Decayed Authors, or a Museum to keep Honest Publishers in? Why should not authors have the kudos of paying off the National Debt? If they are to be the only Socialists in a world of individualists, let them at least have the satisfaction of knowing their money is applied to worthy public purposes.

But I do not agree with you. "The best work at the best prices" is no unworthy motto. The Authors' Society, indeed, tries to put this non-moral principle of valuation upon an ethical basis. It says, for instance, that if the publisher reckons his office expenses in the cost of production, then the author has a right to reckon his, even including any journeys or researches he may have had to make in order to write his book. But this right is not only an ethical fallacy: it is a politico-economical one, because the economical question is only concerned with the distribution of the work, and the money or the heart's blood that went to make it has nothing to do with the question, while the publisher's office expenses are of the essence of the question. Some authors also claim that the publisher has no right to make successful books pay for unsuccessful. But here again he has every right. The publisher is not a piece-worker; he has to keep a large organization going, involving ramifications in every town. It is the existence of this network, of this distributive mechanism, that enables the successful book to be sold everywhere; and the publisher, like every business man, must allow percentages for bad debts and unprofitable speculations. Publishers have a right to capture the bulk of the profits of authors' first books, because they largely supply the author with his public. It is surprising how even good books have to be pressed on an unwilling world, much as cards are forced by conjurers. The number of people that select their books by their own free-will is incredibly small. On the other hand, when a popular author brings a publisher a book, it is he who improves the publisher's distributing agency, by bringing him new clients, and even sometimes strengthening his position with booksellers and libraries, by enabling him, armed with a book universally in demand, to fight against deductions and discounts throughout his business generally. And, just as the publisher may rightly depress the profits of an unknown author, so the popular author has a moral right to larger royalties—which right, however, would avail him nothing were it not backed by might. It is in the competition of rival publishers that his strength lies.

And here comes in the question of the agent. Publishers may rave as they will, but authors have every right to employ agents to save them from the unpleasant task of chaffering and of speaking highly of themselves. And it is the author who pays the agent, not the publishers, their whinings notwithstanding. The agent may indeed squeeze out larger sums than publishers like to disgorge, but how can he obtain more than the market-value? Political economy is dead against the possibility. He cannot, in fact, obtain more than the author may and frequently does obtain for himself. If a competing publisher offers a larger sum than will pay him in coin, at any rate he will not offer more than will pay him in reputation, or in the extension of his clientèle on the lines indicated above. It is still only the market-value. If the reputation honourably built up by the labours of years comes to have a monetary value outside the monetary value of the particular book—a sort of goodwill value, in fact—why should the author or his agent be abused for obtaining it? Will not the publisher in his turn grind down the unknown man to the lowest possible penny? The prostration of the publisher before the celebrity is only equalled by his insolence toward the obscure. Is there any author who has not suffered in his beginnings from the greed of publishers? Far from making money at the start, how many authors have got a hearing without having had to pay for it out of their own pockets? "The wrongs of publishers" is a good red-herring to draw across the track, a smart counter-cry. But publishers have still the game in their hands all along the line. Not a few still keep their accounts secret, still recklessly supply themselves with that opportunity which, the proverb says, makes even honest men thieves. As for America—what goes on across that week of ocean who dares conjecture? And now, what with rumors of wars and free silver—ah me!

In forming a Masters' Union, the publishers have at last abandoned the pretence of being swayed by any but pecuniary considerations in the exercise of their high function. There is something refreshing in this clearing of the air, in this abandonment of the Joseph Surface manner. And yet, I confess, my heart shelters a regret for the old style of publisher, as for the old style of author. Something of picturesque clings even to Jacob Tonson, with "his two left legs." The publisher as the patron of genius, the nurser of young talent, the re-inspirer of old, the scholar and gentleman, at once the friend and the banker of his authors, makes a pleasing figure. It was perhaps more ideal than real, for even of Murray we read in "Lord Beaconsfield's Letters ": "Washington Irving demanded a large price. Murray murmured. Irving talked of posterity and the badness of the public taste, and Murray said that authors who wrote for posterity must publish on their own account." Still, if the publisher would live up to this ideal, his would remain an honorable profession, instead of sinking to a trade. He would rank with the rare theatrical manager to whom art is dearer than profit—if such a one still survives. But the trail of business is over the age: the theatrical manager is a shameless tradesman, and more and more the publisher will become the mere distributer, if indeed he be not eliminated by a mechanical organisation. The popular author needs only a central store to supply the trade with his printed writings, the cost of production of which is covered by the first day's sales. This is, of course, to ignore the publisher in his aspect of initiator of series, art books and encyclopaedias. But to originate is to depart from publishing proper and to become entitled to the profits of the inventor; nay, almost to step over into the province of authorship and the dignity thereof.

But if we can forgive the publisher for succumbing to the business spirit of the age, we cannot as readily acquiesce in the huckstering spirit that has crept over literature. The "battle of the books" has become one of account-books, and the literary columns of the newspapers bristle with pecuniary paragraphs. Even the "chatter about Shelley" was better than the contemporary gossip about the takings of authors, for the most part vastly exaggerated. A paragraph which must have inflated him with pride led to a friend of mine being haled up before the Income Tax Commissioners. "How long have you been an author?" he was asked in addition. "Six years," he replied. "And you have only paid income tax for five!" was the horrified exclamation. Here is the nemesis of all this foolish fuss about L. S. D. The British mind now supposes authorship to be a trade, like any other. You go into it, and you at once begin to make a regular income; and, once successful, you go on steadily earning large sums, automatically. The thing works itself. You are never ill or uninspired; you are never to let your mind lie fallow, never to travel and gather new inspiration, never to shut up shop and loaf. You simply go on making so much a year—for do not the papers say so? And that you should cherish the immoral sentiments contained in the following stanzas, as at least two authors of my acquaintance do, is simply incredible to the envious Philistine.

THE AUTHOR TO THE SYNDICATOR.

Thou lord, of bloated syndicates,
Thou master of the mint,
Who payest at the highest rates
And takest without stint,
Go back, go back to wild New York,
 Go back across the sea;
Go, corners make in beans and pork,
No corners make in me.

For thou art 'cute and thou art smart,
No dead flies hang on thee;
Thou carest not one jot for Art,
But only L. S. D. Go 'back, go back, etc.

Thy aims are low, thy profits high;
Thy mind is only bent,
Whatever live, whatever die,
To scoop in cent per cent.
Go back, go back, etc.

To thee the greatest authors are
Those who most greatly sell;
But he whose soul is as a Star—
Why, he may go to H-ll!
Go back, go back to wild New York,
Go back across the sea;
Go, corners make in beans and pork,
No corners make in me.

An author's income must be indeed difficult to adjudge. He is the manufacturer of a patent article—which only he can turn out. But he is also the vendor thereof, and his transactions involve sales of serial—as well as of book-rights synchronised in two or more countries—a tedious and delicate task. And a great part of his business—"the tributes that take up his time," the MSS. he has to read, etc., etc.—must be conducted entirely without profit, or rather must be run at a loss. Who can determine what are the working expenses of so complex an industrial enterprise? An artist subtracts the cost of his models: may an author subtract the cost of the experiences which supply him with his material, and, if so, how are they to be estimated? Mr. Conan Doyle and Mr. Anthony Hope both write historical novels; but while the former buys and studies large quantities of books, and travels to see castles and battlefields, the latter professedly works from intuition. Are both these men's incomes to be treated alike? Goethe deliberately fell in love so as to write poems when the passion had subsided: how much should be deducted from his gross returns to cover the working expenses of his love-affairs? And even when we do not go about it in such cold blood, our art—is it not woven of our pain and our passion, our "emotions recollected in tranquility"? Do these emotions cost us nothing? Do they not "wear and tear" our system, justifying us in writing off 5 per cent. for depreciation in our machinery? Countless are the problems that arise out of this new view of authorship as an exact trade. Scientifically speaking, the author is a pieceworker, whose productiveness is fitful and temporary. However widely the fame of his business extend, he cannot extend it; he cannot increase his output by adding new clerks or new branches: every order received means work for his own brain and his own hands. If he keep other hands they are called ghosts, and such ghosts are frowned upon even by the Psychical Society.

No, the more I think of it, the more it is borne in upon me that authors should be exempted from income tax altogether—if, indeed, the income itself should not rather be provided for them (free of duty) by a grateful Government. Carlyle is said to have claimed exemption on the ground that the earnings of a writer are incalculable: it seems to me that it is rather the working expenses which are incalculable. "I sometimes sit and yearn for anything in the shape of an income that would come in," wrote poor sick Stevenson on a languorous summer afternoon—by the way, I hope his doctors' expenses were deducted from his gross returns, as incurred in order to keep the writing machinery going; or did he perchance fly to Samoa to escape the tax altogether?—"Mine has all got to be gone and fished for with the immortal mind of man. What I want is the income that really comes in of itself, while all you have to do is just to blossom and exist, and sit on chairs." Poor R. L. S.!—does it not make you think of "mighty poets in their misery dead"? Does it not—if you are more prosaic—bring home to you the absurdity of taxing professional incomes as though they were akin to those which "come in" to the happy folk who have but "to blossom and exist and sit on chairs"? And will you not, whoever you are, rejoice that the work done with so much art and conscience and suffering, obtained, in Stevenson's latter days, its highest possible money-reward through the much-abhorred Agent? Why do not millionaires hear of the woes of authors and send them anonymous bank-notes? Why do not "national testimonials" happen in the author's lifetime in the shape of purses of gold? They are more digestible than posthumous stones. Alas! the author's path is thorny enough. And it is against this jaded, unhappy creature that the publishers have had to make a Union! Well, well, there will soon be no Authors' Union except the Workhouse.

XXVI

THE PENALTIES OF FAME

There is one form of persecution to which celebrity or notoriety is subject, which Ouida has omitted in her impassioned protest. It is interviewing carried one step further—from the ridiculous to the sublime of audacity. The auto-interview, one might christen it, if the officiating purist would pass the hybrid name. Yon are asked to supply information about yourself by post, prepaid. The ordinary interview, whatever may be said against it, is at least painless; and, annoying as it is to after-reflection to have had your brain picked of its ideas by a stranger who gets paid for them, still the mechanical vexations of literature are entirely taken over by the journalist who hangs on your lips; though, if I may betray the secrets of the prison-house, he often expects you to supply the questions as well as the answers. But when you are asked to write your life for a biographical dictionary, or to communicate particulars about yourself to a newspaper, it is difficult, however equable your temperament, not to feel a modicum of irritation. It is not only the labour of writing and the cost of stamps that anger you. Your innate modesty is outraged. How is it possible for you to say all those nice things about yourself which you know to be your due, and which a third person might even exaggerate? What business have editors to expose you to such inner conflict? A scholar I knew suffered agonies from this source. He was constantly making learned discoveries which nobody understood but himself, and so editors were always pestering him to write leaderettes about them. He got over the difficulty by leaving blanks for the eulogistic adjectives, which the editors had to fill in. As thus: "Mr. Theophilus Rogers, the — savant, has unearthed another papyrus in Asia Minor which throws a flood of light on the primitive seismology of Syria." Once a careless editor forgot to fill in the lacuna, and the paper lost a lot of subscribers by reason of its improper language, whilst the friends of Theophilus wanted him to bring an action for libel, unconscious that it would lie against himself.

But perhaps the climax of irritation is reached when, having troubled to write down autobiographical details, having wrestled with your modesty and overthrown it, having posted your letter and prepaid it, the — editor rejects your contribution without thanks. This hard fate overtook me—moi qui vous parle—not very long ago. The conductor of a penny journal, not unconnected with literary tit-bits, honoured me with a triple interrogatory. This professional Rosa Dartle wanted to know—

(1) The conditions under which you write your novels.

(2) How you get your plots and characters.

(3) How you find your titles.

I was very busy. I was very modest. But the accompanying assurance that an anxious world was on the qui vive for the information appealed to my higher self, and I took up my pen and wrote:—

(1) The conditions under which I write my novels can be better imagined than described.

(2) My plots and characters I get from the MSS, submitted to me by young authors, whose clever but crude ideas I hate to see wasted. I always read everything sent to me, and would advise young authors to encourage younger authors to send them their efforts.

(3) As for my titles, they are the only things I work out myself, and you will therefore excuse me if I preserve a measure of reticence as to the method by which I get them.

"What is being interviewed like?" a young lady once asked me, unconscious she was subjecting me to the process. "It is being asked what you drink—and not getting it," I explained to her. The curiosity of the interviewer is indeed boundless. He even asks which is your favourite author, so that you are forced to advertise some other fellow. And yet there is another side to the question, which Ouida ignores. There are two periods in the life of successful persons—the first when they are anxious to be interviewed, the second when people are anxious to interview them. With some there thus arrives a third period, in which they are anxious not to be interviewed, but this is rare. Doubtless there are superior persons who never craved for fame even in their callow youth, and possibly Ouida herself may have taken to authorship as an elaborate means of diverting attention from herself. But the majority of mortals, being fools by edict of Puck and Carlyle, are pleased to fly through the lips of men. Even Tennyson, whose horror of the interviewer almost reached insanity, whose later life was one long "We are observed: let us dissemble," is said to have been disappointed when the casual pedestrian took no notice of him at all. A lady in the Isle of Wight told me that the great poet was wont to put his handkerchief over his face if he met anybody. Naturally this would make the most illiterate person stop and gaze and wonder who this merry-andrew might be. Assuredly this is not the fine simplicity of manners one expects from a great man. "Earl, do you wear one of these?" asked an American democrat of an English peer at his table, as he produced a coronet from a cupboard and stuck the pudding-dish upon the inverted spikes. Tennyson seemed to be always conscious of his laurel crown. The nobler course had been to deck his puddings with the sprigs.

Kind hearts are more than laurel crowns,
And simple mien than Saxon song.

Ouida does a public service by insisting that it is presumptuous of the crowd to judge the conduct of men of genius, whose life is pitched in quite a different key, and runs very frequently in the melancholy minor mode. The travail of soul, the workings of the mind, the agonies and the raptures of genius must be so remote from the common ken, that it is unjust to apply to it the vulgar meteyard; and so, far be it from me to blame the inspired singer of "Crossing the Bar," or to imagine that he could have been other than he was! All the same, it is permissible to regret that he should have throughout his life pandered to the popular conception of a poet. There was something of a robuster quality in Browning, who managed to be a seer and a mystic in despite of afternoon teas. Ouida beats the tom-tom far too loudly. From one point of view the post-mortem revelations of great men's friends, which kindle her ire, perform a public good, even if at the expense of a private wrong. The attempt to apotheosise human nature, to invest our kindred clay with theatrical glamour and to drape it from the property-room, this mythical creation of "a magnified non-natural man," what is it all but the perpetuation of the false psychology of the past? There is no durable good in this childish "make-believe." It is time for humanity to outgrow this puerile self-deception about its powers and characteristics and limitations. A great man is a man as well as great, and he may be all the wonderful things that Carlyle claimed without ceasing to be human and therefore erring. And if he would go about simply and naturally, without developing a self-consciousness as vast and unhealthy as the liver of a goose intended for pâté, he would be happier and wiser, and secure the inattention he yearns for. Moreover, while Ouida is rightly intolerant of the abuse of genius by the bourgeois, the dictionary scarcely affords her own genius sufficient vituperation for the bourgeois. I am at a loss to understand by what logic genius gains the right to hate the bourgeois. It has not the excuse of the bourgeois—stupidity. That the crowd hates superiority and is venomously anxious to degrade it to its own level, is one of Ouida's many delusions about life. Discounting vulgar curiosity, a good deal of the crowd's interest in genius, however annoying and ridiculous the shapes it takes, springs at bottom from a sense of reverence and admiration; and surely it is sheer priggishness, if it be not rank midsummer madness, on the part of genius to regard itself as persecuted by foolish and malicious persons. Methinks the lady doth protest too much. Still it would be unjust to deny her perfect seclusion from the world, if she feels she needs it.

Perhaps the mildest form of persecution is that of the autographomaniacs. "They send me my own books," one of the most popular authors in England complained to me pathetically the other day, "and they ask me to write in them. But to write in them is all that you can do for the books of your friends. If you do this for strangers, what is there left for your friends?" Although far less beloved of the book-buyer than the illustrious novelist, I could yet offer him the sympathy of a minor fellow-sufferer. It is the American reader who is the main persecutor. He is not "gentle," forsooth—a very bully, rather. But why do I say "he," when it is generally "she"? "You have eluded all my wiles hitherto," she wrote me the other day: "now I ask you straight out for your autograph." This honesty would have softened me had I not just had to pay fivepence on the letter—and for the second time that day! Of course her request was not accompanied by a stamped envelope either, though, if it had been, the stamp would have been an American; invalid, a pictorial irony. She has a trick, moreover, of addressing you—most economically—care of your American publishers, who expedite the letter with vengeful empressement, so that you pay double at your end of the Atlantic. And when everything else is in order, her epistle is insufficiently stamped, and your income is frittered away in futile fivepences. It is too much. The cup is full. We must no longer bow our necks beneath the oppressor's yoke, no longer tremble at the postman's knock. We must strike, instead—we other men of letters. For authors, too, are human: manual labourers, overworked and underpaid, with no hope of an eight hours' day. Their pay must not be still further reduced by this monstrous stamp-tax. Will not some Burns—more poetical than John— raise the banner of revolt? Perhaps William Morris may reconcile his hitherto contradictory rôles by placing himself at the head of the movement. Henceforward no author is to despatch his autograph to an admirer, charm she never so cunningly. Beshrew these admirers! a man's personality is in his books, not in his scrawl. Whosoever violates this prescription shall be accounted a blackleg. On one condition only shall autographs be sent—to wit, that they be paid for.

I do not, indeed, propose that the author shall pocket the money, though I see no shame in the deed: everything is worth what it can fetch, and if an adventitious value comes to attach to a signature, the author were amply justified in pocketing this legitimate supplement to the scanty rewards of his travail of soul and body—just as he were justified, should locks of his hair come into demand, in alternating the scissors and the hair-restorer. But as a suspicion still prevails that authors live on ambrosia and nectar (carriage paid), that the butcher, the baker, and the candlestick maker tumble over one another in their eagerness to offer their goods at the shrine of genius, it may be unwise to shock one's admirers too much by pocketing their oboli; and I would suggest—in all seriousness—that a charge be made in the future for all autographs: each celebrity could fix it according to the special demand, and the returns should go for charitable purposes. An "Autograph Fund" should be founded in every profession admitting of notoriety. Among actors the fund could be devoted to that excellent charity the Dramatic and Musical Benevolent Fund; among writers, to the support of decayed critics and neglected novelists. Why not? In days when men cannot bear to see even Niagara wasting its energies in misdirected roars, why should so prolific a source of profit as autographomania be neglected? The authors' strike must be initiated at once: the Autograph Fund demands an instant Treasurer. I don't mind contributing ten signatures to start it, if twelve other writers, of equal eminence and illegibility, will guarantee a like amount.

What profits it to woo the thankless Muse, or to appeal to the autograph-huntress? In a foolish moment of unpardonable sentimentality, I suggested that she should pay for her treasure by a charity contribution; at the very least let her refrain, I prayed, from American stamps. But she does not read me, alas! though my writings are the sole solace of her days and nights; there is no way of attracting her attention. Still, still her stamps flow in. I cry Oyez, Oyez, but she is bent over "Trilby," and I am but the shadow of a name—of a name that is interesting enough tacked on to my favourite motto or a brief autobiography, and may serve to round off her autographic alphabet. Will not Mr. Du Maurier cry aloud to her on behalf of his brother-authors, he whose housetop is the sun, whose voice reaches from the summits of the Rockies to the pampas of La Plata, and echoes from the ice-floes of Labrador to the cliffs of Cape Horn? Will he not tell her that even as "the crimes of Clapham" are "chaste in Martaban," so the stamps of the States are the waste-paper of the London mails. Mr. Kipling, whom I have just quoted, is more fortunate. Breathing the air of Brattleboro', Vermont, he is supplied with native stamps to carry on his correspondence withal. For Mr. Kipling—so he has confided to me in an amusing narrative of his autograph experiences, designed for the warning of fellow-craftsmen to whom my project may have sounded seductive—had actually anticipated my plan: he had sent out two hundred circulars to the admiring crew who ranked him before Shakespeare, proposing that they should send him a donation for a charity in return for his signature. Then the flood-gates—not of heaven—were opened. For weeks abuse rained in upon him, and "thief" seems to have been the mildest rebuke he received. To be asked for an autograph was an honour (even with the stamps omitted). He bowed his head beneath the deluge, praying perhaps—

Of the two hundred grant but two
To take a charitable view.

But no, as one man and one woman they cast him out of grace.

And yet he seems to persevere—for 't is indeed an excellent way of circumventing the wily. In the Chicago Record I read that he wrote to an autograph-beggar that he would send his autograph on receiving proof that the autograph-hunter had deposited two and a half dollars in a certain New York fresh air fund. This is an ingenious variation of the original scheme, for it puts aside the possibility of personal peculation; but I doubt whether it answers. Each celebrity must solve for himself this harassing problem: there be those who simply stick to the stamps ... great free spirits, these, the Napoleons of the pen, Jenseits von Gut und Böse, whose names it is not for me to bewray. Others, like myself, stricken with the paralysis of a Puritan conscience, waver and vex themselves. One ought not to encourage this craze for the external accidents of greatness—the appeal may be fraudulent—and yet what right have you to the stamps?—and after all 't is flattering to be adored from Terra del Fuego; it argues taste—and taste should not go unrecognized in a Philistine world. Eureka! I have found the solution. Don't stick to the stamps, but send them to the funds of a charity.

These views of mine on autographs have greatly distressed the unfair sex. The ladies—God bless them—resent a severely logical view of anything, and to disturb their small sentimentalities is to be cold-blooded and cynical. Once, when I wasj imprudent enough to wonder if the "young person" with the well-known cheek, to which blushes were brought, existed any longer in this age of neurotic novels written by ladies for gentlemen, I received a delicious communication from an Australian damsel informing me that she had been in love with me up till the fatal day on which she read my cynical conception of her sex—which reminds me of another well-meaning young lady who wrote me the other day from America that her epistle was prompted "neither by love nor admiration." If I hint that popular lady novelists do not invariably produce masterpieces of style and syntax, I am accused of inflicting the "tarantulous bites of envious detractors." I am driven—most reluctantly—to a suspicion that has long been faintly glimmering in my bosom, a suspicion that ladies have no sense of humour. It is gravely pointed out to me by incensed writers of incense-laden letters that the demand for a writer's autograph is a mark of veneration; that his letter is reverentially handed about on special occasions quite without a thought of its possible commercial value and that often—though here the argument itself becomes cunningly commercial—it becomes the focus of a local hero-worship that expresses itself outwardly in increased purchases of the author's books. Now, of course every author is only too aware that requests for his autographs are manifestations of reverence, and is only too apt to disregard the supposition of crude curiosity. He knows that it is only natural that people, forewarned by the scarcity of autographs of Shakespeare, should be anxious to safeguard posterity against a similar calamity. But that any author should have humour enough to see the absurdity of the autograph mania, this is what his fair clientèle has not humour enough to understand. Anthony Hope—who, by the way, told me he had received a letter from an unknown lady, the object of which was to abuse me for my heresy on this heart-burning question—says that if to write his name on slips of paper adds to the sum of the world's pleasure, he is ready to do it. This is a noble attitude; but the good people do not always do the most good. Ought one to pamper this interest in mere externals? Here are the man's books, pictures, symphonies: if these have profited you, be content—you have had enough. He has shown you his soul—why should he show you his hand? One knows into what this sort of thing degenerates—into the exploitation of celebrities by smart American journalists, to whom genius and notoriety are equally alike mere possibilities of sensational copy with screaming head-lines. A. Z. has written the opera of the century: the public is dying to know the cut of his trousers and the proportion of milk in his café au lait. X. Y. has murdered his uncle and vivisected his grandmother: how interesting to ascertain his favourite novel, and whether he approves of the bicycle for ladies! For one person who knows anything of the artistic output of the day there are ten who know all about the producers and how much money they are making. Even when our interest in artistic work is intellectual, we are more likely to read criticisms of it than to place ourselves vis-à-vis with the work. Not the truest criticism, not the subtlest misinterpretation, can give us anything like the sensation or the stimulus that results from direct contact with the work itself. As well enjoy the "Moonlight Sonata" through a technical analysis of its form. But this is a venial vice compared with taking your Sonata through the medium of a paragraph about Beethoven's shoe-buckles.

The autograph craze is, I maintain, only another aspect of this modern mania for irrelevant gossip; just as the tit-bits breed of papers is but the outer manifestation of an inner disgrace. We no longer tackle great works and ordered trains of thought: everything must be snappy and spicy; and we open our books and papers, awaiting, like the criminal in "The Mikado," "the sensation of a short sharp shock." To possess a man's autograph may as easily become a substitute for studying his work as an incentive to purchasing it. The critique displaces the book itself: the autograph may displace even the critique. All this without reference to the trouble and expense entailed by an aggregation of the trivial taskwork of signing one's name, addressing envelopes, sticking on stamps, and occasionally paying for them, and not infrequently defraying the extra postage on insufficiently stamped admiration. Henry James, in his latest story in "The Yellow Book," says deliciously: "Lambert's novels appeared to have brought him no money: they had only brought him, so far as I could make out, tributes that took up his time." The earnings of the most popular authors are, I fear me, sadly exaggerated, and their own anticipations seldom realised. As the other American novelist—Mr. Howells—humourously puts it: "I never get a cheque from my publisher without feeling distinctly poorer." The average author is indeed very much in the position of a cabman surveying a shilling. And the even less substantial "tributes," be it noted, are not limited to aspirations after autographs. That would be little to grumble at. But everybody knows that the demands made upon a celebrity—and especially upon an author—are "peculiar and extensive." He is expected to be not only an author—and even, according to the more high-minded among the unsuccessful critics, to be that without fee or reward—but also to officiate gratuitously as publisher's reader to the universe at large—unprinted; as author's agent, hawking unknown MSS. about among his friends the publishers, and placing unknown young men on the staff of the leading journals; as dramatic agent, introducing plays and players to his friends the managers—who will not produce his own works; and, in fine, to act as general adviser to aspirants of every species. Nay, was not Hall Caine recently asked by a lady admirer in poor health, about to visit the Isle of Man, to find lodgings for her? Heavens! who knows what scandal might have arisen had the author of "The Manxman" inconsiderately turned himself into a house-agent! The famous tale of the Nova Scotian sheep in "The School for Scandal" might have been eclipsed by the sequel. Now, the poor lady meant well enough: she may even have thought to show how deep her faith in the novelist's domestic genius and financial impeccability! It simply did not occur to her that she was not the only call upon Mr. Caine's time; and she may have felt as resentful at his reluctance as the beggar who stigmatises Rothschild as niggard because he cannot wheedle a share in his bounty. It may be that I am incapable of envisaging this whole matter fairly, because—to make a clean breast of it—I am one of those Philistine persons who shock Americans by never having been to Stratford-on-Avon. It is true that I have read Shakespeare—and even his commentators, which gives me the pull over Shakespeare himself; it is true that I agree with the persons who haven't read him that he is the greatest poet the world has ever seen or is likely to see; it is true that Shakespeare is part of my life and thought; but somehow my interest in him does not extend to his second-best bed, and I do not greatly yearn to see the room in which Bacon was not born. I do not even care whether Shakespeare was written by Shakespeare or "by another man of the same name." Do you remember that poem of Amy Levy's, telling of how she sat listening to people chattering about a dead, poet they had known, his looks and ways, and thinking to herself—

I, who had never seen your face,
Perhaps I knew you best.

It is this flaw in an otherwise well regulated mind, this "blind spot" in my spiritual eye, that perhaps makes me attach undue unimportance to the attraction of autographs. There is an eminent actress who invariably refuses to send her autograph; but the eminent actor who is her husband invariably sends a letter of apology to the disappointed correspondent. Since I am in the mood for confessions, let me candidly admit that my own attitude has a somewhat similar duality. Though I curse in these pages, I bless like Balaam when it comes to the point. Never have I omitted to return a sufficiently stamped, envelope with the coveted sign-manual—never twice alike. Never have I failed to put my name in a birthday book under a specific date—never twice alike. And though I hate to answer applications for autographs, I should be still more annoyed not to receive them. And as for sneering at the ladies, they have, I vow, no more constant admirer. I could, indeed, desire that when they are next angry with me they would read me before they criticise me; that they would base their denunciations on my text, and my whole text, rather than on some paper's mistaken comment upon another paper's inaccurate extract. But nothing that they can say of me, however harsh, shall, I protest, abate a jot of my respect for them or myself.

XXVII

ON FINISHING A BOOK

Between three and four of the morning the last words of the book were written, and, putting down my pen—without falling asleep, as I should have done had my task been to read the book, instead of to write it—I began to muse on the emotions I ought to have felt, and on the emotions other and greater authors had felt. There was a time, "in the days that were earlier," when the writing of a book was a rare and solemn task, to be approached—like the writing of "Paradise Lost"—after years of devout and arduous preparation, under the "great Taskmaster's eye." Now it is all a rush and a fever and a fret, and the mad breathlessness of the New York newspaper office has spread from journalism to literature, and novelists cheerfully contract to write books in the next century, quite unregardful of whether there will be any books in them by then. That was a very leisurely prescription in the Old Testament: "When a man taketh a new wife he shall not go out in the host, neither shall he be charged with any business; he shall be free at home one year, and shall cheer his wife which he hath taken." Delightful honeymoon of those pastoral days! Now the honeymoon has dwindled to a week, or in the case of actors and actresses to a matinee (for they appear at night as usual), and few of us possess sufficient oxen and sheep and manservants and maidservants to strike work for a year. If only our authors would produce but one book a year, instead of yielding two or three harvests to make hay withal while the sun shines! Nor do they do these things much better in France. From the patient parturition of a Flaubert—the father of the Realists—we have come down to the mechanical annual crop of his degenerate descendant, Zola. Perhaps the age of great works—like the age of great folios—is over, so that none will ever have again those fine sensations that made Gibbon chronicle how he finished his monumental history between the hours of eleven and twelve at night in the summer-house at Lausanne, or that dictated the stately sentiment of Hallam's wind-up of his "Introduction to the Literature of Europe": "I hereby terminate a work which has furnished, the occupation of not very few years.... I cannot affect to doubt that I have contributed something to the general literature of my country, something to the honourable estimation of my own name and to the inheritance of those, if it is for me still to cherish that hope, to whom I have to bequeath it."

Thackeray must have felt something of this fine glow when he finished "Vanity Fair," despite his genial simulation of "Come, children, let us shut up the box and the puppets, for our play is played out." Dickens, who had not humour enough for such self-mockery, took his endings very seriously indeed, and even in the middle of his books had all the emotions of parting when some favourite character had to quit the stage, some poor Dombey or Little Nell. You remember what he wrote in the preface to "David Copperfield" of "how sorrowfully the pen is laid down at the close of a two-years' imaginative task, or how an author feels as if he were dismissing some portion of himself into the shadowy world, when a crowd of the creatures of his brain are going from him for ever." And contrast his superfluously solemn asseveration, "No one can ever believe this narrative in the reading more than I believed it in the writing," with the whimsical melancholy of the "Vanity Fair" preface, the references to the Becky doll and the Amelia puppet. One feels that Thackeray was the greater Master, in that he took himself less seriously, and had the finer sense of proportion. But that he lived with his characters quite as much as his great contemporary may be seen from that charming Roundabout Paper "De Finibus," where he describes the loneliness of his study after all those people had gone who had been boarding and lodging with him for twenty months. They had plagued him and bored him at all sorts of uncomfortable hours, and yet now he would be almost glad if one of them would walk in and chat with him as of yore—"an odd, pleasant, humourous, melancholy feeling." In how much more solemn a mood Dickens finishes "Our Mutual Friend," congratulating himself on having been saved—with Mr. and Mrs. Boffin and the Lammles, with Bella Wilfer and Rogue Riderhood—from a destructive railway accident, so that he cannot help thinking of the time when the words with which he closes the book will be written against his life—"The End." Thackeray needed no railway accident to remind him of "The End," and two lines before the close of "Vanity Fair" we find him writing—in the prime of his life, "Ah, vanitas vanitatum! Which of us is happy in this world? Which of us has his desire, or, having it, is satisfied?" That thought occurred to Gibbon, too, for he had not taken many turns under the silver moon in that coveted walk of acacias, enjoying the spectacle of the lake and the mountains, and the recovery of his freedom and the establishment of his fame, before a sober melancholy was spread over his mind by the idea that he "had taken an everlasting leave of an old and agreeable companion, and that whatsoever might be the future fate of his history, the life of the historian must be short and precarious." When George Eliot put the last stroke to "Romola," the book which "ploughed into her more than any of her books," which she "began as a young woman and finished as an old woman," she exclaimed in her diary—"Ebenezer!" O unpredictable ejaculation! Ebenezer! 'T is true the erudite Miss Evans had Hebrew an knew that it meant "a stone of help." And in the evening she went to her "La Gazza Ladra." Let us hope that some false persuasion of the immortality of "Romola" counteracted that bodily malaise and suffering of which she complained to Sara Hennell. Such pleasant persuasion buoyed up Fielding, as he wrote the beginning of the end of "Tom Jones,"—that almost endless epic—for with a last fling at the critics he cries: "All these works, however, I am well convinced, will be dead long before this page shall offer itself to thy perusal; for however short the period may be of my own performances, they will most probably outlive their own infirm author, and the weakly productions of his abusive cotemporaries."

But it is rather the tradition of Trollope that rules to-day—Trollope, that canny craftsman who wrote every day for a stated number of hours, and who, if he finished a novel twenty minutes before the end of his term, would take up a clean sheet of paper and commence another. Did I say the canny Trollope? Nay, this is rather uncanny, unearthly, unhuman. What! You have lived with your characters day and night for months and months, have thought their thoughts and been racked by their passions, and you can calmly wind up their affairs and turn instanter to a new circle of acquaintances? 'T is the very coquetry of composition, the heartless flirtation of fiction-mongering. Thackeray, indeed, confesses to liking to begin another piece of work after one piece is out of hand, were it only to write half a dozen lines; but "that is something towards Number the Next," not towards Book the Next, for these old giants wrote from hand to mouth. I have always figured to myself Trollope's novels as all written on a long endless scroll of paper rolled on an iron axis, nailed up in his study. The publishers approach to buy so many yards of fiction, and shopman Anthony, scissors in hand, unrolls the scroll and snips it off at the desired point. This counter-jumping conception of the Muses prevails with the customers to-day, with the editors who buy fiction at so much a thousand words. Carlyle—Heaven preserve me from finishing a book as he did his "French Revolution," to lose it and write it all over again!—had the truer idea when he suggested that authors should be paid by what they do not write. But it was reserved for the libraries to reach the lowest conception of literature. Their clients enjoy the privilege of having so many books at a time, a book being a book just as an orange is an orange. If the book the reader wants is not there, why, there is another book for him to take; by which beautiful system the good writer reaps very little advantage over the mediocre, for indifferent books are forced upon the public as the conjuror forces cards on people who think they are choosing them. It is a wonder the libraries do not purvey their literature by the pound.

PART II

HERE, THERE, AND SOMEWHERE ELSE: PHILOSOPHIC EXCURSIONS

[The following pages are not intended as a substitute for Baedeker or Murray. Nor can I solicit your interest on the ground of new places and strange discoveries. To the philosophic tourist all places are equally good to soliloquise in; and in inviting you to accompany my excursions I need scarcely explain that the route is not according to Bradshaw but to the A. B. C., and that you may break the journey at any point.]

ABERDEEN

Critics of London allow too little for the charm of irregularity and historical association—for odd bits and queer views coming unexpectedly round the corner to meet one, for strange ancient gardens and fragments of field in the backways of Holborn, for quaint waterside alleys and old-world churches in out-of-the-way turnings—for everything, in fact, that has the charm of natural growth. If I had my way, I would not give up Booksellers' Row for a thousand improvements in the Strand. Where shall you find a more piquant peace than in the shady quadrangles that branch out of the bustle of Fleet Street, and flash a memory of Oxford spires or Cambridge gardens on the inner eye? What spot in the world has inspired a nobler sonnet than Wordsworth's on Westminster Bridge? Who would exchange our happy incongruity for the mechanical regularity of the mushroom cities of the States? Paris has, no doubt, made herself beautiful; but she could have afforded not to be, much better than she can afford to be. The theorist holds up Glasgow as a model city—a pioneer—and the splendour of its municipal buildings is as the justice of Aristides. But if an ugly woman does not dress well, who should? With all its civic spirit, Glasgow remains grey, prosaic, intolerable—the champion platitude of commercial civilisation. Aberdeen would have been a far finer example of the schematic city of which theorists dream. There is something heroic about the spaciousness of its streets, the loftiness of the buildings, and the omnipresence of granite—a Tyrtaean spirit, which finds its supreme embodiment in the noble statue of Wallace poised on rough craglets of unpolished granite, and of General Gordon with his martial cloak around him. If Edinburgh be the Athens of Scotland, Aberdeen is its Sparta. And yet after a while Aberdeen becomes a weariness and an abomination. For you discover that it is one endless series of geometrical diagrams. The pavements run in parallel lines, the houses are rectilinear, the gardens are squares or oblongs; if by chance the land sprawls in billocks and hollows, nevertheless is it partitioned in rigid lines. The architecture is equally austere. The very curves demonstrate the theorem that a curve is made up of little straight lines, the arches are stiff and unbending, and wherever a public building demands an ornament, a fir-shaped cone of straight lines rises in stoic severity. In vain one seeks for a refuge from Euclid—for an odd turning or a crooked by-way. To match the straight-ness of their streets and the granite of their structures the Aberdonians are hard-headed, close-fisted, and logical (there is a proverb that no Jew can settle among them), and when they die they are laid out neatly in a rectangular cemetery with parallel rows of graves. Even when they stand about gossiping they fall naturally into geometric figures: if two disconnected men are smoking silently in the roadway, they trisect it; and if another man arrives he converts the company into an equilateral triangle. I am convinced the moon shrinks from appearing in Union Street except it is in perfect quarters, and hides timidly behind a cloud unless its arcs are presentable. Professor Bain was born in Aberdeen. This accounts for much in our British metaphysics. Aberdeen produced the man who vivisected Shelley's "Skylark," and explained away the human mind and all that is therein; Aberdeen educated him, graduated him, married him, gave him the chair of Logic in her University, and finally made him Lord Rector. Bain thinks entirely in straight lines. He is the apotheosis of the Aberdonian. Which is a warning against regular cities.

According to the Rev. W. A. Cornaby in "The Contemporary Review," the straight line is an abomination to the Chinese; they avoid it by curves and zigzags, and they think in curves and zigzags. Hence it seems the Chinese suffer from a spurious idealism, just as my Aberdonians suffer from a spurious materialism. If only the maidens of Aberdeen would marry the mandarins of the too Flowery Land, what a perfect race we might expect!

ANTWERP

This is the era of Exhibitions. An epidemic of Exhibitions traverses the world, breaking out now at Paris, now at Chicago, now at Antwerp. To visit them is our modern Pilgrimage; they force us to make the Grand Tour, as our little wars teach us geography. They are supposed to give a fillip to the prosperity of their town, and to nourish the pride and pocket of the citizens. What other function they fulfil is dubious. Time was when "the long laborious miles" of the Crystal Palace were acclaimed as the dawn of the Golden Age, when swords should be turned into the most improved substitute for pruning-hooks, and each man

find his own in all men's good,
And all men work in noble brotherhood.

Unhappily, that millennial vision is still far away—

Far, how far, no tongue can say,

as the canny Tennyson did not forget, even in his rapt prophetic strain. And we have grown chiller. We no longer raise the song of praise because manufacturers of all nations send specimens of their work to a common centre in quest of medals. The world is already federated by the chains of commerce; international barter is an inseparable part of the movement of life, and infinite intertangled threads of union stretch across the seas from shipping office to shipping office. Wherefore the millennium is as likely to arrive viâ Bayreuth or Lourdes, or any other centre of Pilgrimage, as by way of an International Exhibition. No, we must take our Exhibitions more humbly: they are amusing and instructive; they earn dividends or lose capital; they stimulate orders for the goods on view, and they end in a shower of medals. In France, according to Mark Twain, few men escape the Legion of Honor. Is there any artificial product that has escaped a medal at some Exhibition or the other? I cannot recall eating or drinking anything undecorated. They grow on every bush, those medals, copious as the Queen's Arms over the shop-windows of the High Street. No store, however lowly, but the Queen deals there; no article, however poor, but has earned golden opinions, or at least silver and bronze. For the industrial or Gradgrind mind an Exhibition is doubtless a riot, an orgy; for the exhibitors it is a sensational battle-field; for the average spectator it is as exciting as a walk through Whiteley's, or a stroll down Oxford Street.

From the Antwerp Exhibition proper I bear away nothing but an impression of a wonderful paper-making machine, at one end of which the paper enters as liquid pulp, to issue at the other as a solid sheet. A pity the process was not carried one step farther, to the printed newspaper stage—so that what went in as rags should come out as mendacity. Such success as the Antwerp Exhibition has won is a success of side-shows; a panorama of camels and dancing-girls defiles before my eyes, my ears are yet ringing with the barbarous music and incantations of the Orient. Old Antwerp rises picturesque, with its burghers and warriors; the glorious picture galleries stretch away, overladen with artistic treasure; the mimic elephant mounts, mammoth-like, to the skies; the grounds and the façades of the buildings gleam fairy-like in the soft night air, with a million illuminations; and lo! there in the German restaurant the beautiful daughters of the Fatherland smile, in coifs and tuckers and short skirts, Katti and Luisa and Nina, dulciferous names that trip off the tongue as the gentle creatures trip from table to table with flasks of Rhenish wine; the mellifluous voice of Sarah cries cigarettes at her booth in the Rue du Caire—Sarah, the Egyptian Jewess, whose ancestors went back to the land of Pharaoh in defiance of Rabbinic decree—Sarah, with the charm of her eighteen summers and her graceful virginal figure and her sweet unconscious coquetry, as different from the barmaid's as Rosalind's from Audrey's; and Sarah's brother, briskest of business boys, resurges with his polyglot solicitations to buy nougat: a mannish swashbuckler without, a cherubic infant within: I see the Congo negroes, mere frauds from the States, in your opinion, daintiest of American friends, who came all the way from Paris to meet me. But soft! what has all this to do with the Industrial Exhibition?

Rien, absolument rien. Give us these things anywhere, give us lights and gardens and music, give us dances and damsels, give us Congo encampments and "ballons dirigeables," and thither will we troop to make us merry. Ah! but the incurable conscientiousness of the human race insists on pills with its jam. Or is it that it has never yet dawned upon humanity that jam may be taken without pills? There was a time—it lasted seventy thousand ages according to the Chinese manuscript which Elia saw—when mankind ate their meat raw. Then, one day, as every schoolboy knows, Bo-bo carelessly set his father's cottage on fire, and, burning the litter of new-farrowed pigs it held, accidentally invented crackling. So delicious was burnt pig discovered to be that everybody fell to setting his house on fire to obtain it. "Thus this custom of firing houses continued, till in process of time a sage arose, like our Locke, who made a discovery that the flesh of swine, or indeed of any other animal, might be cooked (burnt, as they called it) without the necessity of consuming a whole house to dress it.... By such slow degrees do the most useful and seemingly the most obvious arts make their way among mankind." For seventy thousand ages mankind did without al fresco entertainments. Then some one invented Exhibitions, and mankind found it delicious to promenade the grounds amid twinkling lights and joyous music. But no Locke has yet discovered that musical promenades may be had without elevating a whole Exhibition in the background. At Earl's Court they still keep up a pretence of Industrial Exhibition, though we have long since lost interest in the pretext, and no longer inquire whether the painted scenery that walls in the grounds is called the Alps or the Apennines or the Champs-Elysées. And yet methinks mankind did discover the open-air entertainment, as perchance roast pig was known and forgotten again long centuries before Bo-bo. For what was Ranelagh, what Vauxhall? Were not the gardens of Vauxhall "made illustrious by a thousand lights finely disposed," or, as Thackeray puts it, by a "hundred thousand extra lamps, which were always lighted"? Were not "concerts of musick" given nightly by fiddlers in cocked hats, ensconced in a "gilded cockleshell," and was not the price of admission a shilling? "Vauxhall must ever be an estate to its proprietor," wrote Boswell, "as it is peculiarly adapted to the taste of the English nation; there being a mixture of curious show—gay exhibition—music, vocal and instrumental, not too refined for the general ear; and, though last not least, good eating and drinking for those who choose to purchase that regale." But Boswell prophesied ill. Public gardens were always distasteful to English Puritanism, because they lent themselves to rendezvous; and though Boswell, in protesting against the rise of price to two shillings, certifies to the elegance and innocence of the entertainment, and though Mr. Osborne and Miss Amelia walked unharmed in its groves and glades, and it was not Rebecca Sharp's fault that Jos. Sedley got drunk on the bowl of rack punch, still Vauxhall, like Ranelagh and Cremorne, has come down to us with tainted reputation. It died in the odour of brimstone, and only in the magical ink-pool of literature can we still behold the heralded gallants in the boxes junketing with low-bodiced ladies of quality whose patches show piquantly on their damask cheeks. Rosherville remains in ignoble respectability, the place to spend an h-less day, our one uninstructive institution, for even "Constantinople" and "Venice" have a specious background of geographical and even of industrial information: Rosherville, which only once flowered into poetry, and then under another name—when Mr. Anstey's barber wedded the Tinted Venus with a ring.

And in the magical ink-pool I see you and me still sitting, O Transatlantic Parisienne, as we sat that sunny afternoon—three hundred years ago—in ancient Antwerp, in oud Antwerpen, niched in the windowseat of that quaint hostelry which gives on the great market-place, and watching the festive procession. Do you remember the gorgeous costumes of our fellow-burghers, and the trappings of their prancing chargers in those days when life was not plain, but coloured, and existence was one vast fancy-dress ball? How glad we were to welcome the Archduke Martinias of Austria, our sovereign elect, or was it François Sonnius, our first Bishop, coming to be installed in our glorious Cathedral, amid the joyous carillons of its bells! Can you not still see the Angels hovering over the Virgin, and the Golden Calf, flower-wreathed, and the Flight into Egypt, on that naïve donkey, and "the Flying Dutchman," tugged by a horse, and the gilded galley rowed in make-believe by little children in their Sunday clothes, catching crabs in air, and the incongruous camels bestridden by Arab sheikhs with African pages, and the Persians on ponies, and the Crusaders in their fine foolish coats-of-mail, and the gay courtiers, with clanking swords, and the halberdiers, and the particoloured arquebusiers, and the archers in green and red, and the spearsmen in sugarloaf hats, and the cherubs riding on dolphins? Can you not hear the beating of the drum, and the Ave Maria of the white-robed chorus-boys, and the irrelevant strains of the Danish national anthem, and the japes of the jester with his cap and bells? What happy times for butchers and bakers and candlestick-makers when, instead of working, they could go in processions, bearing aloft the insignia of their guilds, and when middle-class girls, ignorant of the New Womanhood, could loll on triumphal cars with roses in their hair! Do you remember how the topmost divinity smiled to me from her perilous perch, too high to rouse your jealousy, and how the little cherub that sat up aloft besprinkled us mischievously with eau de cologne? Ah, shall we ever again be as happy as we were three hundred years ago? will the wine be ever as red, the potato salad as appetising, or the cheese (did they really enjoy Gorgonzola and Camembert in the sixteenth century?) as delicious as in that ancient Flemish hostelry with its Lutheran motto:

Wie nikt mint Wijn, Wijf en Sangh,
Blijft een Geck sijn Leven langh!

Was it from its inscribed beams that Shelley borrowed his famous lyric "Love's Philosophy"? for did we not read:

Den Hemel drinckt, en d'Aerde drinckt:
Waerom souden wij niët drinckt?

("Heaven drinks, and earth drinks: why shouldn't we drink?") At any rate it pleased us to recall the delectable lines:

And the sunlight clasps the earth,
And the moonbeams kiss the sea;
What are all these kissings worth
If thou kiss not me?

But what does it matter what one did three hundred years ago?

Or, what does it matter what one did that dim Arabian night when we set out with the cavalcade of camels in the marriage procession, and the bride cowered veiled in her corner of the coach, and the plump mother smiled archly at us, and the brother and the bridegroom, mounted on Arab steeds, smacked each other's faces in ceremonial solemnity, exactly like "the two Macs" in the music-hall? Was it then, or in the nineteenth century, that we rode the camel together, I on the hindmost peak? "Oh, the oont, oh, the oont, oh, the gawdforsaken oont!" as the poet of the barrack-room sings. He seems to double up like a garden-chair to receive one; then his knees unfold and the rider shoots up; then the camel rises to his full height, and one ducks instinctively for fear of striking the stars. "Salaam Aleikhoom," I cried to the drivers, airing my Arabic, which I make by mispronouncing Hebrew; and they answered effusively, "Yankee Doodle! Chicago!" Alas for the glamour of the Orient! They had all come from the greater fair, perhaps spent their lives in traveling from fair to fair, mercenaries of some latter-day Barnum.

There was a fine stalwart Egyptian, who stood beating a gong to summon the faithful to improper dances. I gave him a cup of coffee, and he held it on high, and with gratitude effusing from every pore of his dusky face, cried, "Columbus!" Then he mounted a flight of stairs and shouted beamingly, "1492!"

He took a sip, and then his wife called him chidingly, and he fled to her. But he returned to drain the cup in my presence, crying between each sip "Columbus" or "1492." Never before have I bought so much gratitude for ten centimes. Henceforward I found "Columbus" a watchword, and "1492" a magic talisman, causing dusky eyes to kindle and turbaned heads to nod beamingly.

The town-barber of Alt Antwerpen, who was wont to shave me in the sixteenth century, had a beautiful motto:—

I am Hair-dresser, Barber, and Surgeon,
I shave with, soap and much delight,
Although there are barbers who do it
As though they were in a fright.

But it is surpassed by a hundred delightful things in "The Visitor's Handybook," which the touts in New Antwerp, ignorant of its treasures, press upon the traveller gratis. It opens auspiciously: "The opening pages of our little guide we have devoted to a short review of the city of Antwerp, the streets of which still contain elegant specimens of those quaint and handsome edifices of the Netherlands are truly famous, and which in Antwerp, perhaps more than in any other city, seem to abound." Here are some more gems: "Visitors will be naturally anxious to secure a comfortable apartment, in selecting which the following list will be found of service:—see advertisements, all of which can be strongly recommended." "Facing you is the King's Palace; not a very attractive one; however, as a rule, not open to the public, but admission may sometimes be obtained although at great trouble during the absence of the King." "It was formally inaugurated by the presence of the Queen, Princess Beatrice, and a numerous compagny representing the European Benches and Pairs." "A wonderfully painted ceiling, in which the attendant can point out some marvellous effects." "The Visitor's Handybook" is in its thirteenth free edition, and is worth double the price. Antwerp is very strong linguistically. The quatre langues—Flemish, French, English, and German—make a universal confusion of tongues, and the whole town is nothing but a huge open Flemish—French dictionary, every shop-sign or street-name being translated. A few sturdy burghers stick to the old tongue, and sometimes English rules the roast. "The Welsh Harp" (which is Antwerp way) is a sailor's cabaret near the quay. There is even a trace of Irish influence in the etymology of Antwerp as given in the official handbook; for Antigon, the giant who used to cut off the hand of any shipman that refused him tribute, and whose throwing it (Handwerpen) into the river gave the name to the city, is stated beforehand to have lived in the castle of Antwerp. They are not destitute of wit, the Belgians, if I may judge by some specimens I heard. It is a local joke to refer to the famous "dirigeable" balloon, which burst in the latter days of the Exhibition, as the "déchirable" balloon. "They pooh-pooh the past nowadays," said a tram-conductor to me, "but when I look at the Cathedral and Rubens' 'Descent from the Cross' I think our forefathers were assez malins." A seedy vendor of lottery-tickets declared that every one of them would draw a prize. "Wherefore, then, my friend," quoth I, "do you not keep them?" "Je ne suis pas égoïste," he said, with a shrug. To defend myself against his masterful solicitousness, I stated solemnly that lotteries were illegal in England, and that if I returned thither with a lottery-ticket the British Government would throw me into prison. But he was not daunted: "Appuyez-vous sur moi," he replied reassuringly.

BROADSTAIRS AND RAMSGATE

A story is current in the Clubs that Mr. Henry James innocently went to Ramsgate, in order to possess his soul in peace. 'T was the height of the rougher Ramsgate season, and there is something irresistibly incongruous in the juxtaposition of the rarefied American novelist and the roaring sands of Albion. In the which juxtaposition the story leaves him; and we are ignorant of whether he turned tail and fled back to quieter London, or whether he stayed on to collect unexpected material. Our analytical cousin's stippling methods are, it is to be feared, but poorly adapted for the painting of holiday crowds, which require the scene-painter's brush, and lend themselves reluctantly to nuances. The colours have not that dubiety so dear to the artist of the penumbra; the sands are as yellow as the benches are red; and the niggers are quite as black as they are burnt-corked. The love-making, too, is devoid of subtlety. When you see—as I saw last Bank Holiday on Ramsgate beach—Edwin and Angelina asleep in each other's arms, the situation strikes you as too simple for analysis. It is like the loves of the elements, or the propensity of carbon to combine with oxygen. An even more idyllic couple I came upon prone amid the poppies on the cliff hard by, absorbing the peace and the sunshine, steeping themselves in the calm of Nature after the finest Wordsworthian manner. But presently there is the roll of a drum, and the scream of a fife in distress rises from below, and Angelina pricks up her ears. "I wish they'd come up 'ere," she murmurs wistfully; "I'd jump up like steam; I could just do a dance."

Yet all the same their seclusion among the wild flowers on the edge of the cliff showed a glimmering of soul. Not theirs the hankering for that strip of sand near the stone pier, which a worthy dame of my acquaintance once compared to a successful fly-paper. Scientific investigation shows the congestion at this particular spot to be due to the file of bathing-machines which blocks the view of the sea from half the beach. To the bulk of the visitors this yellow patch is Ramsgate, just as a small, cocoanut-bearing area of Hampstead woodland is the Heath, most of whose glorious acres have never felt the tread of a donkey or a cheap tripper. Not that there are many other attractions in Ramsgate, which is administered by councillors more sleepy than sage. Having literally defaced their town by a railway-station, built a harbour which will not hold water, constructed a promenade pier in the least accessible quarter, and provided a band which plays mainly "intervals," they naturally refuse to venture on further improvements, such as refuges on the parade, or trees in the shadeless streets, and, in the excess of their zeal, have even, so I hear, declined the railway company's offer to give them a lift (from sands to cliff), and Mr. Sebag Montefiore's offer to allow the public gardens to be continued right through his estate on towards Dumpton. Even so, these worthy burghers have more of my regard than their brethren of Margate, who have sacrificed their trust to the Moloch of advertisement. Stand on Margate Parade and look seaward, and the main impression is Pills. Sail towards Margate Pier and look landward, and the main impression is Disinfectant Powder.

Baby Broadstairs has known better how to guard its dignity and its beauty; so that Dickens might still look from Bleak House on as dainty a scene as in the days when he lounged on the dear old, black, weather-beaten pier. I spent a week at Broadstairs in the height of a Dynamite Mystery. We were very proud of the Mystery, we of Broadstairs, and of the space we filled in the papers. Ramsgate, with its contemporaneous murder sensation, we turned up our noses at, till Ramsgate had a wreck and redressed the balance. For the rest, we made sand-pies, and bathed and sailed, and listened to a band that went wheezy on Bank Holiday. Broadstairs boasts of one drunkard, who does odd jobs as well. He is tall, venerable, and melancholy, and has the air of a temperance orator. "Joe's one of the best chaps on the pier when he's sober," said his mate to me sorrowfully; "but when he's drunk he makes a fool of himself." This was not quite true; for Joe was not always foolish. Why, when two gentlemen came down from London in a gipsy caravan to teach us Theosophy, and all Broadstairs fluttered towards their oil-lamp, leaving the band to tootle to the sad sea waves, I could not get him to mount the Cheap Jack rostrum in opposition! The most I could spur him to was an indignant defence of London against the lecturer's denunciation of it as an immoral city, a pit of unrighteousness. "'T ain't true!" he thundered raucously. "Many's the gent from Lunnon as has behaved most liberal to me." One day there was an attempt to disturb Joe's monopoly as drunkard, and I am afraid I had a hand in it. A human caricature in broken boots addressed me as I lay on the beach (writing with a stylographic pen and blotting the sheets with the sand), and besought me to buy sprigs of lavender. He proved to me by ocular demonstration that he had no money in his pockets; whereupon I proved to him by parity of reasoning that I had none in mine either. However, I remembered me of a penny postage-stamp (unlicked), and tendered it diffidently, and he received it with disproportionate benedictions. Later in the day he reappeared under my window, hurling up maudlin abuse. He had got drunk on my postage-stamp!

I told him to get along with him, which he did. For some time he staggered about Broadstairs in search of its policeman. He came across him at last, and was straightway clapped into an open victoria and driven across the sunny fields to Ramsgate. Meantime, Broadstairs was left unprotected—perhaps Joe kept an eye on it.

Broadstairs has also a jolly old waterman, who paddles about apparently to pick up exhausted bathers. One morning as I was swimming past his boat he warned me back. "Any danger?" I asked. "Ladies," he replied, ambiguously enough. It thus transpired that his function is to preserve a scientific frontier between the sexes. Considering that the ladies one meets at sea are much more clothed than the ladies whose diaphanous drapery one engirdles in ball-rooms, this prudery is amusing. It is consoling to remember that the Continental practice prevails in many a quaint nook along our coasts, and that the ladies are sensible enough to walk to and from their bathing tents, clothed and unashamed. Strange to say, Broadstairs has placed its ladies' machines nearest the pier, for the benefit of loungers armed with glasses; and I must not forget to mention that the boatman himself holds a daily levée of mermaidens, who make direct for his boat and gambol around the prow. If anything needs reforming in our marine manners, it is rather the male costume. Why we men are allowed to go about like savages, clothed only in skins (and those our own), is to me one of the puzzles of popular ethics. What is sauce for the gander is sauce for the goose. At Folkestone, where the machine-people are dreadfully set against ladies and gentlemen using the same water, promiscuous bathing flourishes more nakedly than anywhere on the Continent; and the gentlemen have neither tents nor costumes. In Margate and Deal the machines are of either sex, and the gentlemen are clad in coloured pocket-handkerchiefs. At Birchington I bathed from a boat which was besieged by a bevy of wandering water-nymphs, begging me to let them dive from it. And they dived divinely!

Though the profanum vulgus takes possession of our strands, and Edwin and Angelina are common objects of the sea-shore, yet I cannot help thinking that there is many a vulgar British beach that would ravish us did we light upon it in other lands. Oh, how picturesque! What a gay grouping of colour! What an enchanting medley of pink parasols and golden sand and chintz tents and white bathing-machines, and blue skies and black minstrels and green waters, and creamy flannels and gauzy dresses! And—ciel! what cherubic children! and—corpo di Bacco!—what pretty women! What frank abandon to the airy influences of the scene! What unconventionality! What unrestraint! See how that staid old signor allows himself to be buried and excavated by the bambino. Watch that charming maman unblushingly bathing bébé. Note that portly matrona careering upon the asino! What cares she for her dignity? Listen to the babel—"[Greek: hokae pokae, hokae pokae]" "Drei shies a pfennig!" "Your photograph, señorita?" Look! the coquettish contadina is slapping the face of the roguish vetturino! How the good-natured crowd, easily pleased, gathers round the Ethiopian troubadour, trolling in unison his amorous catches!—

Daisy, Daisy, donne-moi ta réponse.

And hark! Do you not hear in the distance the squeak of Puncinello? Ah! why have we none of this happy carelessness in England?—we who take our pleasures moult tristement—why have we not this lightheartedness, this camaraderie of enjoyment? Why cannot we throw aside our insular stiffness, our British hauteur, and be natural?

I journeyed to Broadstairs, late at night, riding in a three-horsed brake with many a jocund passenger. And then something happened. Something ineffably trivial, and yet a matter of life and death. We were bowling merrily along the country lanes in the fragrant air. It was a dark, starless night, but so warm that the easterly sea-breeze fanned us like a zephyr. And through the gloom a flash-light leaped and waned, flickered and died and gleamed again with electric brilliance—"the Winnaker(?) light from France," a garrulous inhabitant assured us; a rare phenomenon to be seen only once in a decade, when an east wind clarifies the atmosphere, and allows the rays to pierce through two dozen miles of strait. It seemed like La Belle France winking amicably to us across the waters. And a little to the left twinkled "The Green Man"—no friendly public-house, but a danger-signal from behind the Goodwin Sands, likewise visible but by miracle.

And as we marvelled at these jewels of the night, that shamed the absentee stars, the brake stood still with a jolt and a shock that threw our gay company into momentary alarm. But it was nothing. Only a horse fallen down dead! One of our overworked wheelers had suddenly sunk upon the earth, a carcase. Dust to dust! Who shall tell of the daylong agony of the dumb beast as he plodded pertinaciously through the heat, ministering to the pleasures of his masters? Had he been a man, how we should have praised him, belauded the beauty of his end, telling one another sanctimoniously that he had died in harness. As it was we merely stripped him of his harness and deposited it in the brake! We unhitched the leader and put him between the shafts, side by side with the other horse, both incurious and indifferent, wasting nor glance nor nasal rub upon their defunct comrade. We men feign better. And then we drew him to the edge of the track, a rigid, lumbering mass; and the garrulous inhabitant discussed the value of the carcase, and the driver cracked his whip, and the living horses stirred their haunches, and in a moment we were spanking along, leaving our fellow-creature to darkness and solitude. Only the flash-light from France glimmered upon the poor dead beast, coming all the way to cheer him; only the green eye from beyond the Goodwins blinked upon his unheaving flanks.

And from far ahead came back to his deaf ears with ever-diminishing intensity our noisy madrigal—most music-hall, most melancholy—his only dirge:

Mary Jane was a farmer's daughter,
Mary Jane did what she oughter.
She fell in love but all in vain.
O poor Mary! O poor Jane!

BUDAPEST

The Millennial Exhibition of Budapest—for which the Directors gave me a season ticket as soon as they heard I was leaving—professes to celebrate the foundation of Hungary; but 896 is a very long time ago, and the event does not seem to have been reported in the newspapers of the period. However, as a Hungarian explained to me, when you are counting by thousands you are not particular to a year or two, so perhaps it was not precisely ten centuries ago that the foundation of Hungary was inaugurated by a national assembly that created "the Constitution of Pusztaszer." After all, have not those irrepressible German savants discovered that Christ was born in the year 6 B.C.? At any rate, there is no doubt that the Magyars did steal a country some time or other in the remote past, or in more political language, did obtain a footing in Europe by ousting the Slav tribes that peopled the great plain bounded by the Carpathians and the Danube and the Tisza. They came from Central Asia, on a late wave of that big "Westward ho!" movement of the Eastern peoples, a race of shepherds changed into an army of mounted archers, and pitched their tents first in Galicia, uniting their seven tribes under the great chief Arpád; but, harassed continually by local tribes with unpronounceable names, they moved farther westwards to their present quarters, where, after a vain but spirited attempt to annex Europe generally, they settled down to comfort and civilisation, ceased to offer white horses to idols, and embraced Christianity.

It seems that land-thieves are called conquerors; and after a thousand years of possession of their stolen goods, the glamour of a divine sanctity gets over the past, and high-minded natives live and die for the country which seems to have been theirs from time immemorial, and in which their holiest feelings are enrooted. What makes national robberies moral is the fact that there is honour among the thieves. The morality of crowds is, in fact, as different from that of individuals as "the psychology of crowds" which has just engaged the attention of an ingenious scientist. Into the original conquerors of a country a miscellaneous assortment of other races always gets absorbed, as the Franks by the Gauls, the Turkish Bulgarians by the Slavs. The Hungarians absorbed into themselves Italians, Germans, and Czechs, and the modern Hungarian is, according to Arminius Vambery, a typical product of the fusion of Europe and Asia, Turanian and Aryan. And that is the sort of way in which after a few centuries we get the chauvinistic cries: "Germany for the Germans," "Poland for the Polish," "Hungary for the Hungarians." In truth, no nation has a right to anything it cannot hold by might. And who shall determine what a nation is? Who are the Americans? Who are the English? "Norman and Saxon and Dane are we." And once upon a time some of us threw up our country and sailed away in the Mayflower. For patriotism is not the only bond of brotherhood. Men may be the sons of an idea as well as of a soil. There was a Hungarian girl selling silver at a stall, who had spent four years in Chicago. Never have I heard better American, except it be from a Budapest man who had come back to revisit his native town, and was disgusted with its smallness and slowness. Per contra, I met an American girl in Switzerland who had lived much in Germany, and whose English had such a Teutonic intonation that it was difficult to realise she was not speaking German. And language is but typical of the rest. All other national characteristics are imbibed as subtly. What makes a nation is a certain common spirit—Volksgeist, as the German psychologists have christened it—and this spirit exercises a hypnotic effect over all that comes within its range, moulding and transforming. There is action and reaction. The nation makes the national spirit, and the national spirit makes the nation. The flag, the constitution, the national anthems, the national prejudices, the language, the proverbs—these are the product of the people they produce.

I am inclined to allow more importance to education and environment than to actual birth in a country, and to believe that for a "native," birth is only an etymological necessity. Natives are made as well as born. The "born" native has merely the advantage of prior arrival, and if the "foreign" immigrant is only of a plastic age he may come to love the step-mother-country more than one of her own sons, educated abroad. This consideration would solve every Uitlander question: is the national spirit strong enough to suck in the foreigners? Can the nation digest them, to vary the metaphor—assimilate them to its own substance? I once proposed to a biologist—who flouted it—that a definition of Life might be "the power of converting foreign elements, taken in as food, to one's own substance." Thus, a plant sucks up chemical elements and makes flowers; a man turns them to flesh. Here is a piece of meat: eaten by a dog it runs to tail and teeth, for a cat it makes fur and whiskers, for a bird feathers, for a woman a lovable face. And so the test of life in a nation would be its power of transforming its immigrants into patriots. Only a dead nation is afraid of foreigners.

The figure has its limits, however: one cannot gulp down too large a piece of meat. And there are things inedible—substances which no stomach can digest. The Americans will never make Yankees of their Chinese. On the other hand, nowhere have I found more ardent patriots than among the Jews. Englishmen in England, Americans in America, Italians in Italy, Frenchmen in France, and only not Russians in Russia because they are not allowed to be, they are rabid Hungarians in Hungary; and if I have caught any enthusiasm for Hungary it is from the lips of a young and brilliant Jew, Vidor Emil, who piloted me about Budapest, and who, under Marmorek Oszkár, another young Jew, built "Old Buda," perhaps the most interesting feature of the Millennial Exhibition. This Jewish patriotism, which loves at once Israel and some other nation, may appear curious and contradictory; but human nature is nothing if not curious and contradictory, and this dual affection has been aptly compared to that of a mother for her different children. And besides, in a contest the love of Israel goes down before the more local patriotism. French and German Jews fought each other in the Franco-German war, and probably it is only persecution that accentuates the consciousness of Jewish brotherhood. Wherever the Jews have perfect equality and have been tempted out of the Ghetto, there the beginnings of disintegration are manifest. And who shall say how much Jewish blood dilutes the nations of the Occident, for all their chauvinistic talk!

Mr. Du Maurier, in his unmentionable novel, suspects, like Lowell, that a drop of it has lurked in every artistic temperament. And, in sober truth, the drain from Israel throughout the centuries has been immense. In every age, in every country, Jews have been sucked up into the more brilliant life around them, exchanging contempt and danger for consideration and peace. I know an English gentleman who goes about in fear and trembling lest it transpire that he is of the race of the apostles, and he be driven out of decent Christian society. Cherchez le Juif is, indeed, no empty cry, whenever a new artistic or journalistic planet swims into our ken. That the Jew rules over the Continental press is not quite so untrue as most anti-Semitic cries. "Have you any Christians on your staff?" I said to the editor of the great Budapest newspaper, "Pesther Lloyd," a fine figure of a man, long-bearded and benevolent, like an ancient sage. He pondered. "I think we have one," he said. On the other hand, there are many German and Austrian papers on which there is only one Jew. And in any case the real meaning of the cry is ludicrously untrue.

For the Jew by no means uses his power to help Jews indiscriminately: there is no secret brotherhood of the synagogue. The Jewish journalists have probably never been in a synagogue, except perhaps as children; they are divorced in thought and temper from the body proper. And the only sense in which their pen can be said to have a Jewish bias is in that complimentary sense which makes the Jew synonymous with the champion of sweetness and light, of liberty and reason. In this sense it is true that the Jew is wielding an insidious influence throughout Europe, like the old apostles among the heathen.

"Oh yes, the Jews are very well off in Hungary," said one of the staff of the "Pesther Lloyd." "There are 150,000 Jews in Budapest; they enter all the professions, and supply two members to the House of Magnates, and nine to the Chamber of Deputies, and there are two State Councillors; and you know with us every member of Parliament 'thous' every other in private as an equal. For the laws, liberal as they are, are not so liberal as the spirit of society. I, mere journalist as I am, have the most friendly talks with the Prime Minister, and am a member of the swellest political clubs. We are a good deal like England, by the way: our middle-classes produce our leaders, our aristocracy lacks eloquence and talent, and has only a court influence. Our House of Commons is the most fashionable club. We have no censor, whereas Austria has an oppressive censorship as well as anti-Semitism. In fact, the influence of Vienna has caused a decline in our own tolerant spirit, and at the best of times a Jew needed to have three times the talent of a Christian to make equal progress in any career." A consideration which sufficiently accounts for the superiority of the Jewish remnant. Intolerance and persecution are furnaces which, when they do not destroy, temper and anneal and strengthen. It is as with the bare-footed, half-clad, underfed children of the slums: those that do survive are strong indeed. Let my patriotic cicerone, the Jewish architect, testify. First in all his examinations, a violinist, a bicyclist, a gymnast, he was to be gazetted a premier lieutenant as soon as he had completed his military service. He was a linguist, too (as every travelled Hungarian must be, for Hungarian will carry him nowhere), speaking excellent English and reading our magazines regularly. Humani nihil a me alienum puto might have been his motto. Kossuth himself is said to have had a Jewish grandmother. The Jews are largely responsible for the prosperity of Budapest, as they were for that of Vienna, which now turns round upon them. Fancy a country quarrelling with its coal and iron! And the true wealth of a country is even more in its population than in its dead products. I found the Viennese comic papers full of the old anti-Semitic jokes, hashed up, I have little doubt, by the same journalists who are supposed to judaize the press of Europe. Even so in America, are not the Jewish caricatures in Puck often done by a brother of M. de Blowitz? In something of the same spirit, when the notorious Lueger, whose platform was the extinction of the Jews of Vienna, was up for election as Burgomaster of that town, a poor Jew took a bribe of a couple of florins to vote for him. "God will frustrate him," said the pious Jew. "Meantime I have his money."

The chief surprise of Hungary is its language. Though one knows that Jokaï writes in the strange tongue which sticks its verb into the middle of its noun, yet one vaguely thinks of it as of Gaelic or Welsh— something archaic, kept for Eisteddfods and Renaissances—and it is not till one arrives in Hungary that one realises that it is a living, disconcerting reality. The great European languages have affinities with one another: Latin puts one on bowing terms with French and Spanish, Italian and Portuguese; English is not entirely unrelated to German, Dutch, and even Norwegian; old Greek is the key to modern. But in Hungary one comes face to face with an absolutely new language, in which even guesswork is impossible. When "Levelezö-Lap" means a postcard, and "ára egy napra" means price per day, you feel that it is all up. The nearest relatives of Hungarian are Turkish and Finnish, the Asiatic ancestors of the race having lived between Finns and Turks; and it bears traces of their migrations, and of the great Mongol invasion of Europe by Djingis Khan.

With a language thus handicapped, it was a mistake to have scarcely a word of any other tongue in an Exhibition designed to attract Europe. The only scrap of English I saw was in the "French Theatre," in the show of "Living Pictures," the (London) director of which had forgotten to alter the titles printed beneath the frames. Even in giving the names of foreign authors the Hungarians preserve their habit of placing the Christian name second; so that I saw in the booksellers' windows works by Eliot George, Kock Paul, and Black William.

Hungary is still in the flush of youth, high-spirited, brilliant, enthusiastic, and a little out of perspective in its national consciousness. But who would ever do anything if he saw his true place in the cosmos? The rapid rise of Budapest—unprecedented save in the gold countries—into a capital of European importance, has shed a buoyant optimism, refreshing enough in this jaded century, over the inhabitants of that beautiful city. "We are the Vienna of the future," cried my cicerone, "and already Vienna is feeling our rivalry. The retired Jewish merchants who went there to spend their fortunes are now coming to us; the anti-Semitism of Vienna is at once the cause and the effect of bad business. And Vienna is on the downward grade; we are on the upward. Vienna has never been the capital of Austria—which is a mere federation of races—as Budapest is the capital of Hungary. The German is proud of Vienna, yes; but the Czech looks to Prague, the Pole to Cracow, the Austro-Italian swears by Trieste."

He also complained that there is rather a tendency to think of Hungary as subject to Austria, instead of an associated state; and that this tendency is fomented by the Austrian papers, whose references to Hungary insinuate this conception. The Hungarian papers, whose tone would counteract it, not being in German, are not read by the rest of Europe. Hungary had always beaten Austria. She had never been defeated save by allies of Austria. But Hungary, which is so mettlesome and restive in her patriotism, whose great son, Kossuth, would never even accept the compromise with the House of Hapsburg, has yet no compunction in dominating inferior races, in grinding Serbs, Croats and Roumanians into her own pattern. The Hungarians, who are in the minority, are yet moulding these alien nationalities to their own will. But que voulez-vous? The inhabitants of many nations have adopted Christianity, the nations themselves never. Perhaps the next step for the Christian missionaries is to found international Christianity.

Still the Hungarians have the qualities of their defects. Unlike the Turks, their neighbours, they are a race with a future, and Budapest is from one point of view one of the sightliest capitals of Europe. What town has a fairer situation? With Parisian Pesth sitting stately on one bank of the Danube, and Turkish Buda climbing up the hills in a series of hanging gardens crowned by gilt domes and cupolas on the other, the two joined by wonderful bridges, she exhibits an unsurpassed contrast; and at night, when the long stretch of the river is a-twinkle with lights reflected as shining spears, she may even vie with Venice or the Thames Embankment. From the Andrassy Avenue, a beautiful Boulevard, with its cafés and book-shops, and pleasant interludes of flower-beds and fountains, you may get, in a few minutes—crossing the Danube on a great steamer, and ascending the heights of Buda by a funicular railway—to a spot where, seated in an avenue of chestnut trees and looking on the villa-strewn slopes of sleeping hills, or watching the sun set in splendour behind them, you may forget that you are living in a bustling modern town, and one with an Exhibition to boot.

You may dream of the picturesque days when, as shown in Ujváry's great panorama of the sister towns in 1680, Buda was by far "the better half," and Pesth was a tiny spot. You may visit the tomb of Gul Baba, father of the roses, a shrine of pilgrimage to all good Turks. You may find a good quarter of an hour in the Church of St. Matthias, whose spire comes up white amid the green as you turn a corner; a curious monument, that was three centuries a-building; its interior suffused, like St. Mark's, by a golden glow, its coloured windows original in shape, and no two pillars or capitals alike in design, yet all contributing to a quaint unity and harmony. And it is at Buda that the chief national buildings stand, usually flanked by chestnut trees, and the statues in memory of the wars. Here is the War-Office of the Territorial Army (which is distinct from the joint Austro-Hungarian army); here are the Premier's Palace, the Houses of Parliament, and the King's Palace of many windows set on a breezy hill, and now being enlarged at a cost of thirty million florins. Fortunate Francis Joseph, to command such a panorama from his bedroom window: his hanging gardens, that slope towards the Danube, flowing with molten sparkle, spanned by the great suspension bridge and the railway bridges; and broken by the beautiful Margaret Island; the spires and chimneys and cupolas of Pesth, and the mountains of Buda.

Margaret Island is the "Pearl of the Danube," a charming retreat in spring and autumn, when the heat does not force Fashion to the mountains, and famous for its mineral springs, hot and cold. It belongs to the King's cousin, Prince Joseph, and is a white elephant. The cost of gardening this beautiful island is colossal, and though the Prince has just drained a portion which used to be a swamp, the Danube is a standing danger. It is scarcely surprising that he cannot find a purchaser at three million florins. One of the walls of his private garden (which produces celebrated roses) is the remnant of an old cloister. A tramcar runs through the island, giving one tantalising vistas of glorious stretches of woodland. Altogether Budapest would be an ideal place for a honeymoon but for the beauty of the women, which might make the bridegroom dissatisfied.

But the Pesth part of Budapest is a disappointment. One expects to feel the first breath of the East, and one gets a modern, a Western, almost an American town, with an electric underground railway and a telephonic newspaper which reads itself out all day long to whosoever will clap the cups to his ears—the old town crier in terms of modern science. But it rounds off the day, poetically enough, with music, so that when I sought to hear the latest news, I was treated to Handel's "Hallelujah." How much more soothing than our own "extra special," with its final crop of horrors! Music, indeed, is ever resounding: the gipsy bands are everywhere playing—Hungarian, not gipsy music, as Liszt imagined, for they never play to "the white men." The splendid "Rákóczi" March, which Berlioz introduced into his "Faust," is, however, of gipsy origin, having been invented, says tradition, by Cinka Panna, the faithful gipsy girl of Rákóczi II., after his defeat. There are also Betjár melodies, the songs of the brigand cavaliers, the romantic robbers who took from the rich to give to the poor, like our Robin Hood.

The Exhibition, which I fear will be a financial failure, is only one of the many celebrations of the Millennium, which include the erection of statues and an Arc de Triomphe, the opening of a canal, the construction of two new bridges, of three or four great public buildings, the inauguration of the splendid new Houses of Parliament—situated like our own on the river-side—international congresses, historical cortèges, and the opening of five hundred new primary schools! This programme is a sufficient guarantee that the Exhibition itself is similarly thorough-going, that it represents every side and department of the national life; and if much of it does not differ from other Exhibitions, or even from

Whiteley's Stores, this can only be the more gratifying to the Hungarians, inasmuch as it proves that they have indeed come into step with the general march of European civilisation. For my part I am not sure that I do not prefer Arpád's Hungarians, who believed in one God and one wife, and roved about Europe in the four-wheeled waggons they had invented. And I am certain that in the Exhibition I preferred the beautiful aquarium in the cool dim grotto, which has nothing to do with Hungary, to all the splendours of the Historical Group of Buildings, to the great model steamer, the naval and military pavilions, the very new and very glaring native pictures, and even the wonderful models of the town and the steamer-laden Danube. One great lack in the Exhibition is lavatories. Even at my hotel—a place of gilded saloons—they charged two florins (about 3s. 4d.) for a plain bath, as if in sheer surprise. In "Old Buda" I could only get a bucket from an old woman in which to wash. And the next day, when I repaired confidently in search of this bucket, there was nothing but a tiny saucepan, the contents of which she poured over my hands, watering a garden-plot at the same time. After the first jet I moved my hands away and said that would do. "No, no," she cried: "if you wash, you must wash properly." And I had to stand still and be poured upon till she was satisfied.

Perhaps the most interesting exhibit is the "ethnographic village," designed to represent the life of the Hungarian provinces, though made rather ridiculous by the rigidity of the waxwork figures, arranged about the quaint and impossibly clean houses in their various occupations, but having the air of "tableaux morts" rather than of "tableaux vivants." The best group was al fresco, representing half-naked gipsy-like creatures with coal-black hair squatting outside tents and mud-houses, the women smoking pipes. And this exhibition of unrealities brings me on to the most original feature of the Exhibition, which seems to have escaped all the reporters—to wit, the exhibition of realities. For the committee have hit on a most ingenious notion. The peasants of Hungary marry, and they marry picturesquely. Why should this picturesqueness be wasted, or only be reproduced artificially in comic operas? When a marriage is to be celebrated in any village, let the scene be shifted to the capital: let the wedding-party come up to the Exhibition. Free transit is provided on the railway for the happy couple, the wedding-guests, and all the stage-properties. And so they come up to Budapest—from Toroczkó, Szabolcs, Krassó-Szörény, and who knows what outlandish places, glad of the opportunity of seeing the great capital—and they gather in the Exhibition grounds, the lads with flower-wreathed hats and streamers of many-coloured ribbons, the lasses with gay skirts and tall black combs, the old women with lace head-shawls, carrying bundles of house-linen and stockings for the bride; and the sheepish pair are made one, and the peasants dance and then go in procession to the strains of the Rákóczi March, and are photographed with odd spectators (like myself) tacked on, and they sit down to the wedding-dinner under the trees, and the viands are heaped high on the white table-cloths, sun-dappled with the shadows of the moving leaves. And then they visit themselves in waxwork, and go into ecstacies over the stolid representations of their life and their furniture, and they walk about the town—a sort of grown-up school-procession—and go home to thrill the wide-eyed village with tales of the wonderful city.

But the other instance of converting realities into spectacles is not so commendable. In the supplementary exhibition of "Old Buda" stands a reproduction of an Old Buda mosque, built of stone, majolica and wood, in a mixture of Turkish and European architecture, with minaret and cupolas, and a small kiosk in the Indian style for a sleeping fakir. Here Moslems and Dervishes assemble to say or dance their prayers; and for a florin you may ascend the gallery and watch them below. The mosque opened on the holy night of Bairam, the most solemn feast of the Mohammedan year, and quite a crowd planked down their silver to listen to the pious worshippers. Is it not shameful? I am happy to say I did not pay for my seat. Even in Budapest I was a persona gratis. 'T was certainly a remarkable scene, its solemnity emphasized by the thunder without, that drowned the voice of the muëddin calling to prayer, and by the lightning and rain-torrents that sent the pretty little al fresco waitresses scudding about with their serviettes on their heads to tend the few parties in the leafy square that dined on regardless of diluted wine or under the protection of umbrellas. How the Turks further wetted themselves by complex ablutions in the tank (meydiäh) in the courtyard without, how they removed their shoes and, entering the mosque, knelt on their carpets facing towards Mecca, and turning their backs on me, a serried array of long-robed figures swaying and falling forward with automatic regularity, and showing pairs of heels not always clean, while the Imam chanted heart-breaking dirges overhead, I shall not detail, for everybody has read of Moslem services. But I do not remember to have come across any accurate description of a service of Dancing Dervishes such as followed the more orthodox ceremonial.

All the mere Mussulmans having retired, the Dervishes sat around cross-legged, forming an oval. Presently they began to say some phrase, presumably Turkish (it sounded like es "klabbam vivurah"), which they repeated and repeated and repeated with the same endless, uniform, monotonous intonation, swaying from right to left and from left to right, till I felt the whole universe was this phrase, and nothing else would happen till the end of the world, and the world would never end. At last, when I had reconciled myself to living for ever and ever with this sound in my ears, they broke into a pleasant melody with rhyming stanzas and a refrain of Hazlee. Then they started on another word with endless iteration, and then they repeated Allah, Allah, Allah, swaying and swaying till the universe began to reel. I became aware that their chief, who was seated on a special red carpet, was counting on a rosary, and I drew relief from the deduction that an end would come. It did, but worse remained behind; for the Dervishes got up and formed a ring round their chief, and began swaying right and left and backwards and forwards, unrestingly, remorselessly, getting quicker and quicker, till there was nothing in the world but swayings this way and that way, back and forth.

At last the movements began to slow down and to sweep over larger curves, and suddenly they stopped altogether, only to recommence as the fanatics started singing a joyous hymn. Alas! thought I, one half the world is a laughing-stock to the other half, if indeed not rather a source of tears. For now the chief, whose fine gloomy Eastern face still haunts me, was bowing to his men, and they were responding with strange raucous cries compounded of the roars of wild beasts and the pants of locomotives. Hu! Hu! they roared in savage unison, Hu! Hu! monotonously, endlessly, making strange motions. Hoarser and more bestial grew the frightful roars, wilder and wilder grew the movements, the head-gear falling off, faces growing black, the chief standing silent with his hand on his breast, but in his pale face a tense look of ever-gathering excitement. And then two of the Dervishes held out a curved sword, and the roars redoubled and the chests heaved with wilder breaths; and suddenly the Chief, throwing off his stocking-wraps, jumped on the blade with his naked feet and balanced himself upon it, the muscles of his face rigid, his teeth clenched. Four times he stood upon the bare sword-edge amid this hellish howling and this mad swaying, the perspiration running down the foreheads of the devotees, some of them foaming at the mouth. And then they moved round in a circle to the right, howling He! He! an Armenian Dervish in a tall brown hat varying it by Ho! Ho! and another worshipper singing in a high voice.

The chief bared his breast, and twirling a heavy-hafted dagger, plunged it into his side. When this had been repeated three or four times, pandemonium ceased. The Holy Man, with an air of supreme exhaustion and supreme ecstasy, reclad himself in his white mantle, and the faithful ones wiped their brows, and re-squatting on the ground exultantly vociferated Allah about a hundred times, nodding their heads, and finally changing their cry into Bou! Bou! After a little singing and a shouting of Din! Din! they pressed their foreheads to the ground with a shout of Bou! and suddenly rose and decamped. Other nights other services, and the hysterical worship sometimes embraces a sort of serpentine skirt-dancing with frenzied twirling. There was no blood from the chief's wounds, but the performance does not seem to me to be jugglery. It seems rather akin to hypnotism. The wild cries and gyrations induce a state of anesthesia, just as by the excitement of battle the soldier is so wrought up that he does not feel his wounds. Even in a sham fight a soldier told me he got to such a pitch that he could have done or suffered anything. As for the blood not running from the wounds, I conjecture that the places had become insensitive by frequent stabbing in the same spot. And this is the miracle that testifies to the saintliness of the Dervish and to the truth of his doctrines! I suspect that much of "the wisdom of the East" is of this character: ancient discoveries of the shady side of human psychology, the grotesque aberrations, trances, hypnotic impressionability, double personalities, ghosts, second-sight, what not. And these being misunderstood have always been supposed to trench on the divine. For what is not normal is not human, and what is not human is superhuman. So runs the simple logic. But hysteria can never be a foundation for a creed, and a true religion must always appeal to the common central facts of human experience.

There was another Exhibition going on, as it always goes on, in the town, for the People's Park has very little verdure and consists almost entirely of side-shows and open-air restaurants. I saw swings and merry-go-rounds, a circus, and a marionette theatre, and heard Punch and Judy discussing their domestic differences in Hungarian, and Toby barking in the same uncouth tongue. The joy with which the public greeted each crack on the head administered by Herr Punch's stick showed me how hopeless it was to write literary plays. For the primitive emotions will always be the most captivating. A fight must ever beat the most subtle psychology; and indeed those writers for whom the drama is the art of manufacturing excitement and suspense must find it difficult to compete with a lottery drawing, a prize-fight, or a horse-race, where the issue is known not even to the organiser of the excitement. And this consideration will show why some books are very successful, the art of which is very little. Nothing is harder in real life than to put your back against the wall on a dark staircase and keep three armed men at bay with your whirling sword. But nothing is easier than for the romantic writer to dip his pen in ink and say that his hero did that. And nothing is more stimulating and exciting for the reader than to imagine the hero doing it; and in his gratitude to the giver of all this beautiful breathlessness he is likely, unless he is an analytical person, to mistake a cheap effect for precious art. But the bulk of humanity must always remain at the Punch-and-Judy stage of art. If only the critics would outgrow it! The clowns in the circus who came on with red noses were a further proof of the sempiternal simplicity of our race; and I could have wished for the heart of that urchin whom I saw trying to peer in under the canvas, and whom, with a reminiscence of the young Gradgrinds, I was about to pay for, when he suddenly produced a florin and many coppers and went in like a man. Sitting in the front row, I had a curious presentiment that the daring bare-backed rider would be thrown at my feet; and sure enough he was, and, as I picked him up, I saw by the perspiration what toil his graceful feats concealed. Poor cavalier! I am sure his pride was more hurt than his person, and he excelled himself in galloping round poised on one toe. When he was recalled after his exit, he tumbled his thanks, giving us complex somersaults in lieu of bows. I sometimes fancy he was a holier person than the Chief of the Dancing Dervishes.

CHICAGO

The function and value of literature are curiously illustrated by the passing away of the Great White Elephant. The criticisms by spectators of the World's Fair have not been so comprehensive as the Fair itself, and I feel that I ought to supplement them by the impressions it made upon one who did not see it. For, despite the assurance of the official programme, that I delivered an address in the Parliament of Religions, I was in England, so far as I know, the whole time. The first impression the Fair made upon me was one of sublimity—but of what Sir William Hamilton calls "the material sublime," scarcely at all of "the moral sublime," which was supposed to be its raison d'être. I was, of course, aware that great spiritual facts underlay the physical grandeurs; but spiritual emotion is difficult to get at a distance. One requires the actual objects to impinge on the soul, the architectural glories and industrial splendours to touch through bodily vision. One realises it so vaguely, and fails to get the half-aesthetic, half-religious, uplifting that concrete visualisation should supply. It is, perhaps, a pity that Whitman did not live to see the spectacle, he whose inspiration came so often from synthesis, from a vision of the ALL. The cosmopolitan cataloguer, the man who made inventories almost epical, is the one man to whom the Fair would have been a magnificent inspiration. Judging from the Fair, Whitman would seem justified in claiming to be the voice of America. The Fair was like him both in its moral broadness and its material all-inclusiveness. In his absence no poet has risen "to the height of this great argument," so that now the insubstantial pageant is faded, now that "the cloud-capp'd towers, the gorgeous palaces, the solemn temples," have dissolved, "like the baseless fabric of a vision," they have left not a rack of real literature behind. And to what but literature can one look for a permanent conservator of the eternal lesson of an ephemeral exhibition? Truly, as the Latin poet said, literature is more durable than monuments and dynasties. Except as an object-lesson in the unity and federation of mankind, the Fair had no valuable raison d'être, and, unfortunately, the school-term was short and the number of pupils comparatively limited.

America is a long way from everywhere, even from itself, and the moral heat dissipates in crossing the ocean to the Old World. The Congress of Religions in whose voluminous report the Fair has still a chance of surviving itself, was the most patently spiritual side of the Exposition, and was, undoubtedly, a most valuable index of the progress of human catholicism. That the sects are as narrow as they are numerous, is still largely true, and half the world is still ignorant of how the other half prays, though by a happy accident of birth all the world inherits the one true religion. The greatest force in the universe is the "vis inertiae," and the forces already at work must "dree their weird." To those who are outside all the sects without even circumscribing them, the World's Fair must bring home at once the greatness and vanity of man's life—man who lives like the angels and dies like the brutes—the mortal paradox that has puzzled all thinkers from the Psalmist to Pascal. For the unbeliever this must ever be the ugly reverse of all glories that are merely material, though the sensuous optimist need not allow the skeleton at the feast to spoil his appetite.

The last impression made by the World's Fair upon me was one of sadness—sadness at not having seen it.

EDINBURGH

Till I went to Edinburgh I did not know what "The Evergreen" was. Newspaper criticisms had given me vague misrepresentations of a Scottish "Yellow Book" calling itself a "Northern Seasonal." But even had I seen a copy myself I doubt if I should have understood it without going to Edinburgh and even had I gone to Edinburgh I should still have been in twilight had? I not met Patrick Geddes, Professor of Botany at the University of Dundee. For Patrick Geddes is the key to the Northern position in life and letters. "The Evergreen" was not established as an antidote to the "Yellow Book," though it might well seem a colour counter-symbol—the green of spring set against the yellow of decadent leaves. It is, indeed, an antidote but undesigned; else had not yellow figured so profusely upon the cover. "The Evergreen" of to-day professes to be inspired by "The Evergreen" which Allan Ramsay published in 1724, to stimulate a return to local and national tradition and living nature. Patrick Geddes and Colleagues, who publish it and other books—on a new system of giving the author all the profits, as certified by a chartered accountant—inherit Ramsay's old home. That is to say, they are located in a sort of "University Settlement," known as Ramsay Garden, a charming collection of flats, overlooking from its eastled hill the picturesque city, and built by the many-sided Professor of Botany, and they aspire also to follow in "the gentle shepherd's" footsteps as workers and writers, publishers and builders. In fact, their aim is synthesis, construction, after our long epoch of analysis, destruction. They would organise life as a whole, expressing themselves through educational and civic activities, through art and architecture, and make of Edinburgh the "Cité du Bon Accord" dreamed of by Elisée Reclus. They feel acutely the "need of fresh readings in life, of fresh groupings in science, both now mainly from the humanist's side, as lately from the naturalist's side." In this University Settlement the publishing and writing department is to represent the scriptorium of the ancient monasteries. Of the local and national traditions this new Scottish school is particularly concerned to foster the so-called "Celtic renascence," and—what is more interesting to outsiders—the revival and development of the old Continental sympathies of Scotland. The ancient league with France has deeply marked Scotch history, and even moulded Scotch architecture. As Disraeli said in his inaugural address on his institution as Lord Rector of the University of Glasgow, "it is not in Scotland that the name of France will ever be mentioned without affection." So, among the endless projects of the effervescent Professor, is one for reviving the Scotch college in Paris—the original building happening still to survive—and for making it a centre for Scottish students and Scottish culture in the gay city.

Thus, while the men of "The Evergreen" would renew local feeling and local colour, they "would also express the larger view of Edinburgh as not only a National and Imperial but a European city—the larger view of Scotland, again as in recent, in mediaeval, most of all in ancient times, one of the European Powers of Culture—as of course far smaller countries like Norway are to-day." An aspiration with which all intelligent men must sympathise. The quest at once of local colour and cosmopolitanism is not at all self-contradictory. The truest cosmopolitanism goes with the intensest local colour, for otherwise you contribute nothing to the human treasury and make mankind one vast featureless monotony. Harmonious diversity is the true cosmopolitan concept, and who will not applaud this desire of Edinburgh to range itself again amongst the capitals of culture? Why should it take its tone from London? That centripetal force which draws villages to towns and towns to capitals everywhere tends to concentrate in one city a country's culture, and to brand as provincial that which is not of the centre. But the centre is corrosive of originality, and if now and then a great man does abide therein, it is because he has the gift of solitude amid crowds, and is not obnoxious to the contagion of the common thought. The Scotch School, though its effort to emancipate itself from the intellectual thraldom of London is to be commended, does not escape the dangers that lie in wait for all schools, which upset one convention by another. Still, a school of thought which is also a school of action has in itself the germs of perpetual self-recuperation.

Yes, there can be little danger of sinking into barren formulae, into glib aesthetic prattle about Renascence, in a movement of which one expression is the purification of those plaguy, if picturesque, Closes, which are the foul blot upon the beautiful Athens of the North. Those sunless courts, entered by needles' eyes of apertures, congested with hellish, heaven-scaling barracks, reeking with refuse and evil odours, inhabited promiscuously by poverty and prostitution, worse than the worst slums of London itself—how could they have been left so long to pollute the fairest and well-nigh the wealthiest city in the kingdom? "Do you wonder Edinburgh is renowned for its medical schools?" asked the Professor grimly, as he darted in and out among those foul alleys, explaining how he was demolishing this and reconstructing that—at once a Destroying Angel and a Redeemer. Veritable ghettoes they seemed, these blind alleys of gigantic habitations, branching out from the High Street, hidden away from the superficial passer-by faring to Holyrood. They were the pioneers of the trans-Atlantic sky-builders, were those old burghers, who, shut in about their castled hill by the two lochs, one of which is now the enchanting Princes Street, were fain to build heavenwards as population grew. It was a stormy morning when the mercurial Professor of Botany, recking naught of the rain that saturated his brown cloak, itself reluctantly donned, led me hither and thither, through the highways and byways of old Edinburgh. Everywhere a litter of building operations, and we trod gingerly many a decadent staircase. Sometimes a double row of houses had already been knocked away, revealing a Close within a Close, eyeless house behind blind alley, and even so the diameter of the court still but a few yards. What human ant-heaps, what histories, farces, tragedies played out in airless tenebrosity!

The native writers seem to have strangely neglected the artistic wealth of all this poverty: pathos and humour reside, then, only in villages! Thrums and Drum-tochty and Galloway exhaust the human tragi-comedy. Ah! my friends, go to the ant-hill and be wise! The Professor of Botany (seeming now rather of entomology) explained the principle upon which he was destroying and rebuilding. One had to be cautious. He pointed out the head of a boy carved over one of the archways, the one survivor of a fatal subsidence many years ago, when the ground floor of one of the gigantic houses was converted into a shop, with plate-glass windows in lieu of the solid stonework. "Heave awa'!" cried a piping voice amid the débris: "I'm no dead yet."

The Professor's own destruction was conservative in character: it was his aim to preserve the ancient note in the architecture, and to make a clean Old Edinburgh of a dirty. Air and light were to be no longer excluded; outside every house, as flats or storeys are called, a balcony was to run, giving on sky and open ground. Eminent personages like Lord Rosebery, ancestrally connected with ancient demesnes, long perverted into pigsties, had been induced to repurchase them, thus restoring an archaic flavour of aristocratic prestige to these despised quarters. The moral effect of grappling with an evil that had seemed so hopeless could not fail to be inspiring; and, as we plodded through the pouring: streets, "I will remove this, I will reconstruct that," cried the enthusiastic Professor, till I almost felt I was walking with the Emperor of Edinburgh. But whence come the sinews of war? Evidently no professor's privy purse would suffice. I gathered that the apostle of the sanitary picturesque had inspired sundry local capitalists with his own patriotic enthusiasm. What a miracle, this trust in a man over-brimming with ideas, the brilliant biological theoriser of "The Evolution of Sex" in the Contemporary Science Series, the patron of fantastic artists like John Duncan! Obviously it is his architectural faculty that has saved him. There stand the houses he has built—visible, tangible, delectable; concrete proofs that he is no mere visionary.

And yet we may be sure the more frigid society of Edina still looks askance on this dreamer in stone and fresco; for after all Edinburgh, as Professor Blaekie said, is an "East-windy, west-endy city." Cold and stately, it sits on its height with something of the austere mournfulness of a ruined capital. But we did not concern ourselves about the legal and scholastic quarters, the Professor and I. We penetrated into inhabited interiors in the Closes, meeting strange female ruins on staircases, or bonny housewives in bed-sitting-rooms, in one of which a sick husband lay apologetically abed. And when even the Professor was forced at last to take refuge from the driving rain, it was in John Knox's house that we ensconced ourselves—the grim, unlovely house of the great Calvinist, the doorway of which fanatically baptised me in a positive waterfall, and in whose dark rooms, as the buxom care-taker declared in explaining the presence of an empty cage, no bird could live. It is not only in its Closes, methought, that Scotland needs regen eration. Many a spiritual blind-alley has still to receive sunshine and air, "sweetness and light." So let us welcome "The Evergreen" and the planters thereof, stunted and mean though its growth be as yet; for not only in Scotland may they bring refreshment, but in that larger world where analysis and criticism have ended in degeneration and despair.

FIESOLE AND FLORENCE

At Fiesole I just missed a sensation. Two friends of mine were climbing at midnight the steep hill to the village, when from beneath a dark arch there dashed down towards them two breathless carabinieri, their cloaks flapping in the moonlight like the wings of the demon-bats of pantomime. "Is it your way that the murdered man lies?" they panted. "Murdered man!" At once a hundred shadowy reminiscences stirred in my friends' minds: Prosper Mérimée's novels, stories of vendettas, plots of plays, morceaux d'opéras, even of comic operas; and it was with a feeling in which the latter element predominated that they answered that they had come across no corpse. The police-officers thanked them and hurried off, so my friends soon understood, as far as possible from the scene of the event; for, passing through the arch, the Inglesi came upon a track of blood, black and clotted in the moonlight. But it did not seem real to them—they still had a consciousness of comic opera, a consciousness which was intensified rather than lessened when they emerged upon a group of excited villagers discussing the crime, and learnt its cause. Two rival bands, one from a neighbouring village, had been performing at a local concerto, and the two rival trumpeters had continued to blow their own trumpets after business hours. "Fancy blowing with that little mouth!" said one. "I'm glad I haven't your maw (boccone)!" retorted the other.

From words it came to knives, and ere you could say Jacopo Robinson a trumpeter lay weltering in his blood, or rather in his gore, and the murderer was flying into the arms of the police, who incontinently turned and fled the other way. When my friends passed by the house of the victim, the midnight air was ringing with the horrible curses of his bereaved sister, whose spasmodic face was visible at a window. But the cold-blooded artistic English felt no answering throb of sympathy—it was still a scene in a play to them, still a coup de théâtre—they had lost the primary human instincts, corrupted by a long course of melodrama and comic opera. To-day I myself saw a carnival procession in the village piazza—a veritable survival of the Middle Ages; a triumphal car wreathed in flowers, driven by masquerading mummers and surrounded by Pierrots and peasant buffoons, a thoroughly naïve and primitive bit of religion. But it needed a perceptible effort to shake off the sense of the operatic, to accept the thing as genuine. Ruskin contended (in that olla podrida called "Modern Painters") that the Swiss peasants do not really dance and sing happily in the market-place; and hence he argued—comically enough—that the money spent on the stage reproduction of their happiness should be spent in really promoting their happiness. With my Italian peasants I feel the opposite: that such excellent picturesque effects should not be wasted on mere reality, but should be turned to real use upon the stage. So, too, it is difficult to take a roadside beggar seriously; he seems to ask, not for alms, but for a frame. Happy the unlettered and the inartistic, to whom even the picturesque person is a person, who can think of olive oil when he sees the olive-trees weaving their graceful patterns above the stone walls, and can watch the sun set in lurid splendour behind the purple mountains with never a thought of Turner or Childe Harold!

For modern civilised beings, in incessant relations with the reflections of life through literature and art, it is difficult to receive any impressions which do not re-reflect what lies in the mirror of art. And here is an amusing side-issue. We are presented in plays and books, with numerous situations in which the ignorance of one of the parties is a necessary factor in the particular dramatic situation which it is sought to evolve. But as this person, ex hypothesi, belongs to the class of society which is familiar with this particular plot ad nauseam, is it possible that he or she should go on betraying the same ignorance on which the plot originally was based? Even Marguerite has seen "Faust" nowadays!

This suggests an objection to old plots quite apart from their oldness, for that which started by being probable becomes improbable by age. Even if it were ever possible for a man to be jealous of a woman because he saw her kissing a man whom, after long and weary years of superfluous separation, he discovered to be her brother, it should surely be impossible to-day. If I saw any man kissing my fiancée I should know at once it was my future brother-in-law—or at any rate I should inquire—which the old hero never seemed to do. And yet I will wager that in the course of this year at least a dozen novels and plays will be built up upon this theme. It is, by the way, a noticeable characteristic of people in plays never to have read nor to be interested in any but the petty dramatic matter which is interesting them— and let us hope the audience—at the moment. It may be replied that the economy of the stage demands that everything that is not strictly essential should be eliminated; but yet it ought to be possible, by a few words, to give the idea that the figures upon the boards are doing more than moving to the strings of the playwright. Just so the painter of the gulf should suggest the ocean beyond; the painter of the landscape, the infinity of space and atmosphere in which it is enisled. What the plein air school contended for in painting is no less requisite in literature.

This consideration seems to account for the uneasy sense of unreality which we feel in the modern machine-made Sardou play, in which the characters have the air of existing entirely to themselves, and for the sake of the particular play, and do not give that large sense of being part of the civilised humanity we know that reads and thinks. The men make love or profess hate, repudiate their wives, or cut off their sons with shillings, all with the air of its happening for the first time, and wholly devoid of that sense of the ridiculous which they could not help feeling if they had been accustomed themselves to read novels and sit in stalls.

It is, in fact, impossible for us moderns, educated in a long literary tradition, to live our lives as naturally and naïvely as the unlettered of to-day, or the people of the preliterary geological epoch. This is brought out "ostensively," as Bacon would say, in "Don Quixote," or in the Russian novel "A Simple Story"— apparently so called because it is so complex—in which Gontcharov's hero lives in what Alice might call "behind the looking-glass" of literature. He is a country boy who comes up to St. Petersburg, and after a course of Russian novels is transformed into a series of imitations of their heroes. He does nothing, feels nothing, thinks nothing except after the pattern of these creatures of the quill.

Well! we are all like that, more or less. Though we may not be as chivalrously inspired as the Knight of La Mancha, nor run to the extremes of the simple Russian, we are all to some extent remoulded in imitation of the Booklanders, and this is the truth in the "decadent" paradox that nature copies art. There is a drop of ink in the blood of the most natural of us; we are all hybrids, crossed with literature, and Shakespeare is as much the author of our being as either of our parents. The effect of the stage in regulating the poses and costumes of susceptible souls has not escaped notice; but the effect of novels and poetry is more insidious. Who ever shuddered with bitter alliterative kisses before Swinburne, and who has failed to do so since? What poor little cockney clerk in his first spasms of poetry but has felt, sitting by his girl in the music hall, that if she walked over the grave in which he was planted, his "dust would hear her and beat, had he lain for a century dead" (though how Maud could survive her lover for a century, Tennyson failed to explain)? Per contra, the ingenuous spinster taking her notions of love from Maupassant's "Bel-Ami," or Gabriele d'Annunzio's "Trionfo della Morte," becomes a man-hater. Yes, I fear that the artistic treatment of life has a good deal to answer for. People do not yet understand that the mirror of art does not reflect life unrefracted. The great eternal theme of art is love-making; but even artists have to give up some time to art-making.

But to wind up anent our murderer. He is still at large. The police have given up the chase in despair. But he has never left the village, and we villagers all wink at one another as we discuss his whereabouts; and when we meet him driving his cart or come across him cutting wood in the forest and he genially gives us Buon' giorno we salute him with answering politeness. Only in the village band there is a temporary trumpeter, for even the police might hear of him if he performed in public loudly enough. But Italian justice, though it does really savour of comic opera, is not so farcical as it appears on the surface. It is an unwritten law that the police shall not pigliare him till the sessions are nigh. He is on parole, so to speak, to come up when called upon; if he were really to take flight, he would be declared an outlaw, and the only reason the police cannot find him is that they know where he is. How sensible! Why board and lodge him gratis for weeks? He has outraged the community: shall the community reward him with free meals? Even when he is caught he will be treated with the same economy. Capital punishment there is none in Italy. Why waste a citizen and a tax-payer? Especially when one has already been destroyed! No, he will be sentenced to a term of imprisonment. But he will not serve it. He will escape, or it will be commuted. And while he is in gaol he will have a good time. He will smoke and play cards, or, leaning out of his dungeon casement, hold a levee of his friends. Recently the soldiers at Bergamo mutinied because they were supplied with worse bread than the denizens of the gaol. I trust the ringleaders were sent to prison so as to remedy this dietary injustice.

Please do me the justice to remark that I have been in Italy for several paragraphs without once referring to the Old Masters. But the fact is that I have not been much at the Masked Balls. Does this saying seem cryptic? All it means is that the confusion into which our scientific century has thrown us is worse confounded than usual in the universe of pictures; that the Galleries appear to be made up of pictures masquerading under wrong names. Time was when one might go about comfortably with a Baedeker and a stock of admiration and distribute it as per instructions. But these good old times are over. The Old Masters of yesterday are the young apprentices of to-day. It is pitiable to think how many well-meaning enthusiasts have fallen victims to the careless or crafty curator. Sometimes it scarcely needs a connoisseur to suspect the good faith of catalogues. I, myself, a mere babe and suckling, came to the conclusion, after a visit to the Velasquez Exhibition in London, that Velasquez must have been very versatile. It is too bad that artists should be hanged for crimes they never committed. 'T is to be hoped their ghosts carefully avoid the Galleries. But beshrew your paintings! My eyes make pictures— not like Coleridge's when they're shut, but when they 're open. Who would not rather lie with me in the podere in the shade of the cypress trees, under the blue, blue sky, and behold through a tangle of olive-boughs the marvellous Dome of Florence, as satisfying as the sea, or under a starry heaven the loveliest of cities glittering like a rival firmament with answering constellations? And yet I recant. For if there is one piece of art which is better than nature, 't is Botticelli's so-called "Spring," which, long misprised and now worm-riddled, adds the last magic to the wonderful flower-city. To her that hath shall be given.

GLASGOW

"And what do you think of Glasgow?" said the pretty lady interviewer—I have the right to say she was pretty because she said in print that I wasn't. I replied that of course Glasgow wasn't pretty but—and here would have followed an amiable dissertation upon the municipal superiority of Glasgow. "But," hastily interrupted the lady interviewer, "have you seen the fine vista of St. Vincent Street, the Great

Western Road, the finest thoroughfare in Europe, the charming residential districts of Pollokshields West and Dowanhill, the wide view from the South Side Park or picturesque Camphill?" I tried to edge in an abashed "No," for a monosyllable is the most one can hope to secure of the conversation in an interview; but the pretty lady interviewer went on reproachfully: "Have you seen that stately hill of the dead, the Necropolis, from Cathedral Square? It is itself a quaint and beautiful medley of architecture past and present. Have you seen beautiful Kelvingrove, through which flows the classic Kelvin? In many world-famous cities have I been and yet seen nothing more beautiful than the view on one side of Partick Bridge." I apologised to Glasgow, inwardly confounding the eminent Scotch littérateur who had assured me that Glasgow was the most loathsome den north of Tweed, almost the only such den—his malison upon Glasgow! But although I feel personally nothing but gratitude to Glasgow and its noisy University students, I cannot honestly award it the apple for beauty. After all it is the centre of the town that one naturally gravitates to, and no charm of suburbs can remove the general impression of commercial dinginess.

No, Glasgow must be content with its wealth and its public spirit. If it does not stir the imagination like Edinburgh, it satisfies the brain and the heart, for it is grappling manfully with many social problems, with the opening of parks and hospitals, and especially with the housing of the poor, and is developing an artistic conscience to boot. It owns its gas and water, and I had the felicity of meeting the Lord Provost at the very moment when, his glittering insignia heaving with emotion on his joyous breast, he had to announce to the Town Council that the fiercely-canvassed step of taking over the tramways had resulted in a balance to the good. When the Lord Provost had returned to his chair, I was shown the Councillors themselves at their mahogany tables, in their beautiful Council-chamber, and I made notes— not of the debate, as the lynx-eyed reporter, who counted the number of times I sucked my pencil, imagined—but of the improved appearance of George Square under snow. Seen through the windows the square stretched away pure and beautiful the gloomy statues blanched and Prince Albert's horse gleaming proudly with white trappings. The Municipal Buildings deserve all the praise they have received. The special staircase, which is used only on state occasions, presents from point to point a marvellously proportioned medley of arches and pillars and arcades, with a dominant Corinthian note. It is really "frozen music." And when adorned with tropical plants and lit up with electric lights and pretty faces, it must indeed be a superb sight. Very imposing, too, is the vast Banqueting Hall, from whose platform, to test the acoustic effect of the rows of wires stretched six inches apart under the ceiling to break the sound, I addressed vacancy. The panels of this hall still await their artists. 'T is a rare opportunity for Glasgow to emulate the Parisian Pantheon; and, indeed, there is so much art-work to be done in Glasgow that one begins to understand why it is threatening to become the capital of British Art. The best road in Scotland is no longer that which leads to England. It was curious for a humble author to walk these stately halls, convoyed by courteous officers in red swallow-tails, and to rub shoulders with civic millionaires. An awesome air of wealth hung over the men and the place, a crushing suggestion of vast enterprises, of engineering and railway building and the running of steamers, a subtle aroma of colossal fortunes, wrested from the world by the leverage of an initial half-crown. I have often gone to places with only half a crown in my pocket, but it never seemed to lead to anything. So I surveyed these men with blended reverence and bewilderment, wondering why they bothered themselves to make all that money, and whether they ever suspected they were but tools in the hands of destiny, by whose marvellous alchemy the self-centred ambition of the individual is transmuted to the service of the world. The genial Bailie Simons, who was my host—fancy living in daily contact with a Bailie!—informed me that the grave city fathers are sadly degenerating. Thirty years ago they did not smoke in public: now there is a smoking-room in the sacred building itself; and at least one of them has been seen to leave it in a white hat.

Like the king's daughter, Glasgow is all glorious within, and its inner artistic aspirations make up for and are perhaps inversely inspired by its outer unloveliness. The world must not judge Glasgow's taste by the recent Puritanic rumpus over the nude. The worthy Bailies and the Chief Constable who drew the line at Leighton and Solomon have overlooked the interesting nudities in their own Galleries. The affinity of the Scotch and the French, which has often been noted in history, and which accounts for their swamping the English in literature, has made Style the watchword of the Glasgow School of Art. Whistler's "Carlyle" hangs in the Corporation Galleries, and it was the stylist, Lavery, who secured the tedious commission to commemorate Her Majesty's opening of the Glasgow Exhibition by the usual plethora of portraits. It would have made a more interesting picture had Mr. Lavery perpetuated the fact—so pregnant a contribution to the philosophy of Exhibitions—that a profit of £10,000 was derived from the switchbacks. The picture would then have made a nice supplement to Mr. Lavery's famous studies of "Croquet" and "Tennis." The very slabs of the Corporation staircase are infected with Impressionism, and their natural veinings body forth, here a charge of cavalry, there a march of infantry, and yonder a portrait of Sir William Vernon Harcourt with a prophetic coronet. The stones of Glasgow await their Ruskin. The Exhibition which I saw at the Glasgow Institute of Fine Arts was far more interesting than the last Academy, though it contained some of the same pictures. I was able to tell the Scotch artists an anecdote which no one had heard before, for the simple reason that it was true, and that it happened to me. It was in Perth that, puzzling over a grimy statue, I was accosted by a bare-footed newsboy with his raucous cry of "Hair-r-ald, Glasgow Hair-r-ald!"

"I'll take one," quoth I, "if you'll tell me whose statue that is."

"'T is Rabbie Burns" replied he, on the nail.

"Thank you," said I, taking the paper. "And what did he do, to deserve the statue?"

My newsboy scratched his head. Perceiving his embarrassment, a party of his friends down the street called out in stentorian chorus: "Ay, 't is Babbie Burns."

"But what did he do to deserve the statue?" I thundered back. They hung their heads. At last my newsboy recovered himself; his face brightened. "Well?" said I again, "what did he do to deserve this statue?"

"He deed!" answered the intelligent little man.

Another newsboy, whom I asked if he had ever read Sir Walter Scott, replied, "No, he is ower dreich (over dry)."

Talking of statues, I see that Paisley is going to erect a full-sized figure of the late Thomas Coats, with a bronze high hat under his bronze arm. The history of the Corporation Art Galleries is curious. The nucleus of the collection is the bequest of a coach-builder, who seems to have had a Glaswegian Renaissance all to himself, for it was years after his death before his legacy was routed out from the lumber-rooms to which it had been consigned, and ere its many genuine treasures were catalogued by Mr. James Paton, the learned curator, whose magic-lantern exhibit the other day of the coach-building connoisseur's face was the first display of his lineaments to an ungrateful posterity. The Galleries now claim to contain so many Old Masters that no connoisseur is complete without a knowledge of them. Except Velasquez, there is scarcely one of the great painters who is not represented here, even including Giorgione, of whom, parodying Hegel's remark about the one disciple who understood him ("and he doesn't understand me!"), it may be said that there are only two genuine specimens of him in the world, and that both of these are by his pupils. What Mary Logan would say to these Rembrandts and Rubenses I know not; but there is much of indisputable value in this collection, to say nothing of Flaxman's masterpiece—the statue of Pitt—or the recent accessions, such as the Whistler, or David Murray's "Fir Faggots," or the bust of Victor Hugo by Rodin.

Pictorially the hill of the dead was the most interesting part of Glasgow I saw—a scene which, especially in its simple severe Protestant draping of snow, might well tempt the artist. At its summit John Knox looks down upon the Cathedral, whose altars and images were broken during the Reformation, and whose new stained windows (made in Germany) testify by their preference for Old Testament subjects to the latent Puritanism of Caledonia. Especially interesting is the crypt, with its sepulchral church, whose subterranean service is recorded in "Rob Roy." One of the pillars of the crypt proper is called the Rob Roy pillar, for behind it the great outlaw is supposed to have hidden. Near it is the shrine of St. Mungo, patron saint of Glasgow, who has presumably risen in the hierarchy now that Glasgow has been made a county. Facing the shrine is a window decorated with a portrait of Edward Irving, clothed as St. John the Baptist. The cicerone said it was greatly admired because the eyes followed you about wherever you walked. This is not the first time I have been asked to admire as supreme art what is really one of the commonest of optical delusions. After the Cathedral had closed, it had to be reopened because I had lost a glove within. After a careful search the glove was found in the gloomy crypt, pointing its finger at this miraculous picture, unable to tear itself away. But perhaps the most characteristic thing I came across in Glasgow was an inscription at the end of the bridge leading to the picturesque cemetery. "The adjoining bridge was erected by the Merchants' House of Glasgow to afford a proper entrance to their new cemetery, combining convenient access to the grounds with suitable decoration to the venerable Cathedral and surrounding scenery, to unite the tombs of many generations who have gone before with the resting-places destined for generations yet unborn, where the ashes of all shall repose until the rising of the just, when that which is born a natural body shall be raised a spiritual body, when this corruptible must put on incorruption, when this mortal must put on immortality, when death is swallowed up in victory." There you have Glasgow! An auctioneer's advertisement blent with an edifying sermon, a happy combination of commerce and Christianity, making the best of this world and the next.

I left Glasgow in a choking yellow fog. Five minutes from the city the train steamed into bright sunshine, which continued till five minutes from London, where a sisterly yellow fog was waiting. As Tennyson sings, I had gone "from the night to the night."

HASLEMERE

I am up a "Bô tree." Every schoolboy knows (that is, of course, every Buddhistic schoolboy) that when the Buddha made "the great renunciation," he attained Nirvana by sitting under a "Bô tree." My "Bô tree" is a great oak in the heart of the woods, mounted by a dizzy spiral staircase, at the summit of which you enter Nirvana by means of the "House on the Garden," a glass-house floored with boards and furnished with rustic chairs, a lounge and a writing-table; and here, amid the tree-tops, I write to the music of thrush and blackbird, with restful glances at the sailing clouds or at the sunny weald, that circles for miles around and ends to the south in the "downs" that hide the English Channel. Perhaps it is because my landscape takes in Tennyson's happy Haslemere home that my thought runs so much on him to-day, and then runs back to a cold stone staircase up which I toiled in pitchy blackness to see a great French poet. Taine, who preferred Alfred de Musset to Tennyson, made of a contrast between the two men the most telling pages in his history of our literature, setting in graphic antithesis the dust and flare and fever of the Boulevards against the

English home, gray twilight poured
On dewy pastures, dewy trees,
Softer than sleep—all things in order stored,
A haunt of ancient peace,

where the English Laureate brooded over his chiselled verses. How much more piquant a contrast might be drawn between the jealously-guarded castle in which Tennyson entrenched himself and the accessible garret in the Rue St. Jacques where Verlaine held his court in absolute bonhomie and déshabille.

But, alas! there is no Nirvana on my "Bô Tree"—at least, not to-day. The blatancy of a brass band bursts forth on the breeze. A popular waltz silences the cuckoos. I climb down my spiral staircase and hasten across the wood to discover what these strange sounds portend. In front of the creeper-clad house I come upon a scene of comic opera. This is the village fête day, and here are the festive villagers come to pay allegiance to the lord of the manor. The majority are Foresters, and wear green sashes, and carry banners like to the pictorial pocket-handkerchiefs of Brobdingnag. The music gives over, and my host addresses them from between the roses of his porch, and they laugh at his genial jokes with the unanimity of the footlights. There are tiny tots and old women in the background, and yonder is the Village Beauty—a ripe maid, i' faith, and a comely. There are other girls in her train; but, oddsbobs! what have they done with their tights? and why do they delay to announce her approaching marriage in merry melodic chorus? But I conceal my surprise and, as the cynical Man from Town (gadzooks!), ogle the Pride of the Village, to the disgust of her rural swain, who has started blowing the trombone and dare not desist, though his cheeks get redder and more explosive each instant. In the next Act we all go down to the annual dinner, in a long rose-wreathed tent, and the Parson says grace and the Parson's Clerk "Amen," and the Squire (in corduroy knickerbockers and leggings) bestows his benediction on all the village, while without, the happy peasants project sticks at cocoanuts or try their strength with mallets, and all is virtuous and feudal. In the third Act we are in the Vicarage Garden—a beautiful set, with real rhododendrons. Sir Roger de Coverley takes tea i'fackins with the Parson, and the Stalwart Farmer passes the sugar to the Man from Town, who is gazing out wistfully towards the Village Green, where the Village Beauty foots it featly with the Village Idiot. The last Act passes in the Drawing-Boom of "Bô tree" House, where the Archdeacon's Daughter touches her tinkling guitar and warbles a plaintive ballad:—

O give my love to Nancy,
 The girl that I adore—
Tell her that she'll never see
Her soldier any more—
Tell her I died in battle
Fighting with the black,
Every inch a soldier,
Beneath the Union Jack.

Dear naïve old song, fitting climax of a feudal day, sweet with the freshness of those simple times, when art for art's sake was a shibboleth uninvented, and every other man was not diabolically clever! How many mothers and sisters wept over thy primitive pathos, as they knitted the Berlin wool-work! how many masculine hearts throbbed more manfully at the appeal of thy crude patriotism! To-day we analyse ruthlessly thy metre, proclaiming it the butterwoman's rank to market, and thy sentiment, which we dub pinchbeck, and we remember that the Union Jack is used only in the Navy; we are deaf to thy inspiration and dumb at thy chorus; we are sceptical as to thy soldier's love: Nancy, we know from realistic poets of the Barrack Room, took up with another young man before her month was out; and as for the black, he is the object of our devoutest solicitude. Go to! thou art surely a Gilbertian travesty, a deliciously droll compound of vulgar patriotism and maudlin pathos. And yet somehow there are tears on the smiling cheeks of the Man from Town. Let us go out and hear the nightingales and be sentimental under the moon. Hark how they precipitate their notes in a fine lyric rapture. This is the same "Jug, Jug, Jug," that called forth Keats' immortal ode. We cannot hear the birds' music for itself; it comes to us through melodious chimes of poetry. Nature has been so filtered through human emotion, so passed and repassed through the alembic of poetic passion, that she has ceased to be natural. Little children and fools, on whom, according to the Talmud, the gift of prophecy devolved when the Temples fell, may still see her naked, but for the lettered man she is draped in lyric conventions. There is anthropomorphism in literature as well as in theology: for George Eliot Nature is steeped in humanity; she cannot see anything for itself. "Our delight in the sunshine on the deep-bladed grass to-day might be no more than the faint perception of wearied souls, if it were not for the sunshine and the grass in the far-off years which still live in us and transform our perception into love." I wonder if she ever wrote a pure description of scenery without psychological or mythological allusions. To a soul saturated with literary prepossessions, nightingales, like love and most things human, are apt to disappoint and disenchant.

Heard melodies are sweet, but those unheard
Are sweeter.

The cultured American, who has no nightingales at home—not even big ones—and who arranges to hear an English nightingale between a performance at Ober-Ammergau and an exploration of the Catacombs of Paris, often wants his money back after the songster "on yon bloomy spray" has "warbled at eve when all the woods are still." He has been expecting something like a song of Patti accompanied on the piano by Paderewski. It was an American poetess—Mrs. Piatt—who informed the skylark:

The song thou sang'st to Shelley was not half
So sweet as that which Shelley sang to thee!

After all, birds repeat themselves sadly—they strike one note, like a minor poet, and live on the reputation of their first success. It is amusing for a few minutes to hear a clever bird giving imitations of the cuckoo clock, but the joke palls. The Archdeacon's Daughter has a wider repertoire. And so? though the nightingales are still singing, conversation springs up in the copse as if it were a drawing-room and the singers human. My host discourses of the litter of pigs just arrived from the Great Nowhere, and dilates upon the fact that of the 3,423,807 pigs in England no two tails are curled alike. Perhaps even so no two nightingales curl their phrase identically, and one roulade different from another in glory.

PARIS

Decidedly the Parisian atmosphere is charged with artistic electricity. The play, the novel and the picture flourish on the same stem, and the very advertisement posters tell their lies artistically. Paris is the metropolis of ideas. You may catch them there and set up as a prophet on the strength of a fortnight's holiday. Maeterlinck says he learnt all he knows from a man he met in a brasserie. Fancy picking up ideas in a pothouse! In London you could only pick up "h's." The reverse of the medal is the morbidity that ideas and brasseries engender. In the cafés of the Boule Miehe, where the decadent movements are hatched and the fledgling Verlaines come to drown theusorrows in vermouth, you may see the lacklustre visages and tumbled hair of "diabolical" poets and the world-weary figures of end-of-the-century youngsters pledging their mistresses in American grog.

But the great heart of the People, that beats still to the homely old music, and you shall find no trace of morbidity in the melodramas of the Porte-St.-Martin or the music-halls of the people's quarter. To-day is the Gingerbread Fair—La Foire au Pain d'Épices; and Tout Paris—that is to say, everybody who isn't anybody—is elbowing its way towards the centre of gaiety. Tramcars deposit their packed freights near the Bastile, and where the women of the Revolution knitted, feeding their eyes on blood, bonnetless old crones sit drinking red wine in the sun. The sky is radiantly blue, and there is a music of merry-go-rounds. They are far more elegant than our English merry-go-rounds, these carrousels, hung with tapestry, and offering you circumambient palanquins or even elephants. Before a toy stage, on which a mechanical skirt-dancer disports herself with a tireless smile, an automatic chef-d'orchestre conducts the revolutionary march (none other than "Ta-ra-ra-Boom-de-ay") while grotesque figures strike stiffly at bells. On the pavement an old man has spread for sale a litter of broken dolls, blind, halt and lame, when not decapitated; and in the roadway the festive crowd splits to allow the passage of a child's coffin covered with white flowers. The air thrills with the "ping" of unsuccessful shots: I take a gun, and by aiming at a ball dancing on a fountain jet, hit a bull's-eye two yards to the left. I throw flat rings at a sort of ninepins, five shots for a halfpenny: the first four leave the pins stolid and the public derisive. I throw the last at random, bring down half the pins, and stalk off: nonchalantly, the pet of the fickle French populace. I buy pancakes fried on the stall while you wait—they are selling like hot cakes—and but for the difficulty of finding one with my name picked out in pink on the gingerbread, I would buy a pig and hang it on my breast. Some of the pigs have mottoes instead of names:

De toute la création
C'est moi le plus cochon.

Another asserts:

De la tête à la queue
Je suis délicieux.

I ignore the pigs, but I pacify local prejudice by buying two gingerbread sailors—a Russian and a French—shaking hands in symbolisation of the Russo-French alliance, and I further prove myself a patriot by throwing bright wooden balls into the mouth of a great-faced German, for which I receive the guerdon of a paper rose and a Berlin wool monkey. I purchase a ticket from a clown standing on a platform begirt by noisy cages, and partake in a raffle for a live turkey; but fortunately I am spared the task of carrying it through the Fair, and not wishing to tempt Providence again, I content myself with trying for soap. A pack of cards is spread round a wheel with an index: round goes the wheel, and whoever has the card at which the index stops gets an orange, or if he likes to save up his oranges exchanges them for a box of soap. You get four cards for two sous, but I take all the pack. Round goes the wheel imperturbably. It stops. Amid the breathless anxiety of the crowd I examine my cards, and invariably find myself the fortunate possessor of the winning one. But, by some mysterious arithmetic, which amuses the crowd, every time I win I have to pay several sous. By such roundabout methods I ultimately arrive at the soap. I have my portrait taken, allured by the "only a franc." My image has a degenerate air; the photographer informs me it will not stay unless he fixes it with enamel—which will be another franc. By the time it is framed it has come up to six francs, and then, as I leave, the attendant begs I will remember him! I give him the photograph, and depart, hoping he will remember me. At the Place de la Nation the fun grows thicker: there is a rain of confetti, and everybody comes out in coloured spots; the switchback is busy, chairs mount and descend on ropes, and there is a bunch of balloons; on a platform outside a booth a showman beats a drum, the riding-master cracks his whip, and ladies of uncertain ages and exuberant busts smile all day in evening dress; in the neighbouring Cirque the Ball of the City of Paris is whirling noisily. Yes, life goes on in the old, old way in the land of equality and brotherhood; and the "red fool-fury of the Seine" is but a froth on the surface. The "Twilight of the Peoples" is the morbid vision of a myopic seer. With which reflection we will leave Sanity Fair.

As I write there is an appalling, long-drawn crash, which brings the whole Quarter to its doors and windows. "Bombs" are in everybody's mouth, and I find myself automatically repeating a sentence out of the Latin exercise-book of my boyhood: "How comes it that thunder is sometimes heard when the sky is clear?" I irrelevantly remember that "sometimes" must be translated "not never." In the streets little groups are gathered, gesticulating and surmising. Some say "The Panthéon," others "The Luxembourg"; others trust it is only a gas explosion. I shock my group by hoping it is a bomb, so that I may say I have heard it go off. But I know nothing till I read "Paris Day by Day" next evening in "The Daily Telegraph," and find that my ambition has been gratified, and that the chief victim of the explosion is a Decadent Poet. Has any one been taking seriously Nordau's cry for the extinction of the Degenerates?

The dead have their day in France, but it was not le jour des morts when I bethought myself of visiting the grave of Maupassant. I do not care for these crowded "at homes,"—I prefer to pay my respects in solitude. You will not think this remark flippant if you are familiar with French cemeteries, if you know those great family sepulchres, fitted up as little chapels, through whose doors, crowned with the black cross, you may see the great wax tapers in the candelabra at the altar, the stained-glass windows with the figure of the Madonna and Child, the eikons of Christ, the praying-stools, the vases, the busts or photographs of the deceased—worthy people who not only thought life worth living but death worth dying, and did the one and the other respectably and becomingly. Maupassant lies in one art-quarter of Paris, just as Heinrich Heine lies in the other. The cemetery is off the Boulevard Raspail, within bow-shot of the ateliers of Whistler and Bouguereau, overlooked by an imposing statue of M. Raspail which sets forth that scientific citizen's many virtues and services. He proclaimed Universal Franchise in 1830, he proclaimed the Republic in 1848, and his pedestal now proclaims with equal cocksureness that science is the only religion of the future. "Give me a cell and I will build you up all organised life," cries the statue, and its stony hand seems to wave theatrically as in emulation of the bas-reliefs on its base representing Raspail animating his camarades to victory. But alas! tout passe, tout casse, tout lasse, and not all the residents of the Boulevard are aware of the origin of their address. Chateaubriand survives as a steak and Raspail as a Boulevard.

The cemetery Montparnasse is densely populated, and I wandered long without finding the author of "Boule de Suif." It was a wilderness of artificial flowers, great wreaths made of beads. Beads, beads, beads, black or lavender, and even white and yellow, blooming garishly in all sizes on every grave and stone, in strange theatrical sentimentality; complex products of civilisation, making death as unnatural as the feverish life of the Boulevards. Sometimes the beaded flowers were protected by glass shades, sometimes they were supplemented by leaden or marble images. Over one grave I found a little porcelain angel, his wings blue as with the cold; and under him last year's angel in melancholy supersession. Elsewhere, most terrible sight of all in this ghastly place, was a white porcelain urn on which were painted a woman's and a man's hand clasped, the graceful feminine fingers in artistic contrast with the scrupulously-cuffed male wrist with the motto, "À mon mari, Regrets éternels." Wondering how soon she remarried, I roved gloomily among these arcades of bourgeois beads, these fadeless flowers, these monstrous ever-blacks, relieved to find a touch of humour, as in a colossal wreath ostentatiously inscribed "À ma belle-mère." I peeped into the great family tombs, irresistibly reminded of "Lo, the poor Indian," and the tribes who provision their dead; I wondered if the old ghosts ever turn in their graves (as there is plenty of room for them to do) when some daughter of their house makes an imprudent alliance. Do they hold family councils in the chapel, I thought, and lament the growing scepticism of their grandchildren? Do they sigh to see themselves so changed from the photographs in the family album that confronts their hollow orbits? Do they take themselves as seriously in death as they did in life? But they were all scornfully incommunicative. And at last, despairing of discovering the goal of my journeyings, I inquired of a guardian in a peaked blue cap and a blue cloak, who informed me that it was in the twenty-sixth section of the other cemetery. Wonderfully precise, red-tape, bureaucratic, symmetrical people, the French, for all their superficial curvetings! I repaired to the other portion of the cemetery, to lose myself again among boundless black beads and endless chapels and funereal urns; and at last I besought another blue-cloaked guardian to show me the grave of Maupassant. "Par içi," he said nonchalantly: and eschewing the gravel walks he took a short cut through a lane of dead maidens—

What's become of all the gold
Used to hang and brush their bosoms?—

and, descending an avenue of estimable pères de famille, turned the corner of an elegant sepulchre, to which only the most fashionable ghosts could possibly have the entry. Dear, dear, what heart-burnings there must be among the more snobbish shadows of Montparnasse! My guide made me pause and admire, and he likewise insisted on the tribute of my tear before an obelisk to slaughtered soldiers and a handsome memorial to burnt firemen.

But perceiving my impatience to arrive at the grave of Maupassant, "Mais, monsieur," he protested, "il n'y a rien d'extraordinaire." "Vraiment!" said I, "c'est là l'extraordinaire." "Rien du tout d'extraordinaire," he repeated doggedly. "Sauf le cadavre," I retorted. He shook his head, "Très pauvre la tombe," he muttered: "pas du tout riche." Another guardian, wall-eyed, here joined him, and catching the subject of conversation, "Très pauvre," he corroborated compassionately. But he went with us, accompanied by a very lean young Frenchman with a soft felt hat, an over-long frock-coat, tweed trowsers, and a black alpaca umbrella. He looked like a French translation of some character of Dickens. At last we arrived at the grave. "C'est là!" and both guardians shook their heads dolefully. "Très pauvre!" sighed one. "Rien du tout—rien," sighed the other. And, thank Heaven, they were right. Nothing but green turf and real flowers, and a name and a date on a black cross—the first real grave I had come across. No beads, no tawdry images, nothing but the dignity of death, nothing but "Guy de Maupassant, 6 Juillet, '93," on the cross, and "Guy de Maupassant, 1850-93," at the foot. The shrubs were few, and the flowers were common and frost-bitten; but in that desert of bourgeois beads, the simple green grave stood out in touching sublimity. The great novelist seemed to be as close to the reality of death as he had been to that of life. Those other dead seemed so falsely romanticist. It was a beautiful sunny winter afternoon. There was a feel of spring in the air, of the Resurrection and the Life. Beyond the bare slim branches of the trees of the other cemetery, gracefully etched against the sky, the sun was setting in a beautiful bank of dusky clouds. Life was so alive that day, and death so dead. Outside the tomb the poem of light and air, and inside the tomb—what? I thought of the last words of "Une Vie," that fine novel, which even Tolstoï considers great, of the old servant's summing up: "La vie, voyez-vous, ça n'est jamais si bon ni si mauvais qu'on croit." "Perhaps," thought I, "'t is the same with death." "The Société des Gens de Lettres had to buy the ground for him," interrupted the wall-eyed guardian compassionately. The Dickensy Frenchman heaved a great sigh. "Vous croyez!" he said. "Yes," asseverated the other guardian—"he has it in perpetuity." Ignorant of the customs of death, I wondered if one's corpse were liable to eviction, and whether the statute of limitations ought not to apply. "Je pensais qu'il avait une certaine position," observed the Frenchman dubiously. "Non," replied the wall-eyed guardian, shaking his head, "Non, il est mort sans le sou." At the mention of coin I distributed pourboire. The first guardian went away. I lingered at the tomb, alive now to its more sordid side. Only one row of bourgeois graves, some occupied, some still á louer, separated it from an unlovely waste piece of ground, bounded by the gaunt brick wall of the fast-filling cemetery. As I began to muse thereon, I heard a cry, and perceived my guardian peeping from round the corner of a distant tomb, and beckoning me with imperative forefinger. I wanted to stay; I wanted to have "Meditations at the grave of Maupassant," to ponder on the irony of death, to think of the brilliant novelist, the lover of life, cut off in his pride, to lie amid perspectives of black and lavender beads. But my guardian would not let me. "Il n'y a rien à voir," he cried almost angrily, and haled me off to see the real treasures of his cemetery. In vain I persisted that I must not give him trouble, that I could discover the beauties for myself. "O monsieur!" he said reproachfully. Fearing he might return my pourboire, I followed him helplessly to inspect the pompous bead-covered tombs of the well-to-do, shocking him by stopping to muse at the rude mound of an anonymous corpse, remembered only by a little bunch of immortelles. One of the fashionable sepulchres stood open, and was being dusted by a man and a woman (on a dust from dust principle, apparently). Most of the dust seemed to be little beads. My keeper exchanged a word with the cleaners, and I profited by the occasion to escape. I sneaked back to the grave of Maupassant, but I had barely achieved a single Reflection, when "Holà, holà!" resounded in loud tones from afar. I started guiltily, but in a moment I realised that it was the cry of expulsion. The sunset was fading, and the gates were to be locked. I hastened across the cemetery, evading my guardian's face of reproach, and in another few moments the paths were deserted, the twilight had fallen, and the dead were left alone with their beads.

SLAPTON SANDS

After all the world is a large place. At the moment of writing I have never heard of Home Rule, nor do I care two straws whether the House of Lords is to be blown up on the fifth of November. What moves my interest, what stirs my soul, what arouses the politician that lurks in the best of us, is this question of the crab-pots. Shall the trawlers of Brixham be allowed to slash at our cords and to send our wicker baskets adrift, spoiling our marine harvests and making our larders barren against the winter? They hover about our beautiful bay—these fiends in human shape, with brown wings outspread—and wantonly lay waste our fishing-pots in their reckless course, so that our crabs walk backwards into the sea. We have had gentlefolks down from London about it, men who argue and palaver, and wear high hats and are said to have long bills, and there is talk of a Government cutter to protect us, towed by red tape, and the trawlers are to cast their nets farther asea. But beware of believing what you read in the Brixham papers—we have no voice to represent us in the press, and so these Brixham organs spread falsehoods about us in every corner of the globe. A pretty pretence, forsooth, that it is the steamers who plough up our crab-pots. Why, from Michaelmas to Christmas, when the trawlers are away, not a single pot is disturbed from its station, though the funnels smoke as usual in the eye of heaven. No, no, ye hirelings of the press. Turn your mercenary quills elsewhere, beslaver Mr. Gladstone or belabour him, arbitrate on the affairs of nations, and throw your weighty influence into the scale of European politics. But do not confuse the mind of the country on the question of crab-pots.

We do not get the Brixham papers here, but friends in London tell us that is what they say. It is the same with the crabs—we have to order them from London. All local products come viâ London nowadays: London is like a central ganglion, through which all sensations must travel before being felt at the outside points where they were really incurred. This is the case even with Irish patriots: they are made in Ireland, but if you want them you have to go to London clubs for them. We have only had one funeral here since I came, and then we got our material from London. He had gone up to a London hospital— poor fellow!—and that was the end of him. The village butcher it was, who thus went the way of all flesh, and all of us went to his funeral and wept, for want of something else to do. One cannot always be flippant, even on a holiday. Fortunately the butcher left an aged father, who announced his intention of carrying on the business, so we dried our eyes and dined, sure of the future. We thought of the many creatures the deceased had killed—the Juno-eyed oxen, the tender lambs, the peaceful pigs—and we did not see why we should be so sentimental over the human species. We are all murderers, and yet we are ready to gush over the first corpse that comes along. How I envy the death-bed of a vegetarian!

We are not vegetarians here, but at least we eschew the six-course dinner which so few travellers ever succeed in shaking off, even in Ultima Thule. The most of modern travelling is a sort of Cook's Tour. Everywhere the menu is before you, everywhere waves the napkin, like the flag of civilisation. Nowhere do we eat ourselves into the real life of the people; everywhere the same monotonous variety of fare in kitchen-French. In the remotest Orkneys, in the caves of Iona, in the fjords of Norway, amid the crevasses of the Alps—'t is the same tale of entrées and entremets. When Dr. Johnson made his tour in the Highlands, he was allowed to forget he was not taking a walk down Fleet Street. He interviewed the chiefs in their fastnesses, the cottagers in their crofts. He broke rye-bread with the shepherd, ate haggis and porridge with the peasant, and drank a gill of whisky to see "what makes a Scotchman happy." Behind him he left his dish of tea, and the pet pork that made the veins of his forehead swell with ecstasy. But to-day the dinner-gong resounds where Rob Boy's bugle blared, and you may sit behind your serviette

Where the sun his beacon red
Kindles on Ben Voirlich's head,

or where the monument of a Gaelic poet broods above the heather. The tyranny of the table-d'hôte ceases not even at sea. Every ship bears these monster meals in its belly—from salami to pineapple— whether it walk the Boreal waters, or touch the Happy Isles of Mid-Pacific, or swelter in the Red Sea. Not all the majesties and terrors of naked nature can dock one hors d'oeuvre from the menu. Our stomachs we have always with us—the traveller's only real vade mecum. We change our sky but not our stomach. When Nansen reaches the North Pole, he will, I am sure, be able to put up at the local hotel, and have every luxury of the cosmopolitan cuisine except the ices, which will probably have been all sent up to the London market. It is this sort of thing that makes foreign travel merely an expensive delusion. Your common traveller never gets away from England, fare he never so far. His church, his kitchen and his company are those he left behind him. To get away from England one must go to Devonshire or Cornwall. But even here, amid the combes and the leys, the crags and the quarries, the modern hotel, with its perfect sanitation and imperfect French, is springing up with the rapidity of Badraoulbadour's palace. It spoils the primitiveness of the people, and gives them ideas below their station. They lose their simple manliness and take tips. They corrupt their autochthonic customs, and drink champagne cider. The modern hotel is a upas-tree, under whose boughs poetry withers. One looks to see the ancient ballads lose their blood and brawn. In time we may expect to find Cornwall producing vers de société. As thus:—

And shall Trelawney dine?
And shall Trelawney dine?
Then thrice ten thousand Cornish men
Will order in the wine.

In the absence of six-course dinners and newspapers about Home Rule, we have had to fall back upon literature. We borrowed Zola's latest—from the rector—and read it simultaneously, stealing it from one another. Even the dogs have devoured bits of it. The poodle has taken in most, being French. She is an elegant, tricksy creature, Miss Plachecki by name, but called—for short—"Wopsy." Wopsy's back is arranged in beds like a Dutch garden; she has rosettes of black hair symmetrically disposed about her hind quarters, and her tail is exactly like a mutton cutlet in its frill. She belongs to the Woman of the party. Chum belongs to the Girl. He is a bull-pup, with a frightfully ferocious face, but he never bites unless he wants to hurt you. Girl says she took him to a fashionable photographer's, but the artist refused to pose him. In vain she pointed out that Chum was more paralysed than he; that Chum was trembling all over (I opine 't was at the sight of the actresses' portraits—the young dog!). The photographer steadfastly kept the apparatus between him and the animal, telling Girl a story about a man who owned a bull-dog with a bad memory. The man, coming home late, and entering his sitting-room, was met by an ominous growl in the darkness. Bull-dogs have little smell, and so the man was not recognized. He made a movement towards the mantelpiece, where the matches were, to strike a light and convince the dog of its mistake. But unfortunately the dog guarded the mantelpiece, and every move was answered by a ghastly growl. More unfortunately still, the man's bedroom was only approached through the sitting-room, and its door was only approached through the dog. So, for want of a match, the man passed the night like a Peri at the gates of Paradise. At last Girl posed Chum, herself, her draperies constituting a nebulous background; and the artist, walking warily, adjusted his instrument, and the sun which shines alike on saints and bull-pups, painted the squatter's portrait. But, alas! a woeful disappointment was in store. When the proofs arrived, it was found that all that delightful uncouthness of visage which is Chum's chief charm, all that fascinating ferocity which makes him a thing of ugliness and a joy for ever, had vanished—refined away, idealised into a demureness as of domestic tabby, a platitudinarian peacefulness—nay, a sort of beauty! The camera had been so accustomed to actresses that it could no longer work naturally.

VENICE

I am reading Nietzsche and Tolstoï. Each tells me that the morality of the day is all wrong, and that he has discovered the one true way of salvation. Life, cries Nietzsche, strength, sunshine, beauty. Death, cries Tolstoï, abnegation, pity, holiness. 'T is all as old as the hills, and withal so simple that one wonders why Nietzsche should have needed eleven volumes to say it in and Tolstoï endless pamphlets. I never can understand the lengths to which some authors go in self-repetition. Half the books are written to prove that water is dry, and the other half that it's wet. If you would only stop and think just for one moment, cries Tolstoï, you would at once see what a ridiculous life you are leading and you would refuse to lead it any longer. Stop and think! Ay, but 't is difficult thinking to-day.

It will be all over and done with so long—by the time you read this—that the Triple Alliance may be in three pieces; but for the moment the complications of European politics alternately startle and depress my day with furious cannonades of honour from an Italian gunboat and brazen dronings of national anthems from a German band. For the young man whom Tolstoï has described as the most comic figure in Europe, coming to meet Umberto I. in Venice, inconsiderately stationed his yacht just outside my window; and though he is gone at last, Gott sei Dank, the echoes of him still linger in irrelevant cannon-shots that send the pigeons scurrying in mad swoops; while, as if removed from the oppression of his presence, the band of the Hohenzollern plays London music-hall tunes all day long, commencing, significantly enough, with "Oh, Mr. Porter, what a funny man you are!" I never realised how international is our music-hall till I heard Italians staggering home at midnight, singing "Two lovely black eyes" in choice Venetian. A beautiful yacht this Hohenzollern, as large as an Atlantic liner: I suppose an Imperial yacht is like an Imperial pint. 'T was a great moment when it sailed in round a bend, slow and serene—a glorious white vessel, radiant with flags, stately and majestic in its movement as a sonnet of Milton, and about it a black swarm of gondolas, those of the noble families equipped with half a dozen gondoliers in green, yellow, or blue liveries, and at the stern of each boat a trail of silk. And the dense crowds huzzahed, and the band played "God Save the Queen," only in German, so that it meant, Heil dir im Siegeskranz. And after that came the Italian national air, which isn't an anthem, but a quick march, and so lacks dignity. The "Wacht am Rhein" made a half-hearted effort to be present, but in the night we had the Emperor's own "Sang an Aegir," stuck in the middle of a Wagner programme. Beyond this, compliment could scarcely go.

This brazen air was the one jar on the poetry of a spectacle possible only in Venice. Imagine it! Wagner played on a floating fairy-pagoda, built as of gold flame, and shot with green and red, on the broad bosom of St. Mark's basin, in the divine night, the stars seen hanging diversely in free space, not stuck like gold-headed nails in a dark ceiling; and in the mystery of the darkness, the domes and spires and palaces of Venice, and the dim creeping boats, and the quivering reflections of the illuminated Imperial vessel; and across the narrow track of luminous water made by the Pagoda—that glittered with a fantastic splendour as of Aladdin and Arabian nights—sudden gondolas gliding from darkness to darkness, the beautiful curve of the prow sharply revealed, the gondolier growing semi-transparent and quivering with light, a strange half-demoniac figure bestriding his black bark. And, mingled with the music, the hum of multitudes and the tramp of feet and the silence of the vast night. All as Nietzsche's poem on Venice hath it—"Gondeln, Lichter, Musik." Yes, they play politics prettily on the Grand Canal—the finest street in Europe. Does it matter much what is the game? Cannons and colour, bands and decorations, bread and circuses, emperors uncovering to us, beautiful queens waving dainty handkerchiefs—this is what lies behind the dry Treaties of the history books. A few short weeks back we had been very angry with our King, and had talked of Republics and what not. But the dead men in Abyssinia are dead, and we are alive, and the Bengal fire on the palaces is really very picturesque. If we would only stop and think—just for one moment! But there's the rub.

It's no use stopping and thinking, unless everybody else will stop and think at the same time. For you cannot refuse to lead a life that everybody is leading, unless you are willing to be crushed by the revolutions of the social machinery. Socialists, for instance, are often twitted with not "behaving as sich." But socialists say that socialism should be the law of the land: they do not say that it is practicable for an odd man here and there to be a socialist in a world of individualists. Tolstoï, to be of effect, would have to move all mankind at once to renounce its ways, to abjure the lust of the eye and the pride of life. And he would have to keep on moving it, or back it would roll. Mazzini and the unification of Italy—what words to conjure with! But Mazzini is dead, and how much of Italy is alive! 'T is more like a great show-place, supported by its visitors, than a real, live country. Stop and think! 'T is perhaps better not to think, for fear we should stop. William II., at any rate—he is not likely to stop and think. This young man—from all I have observed since he became my neighbour—lives a highly coloured dramatic existence, in which there are sixty minutes to every hour and sixty seconds to every minute, the sort of life that should have pleased Walter Pater. He must be a disciple of Nietzsche, a lover of the strong and the splendid, this German gentleman who is just off to Vienna to prance at the head of fifteen hundred horsemen. While he lived opposite me, it was all excursions and alarums. As a neighbour an emperor is distinctly noisy. The local comic papers suggested that, as a universal genius, Guglielmo II. would at once set about rowing a two-oared sandolo. But this difficult feat Guglielmo did not essay, being convoyed more comfortably in a long-boat by a brawny crew. Curious, by the way, that transformation of William! They announce plays here by G. Shakespeare, the divine Guglielmo.

'T is all very well for Guglielmo, the gondola of Avon, to invite us to sit on the ground and tell sad stories of the death of kings; and in a city of departed Doges and lost glories't is easy to moralise over earthly greatness. But kings are not always dead, and I daresay as William II. in his cocked hat gazed from the quarter-deck of the Hohenzollern at the marvellous but untenanted Palace of the ancient Bridegrooms of the Sea, he felt that a living lion is better than a dead Doge. And yet it is a strange life, a king's. What an unreal universe of flags and cannons and phrases must monarchs inhabit! Do they think that the streets are always gay with streamers and bunting and triumphal arches, always thunderous with throats of men or guns, always impassable? Do they imagine their subjects spend their whole lives in packed black masses, waving hats? Poor kings! I always class them with novelists for ignorance of real life. And to think that they can only get to know life from novels! If they would only stop, and think! But even when they do stop, they never seem to think. Napoleon on St. Helena never faced realities, aggressively pompous to the end. Then there is Don Carlos, whom I miss in my afternoon stroll. He who might have dazzled us with divinity is visibly a feather-less biped. The poor, mock king had to leave Venice because his brother-sovereigns would not have called upon him. For Don Carlos still keeps up the form and style of a crowned head, and remains the last of the Bourbons, a picturesque ruin, reproach to a blasphemous generation, heedless of the divine right of kings.

And the "divinity that doth hedge a king" can be kept up nowhere so cheaply as in Venice. Venice is the dress-coat of cities, making all men equal. Well might Wordsworth dub her "the eldest child of liberty"! For in the streets of Venice you cannot drive or ride—walk you must. No gleaming broughams, no spanking steeds: nothing—be you monarch or mendicant—but your two legs. 'T is strange, in a land of no horses, to find Venetians styled "Cavalier" for title of honour. They should surely be called "Gondoliers." For the gondola is your only chance of display. Rich Americans may flaunt it with four gondoliers and print "Palazzo" on their visiting-cards. But doctors and lawyers live in Palaces, and even a moderate purse can keep a horseless carriage. And your St. Mark's Square, which is the largest drawing-room in the world, is also the most democratic. Ladies of quality jostle shawled street-walkers, a German sailor galls the kibe of a beautiful Browning duchess, officers with showy epaulettes glitter among respectable shopkeepers; helmeted cuirassiers, Austrian admirals, policemen with coloured tufts like lamp-cleaners, German baronesses, bouncing bonnes with babies, garlic-scented workingmen, American schoolgirls, and kings in exile, are mixed pell-mell, all in perfect freedom and equality, and, though in the shadow of St. Mark's Church, quite Christian. And an Italian crowd is also Christian in its freedom from crush. It does not turn a fete into a fight and a concourse into a competition. Thus, as the Prince Consort was amused to find we English said of our pleasure-parties, all "passes off well." Except when there is rain. And the heavens threw unmistakable cold water on the Triple Alliance. The day of the Emperor's stay was the one wet day Venice had known for months—so dank and chill, with so sooty a sky, that my friend the artist, who had just been reading in the London paper that his work had not caught the glamour and the colour of Venice, that the South had not yet revealed its passionate secrets to him, chuckled grimly. What is all this nonsense about an Italian hothouse? At Florence I was afraid of being snow-bound in the sunny South. For, long and heavily, though the London meteorologists registered sunshine,

Cadeva dal cielo la neve
Con tutta la sua quiete.

(Down from heaven fell the snow
With all its quietness.)

This perfect description of snowfall—which I found rudely chalked on the wall of a Venetian alley—could never have been conceived in the Italy of popular imagination. The superstition about Italian sunshine is like that about Italian beauty. If the country about Florence is the loveliest in Europe, surely the plain of Lombardy around Padua is the ugliest—a land of symmetrical tree-stumps and stony villas flaunting themselves on the roadway in pompous publicity.

In Venice the Emperor seemed specially to irritate the elements. The illuminations were extinguished by a terrific torrent that sent the people pattering away into the black, starless night, gleaming with rain and fire; and to-night when the imperial band attempted to play "Sang an Aegir" again, the heavens fell, and audience and orchestra vanished in the twinkling of a gas-lamp, while the pavement of the Piazza glittered golden as the facade of St. Mark's with dancing reflections, and the lights burnt blue in the wind. Yes, though the papers next day said the Emperor's Song was applauded enthusiastically, Jupiter Pluvius at least never plays the courtier, and Boreas must be a rude reminder to monarchs of their essential humanity. Come, let us sit upon the ground and tell sad stories of the colds of kings. In the daylight I chanced upon a rough wooden platform, bordered with plush and surrounded by tawdry terraces of coloured, glass cups. This was the fairy, Aladdin-like Pagoda. And such, methinks, are kings, on closer acquaintance. How majestic seemed William II., and Humbert, the Kaiserin and Queen Margherita, when, massed in our thousands on the Piazza, we clamoured for a glimpse of them: how inaccessible and star-like when, after much exciting but irrelevant shadow pantomime, they actually appeared on the balcony of the Palace, as if to feed us like the pigeons we had displaced! With what tumultuous rapture did we behold their faces! Stop and think! You cannot stop and think. Enthusiasm is a microbe, and is independent of its object: even so we could yawn over Punch and Judy, if the crowd assembled to yawn. Republicans who came to sneer remained to cheer.

'T is comic this,
And comic that,
And clown on royal pay,
But 't is "Long live unser Kaiser!"
When the band begins to play.

And humanity has need of leaders, heroes—'t is a primal instinct. The Jews had Jehovah himself for sovereign, but nothing would content them but a real man-king, who should rule them and judge them and go out before them in war. Kings were leaders once, but in modern days they are only symbols, just as flags are: the whole force of the nation is behind them, and they stand for home and country. This it is that gives them majesty and divinity. 'T is a case of transformation of function, an old institution adapted to new uses, and valuable partly as giving colour to life, partly for preventing the evils which Gibbon so pregnantly showed to be inseparable from any system of primacy not based on an immutable heredity. The trouble is when the flag wishes to order the march.

An unbroken tradition has kept up the old phrases of loyalty, and so what wonder if a king sometimes takes them seriously! "Le roi le veult" not unnaturally leads sometimes to a king willing. And also we are not quite conscious of the transformation; it has come about so gradually that no one knows when kings ceased to be leaders, and when they became flags, and so with the new feeling blend confusedly strands of the old. We English have abolished the sovereign, but we are too loyal to say so. In Germany the sovereign has refused to be a symbol, and in a country over-civilised in thought and under-civilised in action, he has had a pretty good innings. I must confess I do not find this attitude of his merely ridiculous. It forces clearly upon the modern world the question of kingship, whether it is to be a sham or a reality. Unpopular as William II. has made himself by his martinet methods—ridiculous, if you will— yet there is only one step from the ridiculous to the sublime. In a flippant age he takes himself seriously, has a sense of a responsible relation to his people. Have you seen the cartoon he designed to inspire the nations of the West to league together for the protection of their ideals against the races of the East? The thought may be trite, the philosophy leagues behind the doctrines of the Berlin Aufgeklärter, but it shows a soul above card-playing or court-gossip. What a noble chance there would be for a modern sovereign who should really be the head of his people, on a par with the culture of his age, in harmony with its highest ideals, fostering all that is finest in life and character, in art and thought! Snobbishness would be converted to useful ends, and courtiers would become philosophers out of sheer flattery. But such a Platonic king is scarcely to be looked for: the training is so bad.

The presence of kings makes places abnormal and out of character, but in Venice it rather gives one a sense of the true Venice, she that once held the gorgeous East in fee. For the Venice of every day only escapes vulgarity by force of beauty: she lives up to the English and German tripper, borders her great Piazza with photograph shops, and counts on the sentimental traveller to feed her pigeons. Oh, that trail of the tourist over Europe, falsifying the very things he went out for to see! "Coelum non animum mutant," said the Roman poet long ago of travellers, but the modern traveller carries his sky with him. Instead of "Venice in London" 't is London in Venice. Carefully fenced off from the local life by his table d'hôte, it is rarely that the Briton comes to understand that he and not the native is the foreigner, the forestiere. Cities on show are never real; they are like people posturing before a camera, instead of being taken au naturel. And "the season" is the time in which they are least real. Too many Cooks' tourists spoil the broth. Cities en fête are masked and prankt, and the spring in Italy is like one long Forestieri day. At the church of Eremitani in Padua I was taken to see some Mantegnas at a side-altar while a very devout congregation was celebrating Eastertide, and the verger unlocked a gate and pocketed his tip with undiminished piety. How apt an image of life, these Italian churches—some of us praying and some of us sightseeing! It must be confusing to the celestial bookkeepers to distinguish the Bibles from the Baedekers. And while the real Venice is as unreal as the real Florence or the real Rome, Venice welcoming her king gives one a truer impression of the Venice of our dreams, the Queen of the seas in the brave days of old. Let us forget the steamboats and the iron bridges, let us make believe that the Hohenzollern is the great Bucentaur, in which the Doge went out to wed the Adriatic and which that arch-Philistine Napoleon broke up. For the Venice of every day is a dead city, with nothing left of its ancient glories but wealth. Though the millions be reckoned in lire, there are over a hundred millionaires in Venice. But of that mighty artistic and religious impulse which produced countless churches and palaces, pictures and frescoes, which strewed the very street walls with spirited sculpture, and warmed even parochial offices with priceless paintings, there is as little trace as of the indomitable energy that founded a great Republic on wooden piles and guarded it from the sea by dykes and from its enemies by the sea. The escutcheons of its great families are fast becoming archaeological, and Americans and Jews inhabit their palaces. How great a power Venice was I never realised till I was permitted to see the Archives. It takes three-quarters of an hour to walk through these galleries of town records. Miles of memorandums, wildernesses of reports, acres of ambassadors' letters from every court in Europe, written in cipher with inter-bound Italian translations. I tried to find the report of the ambassador at the Court of St. James anent the execution of Charles I., but gave up hopeless, oppressed by the musty myriads of volumes, and found comfort in the signature of Queen Elizabeth, surely the most regal autograph in the world, like some ship going out against the Armada with swelling canvas and pennants streaming. There's a woman after Nietzsche's heart—strong, splendid, and unscrupulous. If Nietzsche had married her, he might have changed his philosophy. What a diplomatist, this Englishwoman! To this day the Direttore of the Archives of Venice swears by her. Those awesome Archives! The reports of the Council of Ten alone stretch away through vasty halls of death. And then people talk of writing history! How fortunate that the exact details of royal, political and military events are as unessential as they are unattainable! Real history consists mainly of the things that haven't happened—the millions of everyday lives, sunrise and sunset, ships and harvests, the winds and the rain, and the bargains in the market-place. The reading of Clio's blood-stained scroll would be unbearable, were it not for the reflection that all the important things have been left out—the myriads of sunny mornings that dawned on the "Dark Ages," and filled creation with the joy of life; the hopes and loves throbbing in the great obscure mass of humanity; the individual virtues and victories that co-existed with the decadence of great empires; the vast ocean of consciousness of which History just skims the surface. And now all that great Venetian life is over, the dreaded Council of Ten is as the dust that covers its reports, and the Doge's Palace is a spectacle for tourists at a franc a head. Great Caesar dead and turned to show. And those who pay the franc scarcely seem to reflect that princes and artists did not live and die in Italy to help young British or German couples over their honeymoon; that Dandolo and Foscari, Sansovino and Tintoretto, passed away with no suspicion of that latter-day trinity—Bride, Bridegroom, and Baedeker. Strange that that which was so real to themselves is so romantic to us! Such is the transmutation of time, which can colour with poetry things much more prosaic than life in ancient Venice. Nothing of us that doth fade

But doth, suffer a sea-change
Into something rich and strange.

Poets and seers feel the richness and strangeness of the life that is passing under their very eyes. With Maeterlinck it is the mystery, with Stevenson the colour, with Wordsworth the divinity. To see the glamour of the contemporary is the note of your modern. Whitman spent his life trying to see it in the most unpromising materials. The wondering perception of steamships and electric-cables has already grown dulled to us: it requires a Kipling to revivify it. The new photographic process which enables one to carry out Sydney Smith's desire on a hot day, to take off one's flesh and sit in one's bones, alone seems wonderful to us; though to see through a window is just as marvellous as to see through a brick wall. For if nil admirari be the motto of the sage, omne admirari is that of the poet, and the poetry which wafts from the past to the soul of the most commonplace person is seen in the present by him who hath eyes. The pathos of that which must pass away is no less great than the pathos of that which has passed away. And what produces the art-feeling in both cases is the same—the fresh, intense perception of things for themselves alone: only the ordinary man finds it easier to detach his own interests from the past than from the present of which he is part. Romance is not in things, but in the souls that observe. Every place, however enchanted, is inhabited by prosaic persons who earn their living there. My chambermaid was born in Padua—Padua, outside which Donatello could not achieve perfection; Padua, ever dear to us because Portia feigned to have studied law at its University. Alas! alas! the two gentlemen of Verona go down to business in tram-cars, and the

Magic casements opening on the foam
Of faëry lands in perilous seas forlorn

are cleaned and repaired by some one who sends in the bill. Yet, since believing is seeing, let us behold, not the chambermaid and the window-cleaner, but the magic casement and the moonrise. And if to the commonplace our own age is commonplace, yet our age, like youth, is a fault that will mend with time. Our politics, and philosophies too, will crumble and decay, the dust will gather on our books and newspapers, archaeologists will prize our coins, the fashion of our ugly garments will grow picturesque, and samples of our streets will be rebuilt in exhibitions. What is then left to console us for the eternal flux? Only that posterity shall grow old-fashioned too, while we, like antiquity, shall have enjoyed that which never grows old—the sunshine and the stars, love and friendship, the smiles of little children, and the freshness of flowers, aspiration and achievement, thought and worship, struggle and self-sacrifice.

These, these are the eternal things—that persist in every age, in every environment, in old Etruscan villages as in the Paris of to-day: these are the realities to which "the latest scientific conveniences" are but padding, and in which we have had no superiority over our ancestors, even as we shall have no inferiority to our successors, though they riot in "Vril" and balloons, and go on Cooks' Tours to the constellations. The network of nerves in which we live and move and have our being is only capable of a certain quota of sensations, and no invention will really enlarge our enjoyments except it be of a new set of nerves. Persons whose lives have known strange vicissitudes have been astonished to find pleasure and pain about equally distributed in all; and I am optimist enough to think that no age will be really less unhappy than the present. Reformers who imagine they improve on the past age do but alter old institutions to fit new feelings. Reformers are necessary because otherwise the new feelings would be cramped by the old institutions. But there is no addition to the sum of pleasure. Progress really means not lagging behind; and however far we march, the same sunshine will throw the same shadow of pain across our path. The notion of progress, said Spinoza, is a futility, because God, of whom the universe is a manifestation, is always perfect. Later philosophers have found this doctrine a barren blind-alley, and craved for the notion of a more energising God. But both notions seem perfectly compatible. Progress may be just the way perfection manifests itself. The universe moves—and at each point is perfect. It is as good as it could be—at the moment: it could not be any better. For if it could have been, it would have been: it has no interest in being otherwise. That it is not perfect in our sense of the word matters little to the metaphysician. We have such limited experiences of universes that we cannot judge what a really good one should be like; and to say that ours is bad is to foul our own nest.

He had no doubt of the perfection of the universe, that gentle old Franciscan who lives with his twenty-nine brethren on the islet of St. Francesco del Deserto, a rarely visited spot off Venice, that somehow reminded me of the island in Mr. H. A. Jones' "Michael and his Lost Angel." He had never been to Assisi, where his tutelary saint was born. "Have you no wish to see it?" I asked. "My only wish is to obey." Dear old man! He had stopped all his life; but thinking—ah! that is another matter. It was in this island that St. Francis preached to the birds. He was saying the Office when all the birds stopped to listen, and St. Francis took advantage of the opportunity. It was his disciple St. Antony who preached to the fishes, and there is a delicious picture in Padua showing all the fishes perking their heads out of the water and listening in devout dumbness, the very oysters open to conviction. Poor dear fishes! What a delightful change to receive from the upper world something else than hooks! What a sweet simple cloister hath this lonely monastery—a plain stone walk under a red-tiled arcade supported by rough brick pillars, the walls lined by quaint black-and-white engravings of saints engaged in miracles. There is a well in the centre which used to be of sea-water, but St. Bernard of Siena blessed it and it turned sweet. I have drunk of the water, so I can vouch the story is true. And there is a beautiful cypress walk. What a tranquil retreat!

O Beata Solitudo!
O Sola Beatitudo!

as the inscription over the lintel hath it. I do not wonder that St. Francis came here when he was greatly fatigued, "after converting the Sultan of Egypt," as the old Franciscan naïvely explained. 'T is the sort of sanatorium Tolstoï would need, after converting the German Emperor! And despite St. Francis, and his doctrine of brotherhood with birds and fishes, we go on with our cannibal cookery, and even his own Church still teaches that animals have no souls, though that is perhaps because they have no soldi. And despite Tolstoï and his tracts, the people who stop will not think and the people who think will not stop. For to convert the world is the one miracle that the saints have never compassed. Yet is the sunshine of these sweet souls never lost, and the gentle mien of the old Franciscan made me feel at peace even with my sandolier when I found him sound asleep in his boat, wrapped up in my cloak.

And these are the types of character Nietzsche would destroy. They are degenerative, forsooth! They make against life and the joy thereof. Ah, but the joy of life is not only the joy of self-assertion: there is the joy of self-effacement, which is only another form of self-expression, the assertion of a higher self. That was the secret of Jesus, of Buddha. Whereas the doctrine of Nietzsche—c'est le secret de Polichinelle. The man in the street needs no encouragement to enjoyment. It is only by the travail of the centuries that he has been taught to prefer to his own pleasure somebody else's absence of pain. Human nature is like Venice or Holland—a province slowly wrested from the sea, and secured by dams and dykes. Woe to him who makes a breach in the sea-walls! And yet Nietzsche is to be read, though 't is a pity he is to be translated into English for the seduction of unripe minds. The desuetude of Latin as a common language for scholars is to be regretted; it kept the thinkers of Europe in touch, and kept out the profanum vulgus. As I have often pointed out, a truth grows so stale that it is almost a lie, and to invert any conventionality is to produce what is almost a truth. Truth is convex as well as concave.

This method of inversion is Nietzsche's main weapon: as earnest as any of our pulpiteering Puritans, he wears his morality inside out. He denies the copy-book, as Luther denied the infallibility of the Pope. He transposes all moral values, finds virtue often weakness and vice often strength, girds at all the cloud-spinning philosophers, and is one of the most brilliant and suggestive of modern writers, full of epigram and whimsy, and wielding the clumsy German tongue with rare grace and dexterity. But, as might be expected of the son of a parson, he pursues his reaction against conventional cant beyond the bounds of legitimate paradox, replacing the narrow by the narrower. Nietzsche was necessary; some one had to call a spade a spade. The great forces of modern thought, which have been gathering for centuries, had to find shameless expression; and Nietzsche's scorn for those who have tried to patch up hollow truces with bygone beliefs, and dress up new heresies in old Sunday clothes, is amply justified. But what is not justified is his admiration of himself—an admiration so pronounced that it has landed him in a lunatic asylum. Our systems of chronology ought to be recast, cries he; and even as men have dated from A.D., so are they to date from A.N., the year of Nietzsche. Not that he expects immediate recognition: "Erst das Uebermorgen gehört mir. Einige werden posthum geboren." But the bulk of what he tells us is really involved in all modern conceptions of the cosmus—it could have been found long ago in Herbert Spencer.

Anti-Christ he calls himself, and beats the drum and invites you to inspect the greatest philosophy on earth. "Now hold your breath with awe," he has the air of saying, "or if you are not strong enough to hear this fearsome truth, go home to the nursery and read Hegel." And after this fanfaronade, lo! some commonplace that you shall find in a hundred modern poets or philosophers. 'T is like the clown in the circus who works himself up with a mighty pother to mount the bare-backed steed, and then hangs on to the tail. No, no, good Herr Nietzsche, we want our Saints Francis as well as our Napoleons. The one kind is as much in the "order of nature" as the other; and pity and humility, if they are the virtues of "nations in their decline," are preferable to the vices of nations at their zenith. And, good Count Tolstoï, a universe of Saints Francis would be an intolerable bore. The cowl does not cover all the virtues, nor the dress-coat all the sins. 'T is a world we live in, not a monastery; and it is amid the clash of mighty opposites that the music of the spheres is beaten out.

"Everything in Venice is delivered up to the Evil One now," writes John Buskin to Father Jacopo of the Armenian monastery; and such has been the immemorial language of prophets. I sometimes suspect the Evil One deserves more gratitude than he gets. Where would be the play without the villain of the piece? No, the devil is not so black as he is painted, nor the angel so white. And hence these incessant swings of the philosophical pendulum as one truth or the other is perceived. The true ethics of the future will give the devil his due, and deduct a discount from the angel.

The Armenian monastery which has posted up Ruskin's letter is paradoxically proud of its association with Lord Byron, who studied Armenian there; and visitors come there in consequence, and buy books that the monks print. So that Satan has his uses, and Scripture can quote the devil for its own purposes. The book I bought was a charming collection of Armenian folk-songs, and it contains one delicious poem whose refrain has haunted me ever since:

ON THE PARTRIDGE.

The sun boats from the mountain's top,
Pretty, pretty.
The partridge comes from her nest:
She was saluted by the flowers,
She flew and came from the mountain's top,
Ah! pretty, pretty,
Ah! dear little partridge!

Only the highest genius—and what is higher than the folk-genius?—would dare to be so naïve:

Ah! pretty, pretty,
Ah! dear little partridge!

VENTNOR

I did not get to Ventnor without a struggle. Everybody that I met held up hands of horror. "What! Going to Ventnor? You will be roasted before your time." My friends grieved, my very publishers wrung their hands, my newsvendor took me aside and besought me to live on a high hill. Yet through the whole of August I sat coolly writing on a low terrace. There is a superstition about Ventnor, and none of the people who talk glibly about its temperature have ever been there. But I think I have discovered the origin of the great Ventnor myth. The place is a winter resort of consumptives; and Mr. Frederick Greenwood, who was the chief charm of Ventnor, told me that you may take coffee on your lawn in November. The town, then, is warm in winter. The popular mind, with its hasty logic, thinks that this is tantamount to saying it is broiling hot in summer. I fancy there is a similar fiction about Bournemouth.

But as a rule the British climate pays no heed to guide-books. By the natives, Ventnor, though as beautiful as a little Italian town, seems to be regarded as a good place to go away from, for every other man keeps a coaching establishment (I don't mean a school), and you cannot walk two yards without being accosted by a tout, who resents your walking the next two. Its regatta is a puerile affair, its own boating crews going off by preference to rival regattas. But in illuminations it comes out far better than Cowes, whose loyal inhabitants throw all the burden of fireworks upon the royal and other yachts anchored in the bay. And besides, Ventnor has a carnival, which I saw in the shop-windows in the shape of comic masks.

Bonchurch, the suburb of Ventnor, which plumes itself upon a very artificial pond, furnished in the best style with sycamores, Scotch firs, elms and swans, is more interesting for containing the old churchyard by the sea which received the bones of John Sterling and inspired the best poem of Philip Bourke Marston:—

Do they hear, through the glad April weather,
The green grasses waving above them?
Do they think there are none left to love them,
They have lain for so long there together?
Do they hear the note of the cuckoo,
The cry of gulls on the wing,
The laughter of winds and waters,
The feet of the dancing Spring?

I was married in Ventnor. At least so I gather from the local newspapers, in whose visitors' lists there figures the entry, "Mr. and Mrs. Zangwill." I do not care to correct it, because, the lady being my mother, it is perfectly accurate and leads to charming misconceptions. "There, that's he," loudly whispered a young man, nudging his sweetheart, "and there's his wife with him." "That! why, she looks old enough to be his mother," replied the young lady. "Ah!" said her lover, with an air of conscious virtue and a better bargain, "they're awfully mercenary, these literary chaps." The reverse of this happened to a young friend of mine. He married an old lady who possessed a very large fortune. During the honeymoon his solicitous attentions to her excited the admiration of another old lady, who passed her life in a Bath-chair. "Dear me!" she thought: "how delightful in these degenerate days to see a young man so attentive to his mother!" and, dying soon after, left him another large fortune.

SOMEWHERE ELSE

Before I chanced on the great discovery which has made all my holidays real boons, and pleasure trips quite a pleasure, I used to go through all the horrors of preliminary indecision, which are still, alas! the lot of the vast majority. I would travel for weeks in Bradshaw, and end by sticking a pin at random between the leaves as if it were a Bible, vowing to go where destiny pointed. Once the pin stuck at London, and so I had to stick there too, and was defrauded of my holiday. But even when the pin sent me to Putney, or Coventry, I was invariably disappointed. Like the inquisitive and precocious infant of the poem, I was always asking for the address of Peace, but whenever I called I was told that she was not in, while the mocking refrain seemed to ring in my ears: "Not there, not there, my child." And at last I asked angrily of the rocks and caves: "Will no one tell me where Peace may be found? Wherever I go I find she is somewhere else." Then, at last, one nymph's soft heart grew tender and pitiful towards me, and Echo, hardly waiting till I had completed my sentence, answered: "Somewhere Else."

A wild thrill of joy ran through me. At last I had found the solution of the haunting puzzle. Somewhere Else. That was it. Not Scotland, nor Switzerland, nor Japan. None of the common places of travel. But Somewhere Else. Wherever I went, I wished I had gone Somewhere Else. Then, why not go there at first? What was the good of repining when it was too late? In future, I would make a bee-line for the abode of Peace—not hesitate and shilly-shally, and then go to Bournemouth, or Norway, or Ceylon, only to be sorry I had not gone to Somewhere Else direct. In a flash, all the glories of the discovery crowded upon me—the gain of time, temper, money, everything. "A thousand thanks, sweet Echo," I cried. "My obedience to thy advice shall prove that I am not ungrateful." Echo, with cynical candour, shouted "Great fool," but I cannot follow her in her end-of-the-century philosophy. And I have taken her advice. I went Somewhere Else immediately, and since then I have gone there every year regularly. My relatives do not care for it, and suggest all sorts of conventional places, such as Monte Carlo and Southend, but wherever they go, be it the most beautiful spot on earth, I remain faithful to my discovery, and go to Somewhere Else, where Peace never fails to greet me with the special welcome accorded to an annual visitor. The place grows upon me with every season. Sometimes, I think I should like to stay on and die there. No other spot in the wide universe has half such charm for me, and even when I do die, I don't think I shall go to where all the other happy idlers go. I shall go to Somewhere Else.

For Cromer may be the garden of sleep, but you shall find sleepier gardens and more papaverous poppies—Somewhere Else. The mountain-pines of Switzerland may be tall, and the skies of Italy blue, but there are taller pines and bluer skies—Somewhere Else. The bay of San Francisco may be beautiful, and the landscapes of Provence lovely, and the crags of Norway sublime, but Somewhere Else there are fairer visions and scenes more majestical—

An ampler setter, a diviner air,
And fields invested with purpureal gleams.

It never palls upon you—Somewhere Else. Every loved landmark grows dearer to you year by year, and year by year apartments are cheaper—Somewhere Else. The facilities for getting to it are enormous. All roads lead to it, far more truly than to Rome. There can be no accidents on the journey. How often do we read of people setting forth on their holidays full of life and hope—yea, sometimes even on their honeymoon—and lo! a signalman nods, or a bridge breaks, and they are left mangled on the rails or washed into the river. And to think that they would have escaped if they had only gone to Somewhere Else! Too late the weeping relatives wring their hands and moan the remark. Henceforth, among the ten million pleasure-pilgrims, who will be guided by me, there will be no more tragedies by flood or field. Railway assurance will become a thing of the past, and a fatal blow will be struck at modern hebdomadal journalism. To turn to minor matters, your friends can never utter the irritating "I told you not to go there!" if you have been to Somewhere Else. And you need not label your luggage; that always goes to Somewhere Else of itself. Last advantage of Somewhere Else, you may show your face in it, though you departed last year without paying your bill. There are no creditors in this blessed haven. Earth's load drops off your shoulders when you go to Somewhere Else.

I give this counsel in a disinterested spirit. I have not made speculative purchases of land, I am not booming a generous jerry-builder. And yet I cannot help reflecting apprehensively on the consequences of my recommendation. Already I see my sweet retreat the prey of the howling mob; I hear the German band playing on the stone parade, and catch the sad strains of the comic singer. Sacrilegious feet tramp the solitudes, and sandwich papers become common objects of the sea-shore. Shilling yachts will ply where I watched the skimming curlew, and new villas will totter on the edge of the ocean and beguile the innocent billows to be house-breakers. Nay, the place will become the Alsatia of humanity, the refuge for all those men and women people would rather see Somewhere Else, and whose travelling expenses they will perchance defray. Imagination reels before the horror of such an agglomeration of the unamiable. And the terrible thing about my terrestrial paradise is that there is no escaping from it. Everything has the defects of its qualities, and this is the reverse of the dazzling medal—the drawback which annuls all the advantages of Somewhere Else in the event of its becoming popular. In vain shall I then endeavour to flee from it. Though I projected myself from the giant cannon that sent Jules Verne's hero to the moon, I should inevitably arrive—boomerang-like—at Somewhere Else.

PART III

AFTER-THOUGHTS: A BUNDLE OF BREVITIES

Moonshine

Certainly the Moon was very charming that soft summer's night, as I watched its full golden orb gliding nonchalantly in the serene, starry heaven, and keeping me company as I strode across the silent gorse. But—to be indiscreet—I had grown aweary of the Moon, and of the stars also, as of beautiful pictures hung—or should one say, skied?—in a perpetual Academy. Caelum non animum mutant is only tolerably true. A derangement of stars is all the change you get by travelling—everywhere the same golden-headed nails, as Hugo, hard-driven, called them, are sticking in the firmament. This particular moon was hanging, not over a church steeple, like De Musset's moon,

Comme un point sur un i,

but like the big yellow dial of the clock in a church tower. An illuminated clock-face—but blank, featureless, expressionless, useless; in a word, without hands. Now I could not help thinking that if there had really been a Providence it would have put hands to the Moon—a big and a little—and made it the chronometer of the world—nay, of the cosmos—the universal time-piece, to which all eyes, in every place and planet, could be raised for information; by which all clocks could be set—moon time—an infallible monitor and measurer of the flight of the hours; divinely right, not to be argued with; though I warrant there be some would still swear by their watches. This were the true cosmopolitanism, destroying those distressful variations which make your clock vary with your climate, and which throw the shadow of pyrrhonism over truths which should be clear as daylight. For if, when it is five o'clock here, it may be two o'clock there and supper-time yonder, if it is night and day at the same moment, then is black white, and Pilate right—and Heraclitus—and the nonconformist conscience a vain thing.

In supporting correct moral principles, the Moon would be of some use, instead of staring at us with an idiot face, signifying nothing. The stars, too, could be better employed than in winking at what goes on here below. Like ladies' gold watches by the side of Big Ben, they could repeat the same great eternal truth—that it was half-past nine, or five minutes to eleven.

Soon as the evening shades prevail
The moon takes up the wondrous tale,

While all the stars that round her burn,
And all the planets in their turn,
Confirm the tidings as they roll,
And spread the time from pole to pole.

An obvious result of a synchronised universe would be the federation of mankind, Peace on Earth, and all those other beatitudes at present vainly sought by World Fairs, and pig-sticking prophets.

Till we have hands to the Moon I shall not look for the Millennium.

Capital

Suddenly the Moon went behind a cloud, as if to demonstrate that even then there would be difficulties. Besides, I remembered it had its quarter-days. Here my thoughts made a transition to money matters, and, after the manner of Richard Carstone in "Bleak House," I fell to reckoning up the sums I had saved of late. It is a calculation I make almost every week nowadays. I have lost nothing by any of the Jerry-Building Societies, nothing by any of the great Bank Failures. By not having any money one saves thousands a year in these unsettled times. Mr. Hamerton cites with amusement the remark of a wealthy Englishman, who could not understand "why men are so imprudent as to allow themselves to sink into money embarrassments." "There is a simple rule that I follow myself," said he, "and that I have always found a great safeguard: it is, never to let one's balance at the banker's fall below five thousand pounds." The rich Englishman's rule was quite wrong: the only safeguard is to have no balance at all. High and dry on the Lucretian tower of poverty, you may watch with complacency the struggles of the sinking funds. What a burden capital must be to those anxious to find safe investments at high rates of interest! It looks as if interest will sink to freezing point, and capital will have to flow to other planets if that comical claim for "wages of abstinence" is to be met any longer. Perhaps it will flow to Mars, the home in exile of the old political economy. Already a beginning has been made by investments in mines which are not upon this earth.

Credit

Every day makes clearer the evils of our complex credit system—that Frankenstein creation we have lost control over, that ampulaceous growth of capital, most of which is merely figures in a book, and which only exists in virtue of not being asked for, much as the tit-bits on a restaurant menu are "off" when ordered. The real meaning of National Debts is that every civilised country is bankrupt, and only goes on trading because its creditors give it time. To the uncertainties of the weather, and the chances of cholera, war, and earthquake, we have added an artificial uncertainty worse than any of these—we have invented a series of financial cyclones, which sweep round the globe, devastating all lands, and no more to be predicted—despite theories of sun-spots, cyclones and financial crises—than wrecks at sea; indeed, far less predictable, for I believe with the ex-mayor quoted by Bonamy Price, that finance is a subject which no man can understand in this world, or even in the next. The infinite ramifications, the endless actions and reactions, are beyond the grasp of any one but an impostor. The Professor just mentioned thought he had found the right thread of theory in the labyrinth of "Currency and Banking," and really did make a most sensible analysis of what actually went on in financial operations. Only he left out one great factor—the immense influence on the market of other people's wrong theories. No, if there is a right thread of theory, it must be so tangled as to be worse than useless. My friend the business man tells me that for success in business one requires four things: a large capital, industry, insight, and caution—and then it's a toss-up. I am fain to believe this whole system of modern commerce was devised to please the amateurs of the aleatory.

The Small Boy

A plague on both your Houses of Parliament! They legislate day and night, yet leave our lives unmodified. For our lives revolve on the pivot of custom, and our everyday movements are not political. The real ruler of England is the small boy of the streets! And, in truth, is it not so? By the unphilosophic regarded as akin to vermin, existing for the greater confusion of theologians, the small boy looms large to the man of insight, as the true conservator of custom—the one efficient custos morum. He it is who regulates the lengths to which we may go in eccentricity, and, above all, in hair:

Get your hair cut!

He is particular to a shade about clothes, and has a nice taste in hats. One wonders how he acquired it. His patriotic proclivity, his hostility to national costumes other than English, his preference for uncoloured complexions—this one may understand; but his aesthetic instinct is a problem for Weismann. As the interpreter of the conventions, he is of a cast-iron rigidity, for is he not a child of Mrs. Grundy—his mother's own boy? He has no exceptions—it is "one law and one measure." He is the scavenger of manners, as the Constantinople street-dog is of gutters; a natural police des moeurs, infinitely more efficient than any artificial organisation; an all-ramifying association created to keep the bounds of social order, on duty at every street corner, alert to check every outbreak of individuality. Do ladies aspire to ride bicycles? Or wear bloomers? There is the small boy to face. It is a question for him. Conciliate him, and you may laugh at the pragmatic. His, too, is a healthy barbarism, beneficent in its action, that thinks scorn of eyeglasses and spectacles, and leads him to denounce quadruple vision, as, indeed, all departure from the simplicities of physical perfection. A human scarecrow he abhors, and will follow such an one through six streets to express his disapprobation. Extremes of size? whether of tallness or shortness? offend him equally. Whitman was not kinder to "the average man." Nor is the small boy's influence limited to sumptuary and corporeal censorship: by taking up certain songs he "makes" the nation's ballads, and every one knows what that means. Let me train a nation's small boys, I care not who makes its laws. O small boy, true sovereign of England, I take off my hat to thee!—to show thee the maker's name in the lining, and satify thy anxious inquiries as to where I got it.

A Day in Town

I have often wondered what country children do for a holiday. Do good people go round collecting to give them a day in London or Liverpool or Manchester, so that their stunted lives that stretch on from year to year with never a whiff of town fog, never a glimpse of green 'buses, or dangerous crossings, or furnace-smoke, may be expanded and elevated? If not, I beg to move the starting of a Town Fund at once. Nothing can be more narrowing than rustic existence—there are old yokels whose lives have always moved within a four-mile radius, women who have grown gray without ever knowing what lay beyond the blue hills that girdled their native village. I once knew a chawbacon who came to town and was barked at by a street-dog. He stooped down to pick up one of the rough stones lying in the roadway to ward it off withal, but to his astonishment the stone refused to budge, for it was an integral part of the road. "Danged if that baint queer!" he exclaimed. "At home the dogs be tied and the stones be loose. Here the dogs be loose and the stones be tied." Now, if that man had enjoyed a school excursion to the town when a boy, he would have deprived me of a good story. A glimpse of the town in youth might also do good in checking the perpetual urban immigration, which, alas! removes so many of the rustic population from the soil, and places them under it. To this end all school excursions to London should take place in November. Yes, there is a vast future before that fund, and I shall be happy to start it with five thousand pounds, if two hundred and sixty-three one-armed Scotchmen of good moral character will bind themselves to do the same.

The Profession of Charity

Mr. Labouchere is singularly unfair to a new profession. Beggary has long been a recognised profession, with its traditions, customs, and past-masters, and it is time that philanthropy should now be admitted to an equal status. There is no reason in the world why it should be left in the hands of amateurs, who muddle away funds by their lack of science and experience. Supposing a man sees his way to doing good—founding a home for incurables, or drunkards, or establishing a dispensary, or anything you please—why should he not make a living by it? What if he does get five hundred a year, is he not worth it, provided always the institution fulfils a useful function and is not a sham? Surely he does more for Society in return for his money than a Treasury clerk! Probably but for him—but for his wish to earn an income—the charitable institution would never have come into existence. Political economy already shows us how the individual's desire for profit brings humanity all its blessings, opens up new countries for it, and supplies them with wars and railways. If men did not buy shares with a view to a percentage on their savings, the march of civilisation would come to a halt. Since the philanthropy of percentage is so obvious, why should we not recognise the percentage of philanthropy? Charity has gone into business. Why not?

The Privileges of Poverty

The only people who seem to escape the malady of the century are the poor. The Weltschmerz touches them not; however great their suffering, it is always individual. The privileges of poverty are, I fear, insufficiently appreciated in these grasping times. It is not only income-tax that the poor man is exempt from. There is a much more painful tax on income than the pecuniary—it is the thought of those who are worsted in the struggle for bare existence. Vae victis! Yet those who achieve the bare existence, who starve not, neither shiver, have surely enviable compensations. Not theirs the distressful, wearying problems of sociology. Far from feeling any responsibility for their fellow-beings, they do not even fulfil their own personal duty to society—witness the breeding of babies in back streets. They have no sympathy with the troubles of any other class—they eat their hard crust and they drink their bitter beer without a thought of the dyspepsia of the diner-out, and their appetite is not dulled by any suspicion of heart-sickness in good society. Starvation other than physical they do not understand, and spiritual struggles are caviare. The state of the rich does not give them sleepless nights—they have no yearnings to reform them or amend their condition. The terrible overcrowding of the upper classes on Belgravian staircases wakes not a pang; they are untouched by the sufferings of insufficiently-clad ladies in draughty stalls and royal antechambers; and the grievances of old army men move them not. Not theirs to ponder sorrowfully over the lost souls of politicians or the degeneration of public manners. They live their own lives—and, whatsoever the burden, they do not bear any one's but their own.

Salvation for the Seraphim

Herbert Spencer says he knew a retired naval officer in whose mind God figured as a transcendently powerful sea-captain; and we have all heard the story of the English admiral who, when fighting the Dutch, felt sure God wouldn't desert a fellow-countryman. But this ingenuous identification of earthly and divine interests has been carried to the point of imbecility by General Booth in his claim to

"THE LARGEST CIRCULATION."

The War Cry, so the General states,
Among the angels circulates,
To Heaven having gone; but, oh,
That it had first expired below!

Which is uglier—the crude spiritualism of the Salvationist or the crude materialism of the scientist? I receive the same sort of shock when I peruse Mrs. Spurgeon's fond picture of her departed husband waylaying the angels at the shining street-corners to preach the gospel to them, as when I read that woman's poetry is inferior to man's because she exhales less carbonic acid.

Truth—Local and Temporal

The other day I listened to some green-room persiflage between an actress and an eminent actor-manager. The lady said she had loved him years ago, and thrown herself at his head, but had never been able to bring him to a proposal. I asked if she would have been satisfied with the provincial rights. I am not at all sure that the introduction of this principle of legal partition would not promote domestic harmony, especially in theatrical circles, where the practice already prevails in the matter of plays. Indeed, this principle of partition has already been carried beyond its original sphere. Do I not remember a theatrical lawsuit four or five years ago in which the plaintiff sought to restrain the defendant from styling himself part-author of a piece, on the ground that he (the defendant) had not done a stroke of the work, and had been paid ten pounds for it; while the defendant claimed that he had only parted with his rights as regards London, and that in the provinces he was still entitled to claim a share of the authorship? Pascal long ago pointed out, in his "Pensées," that virtue and vice were largely dependent on distance from the equator (a latitudinarianism in morals that does not seem to have shocked his Port Royal friends). But even he failed to reach this daring conception of "local fame." The marvel is that when once reached it should have been let slip again. It seems to me an invaluable remedy for disputes: absolutely infallible. When Mr. Stuart Cumberland wrote from India to claim the plot of "The Charlatan," how simple to accord him the authorship—in India! At once we perceive a modus vivendi for the followers of Donnelly and the adherents of common-sense. In America Bacon shall be the author of "Hamlet," but the English rights in the piece shall go to Shakespeare. In the same spirit of compromise Cruikshank might have been content to be the author of "Oliver Twist" in the Hebrides and the second-class saloons of Atlantic steamers. Herman should be sole author of "The Silver King" in Pall Mall, and Jones in Piccadilly. Some metropolitan streets belong by one pavement to one parish, and by the other to another; so that in the case of parochial celebrities it would be possible for the rival great men to glare at each other across the road—not, however, daring to cross it, for fear of losing their reputation. The Frenchman's long-standing assumption of Parisian rights in the victory of Waterloo would be put upon a legitimate basis.

By a logical extension of the principle we could allow Homer to be born in Chios on Mondays, in Colophon on Tuesdays, and so with each of the seven cities which starved him. They use up the week nicely. On the odd day of leap year we might concede that he never existed, and allow him to be resolved into the pieces into which he was torn by Wolf. Had this pacificatory principle been discovered earlier, "The Letters of Phalaris" would never have fluttered Europe, and Swift would have had no need to write "The Battle of the Books." It is never too late to mend, however, and an academy of leading politicians and ecclesiastics should be at once formed to draw up an authoritative "Calendar and Topography of Belief," fixing once for all the dates and places on or in which it is permissible to hold any given opinion. Although, when I come to think of it, Science and Religion have long been tacitly reconciled on this principle, Religion being true on Sundays and Science on week-days.

The Creed of Despair

I am convinced that optimism is exactly the wrong sort of medicine for our "present discontents." It is time to try homoeopathy. My suggestion is that the religion of the future shall consist of the most pessimistic propositions imaginable; its creed shall be godless and immoral, its thirty-nine articles shall exhaust the possibilities of unfaith and its burden shall be vanitas vanitatum. Man shall be an automaton, and life an hereditary disease, and the world a hospital, and truth a dream, and beauty an optical illusion. These sad tidings of great sorrow shall be organized into a state church, with bishops and paraphernalia, and shall be sucked in by the infant at its mother's breast. Men shall be tutored in unrighteousness, and innocence shall be under ecclesiastical ban. Faith and Hope shall be of the seven deadly virtues, and unalloyed despair of man and nature a dogma it were blasphemous to doubt. The good shall be persecuted and the theists tortured, and those that say there is balm in Gilead, shall be thrust beyond the pale of decent society.

Then, oh, what a spiritual revival there will be! Every gleam of light will be eagerly sought for, every ray focussed; every hint of love and pity and beauty, of significance and divinity, in this infinite and infinitely mysterious universe, will be eagerly snatched up and thrust upon an age hide-bound in orthodoxy; every touch and trace of tenderness that softens suffering and sweetens the bitterness of death, will be treasured up in secret mistrust of the reigning creed; every noble thought and deed, every sacred tear, will be thrown into the balance of heresy with every dear delight of poetry and art, of woods and waters, of dawns and sunsets; with every grace of childhood and glory of man and womanhood. And every suppressed doubt of the hideousness of the universe will sink deep and ferment in darkness, and persecution will sit on every natural safety valve till at last the pent forces will swell and crack the sterile soil, and there will be an explosion that shall send a pillar of living fire towards the heavens of brass. The clerics will be among the first to feel the stirrings of infidel hope—a few will give up their livings rather than preach what they do not believe, but the majority—especially the bishops—will cling to the Church of Despair, hoping against hope that their despair is true. There will be wonderful word-spinnings in the reviews, and the dominant pessimism will be justified by algebraic analogies. But, beneath it all, the church will be infected to the core with faith, and for the first time in history we shall get a believing clergy. There will be secret societies founded to publish the Bible, and Colonel Ingersoll will lecture at the hall of religion, and the prisons will be crowded with martyred iconoclasts incredulous of the gospel of science. No, there is nothing so unwise as your optimistic organized creeds, with their suggestions of officialdom, red-tape, and back-stairs influence. We shall never be perfectly religious and moral till we are trained from childhood to ungodly works, forced to attend long sermons on the error of existence, and badgered into public impiety by force of opinion.

Social Bugbears

First there were the Radicals, who stood for the apogee of human villainy, though it now appears they were Conservatives of the mildest type. Then came the turn of the Atheists, who, for all I have been able to discover, were very respectable creatures full of religious ardour, who spelt God with a small "g" and justice with a capital "J." Then the Socialists had their innings. But "we are all Socialists now," and the empty mantle of villainy has fallen upon Anarchism, which, as far as I can make out, is the simplest and most innocent creed ever invented, and which debars its adherents from exercising any compulsion upon anybody else, relying upon the natural moral working of the human heart. How this is compatible with bombs it is for Messieurs les Anarchistes to explain. Needless to say the assassinous Anarchists are disavowed by their philosophical brethren.

Martyrs

Although we moderns work harder than our fathers for our opinions, we are sometimes taunted with not being so ready to die for them. But, as Renan points out, thinkers have no need to die to demonstrate a theorem. Saints may die for their faith because faith is a personal matter. Even so we are still ready to die for our honour. The Christian martyrs did prove that Christianity was a reality to them; but Galileo's death would have been irrelevant to the rotation of the earth. There is no argumentum per hominem possible here; the truth is impersonal. It is only for beliefs that exclude certainty that a man is tempted to martyrdom. The martyr is indeed, as the etymology implies, a witness; but his death is not a witness to the truth of his belief—merely to the truth of his believing. Blandine at her stake, enduring a hundred horrors unflinchingly, seems in addition to prove that faith was the first anaesthetic. It is curious to note how the word "martyr" has been degraded; so that we have to-day martyrs to the gout instead of to the truth. The idea of suffering has quite ousted the idea of witnessing. What a pity the word got these painful associations! There are "martyrs" to the truth—witnesses who without dying testify to the divine streak in life; and unconscious "martyrs" who, by their simple sincerity, their unpretentious unselfishness, prove more than a bookshelf of theology. I have found "martyrdom" in the grip of a friend's hand, though if I had told him so he would have apologised for squeezing so hard. And is not every pretty woman a "martyr"—a revelation of an inner soul of beauty and goodness in this chaotic universe? There! I have succumbed again to the common masculine impulse to conceive beauty and goodness as a chemical combination, subtly inter-related; whereas the slightest practical experience in the laboratory of life discovers them but a mechanical mixture, dissociable and not seldom antipathetic.

The London Season

I remember being so bored one night at dinner, by the ceaseless chatter about Burne-Jones, that I asked my fair neighbour: "Who is Burne-Jones?" Her reply was as smart as it was feminine. "I don't believe you." There is a moral in this. Why be a slave to the season? Why bother to read all the newest novels, see all the newest plays, hear all the newest musicians, remember all the newest "Reminiscences," and believe all the newest religions, when by pleading ignorance you will pass not only as an eccentric but a connoisseur? On second thoughts, why not eschew the season altogether? God made the seasons and man made the season, as Cowper forgot to say. And a nice mess man has made of it, turning night into day and heating his rooms in the summer. The London Season, not Winter, Mr. Cowper, is the true "Ruler of the Inverted Year."

The Academy

The Academy has survived Mr. Burne-Jones' desertion of his old associates, as it would survive art itself. I for one should regret its disappearance. It is a whetstone for wit, like everything established and respectable. I am only sorry we have no Academy of Letters. It gives one such a standing not to be a member—almost as good a standing as to be one. If you are left out in the cold you loudly pity those asphyxiating in the heat, and if you have a cozy chair by the fireside you fall asleep and say nothing. This promotes happiness all round, and makes the literary man contented with his lot. In England authors have no Academy, and so have to fall back on the poor publishers: Hinc illae lachrymae!

Portraits of Gentlemen

Everybody paints the portrait of nobody. Imagine a great writer being called upon to produce a black-and-white picture of a man of no importance: Let us imagine, say Meredith, being offered a thousand pounds for a pen-and-ink portrait of a provincial mayor—being asked to devote his graphic art, his felicitous choice of words, his gifts of insight and sympathy, his genius, in a word, to the portrayal of a real live mayor—the same to be published in book-form, asked for at the libraries, and discussed at dinner-tables and in the reviews as a specimen of the season's art. Of course Meredith would tell the man to go and be hanged (in the Academy); but if he consented, see what would take place. The literary portrait involves, of course, both mind and body, and practically the work would have to take the shape of a biography. For some weeks the man would come to Meredith's study and give him talkings. At the first talking Meredith would also make a sketch of the outside appearance of his subject. Here the resources of language far exceed those of colour. The happy euphemism of language permits a squint to be described as an ambidexterity of vision; it is even quite possible to omit an ill-regulated feature altogether. Suppose an artist paints a man without a nose—the defect sauterait aux yeux: it would be as plain as the nose not upon his face. But it is quite possible for the literary artist to omit a man's nose without attracting any attention. The reader's imagination supplies the nose, without even being conscious of its purveyorship. As for the psychological portion of the portrait, the author would be entirely dependent on the information given by the subject, so that provincial mayors would develop unsuspected virtues. Where the difficulty would come in would be in the absence of darker qualities, which would make literary chiaroscuro impossible. It is quite likely, though, that as a result of the talkings the subject would unwittingly present the novelist with a real character who would appear in his next work of fiction, and be entirely unrecognized either by the reader of the biography or its subject.

Photography and Realism

No artist of the brush can afford to dispense with models; when he draws from his inner consciousness the composition is tame and the draughtsmanship wild. The novelist, though his object is not portraiture, but creation, can as little afford to keep aloof from real men and women. When George Eliot ceased to draw from models and fell back on intuition and her library, she produced "Daniel Deronda." But I would demur altogether to the use of "photography" in literary criticism as synonymous with realism. The photograph is an utter misrepresentation of life, and this not merely because of its false shades and its lack of colour, but because the photographer is not content with literalness. He aspires to art. So far from being a realist, he is the greatest idealist of all. He not only puts you into poses you would never fall into naturally, he not only arranges you so as to hide your characteristic uglinesses, and bids you call up an expression you never use, but he touches up and tones down after you are gone, and treats his pictures, indeed, as though they were actors and he the dresser. And as each photographer has his own style, no two portraits are ever alike. My portraits of Annabel pass as a collection of pretty actresses. Still, if they are not like one another, they resemble one another in being unlike her. The only good photographs I have ever seen of myself were done by an amateur—most of the others might just as well have been taken in my absence. And there is always a painful neatness about photographs: my humble study was once photographed, and it looked like a princely library. Bags come out with artistic interstices, fustian gleams like satin. It is the true Platonic touch, glorifying and gilding everything. Filth itself would come out like roses. No, no, let us hear no more about Zola's "photography."

The Great Unhung

What becomes of all the old pins is a problem that worries many simple souls. What becomes of all the rejected pictures is a question that seems to trouble nobody. And yet at every exhibition the massacre of innocents is appalling. The Royal Academy of London, which is the most hospitable institution in the world toward "wet paint," still turns away very many more canvases than it admits. Their departure is like the retreat of the Ten Thousand. Into the Salon one year six thousand eager frames crowded, but when the public came to see, only thirteen hundred were left to tell the tale—

All that was left of them,
Left of six thousand.

More ruthless still was the slaughter in the New Salon, the Salon of the Champs de Mars, where the pictures were decimated. Out of two thousand seven hundred works sent in by outsiders, only three hundred survived. It is impossible to believe that ideal justice was done, especially when we consider that the jury took only one day to consider the outcome of so many aspirations, such manifold toil. The pictures were wheeled past them on gigantic easels, an interminable panorama. Even supposing that the gentlemen of the jury took a full working day of eight hours, with no allowance for déjeuner, the average time for examining a picture works out at something like ten seconds. In each minute of that fateful day the destiny of half a dozen pictures was decided. Verily, our picture-connoisseur seems to have elevated criticism into an instinct—he is the smoothest human mechanism on record. One wonders if the critic will ever be replaced by an automaton, something analogous to the camera that has replaced the artist. Meantime, the point is—what becomes of the refused, those unwelcome revenants that return to lower the artist in the eyes of landladies and concierges? Sometimes, we know, the stone which the builders rejected becomes the corner-stone of the temple, and the proscribed painter lives to despise publicly the judges in the gate. But these revenges are rare, and for the poor bulk of mankind the whirligig of time revolves but emptily. The average artist rejected of one exhibition turns him to another, and the leavings of the Salon beat at the doors of Antwerp and Munich, where the annual of art blooms a little later in the spring.

Pitiful it is to follow a picture from refusal to refusal; one imagines the painter sublime amid the litter of secretarial notifications, gathering, Antaeus-like, fresh strength from every fall, and coming to a grim and gradual knowledge of the great cosmopolitan conspiracy. One year the rejected of the Academy were hung in London by an enterprising financier. It was the greatest lift-up the Academy had ever had. Even its enemies were silenced temporarily. But the rejected may console themselves. The accepted have scant advantage over them. To sell a picture is becoming rarer and rarer, and the dealer is no more respectful to the canvas that has achieved the honor of the catalogue than to that which has preserved the sequestration of the studio. Sometimes the unhung picture becomes the medium upon which another is painted (for a picture is always worth the canvas it is painted on), sometimes (if it is large) it is cut up and sold in bits, sometimes it adorns the family dining-room, or decorates the hall of a good-natured friend, and sometimes, after a variety of pecuniary adventures, it becomes the proud possession of a millionaire.

The Abolition of Catalogues

The average Englishman takes his religion on Sundays and his Art in the spring. Influences that should permeate life are collected in chunks at particular seasons. This is sufficient to prove how little they are really felt or understood. The Academy headache is the due penalty of hypocrisy. It is the catalogue that is the greatest coadjutor of cant. If pictures, besides being hung, were treated like convicts in becoming merely numbers, without names either of painters or subjects, what a delightful confusion of critical tongues would ensue! But conceding that a picture should have the painter's name, for the sake of the artist (or his enemies), I would propose that everything else be abolished. It is not unfair to subject pictures to this severe test, because, of all forms of art, painting is the one whose appeal is instantaneous, simple and self-complete. If a picture cannot speak for itself, no amount of advocacy will save it. If it tells a story (which no good picture should), let it at least do so without invoking the aid of the rival art of literature. Literature does not ask the assistance of pictures to make its meaning clear. Nor, too, is anything gained by calling colours harmonies or symphonies. Let such pictures strike their own chords and blow their own trumpets. Catalogues of all kinds are but props to artistic inefficiency. If dumb-show plays did not rely on "books of the words," pantomime would have to become a finer art. If ballets had no thread of narrative attached to them, their constructors would be driven to achieve greater intelligibility, or to give up trying for it—which were the more gratifying alternative. So with the descriptions of symphonies we find in our programmes. Why should good music be translated into bad literature? Surely each art should be self-sufficient; developing its effects according to its own laws! A melody does not need to be painted, nor a picture to be set to music. The graceful evolutions of the dance are their own justification. The only case in which I would allow a title to a picture is when it is a portrait. That is an obvious necessity. Portrait-painting is a branch of art which demands recognition.

The Artistic Temperament

There are two aspects of the artistic temperament—the active or creative side, and the passive or receptive side. It is impossible to possess the power of creation without possessing also the power of appreciation; but it is quite possible to be very susceptible to artistic influences while dowered with little or no faculty of origination. On the one hand is the artist—poet, musician, or painter; on the other, the artistic person to whom the artist appeals. Between the two, in some arts, stands the artistic interpreter—the actor who embodies the aery conceptions of the poet, the violinist or pianist who makes audible the inspirations of the musician. But in so far as this artistic interpreter rises to greatness in his field, in so far he will be found soaring above the middle ground, away from the artistic person, and into the realm of the artist or creator. Joachim and De Reszké, Paderewski and Irving, put something of themselves into their work; apart from the fact that they could all do (in some cases have done) creative work on their own account. So that when the interpreter is worth considering at all, he may be considered in the creative category. Limiting ourselves, then, to these two main varieties of the artistic temperament, the active and the passive, I should say that the latter is an unmixed blessing, and the former a mixed curse.

What, indeed, can be more delightful than to possess good aesthetic faculties—to be able to enjoy books, music, pictures, plays! This artistic sensibility is the one undoubted advantage of man over other animals, the extra octave in the gamut of life. Most enviable of mankind is the appreciative person, without a scrap of originality? who has every temptation to enjoy, and none to create. He is the idle heir to treasures greater than India's mines can yield; the bee that sucks at every flower, and is not even asked to make honey. For him poets sing, and painters paint, and composers write. "O fortunates nimium," who not seldom yearn for the fatal gift of genius! For this artistic temperament is a curse—a curse that lights on the noblest and best of mankind! From the day of Prometheus to the days of his English laureate it has been a curse

To vary from the kindly race of men,

and the eagles have not ceased to peck at the liver of men's benefactors. All great and high art is purchased by suffering—it is not the mechanical product of dexterous craftsmanship. This is one part of the meaning of that mysterious "Master Builder" of Ibsen's. "Then I saw plainly why God had taken my little children from me. It was that I should have nothing else to attach myself to. No such thing as love and happiness, you understand. I was to be only a master builder—nothing else." And the tense strings that give the highest and sweetest notes are most in danger of being overstrung.

But there are compensations. The creative artist is higher in the scale of existence than the man, as the man is higher than the beatified oyster for whose condition, as Aristotle pointed out, few would be tempted to barter the misery of human existence. The animal has consciousness, man self-consciousness, and the artist over-consciousness. Over-consciousness may be a curse, but, like the primitive curse—labour—there are many who would welcome it!

Professional Ethics

There's no knowing where the artistic temperament may break out. "I don't think that a person ought to come to the binder and just say to him, 'Bind that book for so much money.' I think the binder ought to say, 'Is the book worth binding?' and that if it were not he ought to refuse." The applications of this remarkable principle, enunciated by a bookbinder, are obvious. Applied universally it would reform the race. The tailor, when a man came to be measured, would say, "Yes, but are you worth measuring?" and if he was out of drawing would refuse to dress him, thus extruding deformity from the world and restoring the Olympian gods. The charwoman, inspired by George Herbert, would not only "sweep a room as by God's laws," but would inquire whether it was worth sweeping; the wine merchant would refuse wine to rich customers who did not deserve to drink it; and the doctors would certainly not devote their best energies to keeping gouty old noblemen alive.

Lay Confessors

We writers, as Beaeonsfield said to his sovereign, are a good substitute for the confessional; we like to be allowed peeps into the secret chambers of the heart. The most miserable sinners may be as sure of our secrecy as of our absolution. The more terrible the crime the better we are pleased. So come and ease your labouring consciences, and pour your sorrows into our sympathetic shorthand books, and we will work you up the bare material of your lives so artistically that you are the veriest Philistines if you shall not be rather glad to have sinned and suffered. For deep down in our hearts lurks the belief that, as Jerome wittily puts it, "God created the world to give the literary man something to write about!"

Q. E. D. Novels

A novel, like a metaphor, proves nothing: 't is merely a vivid pictorial presentation of a single case. I have just read one novel aspiring to prove that a couple who skip the marriage ceremony cannot be happy ever after, and another aspiring to prove that marriage is the one drawback to a happy union. In reality both novels prove the same thing—that the author is a fool. There is nothing I would not undertake to "prove" in a novel. You have only to take an exceptional case and treat it as if it were normal. Aesop's fables could easily be rewritten to prove exactly the opposite morals, just as there is no popular apothegm whose antidote may not be found in the same treasury of folk-wisdom: "Never put off till to-morrow what you can do to-day," and "Sufficient for the day is the evil thereof"; "Penny wise, pound foolish!" "Look after the pence and the pounds will take care of themselves."

In sooth I suffer from an inability to see the morals of stories—like the auditor who blunts the point of the drollest anecdote by inquiring "And what happened then?" Even the beautiful allegory of the three rings in "Nathan der Weise," always seems to me to throw considerable discredit on the father who set his sons wrangling over the imitation rings. And, inversely, nothing seems easier to me than to invent fables to prove wrong morals: e.g.

The Mouse Who Died

A pretty gray mouse was in the habit of sauntering from its hole every evening to pick up the Crumbs in the Dining Boom. "What a pretty Mouse!" said the Householder, and made more crumbs for Mousie to eat. So great a banquet was thus spread that the Noble-hearted little Mouse cheeped the news to its Sisters and its Cousins and its Aunts, and they all came every evening in the Train of its Tail to regale themselves on the remains of the Repast. "Dear, dear!" cried the Householder in despair, "the house is overrun with a plague of Vermin." And he mixed poison with the crumbs, and the poor little pioneer Mouse perished in contortions of agony. Moral: Don't.

Theologic Novels

Usually the speculations that first reach the great public through the medium of the novel have been familiar ad nauseam to the reading classes for scores of years. Conceive Noah, aroused by the grating of the Ark upon the summit of Mount Ararat, looking out of the window and exclaiming, "Why, it's been raining!" Then imagine Mrs. Noah, catching an odd syllable of her husband's remark, writing a love story to prove that the barometer portended showers. Finally, picture the world looking in alarm for its umbrella, and you have an image of the inception and effect of the modern Mrs. Noah's theologic novel.

MUDIE MEASURE.

Ten lines make one page;
Ten pages make one point;
 Two points make one chapter;
Five chapters make one episode;
Two episodes make one volume:
Three volumes make one tired.

The Prop of Letters

Is it a bright or a black day for an author when he gets so popular that the big advertisers insist on having him in any organ in which they place their advertisements? There can be no question but that it will be a black day for letters when the advertiser becomes the arbiter of literature, as this newest development forebodes. Where is this leprosy of advertisement to stop? Already it covers almost our whole civilisation. Already the advertiser is a main prop of the press.

A SONG OF ADVERTISEMENTS. (After Whitman.)

Give me Hornihand's Pure Mustard;
Give me Apple's Soap, with the negress laving the cherub;
Give me Bentley's Brimstone Tablets, and Ploughman's
Pills—those of the Little Liver.
(O get me ads., you agent with the frock-coat and the fountain pen,
You with the large commissions

And the further discount on cash,
Get me ads., camarado!
Full pages preferred, though little ones not scorning,
For I scorn nothing, my brother.)
Give me the Alphabetical Snuff;
Give me Electric Batteries and False Teeth; also the Tooth-powders;
Give me all the Soft Soaps and the Soothing Syrups;
Give me all the Cocoas and Cough Lozenges and Corsets;
Give me Infants' Food—yea, the diet of babes and sucklings;
Give me the Nibs and the Beef Essences, and do not forget the Typewriters.
(Forget nothing, camarado, for I, the poet, never forget anything.)
Give me of the Fat of your agency, and of the Anti-Fat thereof!
And I will build you magazines, high-class and well illustrated;
Or pictureless à volonté, the latter with heavier articles.
Also newspapers, daily and weekly, with posters flamboyant,
That shall move the state and its pillars,
That shall preach the loftiest morals, elevating the masses,
By the strength of advertisements,
By the mighty strength of advertisements!

It has been suggested that flypapers should be so sprinkled as to produce an aesthetic design in dead flies, so as to introduce beauty into the homes of the poor. It would be more in harmony with the age to lay out our public gardens with floral injunctions to use B's hair-dye and C's corn-plaster. Brag and display are the road to riches, and the trail of vulgarity is over it all. I take credit to myself for having been among the first to cry in the wilderness; but the critics—bless them!—say it is all empty paradox.

The Latter-day Poet

The one exception to the hunger for advertisement is the modern bard. He achieves his vogue by limited editions, and takes pains to prevent himself being an influence. He acquires a factitious fame and an artificial value by printing only a few copies, thus making his paper and print sought after rather than his matter. It is all very well for a book to become rare by the vicissitudes of literary fortune, but this machine-made rarity can only be prized by people who value their possessions merely because other people haven't got them. The old minor poet was frenzied and unbought; the new is calm and "collected." At this rate the greatest poets would be those of whose works only one copy is extant—in MS.

Bend, bend the knee, and bow the head
To reverence the great unread,
The great unread and much-reviewed,
Whose lines are treasured like the lewd,
His first editions prizes reckoned
Because there never was a second.
Obscurely famous in his rut,
Unknown, unpopular, "uncut,"
Where Byron thrilled a continent,

To thrill an auction-room content,
He struggles through oblivion's bogs,
To gain a place in—catalogues!
And falls asleep and joins the dust
In simple hope and modest trust
That, though Posterity neglect
His bones, his books it will collect,
And these will grow—O prospect fair!—
From year to year more "scarce" and "rare."

Have you noticed the Renaissance of alliteration in the new journalism? The early English Poets made alliteration the chief element of their poetry, and in modern times Swinburne has paid more attention to it (and to rhyme) than to meaning, with the result that there has arisen a school of poets who don't mean anything—and say it. In the olden days, a bride was bonny, and was requested to busk herself in consequence; all of which was intelligible. Nowadays, the poet would call a basilisk bonny rather than miss his alliteration. Is it because the new journalism is so imaginative and emotional that it throws off alliterative phrases as naturally and unconsciously as Whittier confesses he did in writing "The Wreck of Rivermouth"? It is sometimes difficult to believe that providence is not on the side of the evening bills. When Balmaceda died he committed Suicide by Shooting himself in Santiago—of all places in the world. Boulanger, if from a local point of view he died less satisfactorily, was yet careful to employ a Bullet. It is for the sake of the phrase-makers that Burglars good-naturedly prefer Bermondsey, and that Tigers do not escape from their cages to play in Tragedies till the show arrives at Tewkesbury. The Baboon is already so largely alliterative in himself that it was an excess of generosity that made one recently attack an infant under such circumstances as to allow the report to be headed, "Baby Bitten by a Baboon in a Backyard at Bow." Alliteration has become a mighty factor in politics: it is fast replacing epigram, while its effects on moral character are tremendous. That "hardened criminal," Mr. Balfour, might have been a good man instead of a "base brutal bully," if his name had only commenced with an X. He is a noteworthy martyr to the mania of the times. I am convinced that the Death of the Duke of Devonshire was accelerated by anxiety to please the sub-editors, and it is a source of real regret to me to reflect that my own death can afford them no supplementary gratification of this nature.

The Humorous

To start anything exclusively funny is a serious mistake. This was why poor Henry J. Byron's "Mirth" was so short-lived. It died of laughing. A friend of mine, with a hopeless passion for psychological analysis, says that the reason people do not laugh over comic papers is that the element of the unexpected is wanting. This, he claims, is the essence of the comic. You laugh over a humorous remark in the middle of a serious essay, over a witty epigram flashed upon a grave conversation, over the slipping into the gutter of a ponderous gentleman—it is the shock of contrast, the flash of surprise, that tickles. Now this explanation of why people do not laugh over comic papers is obviously wrong, because you are surprised when you see a joke in a comic paper; at the same time, it contains an element of truth. The books which gain a reputation for brilliance are those which are witty at wide intervals; the writer who scintillates steadily stands in his own light.

The Discount Farce

Having started your magazine, you will begin humorously enough by affixing a mock price to it. What a strange world of make-believe it is! We are so habituated to shams that we cannot help shamming even where there is nothing to be gained by it. Why is music published at four shillings when you can buy it for one and four, or at most one and eight? Why are novels published at thirty-one and six and the magazines at a shilling? "Shilling shockers" are sold at ninepence, which is as comical as selling "tenpenny nails" at sixpence. The same principle rules in other trades. It almost seems as if there is an ineradicable instinct in humanity for getting things below their price, even if at more than their value. Hence the marked popularity of "sales" and "reductions." The idea of getting things cheap reconciles one to getting things one doesn't want. The craze for cheap things leads one into frightful extravagance. In some shops the weakness of humanity is pandered to without disguise, and every article is ticketed with a little card, from which the first price is carefully ruled out, and even on the second price you get a discount for cash. This same discount for cash is at least intelligible, but business men are painfully familiar with another wonderful deduction. After you wait months for your money, you get a cheque less "discount on payment." This seems to involve an exasperating Hibernicism. "On payment," forsooth! So long as it remains unpaid, the debt due to you is, say, one hundred pounds. But the moment you really get it, it shrinks to ninety-five. Why not call it ninety-five at the start and be done with it? But, no! men will not give up the subtle pleasure of discounts, ineffably childish though it be. The rather deaf lady who being asked six shillings a yard for stuff replied "Sixteen shillings a yard! I'll give you eleven," and who, when her mistake was pointed out, said "I couldn't think of paying more than four and sixpence" was a genuine type of the population of these islands.

The Franchise Farce

One American defense of bribery is as clever as it is cynical. It amounts to this: that universal suffrage is such a peril to the commonweal that having been given prematurely, it must insidiously be nullified in practice, even at the cost of universal corruption; in short, if the old society is to be preserved, universal franchise must be transformed into universal corruption. What an ironic commentary on the constitution that was founded by George Washington, who couldn't tell a lie! The honour of America, it appears, "rooted in dishonour" stands, and "faith unfaithful" makes its politicians falsely true. When one remembers some of the other gigantic evils of the society thus conserved by corruption, when one thinks of the great immoral capitalists, playing their game regardless of whom they ruin or whom they enrich, when one thinks of the squalid slums of the great cities, one wonders whether the society which these things shadow were not better damned. It were cleaner, at any rate, to abolish universal franchise than to flaunt this farce in the eyes of Europe. If universal suffrage was a mistake, if indeed the gift of the franchise does not develop a man's conscience and education—and certainly bribery is not the way to give him a chance of such development—then why not honestly admit that America has made this mistake, that the ideals of the Pilgrim Fathers were inferior to Tammany Hall's, and that even the negro is not a man and a brother?

Does our American reply that it is impossible now to take back the franchise? But on his own showing the electors merely regard it as an opportunity for extracting "boodle." All that would be impossible, then, is to take away this ancient concession without compensation. The electors must be bought out at the full market-value of their votes, with a few cents and corpse-revivers thrown in for their loss of amusement. At every election dollars and drinks for the ex-electors would be circulating freely under the direction of the Treasury. And, ex hypothesi, the bulk, or a number of electors sufficient to annul the danger to society, will accept the liquidation, and thus the dishonest will be honestly weeded out of the electorate. But if the cynics were wrong, and there remained among the poorer electorate men sufficiently honest to retain their votes, and sufficiently numerous to swamp the old society—why, then the devil take the old society! The object of government is only the good of the majority, and these men, being the majority, have every right to select their own form of good. If they were mistaken, nature would soon convince them of their mistake, and the next generation would profit by the object-lesson. Demos would go on, a sadder and a wiser man.

The solution of the question is that the people must not only govern: it must be fit to govern. To corrupt it with dollars, to drowse it with drink, is only to put off the inevitable day. It were far wiser to help it to educate itself for its functions. For, if the revolutionary economic ideas that are in the air are false, they will destroy themselves. And if they are true, they have got to be realised, and will get themselves realised. No amount of corruption will save society in the long run. Meantime, either let universal suffrage operate honestly, or let it be suspended or abolished. Let even those States which have enfranchised the black man, and which now, in accordance with the deep Machiavellian principle, brazenly revealed by our American, dishonestly render his vote nugatory by a reliable inaccuracy in the counting, withdraw their spurious Christianity. A double standard of morals subtly infects the whole core of the nation. Corruption cannot be localised; it creeps and spreads through all departments of thought and action. To give with the right hand, and take away with the left in exchange for a few dollars, is a manoeuvre unworthy of a great nation. The transaction is fair; let it be above board, let it be lifted into the plane of ethics. To found society upon a farce is to lower those ideals by which, as much as by bread, a nation lives.

The Modern War Farce

The horrors of war seem to have reached the vanishing point in our latest African campaign. The smallness of the English losses is appalling. I do not see the fun of fighting (i.e., of paying taxes) if all the spice and relish is to be taken out of the results. I want more blood for my money—hecatombs of corpses. Two men killed in a whole battle? Ridiculous! If I cannot have my war at my own doors, and hear the bands and the cannon I have paid for, I must at least have sensational battle-fields—Actiums and Waterloos and Marengos. What is the use of war if it does not even serve to reduce our surplus population? Soldiering was never so healthy an occupation as to-day; one fights only a few days a year at the utmost, and if the pay is poor, so is that of the scavenger and the engine-driver and the miner, and everybody else who does the dirty work of civilisation, and does it, too, without pomp and circumstance and brass bands and laureates.

Fireworks

If people cannot do without sulphur and noise, there are always fireworks. It is difficult to imagine festivity without them, and yet there must have been a time when rockets did not rise or Catherine wheels go round. You cannot have fireworks without gunpowder, and every school-boy knows that gunpowder was only invented in—I haven't got a dictionary of dates handy. Surely we ought to let off fireworks on Roger Bacon's birthday. "They let off fireworks when he was born," say the French in a slyly witty proverb, which is a circumlocutory way of saying that a man won't set the Thames on fire. For "he has not invented gunpowder" is the French equivalent for this idiom of ours, and it is obvious to the meanest intellect that a man whose birth was celebrated by fireworks could not have been the inventor of gunpowder. And yet there were fireworks of a kind from the earliest times, from the first appearance of stars in the firmament with their wandering habits and shooting expeditions. And, indeed, did not humanity long regard the heavens as a firework show for its amusement, a set piece entirely for its delectation? Mankind has always been fond of playing with fire—ever since Prometheus stole it from heaven and burnt his fingers. I am convinced the ancients only used bonfires for messages so as to enjoy the flare-up on the mountains. Who would not fight when summoned by a tongue of flame?

And the red glare on Skiddaw roused the burghers of Carlisle.

Roman candles were unknown to the Romans, but they enjoyed themselves with torches, and these were the fireworks at wedding fêtes. The golden rain in which Jupiter wooed Danaë was another sort of hymeneal fireworks. There were fireworks at the destruction of Sodom and Gomorrah. The love of fireworks is a natural passion. Does not nature amuse herself with fireworks, especially on tropical summer nights? She loves to flash her lightnings (which are not to be put out by the rain), and to crash her thunder (which, as everybody knows, is only the report of the meeting of two electric clouds). And who does not admire her grand pyrotechnic display—twice daily—at sunrise and at sunset, or her celebrated local effect, the Aurora Borealis?

I have loved fireworks from boyhood, and would rather have had dry bread and fireworks than cake with jam. In manhood often I have listened to the long-drawn ecstatic "aw" of the Crystal Palace crowd. I have even written a poem on fireworks. Here it is:—

A dazzling fiery show of sphery rainbows,
Whereof each wonder, monarch of a moment,
Yields up its glory to the next one's splendour,
And sadly sinks into the arms of darkness.

Is it not a true simile of the favour of the fickle crowd? The most brilliant phenomena are forgotten after a moment. Life and Time are full of such fireworks—religions, philosophies, fashions, dynasties. And overhead the sure stars shine on. In literature fireworks rarely last. They are too clever to live. A humble rushlight lasts longer. "All fireworks are unsound," says Steinitz. He is talking of chess, and chess is very much like life. Whistler has painted fireworks—I mean literally—in his blue and silver nocturne of old Battersea Bridge. Tennyson has painted them in his "Welcome to Alexandra" and elsewhere.

Flash, ye cities, in rivers of fire!
Rush to the roof, sudden rocket, and higher,
Melt into stars for the land's desire!

"Sudden rocket." How good the adjective is! A poet I know spent hall a day in finding the correct epithet for rockets, and was equally pleased and annoyed to discover subsequently that he had chosen the same adjective as the Master.

Nowadays we let off all our fireworks a day before the fair and tug Time by his forelock. A magazine coming out in January must be dated February at the very earliest. We "go ahead" in an Irish-American sense, and cannot endure not to be in advance of our age. We live entirely in the future, and are too busy to live just at present. Christmas falls late in October and extends to the end of November, the period being marked by heavy showers of Christmas numbers. The Jews begin all their festivals the day before, and Christmas is by far the most Jewish of our holidays. Our evening papers come out in the morning, though this will right itself in time, for they are getting earlier and earlier, and will ultimately come out the evening before. Dr. Johnson's line about Shakespeare, "And panting Time toils after him in vain," is truer of the man of to-day. What's that you say? All this has been said before? Naturally.

Diaries

Who is the most marvellous man? He who keepeth a diary. And by keeping a diary I mean keeping it for the whole year, from January 1st to December 31st—keeping it, moreover, by daily entry. Only one year in my life did I succeed in filling up every department of the three hundred and sixty-five, and even then I was often in arrears. Diaries are for those who lead cloistral lives and pure, so that the task is trivial, and whatsoever record of their own leap to light they shall not be shamed. Diaries are not for those whose existence is a whirlpool; for such the blank page is an added perturbation, a haunting whiteness beseeching the blackness of diurnal autobiography, an I O U that calls for instant satisfcation. To the spontaneous vexings of conscience has been added an artificial pricking at the neglect of a supererogatory duty. How have I blonched to see day adding itself to day, unrecorded, time flying without being "kodak'd" on the wing; and each new neglect retarding the day of reckoning even while it aggravated it! Then have I felt myself sinking beneath the self-imposed

Yoke, intolerable, not to be borne
Of the too vast orb of my fate,

yearning for a smaller circumference and a shorter biography. At the outset one begins a diary, as one practises a new virtue, or plays with a new toy—enthusiastically. For the first few days of January the entries are rich in psychological and episodical matter. Then gradually the interest trails off; to the fertile plains of narrative and analysis succeeds a barren desert, relieved only by a few dates of appointments. With Mark Twain it will be remembered the entries were reduced to "Got up, washed, went to bed." The keeping of a diary is generally the first New Year resolution to be broken. How eloquent these old diaries filled up for a month or two—and the rest silence!

On second thoughts there is a more marvellous than the most marvellous man. It is he who keepeth a pecuniary diary. I know one such. He has kept a perfect and absolutely complete record of every farthing he has laid out since the days when farthings were his standard of currency. Which of us would dare do this, or, doing, would dare cast a backward glance on the financial past? There is a crude, relentless actuality about items of expenditure, not to be softened by euphemistic phrasing. Surely a truer proverb than any of its species would be: "Tell me what you buy, and I'll tell you what you be." And to think, in reviewing your pecuniary biography, that, though you owe no man a farthing, you have still to pay the bill; that many things you have bought have yet to be paid for "over and over again," as the Master Builder said, "over and over again."

Looking backward is a luxury which should be indulged in only moderation—say once in fifty years. The preachers will tell you differently. But life is so restless and feverish nowadays that there is no time for obeying the preachers. It is as much as we can do to find time to listen to them. Goethe says, "He who looks forward sees only one way to pursue, but he who looks backward sees many." This is the last word on the subject. It speaks volumes. But as you cannot walk through any of those backways, what is the use of bothering to look for them? True, your own experience enables you to give advice to others. But advice is a drug in the market. What am I saying? A drug! No, no! Even a drug is taken sometimes. Advice never is. We learn only from our own mistakes, and when it is too late to profit by them. No; there is not much profit in looking backwards. Often it tends to make you pessimistic, to sap your energy, to petrify you, as it did Lot's wife. At other times, contrariwise, it makes you expel such salt as is already in you, dissolved in tears—

So sweet, so sad, the days that are no more.

Yet what is this but another form of Buskin's "Pathetic fallacy"? Those divinely sweet, sad days were in reality just as commonplace as to-day.

Life is a chaos of comic confusion,
Past things alone take a halo harmonious;
So from illusion we wake to illusion,
Each as the rest just as true and erroneous.

A familiar form of the new illusion we wake to is seen in the exclamation that so often follows retrospection: "Oh, what a fool I was!" As a rule, nothing can be more conceited than this use of the past tense. A few people, perhaps, can look back complacently upon "a well-spent life" (wherein all the years have been laid out to advantage, and every hour has been made to go as far as seventy-five minutes, and every odd second has been worth a row of pins at least); but I should not care to meet them. For the bulk of us it is best to press on, doing what our hand findeth to do, and letting the dead past bury its dead. It is quite enough to know we cannot escape paying the funeral bills. One of my friends found himself let in for the discharge of a number of extra bills, owing to his retrospective proclivities. He was just beginning to overcome the adverse financial fates when, taking a complacent survey of his past, he was horrified to find it bristling with forgotten debts. Looking backward nearly ruined that man. Another of my friends lost his life entirely through it. He was an old man and a celebrity, and a publisher offered him £2000 for his memoirs. Unfortunately my friend had a very bad memory and no diaries, and, like my other friend, he was conscientious. The publisher's offer tantalized him terribly. He did not know what to do. At last, in despair, he determined to drown himself. On the moment before his death all his past life would come back to him and pass before his mental vision. Of course I was to rescue him the instant he lost consciousness, have him rubbed with hot towels and the rest of it. We went out bathing together, and everything came off as arranged, all except his resurrection. He was too old for such experiments.

A cynical Frenchman has defined life as the collection of recollections for the time when you shall have no memory. It is, at any rate, true (and the preachers are welcome to the moral) that the keenest joys of the senses leave a scant deposit in the memory, and that if sensual pleasures are doubled in anticipation, it is the spiritual that are doubled in looking backward.

Long Lives

Just as there are many persons of whose existence you are unaware till you read their obituaries, so there are many of whose celebrity you are ignorant till you see the advertisement of their biographies. On all sides we are flooded with big books about little people. What is this new disease that has come upon us? Life is short but a "Life" is long. Can there be any one man in this great procession of the suns who deserves the two royal octavo volumes, which is the least monument that the pious biographer builds? The perspective is all wrong. Bossuet got the history of the world into a fifth of the space. How keen must be the struggle for life amid these shoals of "Lives." How futile and vain this aspiration for a "Life" beyond the grave! Vainer still the bid for immortality, when one's own hand raises the mendacious memorial. It is an open question whether even Marie Bashkirtseff's self-hewn shrine will stand—she, who sacrificed her life to her "Life." If it does, it will not be by virtue of its veracity. I would not trust George Washington himself to write a perfectly accurate record of a prior day. As for the average biography, it is but the "In Memoriam" of memory. A friend of mine has written some excellent fiction and some entertaining reminiscences; only he has mis-labelled his books, and called his fiction "reminiscences," and his reminiscences "fiction."

VIVE LA MORT!

Wherefore do the critics rage?
'T is the Biographic Age.
Every dolt who duly died
In a book is glorified
Uniformly with his betters;
All his unimportant letters
 Edited by writers gifted,
Every scrap of MS. sifted,
Classified by dates and ages,
Pages multiplied on pages,
Till the man is—for their pains—
Buried 'neath his own Remains.
Every day the craze grows stronger,
Art is long, but "lives" are longer.
Those who were the most in view
Block the stage post mortem too.
Hark the tongues of either sex—
Reminiscences of X!
Of his juvenile affections
Hundreds write their Recollections,
 (None will recollect their writings)
Telling of his love for whitings
Fried in butter, or his fancy
 For bananas, buns, and Nancy.

Thank the gracious gods on high,
Every day some "Life" must die:
Death alone is our salvation.
Though'tisdubious consolation
That of all these countless "Lives"
   Only the unfit survives.

Men and Bookmen

The literary market is inundated with people who have no right to a stall. Aristocrats are badgered for books merely because they have the titles; and to have achieved success in any other profession than literature is the surest recommendation to the favour of the publishers. If I had to start my literary career over again, I should commence by hopping on one leg through the Pyrenees, or figuring in a big divorce case; anything short of assassination, which makes one's success too posthumous. It is most unfair, this doubling of the parts of doing and writing. Our modern heroes and heroines are quite too self-conscious; amid all their deeds of derring-do they have their eye on Mudie's. The old way was better. Even before the Pyramids were reared, when books were pictures and letters were cuneiform, heroes had their poets and kings their laureates. You can no more imagine Agamemnon, after the fall of Troy, rushing off to write an account of it for "Bentley's," than you can imagine Helen certifying that she found Pears' soap matchless for the complexion. It was better for the heroes as well as for the writers. Aeneas would never have dared to draw such constant attention to his "piety" as Virgil does; and even Louis Quatorze would have hesitated to describe the taking of Namur in the language of Boileau—

Et vous, vents, faites silence:
Je vais parler de Louis.

The true hero nowadays is the man who conquers himself and does not write books.

James I.on Tobacco

But even ancient kings did write sometimes, as witness this of James I: I hold it aye to be a Kings part to the Body-Politicke of all euils & excesses, & would fain demonstrate afresh to my dear Countrey-men how abhorrent to Heauen is this stinking incense that ascendeth day & night; but amid the heat & burden of the day I cannot find an hour to examine into this matter de nouo, & must needs be content with commending to the readers of "Without Prejudice" my booklet, "A Counterblaste to Tobacco," imprinted Anno 1604, wherein they will find the abuses of this foreign custome duly set forth at length. But, on second thoughts, perchance these moderns read nothing but what is under their noses, so I will shortly recapitulate my main positions, merely adding that my objections to Smoak are to-day even stronger than when I wrote. (1) It is a fallacie of the vulgar that because the braines of men are colde & wet, therefore Tobacco Smoak, being hote and dry, is good for them; a conclusion which no more followeth on the Premiss than the Ratiocination of one who should apply a cake of cold lead to his stomacke, because the Liver, being the fountaine of blood, is always hote. Moreover, the Smoak hath also a venomous qualitee. (2) It is a vulgar fallacie that the affection of mankind for the Practise is a proof that it is good for them; inasmuch as men are ledd astray by a mode, & furthermore, the affectation & conceit of the patient persuadeth him he is benefited; yet how shall one drug cure of all diseases men of all complexions? (3) Men are by this custom disabled in their goods, spending many pounds a year upon this precious stinke, and are no better than drunkards. (4) It is a great iniquitee & against all humanity that the husband shall not bee ashamed to reduce thereby his delicate, wholesome and cleane complexioned wife to that extremitee that either shee must also corrupt her sweete breath therewith, or else resolve to live in a perpetual stinking torment. In short, tis a custome lothsome to the eye, hateful to the Nose, harmefull to the braine, dangerous to the Lungs, & in the blacke stinking fume thereof neerest resembling the horrible Stigian smoke of the pit that is bottomeless.

A Counterblaste to James I

So please your Majestie, I would beg leave in all loyaltie & service to cry you mercy on behalf of the foreign weed, Tobacco, which stands for all time condemned by the potent Counterblaste of a monarch, the maruelle of Christendom, whose brow hath borne at once the bays of Apollo, the laurels of Mars, & the crownes of Scotia & Anglia. And imprimis I would venture humbly to obserue that your Majesties arguments are to the last Degree asinine. Euen the title—which, as is customarie with great personages, is the best part of your Majesties book—is marred by an unseemlie concession to paronomasia. That your Majesties manifold abuses of the Logicks may be better espied, I will take them seriatim. (1) The ground founded upon the Theoricke of a deceiuable apparence of Reason—your Majestie is mistaken in thinking that I hold it a sure aphorisme in the Physickes. For the braines are neuer colde & wet saue when there is water on them; & those who do not Smoak haue no braines for Tobacco to benefit. (2) Your Majesties argumentation proueth how zealously your Majestie striueth to liue up to the nickname of the British Solomon. And, of a veritie, I could not myself run atilt more cunningly at this popular fallacie; though I might back up your Majestie with a most transparent illustration—to wit, that the affection of Mankind for monarchs is no proof that they are good for them. (3) I denie that Tobacco wastes ones substance, & I would refer your Majestie to my demonstration of the Extrauagance of not smoaking. (4) And is it not an advantage that it resembleth to the Stigian smoak of the pit? The more we accustom ourselves thereto, the lesse we shall suffer when we join your Majestie. Will your Majestie kindlie recommend a Brande? Nor can I conclude without a word as to the ill-taste of that supplement to your Majesties booklet—a tax of Six Shillings & Eighte-Pence upon euery Pounde-Waighte of Tobacco, ouer & aboue the Custome of Two Pence upon the Pound-Waighte usuallye paide heretofore. Did your Majestie hope to effect so little by Reason that your Majestie must needs fall back on Reuenue? Hauing challenged this habit by the Kings pen, how unmannerly to resort to the coastguards cutlass & fight the custome at the Custome House. Was it, perhaps, that your Majestie was wishful to promote English Agriculture or was getting up a cornere in Cabbaiges?

Howsoever, Smoak hath suruiued the Stuarts.
May I offer your Majestie a Cigarre?

Valedictory

And now, gentle reader, the hour has come for parting. You have kept me company a long time; tolerant of all my whimsies and vagaries, and not too restive when I became serious and heavy. I have written for you in many places and in many moods, and I cannot hope to have escaped the mood of dulness.

Up! up! my Friend, and quit your books;
Or surely you'll grow double;
Up! up! my Friend, and clear your looks:
Why all this toil and trouble?

Ah, dear Wordsworth, 't is easy enough to answer your question. Still, at last the pen falls from my tired fingers.

Books! 't is a dull and endless strife:
Come, hear the woodland linnet!
How sweet his music!
On my life, There's more of wisdom in it.

Yes, I will go down and hear the woodland linnet, there is one in the bird-shop round the corner. Ah me! he will not pipe—his is the wisdom of silence. Never mind; the pavements are flooded with sunshine, and the folk are walking gaily, and the omnibuses roll along top-heavy, and there is a blue strip of sky over the Strand. Yes, Spring is here, and the violets are blooming in the old women's baskets. How happy everybody seems! Even the sandwich-men have lost their doleful air. The sap is stirring in their boards. They are dreaming of their ancient springtides, when they edited magazines or played "Hamlet." And so, having taken up my pen again to tell you how I dropped it, let me not lay it down without bidding you a fond and last farewell—without prejudice.

Israel Zangwill – A Short Biography

Israel Zangwill was born in London on 21st January 1864, to a family of Jewish immigrants from the Russian Empire. His father, Moses, was from modern-day Latvia, and his mother, Ellen Hannah Marks Zangwill, from modern-day Poland.

Zangwill was initially educated in Plymouth and Bristol. At age 9 he was enrolled into the Jews' Free School in Spitalfields in east London. The school was for the children of Jewish immigrants and added to its teaching, of both secular and religious matters, with supplies of clothing, food, and health care. Zangwill excelled here. He began to teach part-time at the school and eventually full time. Whilst teaching he also studied with the University of London and by 1884 had earned his BA with triple honours in philosophy, history, and the sciences.

He had already co-written a tale entitled 'The Premier and the Painter' when he resigned as a teacher owing to differences with the managers of the school. Zangwill now turned to journalism for his new career path, initiating Ariel, The London Puck, as well as working in various capacities for the London press.

His writing earned him the sobriquet "the Dickens of the Ghetto" primarily based on his much lauded novel 'Children of the Ghetto: A Study of a Peculiar People' in 1892 and its glimpse of the poverty-stricken life in London's Jewish quarter.

As a writer he was keen to reflect on his political and social outlooks. His simulation of Yiddish sentence structure in English aroused great interest. His mystery work, 'The Big Bow Mystery' (1892) was the first locked room mystery novel. Social satire flowed with 'The King of Schnorrers' (1894). A follow up to 'Children of the Ghetto' was 'Ghetto Tragedies' in 1894 and 'Dreamers of the Ghetto' in 1898 which included essays on famous Jews such as Baruch Spinoza, Heinrich Heine and Ferdinand Lassalle.

Zangwill was also involved with narrowly focused Jewish issues as an assimilationist, an early Zionist, and later a territorialist. In the early 1890s he had joined the Lovers of Zion movement in England. A few years later, in 1897, he took part in the "pilgrimage" of English Jews to Palestine. That same year he also joined Theodor Herzl (considered the father of modern political Zionism) in founding the World Zionist Organization and would take part in the first seven Zionist congresses. Zangwill was much admired as an orator and spoke movingly and eloquently on the issues he was passionate on.

In 1901 he had written that "Palestine is a country without a people; the Jews are a people without a country". On Herzl's visits to London, they worked closely together. In a debate at the Article Club in November 1901 however Zangwill was still mis-using the facts: "Palestine has but a small population of Arabs and fellahin and wandering, lawless, blackmailing Bedouin tribes." And made a direct plea to "restore the country without a people to the people without a country. For we have something to give as well as to get. We can sweep away the blackmailer—be he Pasha or Bedouin—we can make the wilderness blossom as the rose, and build up in the heart of the world a civilisation that may be a mediator and interpreter between the East and the West."

In 1902, Zangwill wrote that Palestine "remains at this moment an almost uninhabited, forsaken and ruined Turkish territory". But from this point on Zangwill began to see things differently which would, in 1905, result in his breakaway from Zionism.

Zangwill quit the established philosophy of Zionism when his plan for a homeland in Uganda was rejected and instead founded his own organisation; the Jewish Territorialist Organization. Its stated goal was to create a Jewish homeland in whatever territory in the world could be found for them. At that point in time suggestions were as varied as Canada, Australia, Mesopotamia, Argentina, Uganda and Cyrenaica.

Amongst the challenges in his life he found time to write poetry. He had translated a medieval Jewish poet in 1903 and his own volume 'Blind Children' in 1908 shows his promise in this new endeavour.

In 1908, Zangwill told a London court that he had been naive when he made his 1901 speech and had since recognised that the Arab population was twice that of the United States.

Zangwill was a supporter of both feminism and pacifism, but his greatest effect was as a writer who gained a wide audience with the idea of combining ethnicities into a single, American nation. The hero of 'The Melting Pot', proclaims: "America is God's Crucible, the great Melting-Pot where all the races of Europe are melting and reforming... Germans and Frenchmen, Irishmen and Englishmen, Jews and Russians – into the Crucible with you all! God is making the American."'

'The Melting Pot' made Zangwill's name as an admired playwright. The title itself was popularised as the phrase to use to describe American absorption of immigrants when it ran in the United States.

When the play opened in Washington D.C. on 5th October 1909, former President Theodore Roosevelt leaned over the edge of his box and shouted, "That's a great play, Mr. Zangwill, that's a great play." In a later letter in 1912 Roosevelt went further "That particular play I shall always count among the very strong and real influences upon my thought and my life."

'The Melting Pot' shone a spotlight on America's growth through the input of its new waves of immigrants. Zangwill was writing as "a Jew who no longer wanted to be a Jew. His real hope was for a world in which the entire lexicon of racial and religious difference is thrown away."

According to Ze'ev Jabotinsky, Zangwill told him in 1916 that, "If you wish to give a country to a people without a country, it is utter foolishness to allow it to be the country of two peoples. This can only cause trouble. The Jews will suffer and so will their neighbours. One of the two: a different place must be found either for the Jews or for their neighbours".

In 1917 he wrote "'Give the country without a people,' magnanimously pleaded Lord Shaftesbury, 'to the people without a country.' Alas, it was a misleading mistake. The country holds 600,000 Arabs."

With the end of World War I, and a more clearly defined idea of a Jewish settlement in Palestine, Zangwill once more returned to the Zionist effort and made efforts on behalf of the Balfour Declaration, proclaiming the right of a Jewish homeland in Palestine

In 1921 Zangwill wrote "If Lord Shaftesbury was literally inexact in describing Palestine as a country without a people, he was essentially correct, for there is no Arab people living in intimate fusion with the country, utilizing its resources and stamping it with a characteristic impress: there is at best an Arab encampment, the break-up of which would throw upon the Jews the actual manual labor of regeneration and prevent them from exploiting the fellahin, whose numbers and lower wages are moreover a considerable obstacle to the proposed immigration from Poland and other suffering centers".

Despite his advocacy on Jewish matters he would be disappointed to know that despite Israel now being established the quarrels of the Middle East continue to divide.

Israel Zangwill died on 1st August 1926 in Midhurst, West Sussex.

Israel Zangwill – A Concise Bibliography

The Bachelors' Club (1891)
The Old Maid's Club (1892)
Children of the Ghetto: A Study of a Peculiar People (1892)
Grandchildren of the Ghetto (1892)
The Big Bow Mystery (1892)
Merely Mary Ann (1893)
The King of Schnorrers (1894)
The Master (1895) (based on the life of George Wylie Hutchinson)
Without Prejudices (1896)
Dreamers of the Ghetto (1898)

Ghetto Tragedies, (1899)
"The Return to Palestine", New Liberal Review, (Dec. 1901)
Children of the Ghetto (1902)
"Providence, Palestine and the Rothschilds", The Speaker, vol. 4, no. 125 (22 February 1902)
Selected Religious Poems (1903) Translation of the Jewish Medieval Poet Solomon in Cabirol.
The Grey Wig: Stories and Novelettes (1903)
The Serio-Comic Governess (1904)
Merely Mary Ann (1904)
Ghetto Comedies, (1907)
Blind Children (1908) Poetry
The Melting Pot (1909)
Italian Fantasies (1910) Travel
Chosen Peoples, (1919)
The War For The World (1916)
The Principle of Nationalities (1917)
Chosen Peoples (1918)
Hands Off Russia: Speech by Mr. Israel Zangwill at the Albert Hall, February 8th, 1919. London: Workers'
Socialist Federation, n.d. (1919)
The Voice of Jerusalem. (1921)

Filmography

Children of the Ghetto (1915, based on the play Children of the Ghetto)
The Melting Pot (1915, based on the play The Melting Pot)
Merely Mary Ann (1916, based on the play Merely Mary Ann)
The Moment Before (1916, based on the play The Moment of Death)
Mary Ann (1918, based on the play Merely Mary Ann)
Nurse Marjorie (1920, based on the play Nurse Marjorie)
Merely Mary Ann (1920, based on the play Merely Mary Ann)
The Bachelor's Club (1921, based on the novel We Moderns)
We Moderns (1925, based on the play We Moderns)
Too Much Money (1926, based on the play Too Much Money)
Perfect Crime (1928, based on the novel The Big Bow Mystery)
Merely Mary Ann (1931, based on the play Merely Mary Ann)
The Crime Doctor (1934, based on the novel The Big Bow Mystery)
The Verdict (1946, based on the novel The Big Bow Mystery)